A COIN FOR THE FERRYMAN

IMBRIFEX.
BOOKS

ALSO BY MEGAN EDWARDS

Full Service Blonde: A Copper Black Mystery

Getting Off on Frank Sinatra: A Copper Black Mystery

Strings: A Love Story

*Roads from the Ashes: An Odyssey in Real Life
on the Virtual Frontier*

A COIN FOR
THE FERRYMAN

—— A NOVEL ——

MEGAN EDWARDS

IMBRIFEX BOOKS

IMBRIFEX BOOKS
8275 S. Eastern Avenue, Suite 200
Las Vegas, NV 89123
Imbrifex.com

IMBRIFEX.
BOOKS

A Coin for the Ferryman: A Novel

Library of Congress Cataloging-in-Publication Data

Names: Edwards, Megan, author.
Title: A coin for the ferryman : a novel / Megan Edwards.
Description: Las Vegas, NV : Imbrifex Books, [2022] | Summary: "A
    time-travel experiment that transported Julius Caesar from his last Ides
    of March to a covert lab in Pasadena in the year 1999. The plan is for
    him to stay in the lab for four days and then return to Rome to meet his
    fate"— Provided by publisher.
Identifiers: LCCN 2021016817 (print) | LCCN 2021016818 (ebook) | ISBN
    9781945501159 (hardcover) | ISBN 9781945501173 (epub)
Subjects: LCSH: Caesar, Julius—Fiction. | GSAFD: Biographical fiction. |
    Science fiction.
Classification: LCC PS3605.D8898 C65 2022 (print) | LCC PS3605.D8898
    (ebook) | DDC 813/.6—dc23
LC record available at https://lccn.loc.gov/2021016817
LC ebook record available at https://lccn.loc.gov/2021016818

Jacket design: Jason Heuer
Book Design: Sue Campbell Book Design
Author photograph: Benjamin Hager
Editors: Nancy Zerbey, Kristen Weber

Typset in: Berkley Oldstyle
Printed in the United States of America
Distributed by Publishers Group West

First Edition: March, 2022

For Mark

Nunc scio quid sit amor. —Virgil

I

ID. MART. DCCX A.U.C.

"Juli."

He heard the first whisper but waited for the second.

"*Juli. Are you awake?*"

Julius Caesar had been awake for nearly an hour, though dawn was just breaking.

"I am awake," he said as she reached his bed. She sat on the edge. He smelled the rosemary before she held it near.

"My darling," she said. In the dim light, he watched her hold the rosemary first to her own nostrils, then to his.

"Calpurnia," he said.

She kissed his brow. "Juli," she said again. "Will you stay with me today?"

Caesar considered her request for a brief moment. These moments of lucidity visited his wife ever more infrequently. He had no way of knowing when the madness would descend again, when he would no longer be her "Juli," but once again her captor and tormentor.

"We can ride out the Appian," she said, wheedling now. "Terentia says the hyacinths have already begun to bloom."

It was still too early for wildflowers, Caesar knew, but what did it matter? He had no time for a picnic or a stroll. He would be leaving for Parthia in April, and it was already the Ides of March.

"No, my dove," he said. "I am expected in the Senate."

"I know that." Calpurnia sighed. "It was a wish, not an expectation."

She tucked the sprig of rosemary under his pillow and departed.

By the time Caesar was ready to leave for Pompey's Theater, madness had once again overtaken his wife. Her shrieks echoed through the house. Not for the first time, he wondered whether he had succeeded in keeping her strange fits and rages a secret. Anyone walking by outside could hear her wails.

"Do not depart this house!" she cried as Caesar crossed the atrium. "They will ensnare you! You will never return!"

Terentia rushed into the atrium and tried to restrain her, but Calpurnia wrestled free and threw her arms around her husband.

"Juli! Juli! Do not abandon me!"

Calpurnia had often screamed at him in her madness, accusing Caesar of harming her in countless terrible ways. "Get away, you brute!" she would screech, day after day. "Don't touch me, foul dog of Orcus!"

What is so different about today? he wondered. Why all the pleading instead of her usual anger?

"If you must go, take a dagger!" Calpurnia cried. "Do not go unarmed, I beseech you!" Her eyes wild, she clutched his arms. "There will be blood! I see it! I see it everywhere!"

Madness, Caesar told himself. Her words carried no special knowledge. She was raving, nothing more.

He departed, though the sun had not yet reached above the garden wall. Nothing could be gained by remaining with his poor suffering wife, and he could use the time to clear his head before he faced the tasks of the day.

As was Caesar's custom when he could spare the time, he walked to the Cestian Bridge. He paused there to look over the Tiber, thinking—as he always did—about the memorable day he had chanced to meet Servilia in this very spot so many years before.

Their meeting at the bridge had been a coincidence. Servilia and Caesar had always taken the utmost care never to be seen together inappropriately in public. Fortunately, it was early morning. Just like today, there were no passersby.

Caesar looked down at the water. Swollen by recent storms in the hills, the river was rough and dark. Utterly unlike the day of that chance meeting long ago. The Tiber had been blue and placid that other day, as calm as Servilia, as docile as the baby perched on the stone railing next to her.

"Juli, meet Marcus," Servilia said, once they had both concluded it was safe to acknowledge each other. "At long last."

At last, indeed. This was Marcus Brutus, the child who had kept the lovers apart for so many months. Caesar had attended his *lustratio*, of course, but that had been nearly a year before.

Caesar stared at the boy, impressed at how straight and tall he sat for one so young. He met Caesar's gaze solemnly with unblinking black eyes.

"He is a willful one," Servilia said. "But I suppose that comes as no surprise."

She laughed, then bent down to adjust her sandal.

Just that. A simple thing. A task that took a moment, no different from the myriad of mundane occurrences that make up a lifetime. What if Caesar had not chosen to pass by the Cestian Bridge that morning, or if he had arrived at a different hour? But it was pointless to wonder. He was there when the baby, one moment strong and still, began to fall backward. Caesar stepped forward and grasped the child's left arm. By the time his mother rose, he was sitting straight again, Caesar's hand supporting his back.

Servilia looked from the baby to Caesar. When their eyes met, she smiled.

"I am so happy you and Marcus have met," she said.

Caesar nodded and smiled at the baby. The boy stared back at him, utterly unaware of his brush with death. Reluctant to spoil the brief time he was enjoying with his mother, Caesar said nothing about it to her.

"I am so happy I decided to walk past the Cestian Bridge today," he said instead.

And today, Caesar thought as he continued on his way to the Senate, I am happy again, in spite of Calpurnia's lunacy and in spite of all the whining demands and self-centered grievances that awaited him at Pompey's Theater.

Because Marcus Brutus would be there, too. In the gifted statesman he had become, Caesar would always see that tiny, dark-eyed boy sitting calmly on the stone railing of the Cestian Bridge. He would once again remember how, on a cool spring morning long ago, fate placed his hand at a baby's back while his mother tied her sandal.

◎◎◎

Caesar reached the Forum. As he passed the Temple of Vesta, the old soothsayer Spurinna plucked at his arm.

"Take care," he said, his voice so hoarse that Caesar could barely make out his words. "It is the Ides."

As if Caesar did not know what day it was. He shook the old man off but thought again about Calpurnia's attempts to keep him home.

What is so special about today?

Caesar found out, of course, rather quickly. He had no sooner entered the theater when Quintus Pollio rushed toward him. Before he could escape, Pollio was in his face, launching into his standard list of querulous demands.

And then—he was silent. And not only silent, but gone—along with the stench of garum and garlic. In his place was Venus, gazing into Caesar's eyes and reaching her hands toward him.

II

JUNE, 2003

C assandra stared at the ceiling. She couldn't decide whether the old glow-in-the-dark stars still clinging to its yellowed surface were sweet or pathetic. Whatever they were, this would be the last time she'd stare up at them. Tomorrow was moving day. This was the last night she would ever spend in her crappy old room and her crappy old bed in her mother's crappy old double-wide in Carefree Canyon Mobile Home Resort. Perhaps it wasn't surprising that she couldn't sleep.

Propping herself up on one elbow, Cassandra looked down at Julian, asleep in his sleeping bag on the floor next to her. She knew she should be doing the same. But even though she was exhausted, her mind refused to slow down.

Maybe some reading would help. Cassandra groped for the flash-light on the nightstand. She clicked it on, careful to avoid shining it on Julian. Silently, she slipped out of bed and moved toward her crappy old bookcase.

She raked the flashlight beam across the shelf, passing Homer, Tolkien, and Robert Graves. She paused on a blue spine with gold lettering. She pulled the book from its spot and turned the flashlight on the cover.

Out of Place and Out of Time: My Quest for Truth,
Beauty, and the Meaning of Life

The author's name stood out below in large gold capital letters.

PHILIPPA KENYON SYKES

Cassandra sighed. The book shouldn't be here. Her mom had promised to give it to her stepdad ages ago. But here it still was, like a message from beyond the grave. Pippa Sykes had lived more than a year longer than doctors had predicted, but bile duct cancer had won out in the end. Not even a month had passed since Cassandra had read her obituary in *The New York Times*.

Cassandra opened the book to the title page. It had been nearly five years since she first saw the legible but spidery cursive.

For Cassandra—Never doubt your vision.
Yours in beauty,
P. K. Sykes

The first time Cassandra read the inscription, she dismissed it as a clever reference to her mythological namesake. People had been ribbing her about her name for as long as she could remember. At least Pippa's comment was encouraging, she thought now. It was almost a compliment.

A wave of sadness washed over her. Pippa was dead, and Cassandra had never even bothered to read her memoir. Like every other academic she knew, she had dismissed the book as the work of a nutcase, a formerly respected archaeologist who, thanks to a sudden inexplicable interest in space aliens, had sold out to talk shows and the tabloids. The book was a party favor, and she had saved it only because she knew her stepdad would get a kick out of Pippa's autograph. Malcolm was an unapologetic celebrity addict.

Cassandra was about to slide the book back into its spot on the shelf when she changed her mind. This might be just what I need, she thought. If I'm lucky, it'll be so boring I'll fall asleep. She climbed back into bed, settled in against her pillow, positioned the flashlight, and began to read.

III

I t's time to tell the story that started it all: how I became interested in out-of-place artifacts, and how they ultimately caused the academic world to shun me. It's strange and it's tragic, but it's also cathartic to be telling the truth at last.

It was the end of the summer season in 1974, and I was on my way back to New York from my last season at Knidos in southern Turkey. I stopped in Rome, where the English archaeologist Paul Mardling was wrapping up his summer's work at the Theater of Pompey.

I think it's permissible to reveal—now that all the parties whose privacy might be invaded are no longer alive—that Paul and I were lovers. We kept our relationship quiet to protect his marriage and reputation. While it spanned the better part of a decade, the actual affair was limited to short trysts at academic conferences and occasional stolen weekends. We were both very careful to avoid becoming the subjects of gossip.

Paul and I had planned to meet in Rome the week before he left for England. We would stay in his small apartment near the Theater of Marcellus for a few blissful days before he headed home to Cambridge, and I would leave for New York. He still had end-of-season work to complete at his dig, and I offered to help in any way I could. His colleagues and students had already dispersed. Except for two Italian laborers and a guard, we would be alone on the site.

Paul asked me to spend what time I had on a small area where a marble slab floor had just been lifted. The strata dated to the first century BC.

"I would appreciate your assessment of that quadrant," Paul said. "It's where I plan to begin work next summer—but I'd like to know what you think."

I got to work immediately. After surveying the whole quadrant visually, I began work in one corner with a small pick and brushes. I soon found myself in that wonderful meditative state only archaeology provides me. I was one with my little tools, the dirt, and the warm sun. If I had one day left on Earth, it is a day like that one I would wish for.

It's difficult to recall just how long I had been working when my pick nicked against something that felt different from the packed soil surrounding it. Carefully, I brushed dirt away from the spot. Soon, I saw the glint of yellow metal.

Gold.

Any kind of metal is noteworthy at an archaeological dig, but gold is always in a class by itself.

I rose to my feet and called across the enclosure to Paul. Within a minute, he was at my side.

"Take a look," I said. "I think it's a gold coin."

Paul crouched down. He brushed away a bit more dirt with his forefinger. He turned to smile at me.

"I don't know how you do it, Pippa," he said. "I've been working here for four years without turning up a find like this. How long have you been here? Two hours?"

I laughed. "I'd better get back to work," I said. "It would be nice to know whose face is on that coin."

"Indeed," Paul said. He patted my shoulder and went back to his own work.

An hour later, there was no doubt. My find was not only a coin, but a large one. It was on its side, and there was no mistaking its curved edge. It troubled me, however, that the edge was oddly fine. A coin from the first century BC would have an irregular but smooth edge. The coin I was excavating had a sharp rim and a milled edge. It looked nothing like an ancient coin and far too much like a modern one.

I kept working. The truth would be obvious once I revealed the coin's face.

Just as the sky was beginning to darken, I brushed the last bit of soil away from what I guessed was the obverse of the coin. The words I had been steadily revealing all afternoon were now clear.

"CAESARS PALACE," read the legend around the rim. "LAS VEGAS." The words surrounded an image obviously inspired by the Augustus of Prima Porta.

I hadn't called Paul over to look at the coin as I was revealing its disappointing face. I knew all too well how unhappy he would be to learn of its presence. It must be an intrusion, even though its position and matrix did not suggest it. There was no other explanation for the presence of a modern coin in strata that otherwise dated to the first century BC.

He should be here when I lift the coin, I told myself. He should see it in situ. Before I called him, I extracted my Kodak Instamatic from my shoulder bag and snapped a picture.

"Bugger!" was Paul's first comment when he arrived at my side. "Everything's been pristine so far. Are you sure you didn't put this atrocity here as a prank?"

"You know me better than that," I said. "Are you ready to see the reverse?"

"Go ahead, my love."

Using a dental tool, I carefully pried the coin from its resting place.

"It's heavy," I said. I turned it over. Paul and I both saw the coin's reverse side at the same moment.

"HAYCOCK-FLORES," read the legend. "DECEMBER 17, 1998." An image filled the field in the center, this one the profiles of two men facing each other. Neither evoked comparison to anything in ancient art.

Paul snorted in disgust. "Intrusions are such a bore," he said.

"An intrusion from—the future?" I said. I was still attempting to make sense of the date on the coin, twenty-five years hence.

"Anyone can strike a coin," Paul said. "The date is obviously false." He looked at me, contempt written on his face. "Pippa, it's from Las Vegas. What do you expect?"

I don't know what I expected, but what I did not anticipate were Paul's subsequent decisions and actions. He picked up the coin and slipped it into the pocket of his trousers.

"At least I don't have to report it," he said. "Nothing contemporary has to go into the record for the Italians."

I looked around. Had either of the laborers observed the find? Neither one was anywhere in sight. Intent as I had been on my work, I hadn't noticed *their departure.*

"What about your own record?" I said. "Even if it's an intrusion, you should document it."

"This is my dig," Paul said, and our conversation deteriorated from there.

By morning, the coin had cost us our relationship. I might have agreed to disagree with Paul about whether the coin had somehow traveled from the future, but what I could not tolerate was his refusal to acknowledge the find. There had to be a reason the coin was there, even if neither of us could explain it. We both knew that the responsible—and professional—thing to do would have been to catalog it and allow for future evaluation.

In spite of this, Paul was adamant in his refusal. Looking back, I believe he just couldn't face the unwanted publicity that was sure to ensue if he published the find. He was nearing the end of his career and was perhaps understandably concerned that a distraction of this nature could bring the wrong kind of attention to him and his life's work. Perhaps I should have backed down, but my own professional pride wouldn't let me.

What made things even worse was Paul's decision to pin the blame on me.

"You know you planted the coin," he said. "Admit your joke, and let us move on."

"I would never do such a thing," I protested again and again. But Paul persisted with his ridiculous accusations.

"Why would I do that?" I asked. "What could I possibly gain?"

"I don't know," Paul said. "I haven't the faintest inkling why you would want to hurt me."

"I would never hurt you," I said. "I just think there must be an explanation—"

"I already know the explanation," Paul said, and he again accused me of trying to scuttle his reputation and destroy his career.

Of course, I was eager to examine the coin again, but I was not surprised that Paul refused when I asked. I never saw it again, and I saw Paul only once, and only from a distance. He died of pneumonia at home in Cambridge in 1979.

In spite of what happened that fateful day in Rome—and even though he treated me unfairly—I still think of Paul as the love of my life.

After our nightlong argument, I could no longer stay with Paul in Rome. Instead, I caught a train to Germany, where Drew Bridges, a friend from New York, was wrapping up a summer of silverpoint sketching in the Bavarian Alps. Eager to spend what time I had with Paul, I had declined Drew's earlier invitations to visit on my way back home. Now, with my relationship suddenly terminated, a short stay in the mountains held irresistible appeal.

On the train—though awash in tears—I sketched what I remembered of the coin's reverse. It had cost me my relationship with Paul, but the coin still intrigued me. My mind would not let go of the puzzle of its unfamiliar names, portraits, and future date. What was the story behind the strange artifact? I was curious, but it wasn't until after my brief visit to Garmisch-Partenkirchen that I became obsessed.

Because my artist friend spent his days drawing mountain scenes, I had to entertain myself until the evening hours, when he was free to eat, drink, and converse. This was not a problem. I enjoy hiking, and the Alps are particularly beautiful in the waning weeks of summer. The first day of my visit, I purchased a new pair of hiking boots in the town. I took a short cable car ride up the Zugspitze and joined the throngs of hikers enjoying the warm, clear day.

I can't recall the exact details of what happened on the rocky trail overlooking the gorge. I think now that I had failed to tie the laces of my new boots securely. Whatever the reason, I tripped as I was passing a family on the trail. We had just exchanged friendly "Grüss Gott"s when I stumbled. I am not certain of the exact chain of swift events, but there is no doubt that I set them in motion. In the aftermath, the conclusion was that I struck the small boy as I tumbled. The child lost his footing and toppled over the cliff. Reacting instinctively, the boy's father lunged to catch him. Both father and son went over the edge, plunging hundreds of feet into the rocky canyon below.

What I remember with crystal clarity is the face of the young woman left alone on the alpine trail. As I pulled myself to my feet, our eyes met. We stared at each other for a fleeting moment that will linger in my mind's eye forever. Then she began to scream.

Yes. In one irreversible second, I had killed two-thirds of a family. I was not charged with a crime, but many are the times that I wish I had been. Punishment might have eased the horror and helplessness I have lived with ever since.

You may wonder what connection this terrible story has with my interest in out-of-place artifacts. I can't guarantee that you won't still wonder when I attempt to explain.

I shouldn't have been on that mountain trail. I should have been in Rome, in the arms of my lover or out at the Theater of Pompey, working on his dig. If I hadn't uncovered that odd Las Vegas coin, I would have been. It was as though that coin, itself so strangely out of place, had set in motion a horrible *chain of events. Had it done so from the future? Was there an explanation? Does everything happen by sheer chance, or are there forces at work that we—with enough diligence and thought—can understand? I couldn't repair my relationship with Paul. I couldn't speak of the anachronistic coin without sacrificing my career. That was Paul's final threat.*

"Speak of this coin to anyone, and I will see to it that you are labeled a lunatic," he said.

Because I wasn't supposed to be working on Paul's site, and he would deny it if I tried to claim that I was, the coin's presence was not a subject I could investigate. Learning how it found its way into ancient strata was as impossible as restoring a German family to wholeness. Paul never attempted to have me labeled a lunatic, but the events of the summer of 1974 have never stopped driving me crazy.

You have probably already recognized the names on the mysterious coin, but in 1974, neither "Haycock" nor "Flores" meant anything to me or anyone else. You may easily imagine my fascination when those names began appearing on sports pages a few years ago. You may even more easily imagine my fascination when I read that Sam Haycock and Rolando Flores faced off against each other on December 17, 1997, at Caesars Palace in Las Vegas. My only regret is that I did not write this memoir earlier. Had I done so, no one could accuse me of fabrication. To doubters, I can say only what I told Paul Mardling all those years ago.

I would never do such a thing

Philippa Kenyon Sykes
February 28, 1998

Cassandra could not stop the tears as she closed Pippa's book. She wiped them away as she looked once again down at Julian. The little boy was still sleeping soundly.

If only I had read those pages sooner, she thought. *If only I had known the secrets Pippa had been keeping all those years. I could have* explained everything she sacrificed her career to investigate, Cassandra thought as she looked down at her sleeping child. Pippa wasn't crazy. She just didn't have all the facts.

Cassandra lay back against her pillow. Sleep still eluded her.

IV

MAY, 1998
LAS VEGAS, NEVADA

C assandra studied the gold coin on the table in front of her.
        "Dude told me it was a Krugerrand," Tanya said. "Said it was worth about two grand."

"Better tip than I've ever gotten," Cassandra said. "But then, I only sling drinks."

"Nope. He lied. It's a fake." Tanya set down her Guinness and picked up the coin. "I'm going to have it made into a pendant," she said. "I'm going to wear it around my neck every day forever."

"Why, if it's a fake?" Cassandra said.

"To remind me that men are more worthless than pigs," Tanya said. "With pigs, you at least get bacon."

Cassandra thought Tanya's views—and her decision to work as a call girl on the Las Vegas Strip—were the result of growing up with

27

an awful father. Cassandra worked on the Strip, too, as a cocktail waitress at the Monte Carlo. She and Tanya would get together every couple of weeks at the Crown & Anchor. It was there that Cassandra tried to convince her friend that the man Cassandra had been dating was not a pig.

"There really are nice guys out there," Cassandra said. "Peter is one of them. He's everything I've been looking for."

Tanya rolled her eyes. "Cassie, he's *married*."

Cassandra regretted telling her that part.

"He'll finalize his divorce in two years—when his son turns twelve," Cassandra said. "I actually love that he cares so much about Conrad."

"Seriously, Cass," Tanya said, "you're a cheatin' dude's dream come true. He gets you Monday to Thursday and then goes home to wifey for a nice long weekend by the bay. No fuss, no muss, no chance of you two bumping into each other at the gym."

Cassandra didn't like her description, even though it was accurate. Peter Horton-Metz commuted from San Francisco every week to his job as a consulting architect at the Imperial Palace.

"We're exactly alike," Tanya went on, "except I get paid for what you're giving away for free."

"No," Cassandra protested. "We are not at all alike. Peter and I love each other. I'm sorry you're so disillusioned that you can't believe in love."

"Wrong. I love my mom. I love Ashley. I love my condo and my car. Most of all, I love knowing that in a year or so, I'll be able to buy my Master Massage franchise and become a respectable Las Vegas businesswoman."

It was true that Tanya had been supporting her disabled mother and younger sister ever since her father died at the end of senior year. Her condo was a chic showplace in the Polo Towers, and her new Porsche was a far cry from Cassandra's aging Ford.

"Do you have any idea how much money you could be making for doing exactly what you're already doing?" Tanya asked. "And it wouldn't be so different. You're already lying to your mom about where you spend the night."

Cassandra couldn't argue that point. She was keeping Peter a secret until he was divorced. As soon as she could flash an engagement ring, Cassandra would announce her plans to get married, move to California, and finish her degree.

"Berkeley or Stanford," Peter had promised. "Your choice."

Cassandra believed Peter until the day everything changed.

She worked at the Monte Carlo, but every so often, she'd get a call from Samantha, another high-school friend who was a banquet manager at the Imperial Palace. Cassandra was on Sam's list of people willing to pinch hit when she got caught shorthanded.

Sam called on a Friday afternoon. "I've got a wedding reception tomorrow," she said. "Any chance you can work it from three to eight, maybe nine?"

Ordinarily, Cassandra worked swing on Saturdays, but she'd done some vacation swapping and happened to be off.

Guests had been trickling in for about twenty minutes when Cassandra caught sight of a double stroller entering the room. Two curly-haired toddlers were being pushed by an older boy with the same hair. She had just turned to go in search of a couple of booster seats when she heard a man's voice say, "Slow down, Conrad! You're bumping into people."

Cassandra jerked her head around just in time to lock eyes with Peter and take in the pretty, curly-haired brunette on his arm.

His deer-in-the-headlights expression told her everything she didn't want to know.

Tanya never said, "I told you so." She was very sweet, in fact. She comforted Cassandra while she cried and listened while she raged.

About a month after Cassandra dumped Peter, she was at Tanya's condo in the Polo Towers. Tanya had just handed her a glass of white wine and opened a Red Bull for herself. The two chatted while Tanya got ready for her "date" that night.

"This guy's from Argentina," Tanya said. "I wish I spoke more Spanish than taco and margarita."

"He doesn't know any English?" Cassandra asked.

"His casino host says he knows a little. We'll have to play charades."

"I'm sure you'll do just fine."

"Easy for you to say," Tanya said, her eyes locking with Cassandra's in the mirror. "Conversation is more important than you think. Which is why you'd be so great, with your French and Latin and all."

"Nobody speaks Latin anymore," Cassandra said, but she was really just trying to change the subject. Tanya hadn't tried to sell her on becoming an escort since she'd learned the truth about Peter, and Cassandra didn't want her to start.

"I'm serious, Cass," Tanya went on anyway. "Time is not your friend, but you still have what it takes to be fabulous in this line of work."

"It just goes against everything I ever believed in." Cassandra said. "I'm not being critical—I know it works for you—"

Tanya set her hairbrush down, turned around, and laid a hand on her friend's shoulder.

"Do you really want to be over the hill *and* still in town?" Tanya asked.

As always, she knew exactly which of Cassandra's buttons to push.

"Fairy tales are wonderful, but this is real life," she went on. "So let me talk to Dorian, okay? He's my contact at Caesars."

V

Dorian set everything up perfectly, just as Tanya had promised.
"You're gonna be fine, Cass," she'd said. "Just remember
everything I told you." Cassandra wasn't so sure, but here she was at
Caesars Palace, nervously scanning the perpetual twilight of Cleopatra's
Barge in search of her first client.

He was sitting at a table for two, a glass in front of him, his hands
on the table. The candlelight caught the ring on the fourth finger of
his left hand.

A wedding ring.

It wasn't a surprise. The guy had no reason to hide his marital
status. He—or, more accurately, the casino—was paying for his female
company. Cassandra's stomach clenched as she thought about what the
ring meant. This guy would get lucky without pretending to be single.

Cassandra sat down.

The man leaned toward her, but her eyes were still on his ring. It
was a wide gold band with ... yes, an inscription. She could almost
make out a few letters from across the small table.

"Your ring is beautiful," she said. "What does it say?"

Surprised, the man pulled his hand away.

"Oh, just something in—" he paused before continuing. "Something in a language you wouldn't understand."

"May I see?"

Cassandra reached across the table. With a smile just shy of condescending, the man stretched his manicured hand out over her palm. She drew it closer.

"*Vivamus atque amemus*," she read aloud, turning his hand to read the words that circled the band. "Let us live and let us love."

Ignoring the startled look on her companion's face, Cassandra continued. "Catullus, Poem 5, except you left out '*mea Lesbia*.'"

The man disguised his surprise with a laugh.

"My wife left it out, you mean. My name's Alex, so a little editing seemed appropriate." He smiled. "You're Cassandra, right?"

She nodded. She'd told Dorian to use her real name even though Tanya had advised using an alias. A fake name felt too uncomfortable, and she was already too uncomfortable.

"I use Nirvana," Tanya had said, "but I think you need something snootier or French, like Anastasia or Antoinette. Or—I know! Athena!"

Like she'd name herself after a goddess.

A cocktail waitress appeared. Cassandra ordered a glass of pinot grigio, then fixed her gaze on the man's face. She could almost hear his thoughts.

A Vegas call girl who can quote Catullus?

"How old are you?" he asked.

The question bordered on rude. But hell, he was the client. Cassandra wouldn't get paid if she didn't keep him happy, and her knowledge of Latin was not what he was paying for.

"I turned twenty-six in October," she said, forgetting Tanya's advice to shave off a few years.

"My daughter's age." Alex looked down. "She would have turned twenty-six yesterday."

Would have … Oh, Christ.

"And my wife would have been fifty-eight. They shared a birthday."

Damn! Tanya hadn't covered dialog like this. She'd been very thorough about money and condoms, but a dead wife and daughter? Cassandra was off the map without a compass.

Having no idea what to say, she took a sip of wine. There went another of Tanya's rules. "Order it, but don't drink it," she had said. "They're playing, but you're working."

"I knew this wasn't a good idea." Alex sighed and ran a hand through his hair. "I'm sorry."

Damn again! She'd just blown her first gig. It'd probably be her last, and Tanya would never forgive her. Cassandra had promised not to let her down.

"You'll be paid," Alex said. "Don't worry about that. This isn't your fault."

"Yes, it is," Cassandra said. "I never should have—I wasn't supposed to—" She paused. "I—I'm really sorry about your wife and daughter."

Alex's face softened, and his eyes looked off to that point in the distance where memories live. "They died four years ago. I come to Vegas on their birthday—too painful to stay home." He knocked back a slug of his highball. "I've never let my casino host talk me into this sort of thing before, but this time he was just so convincing." Alex smiled. "You're everything he said you would be, Cassandra. It's just that—"

"I know, I know. I shouldn't have been such a show-off—"

"When did you learn Latin?"

"I started in ninth grade—a special program my mom got me into. It was great—my teacher was a former Jesuit priest who used to teach at Georgetown. The funding for my program ran out, but he kept tutoring me. He still does, because you can't major in classics at UNLV—" God, she was rambling. "I'm sorry. It's just that I've never done anything like this before, and—"

Oh, right. Might as well try telling him I'm a virgin.

She was about to fill the vacuum with the next stupid thing when Alex laughed again.

"I've never done this, either," he said. "As I was saying, Dorian—my casino host—talked me into it."

Alex lifted his glass. He waited until she raised her own.

"To new experiences," he said, clinking his glass against hers. "*Ad astra per aspera.*"

Through hardships to the stars.

Holy crap. The guy had just quoted the motto Cassandra had inscribed inside every one of her college textbooks.

"I've had enough hardships," she said. "And as for stars, all I want is to go to college at a place where I can *really* study Latin. I'd do anything for that."

Like have sex for money. So here she was, screwing up her first assignment.

Alex leaned closer. "Do you mean that?" he asked. "Anything?"

Jesus. Is he some kind of disgusting pervert? Tanya had done her best to prepare her for the kinky stuff—

"Would you move to Arkansas?"

If Cassandra had surprised Alex by translating a line from Catullus, he had just trumped her.

"Um ..."

Alex laughed a victor's laugh.

"Just say yes. Come on. I dare you."

"You're telling me that if I moved to Arkansas, I could get a degree in classics?"

Alex nodded, smiling broadly.

Cassandra searched her brain and came up empty. Was the University of Arkansas an improvement over the University of Nevada?

She had no idea. And ... was he even talking about academics? She was new at this. There was still the possibility they were somehow discussing sex.

Alex's face grew solemn again.

"My daughter had just been accepted to medical school at Columbia when she died. My wife had a doctorate in art history. I'd give anything to bring them back."

He couldn't be talking about sex, but—

"Since I can't, I set up a foundation in their memory in Yell County, Arkansas. Any kid who lives in Yell County can go to college if they want to. The foundation will pay for it." He paused and looked straight into Cassandra's eyes. "Are you serious about studying Latin?"

She nodded. "If I'd chosen something practical, I could probably get a scholarship. Money's tight when it comes to dead languages."

"I think you just moved to Arkansas."

Cassandra still wasn't completely sure what Alex was talking about, so she didn't say anything. Who was this guy, anyway? Someone with enough money to set up a scholarship program for an entire county had to make the news at least once in a while, even if it was only on a *Forbes* list.

"Would you care to dine with me, Miss—?"

"Fleury," she said, leaving Tanya completely behind.

"Cassandra Fleury," Alex said. "I'm very happy to meet you. I'm Alex Hunt."

Alexander Hunt. The name sounded vaguely familiar, but it was that sort of name. Fortunately, Alex didn't seem to expect recognition.

"Shall we retire to my suite?"

Wait a second! Hadn't he said dinner?

Alex smiled as he read the surprise on Cassandra's face.

"To dine, my dear. Not only will we enjoy the best food in Las Vegas, we shall have the best view."

Cassandra couldn't think of any reason to turn down Alex's invitation. If things had gone as planned, she'd be heading to his suite anyway. The worst that could happen was—well, she'd already agreed to that. And this way, if Dorian saw them—

"I'd love to."

VI

"I don't know how to thank you, Mr. Hunt, but I won't stop trying until I find a way."

Alex Hunt offered to escort Cassandra to her car, but she had no intention of making her new benefactor walk all the way from the Palatine Suite to the self-parking garage at one in the morning.

"You don't need to thank me," Alex said. "You don't even have to be a star. Just go to school and see where it takes you." He patted her shoulder. "And please—call me Alex."

Is this guy for real?

Here she was, ready to sell her body to pay for college, and—first time out of the chute—she'd scored a guy who wanted to finance her degree and expected nothing in return. More unlikely than winning Megabucks millions.

Of course, he might still be a fraud. This was Vegas, after all, the city where everybody's expecting something for nothing, and nothing in the whole damn place is free.

Was Alex Hunt a clever predator or a genuine altruist? Cassandra figured she'd find out when she cashed the personal check she had in her purse. Two thousand bucks to "get things started—application fees, whatever." If the check bounced, well, that would be the end of it. If it didn't, she still wasn't out of the woods. She was fully aware that con men sometimes give their marks money at the outset to gain their trust.

Cassandra also knew that con men make a point of choosing marks with assets. Except for a bedroom full of books, all she owned was an elderly Ford whose transmission had just sucked down a significant portion of her savings account.

As she walked back through the hubbub of the casino and on out to the parking garage, Cassandra tried to wrap her head around what had just happened. Alex Hunt had asked for nothing except that she enjoy her Chateaubriand and tell him how she had learned the language of the Caesars in the shadow of the Strip. He shared his own stories about studying Latin in high school, but then majoring in business when he went to Tulane.

"I loved reading Caesar," he said. "But I'd known since I was five that my future lay with the family business."

Vietnam had intervened. Alex served as a helicopter pilot and then came home to take the reins of Chasen Chicken.

Chasen Chicken! A recognizable name!

"Chasen Chicken is your family's company?"

"Yep, we're a bunch of Arkansas rooster wranglers," Alex said.

Holy crap. Cassandra was having dinner with the CEO of the world's largest distributor of processed poultry. If he wasn't a fake, the guy really did have enough money to send a whole county to college.

After she climbed into her Escort, Cassandra pulled Alex's check out of her handbag.

"Alexander Hunt," it said, "Seven Hills, Arkansas 72126."

There was no way of telling whether the small piece of paper was a life changer. For now, all it was good for was an interesting conversation with Mom. Cassandra started her car and headed straight for Carefree Canyon.

By the time she turned the corner onto Leisure Lane, it was after 1:30. There was a chance her mother might still be awake. Cassandra hoped so. She was way too wired to sleep and too busy hoping that Alex Hunt wasn't a con man. She needed someone to talk to.

Cassandra was still a few hundred feet from space number 173 when her heart sank. Mom was probably awake, all right. Cassandra's stepfather's car was parked in the driveway, right next to Mom's VW. That always irked Cassandra. That was her own parking place, but if Malcolm showed up when she wasn't home, he took it like it belonged to him.

Except for the first two or three years, Cassandra's stepfather had never actually lived in the mobile home on Leisure Lane. Malcolm only appeared when he needed money, although of course he would never admit that was his mission at first. He'd arrive with roses for Margot and a book for Cassandra. Even now, there was probably a gift inside waiting for her—the latest commentary on the *Aeneid* or a beautiful new edition of Plato's *Republic*. Cassandra had to give him this much: he always encouraged her interest in the ancient world, and his stories about his ivy-covered years at Oxford were what first kindled her academic dreams.

Malcolm Lewis was probably sitting on Margot's sofa right this second, drinking her port and telling her how much he'd missed her. Sometime tomorrow, the inevitable truth would come out, and the rest of the weekend would be a huge drama of yelling, accusations, threats, ultimatums, and tears. Malcolm would roar off Sunday afternoon with less cash than he'd angled for, and more than Margot wanted to part with.

When Cassandra was little, she worried nonstop that Mom and Malcolm would get divorced. Now she couldn't understand why her mother didn't sever all ties.

She paused in front of the trailer next to Margot's. She had been ready to share her news with Mom, but Malcolm put a kink in the plan. He had always encouraged Cassandra to study ancient languages, but his own biggest interest—next to playing high stakes poker—was rich people. He would be far more interested in meeting Alex Hunt himself than thinking about Cassandra's future. It was almost funny, really. His wife and stepdaughter lived in a broken-down old double-wide while Malcolm mingled with tycoons. The two cars in the driveway said it all: Mom's green 1977 Volkswagen beetle next to Malcolm's new shiny black Mercedes coupe. Margot had owned Jeremiah—that was her nickname for her old bug—since college. She always said that if she bought a better car, Malcolm would talk her out of it. The same went for a better home.

"You can't take out a mortgage on a run-down mobile home sitting on a rented space," she'd say. That might be true, but ever since Cassandra learned about real houses and leafy backyards, she'd dreamed of the day she'd have a real address instead of a space number on Leisure Lane in a godforsaken gravel pit called Carefree Canyon.

Cassandra was just shifting into reverse when another thought struck her. Maybe Malcolm knew something worth knowing about Alexander Hunt. All she had to do was change her story a little.

Margot and Malcolm were sitting on the living room sofa, as Cassandra had expected. There were empty glasses on the coffee table in front of them, along with an ostentatious vase full of at least two dozen long-stemmed roses.

Yup, he was here to separate Margot from some of her cash.

"Cassandra! You look like you've been having some fun," Mom said.

"Just a little clubbing after work," Cassandra said, glad she had thought of a cover story for her cocktail dress and overdone hair.

"I was hoping I'd see you tonight," Malcolm said. "I brought you something."

But it wasn't a scholarly tome. Much to Cassandra's surprise, the small box Malcolm handed her contained a pendant on a silver chain.

"There's a new shop at Caesars," Malcolm said. "All the jewelry is made from ancient coins."

"Marc Antony," Cassandra said as she examined the coin dangling from the chain. "Is it real?" She couldn't help thinking about Tanya's Krugerrand.

"So the proprietor assured me," Malcolm said. "He's very well connected. Works with an antiquities dealer in Beverly Hills."

No surprise that Malcolm would be aware of such a detail. He probably knew a lot more than that. Cassandra might have found the topic mildly fascinating any other night, but the ancient bling would have to wait. Right now she needed intel on her generous billionaire.

"You were at Caesars—today?" Cassandra asked.

God. What if she had run into Malcolm while she was with Alex Hunt?

"No. Last week. Why?"

"I was there tonight," Cassandra said, trying not to look relieved. "With friends, at Cleopatra's Barge. We met—" she paused. "We met someone quite interesting."

"Do tell," Margot said. "You want some port?"

Cassandra shook her head. "We met a man named Alexander Hunt."

Margot's face remained blank, but Malcolm's lit up like Christmas. "Alex Hunt, the chicken mogul?" he said. "Really?"

"That's the one. He said he comes to Las Vegas every year around this time—"

"Do you know who he is, Margot?" Malcolm interrupted. "Did you ever read about that horrible plane crash?"

As Cassandra had expected, Malcolm knew all about the stormy night in Arkansas in 1993, when Alex's life changed forever.

"Adrienne—that was his daughter—had just gotten her pilot's

license. Her mother was the passenger. It was a single-engine Cessna, if I remember correctly. Crashed while trying to land at Hunt's estate."

"I think I do remember that," Margot said. "So, so sad."

"Afterward, Hunt built an air traffic control tower for his landing strip," Malcolm went on. "He keeps it staffed twenty-four-seven. Anyone who wants to can land there any time—safely. He's got a big heart."

"Doesn't bring his wife and daughter back, but it's nice," Margot said.

"He also set up a foundation," Malcolm said. "If you're lucky enough to grow up in Yell County, Arkansas, you can go to any college you can get into—all expenses paid."

Cassandra successfully suppressed a shriek.

Hot damn! Malcolm had just confirmed everything Alex Hunt had told her. She was on her way to a university with a classics department!

Cassandra almost blurted out the details of her astonishing news to her parents.

"Oh my God!" she said instead. "I left my ID at work. I've got to run back to the Strip."

It was a lie, but it got her outside, into her car, and back onto Boulder Highway. If Cassandra couldn't tell Margot about her miraculous good luck, she'd tell the one other person who would share her delight wholeheartedly. Her Latin teacher might be surprised to find her at his door in the middle of the night, but she was willing to bet that Dr. Dennis Martinelli would forgive her if she woke him up.

VII

Cassandra had first glimpsed Dr. Martinelli after Christmas vacation her freshman year of high school. Her mother, who taught French at Chaparral High and knew how to pull strings with the school district, had managed to enroll her in a brand-new "magnet" humanities program for college-bound students. It was a long bus ride every day to Rancho High on the other side of town. It meant getting up at four o'clock every morning, but Cassandra didn't mind at all. "College" epitomized everything that life in Las Vegas—and especially Carefree Canyon Trailer Resort—was not.

Cassandra signed up for both French and Latin, though she was required to take only one foreign language. She figured French was an easy A, because her mom, who had grown up bilingual in Ottawa, had been speaking French to her from the day she was born. Latin, on the other hand, sounded exotic and difficult—just what someone bound for college ought to be taking.

"*Salve*," Dr. Martinelli said when Cassandra entered the classroom. "*Nomen mihi est Martinelli. Quid nomen tibi est?*"

Cassandra looked over her shoulder. No one was behind her. She looked back. There was no doubt about who the man was talking to. Fortunately, Dr. Martinelli broke into English long enough to reveal that he was the new Latin teacher.

Hooray! A real Latin teacher. The old one had left suddenly in early October to chase his Thai contortionist girlfriend home to Bangkok. The class had been muddling along with a Filipino substitute who might have known Latin but didn't speak much English. By Halloween, most of the students had switched to other languages. Now, Cassandra realized as the bell rang and she took her seat, she was the only kid left in Latin I. Later, she learned that the school would have canceled the class if the program hadn't been brand new and well funded. As it was, Cassandra was treated to a six-week private tutorial with a former Jesuit priest who refused to accept that Latin was a dead language.

Besides memorizing declensions and conjugations and deciphering sentences from Caesar's *Gallic Wars*, Dr. Martinelli expected Cassandra to leave English behind when she walked through his classroom door. If she wasn't exactly fluent by the end of that first semester, she could have held up her end of a polite interchange in the Vatican City. Even her mother, who had serious doubts about the value of conversing in a dead tongue, was impressed.

"French will always be more useful," she said, "but speaking Latin is a fantastic parlor trick."

Most high-school freshmen would probably hate having one-on-one instruction, but thanks to Malcolm's stories about his Oxford tutors, Cassandra loved it. Of course, other students joined Dr. Martinelli's Latin classes as the months went by, but he kept tutoring Cassandra privately.

"You've got a real ear for languages," he told her more than once. "It is a gift you must not squander."

Cassandra thrived on the personal attention and the stories Dr. Martinelli told her about college life. Latin came easily to her, and if it could pave her way out of southern Nevada, that was more than enough to recommend it.

Cassandra continued her tutoring arrangement with Dr. Martinelli after she graduated from high school. Her dream had been to go to college somewhere else, but UNLV was the only affordable option. It was disappointing, not only because it wasn't ivy-covered and in another state, but also because Cassandra couldn't major in Latin. Even so, by the time she had racked up enough credits to call herself a junior, she'd read as much Roman literature as anyone in a bona fide classics program. Thanks to Dr. Martinelli, she was equally proficient in ancient Greek.

Still, though they had spent countless hours together over the last decade, Dr. Martinelli was a teacher, not a buddy. Cassandra could only hope that her amazing news would excuse a knock on the door at two in the morning.

As her knuckles pulled back from the door of Unit 12 at Flamingo Heights Estates, Cassandra suddenly realized that explaining how a high-rolling tycoon would be funding her education might force her to make some embarrassing admissions.

Damn! Why had she been so eager?

Too late now. The smell of cigar smoke wafted around her as the door opened.

"Cassandra!" He pronounced it like an Italian—the way Cassandra always thought an ancient Roman might have, too.

"*Salve,*" she said. "I hope I haven't disturbed you."

At least she hadn't awakened him. Dr. Martinelli was wearing a camel sport coat and a tie.

"Not at all. Please come in."

Dr. Martinelli appeared to take no notice of Cassandra's apparel. That didn't surprise her. The man was a model of decorum. If his protégée turned up in the middle of the night wearing a strapless minidress, nightclub hair, and stiletto heels, he would display no lout-ish curiosity. Maybe she wouldn't have to reveal how she had managed to attract an academic sugar daddy.

Cassandra stepped into Dr. Martinelli's condo, which looked more like the stacks at a research library than an apartment living room. Four rows of back-to-back bookcases were arranged perpendicular to the left wall, leaving a narrow passageway on the right, where he had squeezed in a La-Z-Boy recliner and a small table. On the table, a still-smoking cigar sat on the edge of a Caesars Palace ashtray. Next to it was a snifter with a bit of brown liquid in the bottom. Next to that, a book.

"Plutarch," Dr. Martinelli said as Cassandra looked at it. "I felt like some *Parallel Lives* tonight."

He turned. Their eyes met. Cassandra easily read the question in them.

"I have news," she said, answering his query while it was still only a thought. "I've got the money for college."

Dr. Martinelli's eyebrows rose over his thick-rimmed glasses. They matched his hair—a slightly wild salt-and-pepper thatch.

"Let's sit down," he said, which meant they had to move into the kitchen. Cassandra waited while he moved a few stacks of books and magazines, freeing up two chairs at the table in his breakfast nook.

As Dr. Martinelli's eyebrows rose and fell across the table from her, Cassandra explained how an honorary Yell County residency was going to finance her degree.

"The Hunt Foundation will pay for everything, and I don't even have to move to Arkansas," she finished.

"I can understand why you couldn't wait till morning with news like this," her teacher said, "but I will wait until a reasonable hour to call John Reynolds."

He smiled, and Cassandra smiled back.

Hallelujah! It was finally going to happen.

Cassandra had been hearing about John Reynolds for years. He and Dr. Martinelli had both been classics majors back in the seventies at College of the Holy Cross in Massachusetts. Both had gone on to graduate school and then academic careers. Fast-forward a few decades. Reynolds was now chairman of the classics department at the University of Southern California. Dr. Martinelli, who had become a Jesuit, taught at Georgetown until he moved to Las Vegas. The two classmates had stayed in touch, and Dr. Martinelli had promised Cassandra that when the time was right, he would put in a word with his old friend.

"Your credentials will be unorthodox," he'd said, "but I'll do my best to make sure you're taken seriously."

At last! Armed with straight A's and Dr. Martinelli's endorsement, Cassandra had always figured she could at least spin a cherry. Now, with Alex Hunt's gazillions behind her, she was looking at a row of sevens.

VIII

I t was a little past seven when Andrew Danicek pulled into the small parking lot at 950 South Raymond Avenue. The neighborhood was familiar enough to him, but he had never noticed this particular building before. No surprise. It was a plain gray concrete tilt-up surrounded by similar nondescript structures.

Perfect, he thought, at least from the outside. Completely boring, and no exterior clues as to its contents.

Andrew stepped out of his Mercedes into the chilly morning air and climbed three concrete steps to a pair of metal double doors. The key turned easily in the lock, but the left-hand door squeaked on slightly rusty hinges as he pulled it open. Inside, Andrew found a light switch and flipped it on. Fluorescent light panels suspended among a maze of air ducts on the ceiling buzzed and flickered above him. They bathed the entire interior of 950 South Raymond Avenue in bluish light. It was one big empty box, just as he had been promised.

"It used to be a custom bronze foundry," Sonia Illingsworth had told him, and the evidence was there. While the building was mostly empty, Andrew recognized a cracked crucible next to one wall, and the floor was littered with scrap metal.

Counting his paces, Andrew walked the length of the building. He paused at the far wall next to an emergency exit door. The space was roughly 100 by 100, or about 10,000 square feet Again, perfect. Relief rippled through him. There would be no argument with his patroness. Sonia, while generous to a fault, enjoyed being part of Andrew's decision-making processes, even though she held no qualifications other than having been married to an engineer. She acted as though she had inherited her late husband's doctorate upon his passing. In truth, her assumptions and suggestions were often ridiculously off base. Andrew did his best to indulge her, even though it was tedious and wasted enormous amounts of time. But granting Sonia Illingsworth the privilege of feeling like a respected scientist was hardly a high price for the millions she had already invested in Andrew's research and the millions more it was going to take to achieve his goals.

Andrew lowered himself onto a wooden shipping crate next to the emergency exit on the back wall. His head throbbed. He fished a pack of Marlboros and a lighter out of his jacket pocket. He hated himself for falling back into his old habit, but the headaches were coming more often now, and smoking was the one thing that helped. He lit up and took a long, slow drag. As the pain behind his temples subsided a little, he closed his eyes. He leaned back against the wall as a familiar melody drifted soothingly through his mind.

IX

Ich weiß nicht, was soll es bedeuten,
Daß ich so traurig bin,
Ein Märchen aus uralten Zeiten,
Das kommt mir nicht aus dem Sinn.

The lyrics always accompanied the melody. Andrew wished he knew how he had learned the song, but he had no conscious memory of it. Someone—his mother perhaps—must have sung it to him often enough to etch the words and melody into his infant memory, and subsequent events anchored it to his earliest recollections.

I do not know why I am so sad. An ancient story haunts my mind.

It was only after he got his first library card at the Basking Ridge library that Andrew found the English translation of the lyrics and learned that they are from Heinrich Heine's "Die Lorelei." It was a song any German child might know.

Andrew knew beyond a doubt that he had begun life as a German child. In addition to having "Die Lorelei" hidden in his head, he had another secret. His name was not Andrej Novotny as his adoptive parents were told. His name was Dieter Baumann.

As Andrew massaged his aching forehead, early memories flooded his mind. He was back in Germany, no longer Andrew Danicek, the Nobel laureate who was developing technology to conquer the space-time continuum. He was skinny little Dieter Baumann, sucking on the filthy remnant of a hand-rolled smoke that Andrej Novotny had found behind the *Scheisshaus*.

"Hey!" Andrej said. "Don't hog it all!"

Andrej was skinny, too. According to Frau Traugott, he was a year older than Dieter, but they were exactly the same height.

"*Traugott!*"

Andrej snatched the butt and stuffed it into his pocket. Why it didn't set his shorts on fire, Dieter would never know. Sprinting nimbly on their grimy toothpick legs, the boys managed to disappear into the barn before Frau Traugott could lay a beefy paw on either one of them.

Smoking behind the pig barn was the fondest memory Dieter would have of the years he spent under Frau Traugott's iron fist. His earliest was of an especially brutal whipping, although he could not recall the heinous crime he committed as a three-year-old to deserve it. How and when he arrived at that evil woman's swine farm, he had never been able to learn. Years later, he spent many hours in libraries trying to discover who his real parents were, but even a summer in Europe after his junior year at Princeton yielded next to nothing. He managed to cross into East Germany and get back to Kegelsruhe—he figured out where Traugott's sties had been—and even found an elderly woman who remembered the ragtag band of undernourished young-sters who tended the pigs right after the war.

"The children came from Warsaw, I believe," she said. "Also perhaps Prague."

Perhaps. But Dieter Baumann was an indisputably German name, not Polish or Czech. Nothing added up, and no paths led anywhere but into the darkness of the unrecorded past.

Andrej Novotny, on the other hand, claimed he was from Brno.

"My mother will come for me," he said. "When she does, she will take both of us. I promise."

Before Andrej joined the tribe of child slaves at Traugott's farm, Dieter had never thought about a day when he might leave. He had no memories before the farm and the sting of Traugott's leather strap. Andrej changed everything.

Two days after Traugott almost caught the boys smoking, Andrej said, "I know how to get more food."

Andrej's plan involved a convict work project across the road from Traugott's barn. At around the same time that the children slopped the pigs each morning, the prisoners arrived. Chained together in a long, bedraggled line, they stood at attention while two guards unlocked their shackles and barked the day's instructions.

"The woman who brings their food always leaves the wagon in the same place," Andrej whispered when Traugott was out of earshot. He pointed toward the brick wall that they were constructing. "When the wall was low, the food was safe. Now the wall is high."

Dieter looked across the road. Andrej had a point. For the few minutes it took for the guards to unlock the work crew's shackles, the food wagon was left unguarded behind the freshly laid courses of brick.

"Bread," Andrej said. He smiled and rubbed his belly. "I'm going for the bread."

His plan was simple enough. While the guards were busy with the prisoners, Andrej would cross the road and grab whatever food he could stuff under his shirt.

"All you have to do is cover for me," Andrej said. "Make a ruckus if anybody notices I'm missing." Andrej patted Dieter on the shoulder. "You have the *easy* job," he said, "but we'll both get bread."

The plan worked. Andrej was fast, and his timing was perfect. Later that day, the boys split a small loaf of *Vollkornbrot* out behind the barn. It was riddled with gray mold, but Dieter had never tasted anything quite so wonderful.

Andrej's second trip across the road yielded a boiled potato and more moldy bread.

"I keep looking for cheese," he said, "and hoping for meat."

Dieter was happy enough with the bread.

Traugott lurked too closely for the next two days, and then it was Sunday. When a summer rainstorm struck Monday morning, the boys knew they'd have another chance. Traugott stayed in the house when it rained. Lena, the girl she sent in her place, preferred reading *Romane* in the hayloft to watching pigs eat.

At the perfect moment, Andrej sprinted through the downpour across the road. Dieter kept watch. The rain made it difficult to see, and his view was further obstructed when a small mule-drawn wagon piled with firewood moved past at a snail's pace.

"Jozef Grech!" It was Lena's voice. Dieter whipped around to see her standing at the barn door, reading from a scrap of paper. "Mattias Kraus!"

What was happening? Dieter turned back toward the road again, but the wagon, one wheel now stuck in a muddy rut, still blocked his view.

"Andrej Novotny!"

Oh, no! Josef and Mattias had already dropped their pails and were scrambling to stand in front of Lena.

"Andrej Novotny!" she shouted again.

At Frau Traugott's farm, there was only one reason boys were called by name, especially during chores. Josef, Mattias, and Andrej had obviously done something to warrant a whipping.

All you have to do is cover for me. But how?

"Andrej! Where are you? Get over here this instant!"

Dieter dropped his pail. "I'm coming!"

His feet slipping on slick skids of pig manure, the boy scrambled around the troughs and stood next to Mattias. Lena glowered down at him.

"You're not Andrej," she said.

"Yes, I am!" He shouted it.

"Liar. Where's Andrej?"

"I'm Andrej," he said again, hoping against hope that the other boys wouldn't say anything.

Lena raised an eyebrow, then shrugged. "Have it your way, *Dummkopf*," she said. "All you *Schweinkinder* are the same to me."

Lena shooed the boys up the hill toward Traugott's house. They were drenched to the skin by the time a man stopped them on the muddy path. They had never seen him before.

"Come with me," the man said. Five minutes later, the three boys were sitting on metal benches in the canvas-covered back of a dirty brown truck, each wrapped in a green wool blanket.

"U.S." Jozef said, pointing at the black letters stenciled on his blanket. "*Amerikanische.*"

Fourteen days later, Dieter was *Amerikanische*, too. In two transformative weeks, he had crossed the Atlantic, tasted his first orange, and watched his first Hollywood movie. He had met his adoptive parents and older sister. He had taken up residence in his own bedroom—with a cowboy lamp and a wagon wheel headboard—in a white two-story house in Basking Ridge, New Jersey. He had also acquired a new name.

Andrew Danicek.

"Andrew is American for Andrej," his adoptive father—who spoke some German—explained. "Your new last name is still Czech, though. Welcome to the family, son."

He should have said it then. *I'm not Andrej. You got the wrong boy.*

But he was too afraid.

Or too weak.

Or too selfish.

And then it was too late. Once he had allowed himself to take Andrej's identity—and his father and mother and sister and cowboy lamp—how could he admit his awful crime?

As time went by, Dieter-now-Andrew learned that his new father was a second-generation Czech-American who wanted to help war orphans. He and his wife had adopted a girl—his older sister, Mary— through the Bohemian Society of New Jersey. The same network had arranged for Andrej Novotny to come to the U.S. and join the family. No one ever learned about two hungry little boys and the rainy Monday morning when Dieter Baumann thought he was stepping up to take a beating for his friend.

Andrew swore he'd go back when he was old enough. He'd find Andrej and make everything right.

Because everything was right for Andrew Danicek now. His mother, who had a history degree from Vassar, helped him learn English and catch up in school. His father, who was a research scientist at Bell Labs, bought him a chemistry set and helped set up a lab in the garage. Later, they rented an apartment in New York so Andrew could qualify for admission to the Bronx High School of Science. From there, he went on to Princeton, MIT, and Caltech, where he soon held the Charles and Sonia Illingsworth Chair in Physics. When he won the Nobel Prize in 1982, he was grateful that his adoptive parents were both still alive to hear the news. It was all for them, after all.

Or was it for Andrej?

It was Andrej, after all, who had first inspired Danicek's interest in the mechanics of time. If things had gone the way his eleven-year-old mind had dreamed them, Andrej would have been the reason he was building this lab, not Julius Caesar.

X

A week later, Andrew sat at the head of a folding table in the vacant building, scowling at the newspaper in front of him.

"DANICEK PARTNERS WITH ILLINGSWORTH IN NEW VENTURE" read the headline above a short report that revealed Illingsworth's purchase of "an industrial property in Pasadena."

Andrew was well aware that word would eventually leak out about his connection with the Illingsworth Corporation, but he certainly hadn't expected media coverage this soon.

He sighed and took a sip of coffee. On his left, Eric Barza took a bite out of a sesame seed bagel.

"You did a great job getting this place cleaned up," Andrew said. The building was still empty except for the table and chairs, but the litter was gone and the floor swept clean.

"Thanks," Eric said, brushing a crumb out of his beard. "I hired a day laborer, and it only took a couple of hours."

Andrew often felt lucky to have Eric as his assistant. Not only did the younger man possess every necessary academic qualification, he was also a naturally gifted logistician. Andrew had been exploiting this talent for years. Back when Eric was a graduate student, Andrew learned to rely on him whenever he needed help setting up an event or arranging a meeting. More recently, he had learned that Eric had experience in food service, too. He had grown up making cheese steaks in his uncle's sandwich shop in Philadelphia, and he had also worked as a waiter at the MIT faculty club when he was an undergraduate. This discovery made Andrew feel even more fortunate that Eric would be his right-hand man for this new phase of research.

"Thanks for breakfast," Andrew said.

Eric nodded. "I brought a croissant for Sonia," he said.

A perfect example of Eric's attention to detail, Andrew thought. He had no doubt that whatever beverage the Starbucks cup with her name on it contained was her favorite, too.

The metal door squeaked. Andrew rose and moved toward it. He pushed it open to admit a petite silver-haired woman in a bright red coat that matched her lipstick.

"Good morning, Sonia!" Andrew said.

"*Hola*, Andrew!" Sonia said as he bent down to kiss her on each cheek. He pulled out her chair. "It's a bit chilly in here," she said. "I think I'll keep my coat on."

"Coffee might help warm you up," Eric said. "I brought you a double latte with three sugars and a shake of cinnamon."

"*Perfecto!*" Sonia said. "Eric, you are such a sweet boy to remember." She sat down.

"Is that today's?" she asked, pointing a scarlet fingernail at Andrew's *Los Angeles Times*.

Andrew nodded. "I am uncomfortable with news coverage at this point," he said.

"I know that," Sonia said. "But the purchase of this building is public record. I can't help it if a reporter found it newsworthy."

"I understand that, but how did the reporter know about my

involvement?" Andrew said.

"I told her," Sonia said. "She asked me about the building's purpose, and I didn't want her thinking that I was trying to cover something up. In my experience that only makes journalists more curious. At least she honored my request to withhold the address."

"I've ordered security to begin today anyway," Andrew said. "And I know my phone will start ringing. It doesn't take much. I got calls when I adopted a cat from the Humane Society."

Sonia laughed. "The perils of being a celebrity, *querido*," she said.

"We knew this would happen," Eric said. "We just didn't expect it this early. But we're ready. We've just got to start using our cover story."

"I was ready to do that," Sonia said, "but the reporter didn't ask. It's not a full feature article. Just a little notice in the metro section."

"They'll be back," Andrew said. "But in the meantime, if anybody asks, we're testing groundbreaking new technology for dating ancient artifacts. We're going to begin our tests with Roman antiquities from the first century B.C. Why? Because we can test the new data against existing knowledge."

Eric and Sonia both nodded.

"Okay," Andrew said. "Let's move on. We wanted to show you a preliminary drawing."

Eric pulled a manila folder from his day pack and extracted a sheet of graph paper. Andrew pointed at the pencil sketch.

"We'll have the CAD drawings in a week or two, but you can see from this what we've got in mind. A foyer, a common area, staff residences, the main lab and offices, a kitchen, a dining room, and the medical facility." He touched his forefinger to the center of the drawing. "And our visitor's suite, of course."

Sonia smiled. "You've chosen a contractor?"

Andrew nodded. "Penrose and Lee," he said. "They're on your list. They're the best fit, given our power and air-filtration requirements."

"Good choice," Sonia said. "I know Chip would have agreed, too. Which reminds me. I have a request."

Andrew suppressed a grumble. When Sonia Illingsworth had a request, an argument rarely failed to ensue.

"*Querido* Andrew, I would be so thrilled if our new facility could be called the Illingsworth-Danicek Exploratory Studies Laboratory." She paused and smiled. "The IDES Lab for short."

Andrew failed to prevent his eyes from rolling. Was she serious? Did she think this was a child's game?

"What about just Illingsworth-Danicek Laboratories?" he said, trying to hide the exasperation in his voice. "The I.D. Labs."

Sonia pouted. "I like the IDES. Don't you get it? Like the Ides of March?"

"Of course I get it," Andrew said. "And I don't like it. Too risky, and for no good reason."

"It will be our secret," Sonia said. "No one else will have any reason to suspect anything."

"But what's the point?" he said. "To be cute?"

"It would have pleased my husband," Sonia said. "And it would please me."

Andrew let out an irritated sigh. He hated it when Sonia invoked her dead husband to get her way. She had already done it once. When Andrew first decided on Julius Caesar as the subject of phase three, Sonia wanted to be a member of the team that would interact with him, even though she lacked the academic and linguistic credentials. As a compromise, Andrew acquiesced to her counterproposal.

"I understand your arguments against my taking a spot on the team, *querido*," she said. "Instead, please allow me the privilege and pleasure of entertaining Julius Caesar in my home. I only wish that Chip could be there to enjoy it, too."

Taking Caesar out of the lab was the last thing Andrew wanted to do, but in the end, he decided that a short excursion was preferable to four days of nonstop Sonia as a member of the team. At least his patroness had held up her end of the bargain by finding an appropriate building for the lab that was only two miles from her house.

Now he was forced to decide whether denying this new wish was worth the additional guilt trip she would try to impose on him.

"I have an idea," Eric said. "Why don't you flip for it?"

"*Ay, perfecto!*" Sonia said. "*Cara o cruz!*"

More and more ridiculous, Andrew thought, but the coin toss was actually a pretty good idea. He had a fifty-fifty chance of prevailing, and if he did, Sonia couldn't hold it against him. He nodded.

Eric extracted a quarter from his change pocket. "You call it, Mrs. Illingsworth," he said. He flipped the coin into the air.

"*Cara!*" Sonia cried. "*Disculpe!* I mean *heads!*"

The coin bounced on the table and landed.

"Heads," Eric said. "Welcome to the IDES Lab."

XI

Later that same day, Eric carried his bike down the steps and into the lab he and Andrew Danicek would vacate as soon as the 950 South Raymond Avenue was ready for occupancy. Located in the basement of an industrial building in east Pasadena, the old lab had been an excellent home for Andrew Danicek's research until a certain seminal experiment ended successfully. On June 27, 1996, the Temporal Episode Signature Actuator—TESA for short—successfully located a nickel that Andrew Danicek had placed in a Petri dish on a shelf in the lab's storeroom six months earlier. Operating according to protocols developed by Andrew and Eric over the preceding four years, TESA excised the nickel from its location in both space and time and transported it to TESA's central core, a thick-walled container about the size of a kitchen microwave. Eric removed the nickel and marked it with a red Sharpie. Two minutes and thirty-one seconds later, he placed the coin once again inside TESA's central core and initiated the reinsertion protocols. Then he and Andrew went into the storeroom. The Petri dish contained a nickel, just as it had for the last six months. Andrew picked the coin up. Eric watched as he turned it over in his palm. He did not scream when he saw the red X on Jefferson's cheek, even though he felt like it. Both men just stood there until Andrew broke the silence.

"I do believe we're ready for the next phase," he said. He sounded matter-of-fact, but his huge smile let Eric know that he probably felt like screaming, too.

Later, Eric popped the cork on the bottle of champagne that Sonia Illingsworth brought to the lab. The champagne was nice enough— Veuve Clicquot—but it wasn't cold enough, and they had to drink it out of Styrofoam cups. The irony of this was not lost on Eric. He and Andrew had just succeeded in conquering the space-time continuum, and the world would remain ignorant while two guys and one old lady toasted with warm champagne in a basement.

Though he had felt like celebrating when he saw the red X, a vague feeling of dread soon mingled with Eric's excitement. "The next phase," as Andrew called it, was a giant step. Eric wasn't totally sure he wanted to take it, but the longer he stayed with Andrew, the more inextricably tied to his research he became. Joining Andrew's inner circle had turned out to be like being inducted into a gang or the mafia. Once you were in and knew all the secrets, you couldn't leave. And even if he had been able to bow out, he couldn't revert to ignorance of the work that would continue without him. There was no way he could turn his back on an experiment that would ultimately attempt to transport a human being from the past to the present. So much could go wrong, and too much was at stake. It might be a deal with the devil, but Eric would stay the course.

It had been eight years since Andrew first invited Eric to his unmarked basement lab. Until then, Eric knew only of Andrew's official lab at Caltech, where Eric had earned his doctorate under Andrew's guidance. In this secret place, Andrew showed Eric TESA's ancestor, a device that looked like a water heater with a small television screen set into the side. Eric had looked at the screen to see a grainy image of a boy playing a piano. He was pretty sure it was Andrew—the intense dark eyes and angular nose were the same, even if the hair was now thinner and streaked with gray—but so what?

"You are not looking at a photograph," Andrew had said. When Eric still looked blank, Andrew spoke again. "Do you understand what I'm getting at? It's not a photograph from when I was ten years old. It's an image of me at age ten—in real time."

And so Eric was drawn into Andrew's inner circle, an elite coterie that included only two other people. Charles Illingsworth, chairman of the board of the Illingsworth Corporation, was the first one Eric met. Chip was a Caltech alum who had gained fame and fortune as a young engineer when he developed an innovative braking system for the electric locomotives that towed ships through the locks on the Panama Canal. The Illingsworth Corporation had grown into a global engineering firm. He and Andrew Danicek met when Andrew became the first professor to hold the chair Chip and his wife endowed at Caltech.

Chip Illingsworth did not live to see the nickel with the red X, but fortunately for Andrew, his wife was committed to continuing the financial support necessary for Andrew to move forward with his work.

Eric sat down at his computer. He pulled up the to-do list he was working on to keep himself organized during the transition. It was already lengthy and still far from complete. He had just added, "Define HVAC specs" when he heard the door open.

"Glad you're here," Andrew said. "I have news."

Eric swiveled around in his chair.

"We have our doctor," Andrew said. "I had a message waiting when I stopped by campus. Faith Hopper has accepted my offer."

"That's great," Eric said. Faith had been their first choice among biochemists with medical degrees. She headed a research team at Johns

Hopkins. "When does she arrive?"

"December first," Andrew said.

"We've got to move quickly to get her lab set up by then," Eric said. "One more crunch caused by the timeline change."

The timeline change contributed greatly to Eric's increasing feelings of unease, but he couldn't complain. It was Eric who had raised the alarm about computer malfunctions that could occur when clocks ticked over to the year 2000.

"I thought we had everything taken care of," he had told Andrew, "but given the number of variables, I'm concerned we might have missed something. I think we should postpone until any millennium bug issues are resolved."

Andrew thought this over. "When is the next available synch?" he asked.

"February 11, 2001."

"What's available in 1999?"

"March 12."

"Why wait?" he said. "We're ready."

Eric had argued strenuously against this new target date, but it only made Andrew dig his heels in.

"If you can name one concrete reason we can't initiate on the earlier date, I'll listen."

Andrew did not consider extra work for Eric a concrete reason. So here Eric was, in a race against time to prepare for a time-travel experiment. He couldn't figure out why Andrew chose to add this extra element of risk to their project. In the past, he had always said things like "Haste begs calamity," but now he said things that were once uncharacteristic, like "Hire whatever help you need." Once he even said, "Don't sweat the details."

But it was all details, and Eric was sweating more every day.

"Have you had a chance to work on the academics?" Andrew asked.

Eric clicked over to a different file. "Yes," he said. "I've worked up a list of classicists who specialize in Roman history. Two in the UK are worth looking at, a guy in Wales and a woman in Cambridge, both Julius Caesar experts. In the U.S., Bernard Kingsley at Cornell is a good fit. And then there's John Reynolds at USC. He's pretty well known as the author of *What Would Julius Caesar Do?* Came out in 1990 and is now being made into a documentary for the History Channel. I've got full bios on them—and a bunch more—for you to read."

"I don't want to settle for anyone but the best," Andrew said, "but it would be very convenient if our consultant were local. Would John Reynolds be your first choice?"

"He could be," Eric said. "All the ones I mentioned are extremely well qualified professionally. Going forward, I think personality is going to be what matters. And gender. Do you want a man or a woman?"

"Good question. I'll think about that as I read the CVs. In the meantime, why don't you go ahead and get a background check started on Reynolds? And then focus on the new facility. Faith Hopper arrives in three months, and I want to conduct phase two as soon as possible after that.

XII

D r. Faith Hopper recognized Andrew Danicek the moment the escalator descended far enough to reveal the baggage claim area. Even in a crowd, he stood out like a giant. But only to Faith, she noted, as she continued her downward journey. Interested only in jostling for front-row spots at the baggage carousels, the people in the crowd had no idea they were rubbing shoulders with one of the most brilliant minds of the twentieth century.

Faith hadn't expected Andrew to meet her at the airport. All he had told her was that someone would be there to transport her and her luggage to Pasadena. She was looking for a taxi driver holding a sign reading "HOPPER" when her eyes fell on a profile she would have recognized anywhere.

The man himself.

Andrew still hadn't seen Faith as she crossed the terrazzo floor, her carry-on case rolling behind her. She laid a hand on his shoulder.

Andrew turned. Faith would never forget the way his expression morphed from mild surprise to enthusiasm.

"Faith!" Before she could say a word, Andrew grabbed her by the shoulders and planted a kiss on each cheek. "Welcome to my world!" he cried.

If that sounded a bit narcissistic, Faith chose not to notice. He was Andrew Danicek, after all. Shouldn't a titan like him be forgiven a little arrogance? The next half hour was a blur. They must have retrieved her bags and found their way to the parking garage. Faith must have said something, but what? Later, she ran the scene through her head a thousand times, but the details were lost.

Andrew pointed out landmarks on the way to Pasadena—the Hollywood sign, L.A. City Hall, Chinatown. This wasn't Faith's first trip to Southern California, but her previous visits had been to attend conferences in Anaheim and Irvine. This was her first introduction to the real Los Angeles.

Faith loved the apartment that Andrew had arranged for her in a vintage tile-roofed building. He helped carry her bags up the stairs to an airy unit with a balcony overlooking a courtyard ringed with palm trees.

"It's completely furnished," he said. "I wanted to make your move here as smooth as possible."

Faith was grateful for that. While she had left some belongings in a storage unit in Baltimore, she was eager to leave her old existence behind. Divorce finalized, she was more than ready for the next phase of her life to begin.

"I'll show you the lab tomorrow," Andrew said while Faith was still checking out her new digs. "And we can take care of all the paperwork then, too."

Faith knew he was referring to the nondisclosure agreement she would be signing. She looked forward to finding out why Andrew's artifact-dating project required someone with her skill set.

Andrew opened the refrigerator. "My assistant bought some groceries for you," he said, "but I'm hoping you are willing to join me for dinner."

"Willing?" Faith said. "Will 'eager' do?"

Faith saw the color rise in Andrew's cheeks as her own cheeks warmed.

Damn! Did I really just flirt with a Nobel Prize winner?

Andrew departed after they agreed he'd return in two hours to take her to dinner at Caltech.

Caltech's faculty club was housed in a vine-covered Mediterranean villa with ATHENAEVM carved into a huge stone lintel above its outsize paneled door. When they stepped into the foyer, the small group of people assembled there immediately fell silent. A colleague greeted Andrew, and the others smiled and nodded. It was like being with a movie star, Faith thought, or maybe the president. The quiet but palpable attention continued as they walked toward the main dining room, a grand hall with massive chandeliers suspended from its high coffered ceiling. The room's mahogany paneling and oriental carpets made it warm and inviting despite its size. A host seated them at a table between two huge arched windows. He handed them both menus and gave Andrew a wine list. "We have one bottle left of the Chateau Montrose eighty-nine," he said. "I held on to it in case you're interested."

"Thank you for thinking of me, George," Andrew said. "That would be perfect."

The host departed. Andrew moved the small vase of flowers from the center of the table to the side. He leaned forward. "I can't tell you how glad I am to be sitting here with you," he said. "For me, it's an evening for celebration."

Faith felt her cheeks warm. This felt so intimate somehow. Maybe too intimate.

When the wine arrived, Andrew tasted it and pronounced it excellent. "It will go perfectly with the filet," he said. "I hope you eat beef."

"I'm originally from Wyoming," Faith said. "Not eating beef there is grounds for deportation."

The wine was, as Andrew had announced, excellent. But as the evening progressed, it was Andrew's rapt attention that was intoxicating. As she basked in it, Faith felt her old life completely fall away. She had looked forward to new surroundings and a fresh start, but she never dreamed it might be so much more. Maybe the euphoria would wear off someday, but so far, moving to California felt like the best decision she had ever made.

"Einstein stayed here," Andrew told her as they sipped their after-dinner coffee. "He thought Pasadena was like paradise, with its sunshine and gardens and palms. It's smoggier now than in his day, but for the most part, I agree with him."

"I still have a lot to learn," Faith said, "but so far, I agree with him, too."

"I hope you will let me be your cicerone," Andrew said. "Tomorrow we'll meet at the IDES lab, but once we've taken care of business, it would give me great pleasure to show you more of your new city."

Faith smiled but kept her lips pressed firmly together. She was afraid that if she opened her mouth to tell Andrew that the pleasure was all hers, she just might squeal.

XIII

Eric made himself a double cappuccino after he finished his morning conversation with the contractor. Things were progressing pretty well at the IDES Lab. He was glad the kitchen was finished enough to bring in the espresso maker. In fact, having all the plumbing complete was a major milestone. Along with the kitchen, one of the restrooms was usable now, even though it still needed flooring and paint. The timing was just about perfect for Faith Hopper's arrival. Her input would be vital as they set up her lab and the rest of the medical unit.

Eric sat down at the folding table that was still in use in the common area. He looked over his notes as he waited for his colleagues.

Andrew arrived first, carrying a stack of food containers. He had informed Eric the night before that he would be bringing breakfast. Eric was surprised. In all the years the two men had worked together, Andrew had never once offered to do food procurement. Last night, he had insisted.

"Are you sure?" Eric had said. "I'm happy to—"

"It will be my privilege and pleasure," Andrew said.

Weird. But here he was, with fruit compotes and pastries for three, along with plastic utensils and paper napkins. Good thing. Coffee cups were the only tableware Eric had acquired for the lab so far. He was waiting for the rest of the kitchen cabinets to be installed.

"I'm very pleased with Dr. Hopper," Andrew said. "I haven't shared specifics with her yet, of course, but I got to know her a little over dinner last night. I think you'll agree that we chose well."

Eric hoped so, even though he'd had little to do with the decision. Andrew's use of "we" was almost always the royal kind.

While Eric arranged breakfast on the table, Andrew retrieved his briefcase from his car.

"We'll eat first, then get down to business," he said when he returned.

Just then, the door squeaked. Andrew leapt to his feet and rushed to open it. When Faith Hopper entered the room, he greeted her with a kiss on each cheek.

Seriously? Eric thought. He could understand Sonia being into that sort of thing, but she was old and Costa Rican. Faith was thirty years younger and all-American. She seemed to like Andrew's old-school move, though. She was all smiles as Andrew led her to the table where Eric was standing.

Before she sat down, Faith paused to look at her surroundings. Eric watched her take in the size of the building through the framed walls that had yet to be drywalled. She looked up. The framework that would hold the dropped ceiling was in place, but above it the ducts and cables and conduits formed an extensive and complicated maze.

"This place is enormous," she said. "I had no idea."

"You'll know why before you leave today," Andrew said. "But first, meet Eric."

After a few pleasantries, Eric offered to make Faith a coffee. "Our kitchen is far from finished," he said, "but we just got our Gaggia.

Consider me your barista."

Faith laughed. She was quite attractive, Eric thought. He'd seen her picture, of course, and knew about her mass of wavy red hair. But the photograph had not revealed the sparkle in her piercing blue eyes. Eric knew she was thirty-five, but she seemed younger than that—closer to his own age of twenty-eight. She was lean and fit, too. He wondered if she might be a runner.

After they ate—and Eric had cleared the table—Andrew opened his briefcase and pulled out a manila folder. He extracted a stack of pages held together with a black binder clip.

"Ah, the NDA," Faith said with a smile.

Andrew nodded. He unclipped the stack of pages and pushed them toward Faith along with a ballpoint pen. "Please initial each page," he said, "and then sign the last one."

It took a while, but Eric waited silently. When Faith reached the last page, she paused a moment after she signed her name. "Will you be the witness, Dr. Danicek?" she asked.

"No. Eric will," he replied. "I'm just an observer. And you are more than welcome to call me Andrew."

You are more than welcome to call me Andrew.

Sheesh, Eric thought. Coupled with Andrew's unusual insistence about bringing breakfast, this seemed uncharacteristically ingratiating. He shrugged it off, though. Too many other things to think about.

"Before I give you the tour, you need to know more about our work here," Andrew said, "and why confidentiality is so important."

Faith nodded as Andrew paused and took a sip of coffee. "You know we will be testing new technology for dating objects from the past."

Faith nodded again.

"We have completed one test of our newest protocols," Andrew went on. "We identified the location of a nickel six months in the past."

Eric watched a quizzical look pass across Faith's face, but she said nothing.

"We then transported the nickel to the present, where it stayed for a few minutes," Andrew went on. "Then we reinserted the coin into its original time and place."

Faith's eyes widened as she stared at Andrew. Then she looked down.

Andrew opened his mouth to speak again when Faith raised her eyes. "You're seriously telling me you've got a time machine?" There was a note of skepticism in her voice.

It was Andrew's turn to nod. "We don't call it that," he said.

"What do you call it?" Faith said.

"TESA," Andrew said. "Stands for Temporal Episode Signature Actuator."

Another tense pause.

"So this story about dating artifacts is just a clever cover," Faith said at last.

This time Andrew shook his head. "Unlike other dating methods, TESA can date things with perfect precision. At first, looking at objects in the past was all she could do. We identified date and time. She showed us what was there.

"She."

"TESA sounds female, wouldn't you agree?"

Faith didn't reply. She pushed her chair back and stood up. She paced a bit.

"So you've transported a coin," she said at last, resting her hands on the back of her chair. "What's next?"

"Phase two," Andrew said. "An animal."

Eric watched Faith think that over.

"It's beginning to make sense," she said. "If all this is true, I'm beginning to see why you want someone like me on your team."

Andrew smiled. "I know it's a lot to take in all at once. You can ask all the questions you want while we show you around."

Andrew did his best to explain what the various rooms and spaces would look like once construction was finished as they headed to the far left corner of the building. "This will be your lab and the medical unit," he said. "We were eager to have you on board while we are still in the design phase. Everything will be built and furnished to your specifications."

"There's plenty of room," Faith said. "That's good to see."

"We want a fully functional operating theater," Andrew said.

"What kind of animal are you thinking about?" Faith asked.

"Haven't decided about phase two yet," Andrew said, "But phase three will be human."

XIV

Andrew drove Faith to her apartment after the meeting at the IDES Lab.

"I hope you will do me the honor of joining me for dinner again tonight," he said as he held the passenger door open for her.

The invitation surprised Faith nearly as much as it pleased her. She had so many questions left to ask him, so much more she wanted to know about this man who had—unbeknownst to the world—apparently conquered time.

That night, Andrew took Faith to The Derby, a restaurant near the Santa Anita Racetrack where horse race aficionados rubbed shoulders with jockeys and trainers. The evening after that, he drove her around Hollywood and then to Musso and Frank for dinner. The next afternoon, they took Sunset Boulevard all the way to the coast. They walked on the beach in Malibu, then had dinner at a cozy seafood spot with a view of the water. They watched the surfers and pelicans as the sun went down.

The following morning, the IDES team was at work in the lab. Around noon, Andrew walked out of his office and sat down across from Faith at the folding table, where she was working on her laptop.

"Sorry to interrupt," he said.

"It's perfectly fine with me," Faith said, looking up with a smile. She didn't add what she was thinking—that being interrupted by Andrew Danicek was the best thing in her life right now. The last three days had been nothing short of blissful.

"I'm wondering if you'd care to join me for lunch at my place," he said. "I've got some foie gras and some very nice camembert, among other things."

Faith hesitated, a little confused. Every day since she'd arrived, Eric had brought in sandwiches, and they'd eaten them together around the folding table.

"You'll be doing me a favor. I need to check on my rufous."

"Let me grab my bag," Faith said. She wondered who Rufus was but decided not to ask.

A half hour later, Faith stood on the deck of Andrew's multi-level log house in the hills with a view of the entire valley.

"Good thing it's a clear day," he said. "That's Catalina Island out there."

Faith gazed out over the panorama and wondered—as she had so many times over the last few days—what she had done to deserve the attentions of this remarkable man.

She followed him into the kitchen, where he moved to the windowsill and gently pulled back a cloth from a small basket to reveal a tiny scarlet-throated hummingbird with an injured wing.

"My rufous," he said. "He crashed into my living room window a few days ago."

Faith watched as he used an eyedropper to feed the tiny bird. "He's responding well," Andrew said. "And his wing is stronger today. He just might make it."

With its oversize stove, huge stainless steel sinks, and built-in refrigerator, Andrew's kitchen looked like it belonged in a five-star restaurant. He moved around in it with the ease and confidence of a chef. In a few minutes, he and Faith were seated at a table by the window with a well-crafted charcuterie board between them. As promised, there was the foie gras and the camembert, surrounded by an artistic array of other meats and cheeses, some tiny pickles, olives, grapes, nuts, and several kinds of crackers.

If she hadn't been wined and dined by the man for three days prior, Faith might have been surprised. As it was, Andrew's culinary skills, and even his temporary role as veterinarian, all seemed to fit. *The guy's amazing,* Faith thought. *I am so, so lucky to be part of his inner circle.*

After they ate, Andrew showed Faith the rest of the house. As she followed him up and down stairs to living room, library, study, and bedrooms, she found herself wondering whether Nobel Prize winners put their medals on display. But after the tour was complete, and they were back on the deck outside the kitchen, she had not spied a single bit of evidence that Andrew was a celebrity. She had seen no evidence of anything except his good taste in home decor. Even though he had every right, he obviously wasn't a show-off.

As they stood looking once again over the valley, Andrew put his arm around Faith's shoulder. Andrew had touched Faith before, of course, but only in greeting. This felt decidedly different. A delicious feeling of nascent intimacy rippled through her.

"I've been doing all the talking," Andrew said. "It's now your turn. Tell me everything you know about Faith Hopper, M.D., Ph.D."

It sounded like a signal for Faith to begin her life story with medical school, but Andrew interrupted when she began there.

"No. From the beginning," he said. "What's your earliest memory?"

Ooh ... bad question.

Faith watched Andrew read the discomfort on her face.

"My earliest memory is of being lashed with a leather strap," Andrew said. "Why do I get the feeling yours might be similar?"

"A leather strap?" Faith asked, shocked. "How old were you? Who did it?"

"Long story," Andrew said. "I was about three. My parents weren't involved. I'll tell you, but—you first."

Christ. A brutal whipping at age three. Faith's story, as troubling as it was to her, could not compete.

"I don't have a conscious memory of it, but my identical twin sister drowned when we were two."

They retreated to Andrew's cozy living room, where Faith let her whole story pour out.

Andrew listened intently as she told him how she had decided to read *The Lion, the Witch and the Wardrobe* at her aunt's house the summer she turned eight. Somewhere around page 25, Faith came across a card with a photograph of a little girl printed in color on the front. She immediately recognized the smile and red curls as her own. Then she opened the card.

In Loving Memory of Hope Marguerite Hopper
July 9, 1964 – August 27, 1966

A poem about "Little Angels" and another about "Tiny Footprints" faced information about "visitation" and a memorial service at St. Catherine's Catholic Church.

Faith would never forget the paralyzing shock that gripped her as the meaning of the card sank in. She didn't remember her twin, but the moment she learned of Hope's existence, she understood a host of other previously inexplicable feelings. She was only eight, but Faith knew the cloud of sadness that hung over her set her apart from other children. When other girls her age dressed up as brides and played wedding, Faith searched for dead birds in the yard and played funeral.

Faith sat next to Aunt Amy's fireplace and gazed at the card and her sister's face. Her own face.

"Oh, baby, I'm so sorry you had to find out this way!" Aunt Amy cried when Faith showed her the card. "We were waiting until you were older to tell you."

"What happened to her?" Faith demanded.

Held tight in Aunt Amy's embrace, Faith listened to the story of how a babysitter had stepped away while two little girls played in an inflatable backyard wading pool.

"When she got back, you were playing with a rubber ducky, but Hope was face down in the water," Aunt Amy said. "The paramedics came, but it was too late." She hugged Faith even tighter as she added, "It wasn't your fault, sweetie. It wasn't your fault."

Faith allowed the terrible information to sink in.

I was there. I watched her die.

Squirming out of her aunt's embrace, Faith looked directly into Aunt Amy's wet eyes.

"Why didn't anyone tell me?"

"Oh, baby, your mom was waiting for the right moment. She didn't want to hurt you. You didn't remember, so she decided it was best to leave it that way."

Aunt Amy's distress was nothing compared to Mom's when Faith hopped out of Aunt Amy's car that Sunday afternoon with the card in her hand.

"You should have told me," Faith said as her mother's face crumpled.

"Yes, honey, yes," she said. "I should have told you. I was just so—so—"

She dissolved into tears. Faith stared at her mother's heaving shoulders, but she didn't cry until later. When she was alone in her bed, she lay looking at the other bed in her room. Mom had insisted the room needed the other bed, even though Faith had begged for a desk instead.

Now, as the tears flowed, Faith understood. It was Hope's bed.

It wasn't your fault.

Her aunt's words repeated themselves in Faith's head.

But it *was* her fault, Faith decided as she lay there in the darkness. It wouldn't matter how many times people told her it wasn't.

I was there, and my sister died.

The weekend after she learned about Hope, Faith found a card at her place at the breakfast table. There was a string attached to it.

"Follow the string," the card read.

Winding the string as she went, Faith followed it through the kitchen and out onto the back porch. There, sitting in her mother's lap, was a black puppy.

"His name is Skipper," Mom said before Faith could say a word.

Because he's a boy, she decided. Which was probably a good thing. If the dog had been a girl, Faith would have been tempted to name it Hope.

Faith thought about Skipper as she snuggled next to Andrew in the deepening darkness. The sweet black puppy had comforted her as a child. He was the best friend she ever had, and everything about him fascinated her—a living creature, so different from her, and yet connected. He was the reason Faith became a scientist. As a child, she had wanted to be a vet, a dream that led to biology and then medicine.

"I owe my career to a cocker spaniel," she said.

"And your sister," Andrew said.

Tears instantly rose in Faith's eyes. "It's always been about her," she said. "How did you know?"

"Simple. My story is the same. For me, it's always been about Andrej."

It was Andrew's turn. There, looking out over Los Angeles, Faith listened to the strange tale of a boy whose identity belonged to someone else.

XV

"Back when I was in college, I searched for Andrej," Andrew said after he'd finished his story. "I spent a summer in Europe and endless hours in libraries. I searched phone books, street censuses, marriage licenses, death certificates. Novotny is a common enough name, but I turned up nothing. After the Berlin Wall was built, access to records was even more difficult. I knew my chances of finding the right boy using traditional methods were next to zero."

Andrew turned to face Faith, and their eyes locked. When she saw the pain and earnestness there, she felt tears rise in her own eyes.

"My only hope was a path I knew would be long and difficult," Andrew said. He looked down. "I told no one, but I started grappling with time travel while I was still an undergraduate."

Faith had nothing to say.

"What other choice did I have, in a world full of Andrej Novotnys who weren't the right one? I got the idea on a train from Prague to Krakow. As I watched those old farms speeding by, I felt as though I was traveling back in time …"

Faith watched the memories swim behind his eyes. "If only I could,

I kept thinking. If only I could go back and set things right."

"Is there anyone who hasn't wished that?" Faith asked as her own thoughts traveled to a backyard wading pool.

"Probably not." Andrew ran a hand through his hair. "But I'm the only one who has actually done anything about it."

"Are you telling me you found Andrej?"

Andrew shook his head. "Alas, no. That goal has remained elusive."

Just then, a hummingbird buzzed past Faith's head. It was heading for the feeder next to the kitchen door.

"Ah, my Anna's is back," Andrew said. "He's been a regular for at least six weeks now."

The bird's iridescent magenta head caught the afternoon light as it hovered.

"He's beautiful," Faith said. Her eyes met Andrew's again. His gaze felt like physical contact. Oh my God, Faith thought. Is this really happening?

"I have a lovely bottle of pinot gris in the refrigerator," Andrew said, breaking the spell. "Unless you feel it imperative to get back to the lab—"

It was only three o'clock, and it wasn't even Friday. Should I excuse myself? Faith wondered. Is this a test of my professionalism? If it is, she decided instantly, I'm about to fail.

"You're the boss," she said. "You tell me."

A few minutes later, they were sitting side by side downstairs in Andrew's living room. The leather sofa faced a large window with the same view as the deck above them. They each held a crystal glass of white wine, and Ravel wafted over them from speakers built into the raftered ceiling.

Enchanted afternoon gave way to enchanted evening. Looking back on it later, Faith couldn't remember all the things they talked about or even all the secrets they shared. They were only details anyway. The only important thing was their connection. It was far more dizzying than the wine.

When Faith woke up the next morning, dawn was leaking around the edges of the window blinds. As she watched Andrew breathe, she tried to assess what had happened over the preceding twelve hours. Or really, the last three days, she thought. She hadn't realized it at the time, but all this had really begun at the airport.

Andrew stirred. Faith watched as his eyes opened and slowly focused. A smile spread across his face.

"You are so much more than I ever dreamed," he said. He touched her cheek. "So much more."

Faith melted into Andrew's embrace. Two hours melted away, too.

"Are you hungry?" Andrew asked at last. "I would love to cook you breakfast if you are."

"I am," Faith said. She kissed him, and another hour vanished.

XVI

I t was midmorning when Faith followed Andrew into the kitchen and watched him feed his injured hummingbird. How could she have guessed, when she arrived the day before, that she would still be here this morning, clad only in a flannel pajama top? She loved that he was wearing the bottoms, his chest bare. It felt so sweetly intimate.

Faith watched dreamily as Andrew moved around his kitchen. He soon had a pot of oil sizzling on the stove.

"Tell me more about your research," Faith said. "I know you didn't find Andrej, but I wouldn't be here if you hadn't succeeded at other things."

"The first protocols we developed allowed us to look into the past," Andrew said. "But all we had was a tiny, immobile peephole." He removed a beignet from the pot with a pair of long tongs. He pointed the tongs at a metal shaker sitting on the counter. "Sprinkle on the powdered sugar," he said as he placed the hot fritter on a plate next to the stove.

"Looking into the past is immensely useful, of course, but we were limited to one precise moment." He lowered another piece of dough into the pot. "Basically, that's all our new protocols can do, too, except—" He looked at Faith. "As you know, the big difference is that TESA can transport. Phase one—transporting and reinserting the coin—was a success."

Over the fresh beignets and French Market coffee, Andrew told Faith more about phase two.

"As I've mentioned, our next subject will be a living creature. An animal."

"What kind?" Faith asked.

"The species is less important than the where and when," Andrew said. "We knew exactly where to find the nickel—our first target—and we knew exactly when, because I placed it in the Petri dish myself and recorded the time."

"I know the exact location of many a lab rat," Faith said, thinking back on all her research as a graduate student.

"Exactly where they were when they died?" Andrew asked. "And do you know the exact moment of their deaths—at least ten years ago?"

"Their deaths? What does that have to do with anything?"

Everything, it turned out. As Andrew explained why he needed to identify an animal about to meet an untimely end, Faith immediately thought of Skipper.

"I know exactly when my dog died," she said. "And exactly where."

"Really?" Andrew asked. "Within twenty meters?"

Faith nodded and described how Skipper had died at the corner of Sheridan Avenue and 10th Street in Cody, Wyoming, on the morning of April 7, 1975. They were half a block away when Skipper pulled his leash out of Faith's grasp to chase a big cheddar-colored cat. By the time she reached the corner, she had already heard the screeching tires.

"It was 10:16 by the courthouse clock," Faith said. "I looked at it as soon as I saw Skipper in the road. Don't know why, but the time stuck in my mind. Is that exact enough?"

"We can hope the courthouse clock was accurate," Andrew said. "Would you like to see your dog again? If only for about five minutes?"

Faith thought for a moment. It could be difficult, knowing that Skipper would be returning to sudden death. On the other hand, five more minutes with her best friend would give her the chance to say good-bye she'd never had.

"Yes," Faith said. "I'd like nothing more than to hug him one last time."

XVII

As he had each morning since Faith arrived, Eric arrived at the IDES Lab on Thursday with breakfast for three. The other mornings, Faith had arrived almost exactly when he did, at nine o'clock. This morning, though, she was nowhere to be seen, even though it was already closer to 9:30. No big deal. The team meeting with Andrew wasn't until ten.

Eric set the food on the kitchen counter and headed into the TESA unit. When he logged in to his workstation, he saw he had email waiting. "Change of Meeting Time," one of the subject lines read. He clicked the message open.

> Eric and Faith—
> Today's meeting scheduled for 10:00 a.m. will now take place at 3:00 p.m. at the IDES Lab. Sorry for any inconvenience. See you later.
> A. Danicek
> Director
> Illingsworth-Danicek Exploratory Studies Laboratories

Eric checked the time stamp. Andrew had sent the message the night before, just before midnight. He wondered what had come up in the middle of the night to make Andrew change the meeting time but knew he'd probably never find out. He sighed. What difference did it make, anyway? Andrew was the boss. Eric had been dealing with his personality quirks since he was a graduate student. Some of them required a lot more patience and understanding than an unexpected schedule change.

Eric was talking with an electrician a little before three when the main door opened. Andrew and Faith entered the room together. Eric couldn't explain his sudden surprise at their simultaneous arrival. They were both on time for the meeting he would be attending, too. Still, there was something about them that was, well, different. Why did they seem so friendly? But that wasn't quite the right word. They seemed more like accomplices, like partners in a practical joke or two teenagers who thought they had just fooled a teacher.

Just my imagination, Eric decided. Andrew was perfectly professional as he called the meeting to order. Apart from an obvious good mood, there was nothing unusual about Faith or her behavior.

"I think we've got our subject for phase two," Andrew said after Eric had given him the construction update. He explained how Skipper had been hit by a truck while chasing a cat in 1975, and that Faith could identify an adequately precise location and time.

"What do you think, Eric?" Andrew asked. "Seems to me that Skipper's an ideal subject, but I'd like your thoughts."

Eric's thoughts included a question about how Andrew had learned about Faith's childhood pet, but he set his curiosity aside to answer.

"I'll run the preliminaries," he said. "Then we'll know for sure. A cocker spaniel should make a good target—big enough to home in on when our coordinates are not as precise as they were in phase one."

"I thought a dog would be a good choice," Andrew said. "A good step toward phase three."

Eric nodded, but he wondered how much Faith knew about the experiment. Since they had no way of knowing what effect time travel might have on a living subject, one of phase two's purposes was to find out whether it would be harmful or even fatal. Had Andrew informed Faith of this possibility? Did she know TESA might injure or kill the dog in the process of transporting him? He decided to assume that Faith knew the risks. The worst TESA could do would be to shorten the dog's life by a few minutes. And who knew? Maybe death on a time trip was preferable to getting flattened by a pickup truck.

"So now our focus is getting everything ready for phase two," Andrew said. "The medical unit must be completed in no less than eight weeks." He looked from Eric to Faith and back. "Doable?"

Faith answered immediately. "Yes. I've already spec'ed the lab, and I'm halfway through the medical unit."

Eric took more time to respond. It was one thing to "spec" and quite another to procure, install, and test. The lion's share of the work fell—as usual—on Eric's shoulders.

"If everything goes smoothly," he said, "we should be fine. First I need to run preliminaries on Skipper and see if we really do have a viable subject."

"Of course," Andrew said.

"What's involved with that?" Faith said. "Can you give me an idea of how TESA works?

Eric pushed his chair back and folded his hands behind his head. He wouldn't dream of intruding on one of Andrew's favorite tasks: explaining TESA in layman's terms. Andrew had had the opportunity only twice before. He had developed the story originally for Charles Illingsworth and then used an improved version to explain TESA's protocols to Sonia. Now that Faith had been inducted into the inner circle, he could spin his tale again.

"Imagine that Skipper's location in space and time is a piece of paper in a file folder," Andrew began. The file folder is in a file drawer in a filing cabinet, and the filing cabinet is in a storage room in an office building. Because the point in time we are looking for is in the relatively recent past, imagine that the office building is in—" he paused for effect. "Let's say Barcelona."

"*Barcelona?*" Faith said.

"Because we know where Barcelona is, but it's not right nearby. First we have to go to Spain."

Faith nodded.

"Then we have to find the right office building. Then the correct storage room, and the right filing cabinet, file drawer, and file folder. There's still some searching after that, but eventually, we find it. The piece of paper we were looking for."

"It does sound like a lot of steps," Faith said.

Andrew nodded. "I could just as easily have used the needle-in-a-haystack metaphor."

"That's what you had to do to find the coin you transported in phase one?" Faith asked.

"No. Phase one was more like going to Phoenix. The further back in time you go, the more scattered the temporal signatures are. In the recent past, they're more dense and ordered. It's as though time's filing clerk is really conscientious at first, but gets more careless as time goes by."

"Then why not stick with more recent events? Why not locate a dog that died last year?"

"Good question," Andrew said. "And that's essentially what we did with the nickel we transported in phase one. We went back only six months, but that meant that the nickel could stay in the present for a little under a minute. If we'd kept it longer, we wouldn't have been able to reinsert at all."

This was not entirely true, but Eric knew better than to contradict Andrew. And it was enough for now, Eric decided. Faith had so much more to learn, this one detail hardly mattered.

"Why reinsert?" Faith asked. "Why does Skipper have to go back and die?"

"The truth is, he doesn't," Andrew said. "We could keep him here. It's our choice."

Faith dropped her eyes, then raised them. Her unspoken question hung in the air.

"We don't know what would happen if we don't send him back. Maybe nothing at all." Andrew paused. "Or," he went on, "Maybe we'd all cease to exist."

XVIII

That night, Andrew took Faith to dinner at the Parkway Grill.
"I didn't want to bring up phase three at our meeting earlier,"
he said. "I wanted to have the chance to discuss it with you privately
first. So you'd feel freer to ask questions."

That was sweet, Faith decided. "Thank you," she said as the waiter
arrived to twist an enormous pepper mill over their salads.

"As I mentioned after you signed the NDA, phase three involves a
human target," he said quietly, after the waiter left. "Our challenge is
to select the perfect subject."

Faith said nothing.

"Time, place, and imminent sudden demise," he went on. "Those
are the only hard and fast requirements." He paused. "So who shall
it be?"

Faith remained silent. He must have someone in mind already, she
thought. Or at least a short list.

"Kennedy comes to mind," Andrew said. "Or Martin Luther King,
Jr."

"Somebody on the *Titanic*, maybe?" Faith said, figuring she might as well take the bait.

"I doubt we can pinpoint the location of a specific person," Andrew said.

"Okay, James Dean? Or Carole Lombard. Or Buddy Holly."

Andrew chuckled.

"They do qualify with respect to imminent demise," he said. "But I'm eager to select someone truly worth talking to. And I would prefer a stationary target. No ships, planes, or automobiles."

"An academic," Faith said.

"Not necessarily, but someone who might shed light on historic mysteries, or clarify scholarship. It would be easier to select a random nobody, but why not add to our intellectual knowledge in addition to testing the science?" Andrew went on. "I want to make this next experiment a cross-disciplinary effort. Get some historians involved, or whoever could make the most of interacting with our subject."

"Marilyn Monroe," Faith said, thinking of the photo she'd seen on the bookshelf in Andrew's office. "There are plenty of unanswered questions about how she died."

Andrew smiled. "I am an admirer of hers," he said, "but I want to go farther back. The farther back in time we go, the longer the subject can stay in the present."

"Marie Antoinette," Faith said. "Anne Boleyn."

"Good thoughts," Andrew said as their fillets arrived.

"Wouldn't it be best to choose someone we can talk to easily?" Faith asked. "I don't speak French. Do you?"

"Some. My German is better."

"Oh my God. You're not thinking Hitler, are you?"

Andrew answered with a frown.

"Wait! How about Abraham Lincoln?" Faith asked. "He might be perfect. Don't we know exactly where he was when Booth shot him—and when?"

"Yes. I've thought of him, too. I'd like to go farther back. Far enough so that our subject could remain with us for a few days."

"How far back would that have to be?" Faith asked.

"Early medieval times, at least."

Faith took a bite of steak as she pondered this.

"How did Charlemagne die?"

"In his bed," Andrew said. "Of pleurisy. And we don't know exactly where his bed was."

Clearly he had already done some research.

"Frederick Barbarossa?" That was the only other antique German Faith could think of.

"He drowned," Andrew said, "but a heart attack might have caused it. We don't want someone on the verge of natural death, and again, we don't have good enough coordinates."

The waiter turned up to refill their wine glasses.

"Do you really want to keep someone for *days?*" Faith asked after the waiter left. "Where will he—or she—stay? What if something unexpected happens, like a fire—or an earthquake? Seems like the shorter the stay, the better, from a safety point of view."

The words were no sooner out of her mouth when a flood of other thoughts began whirling in her brain.

"And what about exposure to bacteria or viruses? I doubt that people from the distant past can even eat modern food safely. Oh my God! We'd have to keep them in a bubble and feed them—I don't even know what! Or—Jesus Christ! What would happen if they—?"

Faith paused, her mind still spinning.

"Now you understand even more clearly why you are here," Andrew said. "You are vital to our success."

Faith willed her heart rate to slow down. She took a drink of water.

She forced her thoughts back to the subject at hand—important people from the distant past whose whereabouts when they died sudden deaths were known.

"Jesus," she said, this time not as an expletive. She looked at Andrew.

Andrew's face registered surprise, then softened. "I'd get him if I could, but his dates and places are just too vague. You're on the right track though."

Faith thought a moment, then tried again. "Beware the Ides of March," she said.

A huge smile spread across Andrew's face. "Now you're talking."

"You like the idea of Julius Caesar?"

Andrew nodded. "So much that I'm already in discussions with John Reynolds," Andrew said. "He's chairman of the classics department at USC and an authority on Caesar."

"You've already decided? Why didn't you tell me?"

"I planned to. I didn't expect our conversation to unfold as it did." Andrew reached across the table and took Faith's hand. "You were so quick to accept the mental challenge. I loved watching your mind at work." He paused as he looked deeply into Faith's eyes. "Sometimes I can't help believing in destiny," he said. "We were meant to be together."

Faith said nothing as a feeling of wondrous disbelief engulfed her. Andrew Danicek had been miracle enough, and now she was going to meet Julius Caesar.

XIX

"Whoa!"

Or maybe it was, "Wow!" Whatever Andrew yelled, it expressed everything Faith could not. Skipper's appearance struck her utterly dumb.

There was no warning, no sound, no gradual coalescence of molecules. Not even the tiniest air disturbance. Faith had no metaphor to explain how shocking it was to be alone with Andrew in TESA's translocation chamber one moment, and then—a nanosecond later—to be staring at the back end of a dog that had died twenty-five years earlier.

"Sorry," Andrew said. "It's just so—so astonishing!"

Skipper whipped around, his toenails scrabbling on the polished concrete floor. His eyes bulged in fright.

Oh, God! What have I done?

How could Faith have thought it a good thing to snatch her sweet friend from familiar surroundings? She couldn't change the fact that he was about to die. Why subject an unwitting dog to terror in the few moments he had left to live?

Skipper looked at Andrew first. He panted, his tongue flapping out the left side of his mouth.

Then Skipper turned his head, and his eyes met Faith's. Would he recognize her? She was twenty-five years older. She looked nothing like the eight-year-old girl he knew.

Before she could ask another mental question, Faith's arms were full of cocker spaniel. Skipper whimpered joyously as he licked her entire face.

You are all that matters.

No, Skipper could not talk, but his message to Faith could not have been clearer.

You—not my sudden displacement, strange surroundings, odd sounds, and peculiar odors—you are all that matters. If you are here, my dearest friend, all is well.

And all was indeed well for the next six minutes and thirty-seven seconds. Followed closely by Andrew, Faith carried Skipper into her lab. She took his vitals and did a quick exam. Eric took photographs, and Andrew took notes. In all, she had about three minutes to do nothing more than try to communicate to her dog that she loved him as much as he loved her.

"It's time," Eric said too soon. Faith gathered Skipper into her arms again, breathing in the fragrance of the lilac bush he liked to hide under. She carried him out of her lab and back toward TESA. He panted in her right ear and licked it in between breaths.

Andrew opened the door, and together they walked into TESA's control room. They crossed to the other side while Eric opened TESA's antechamber. When the doors slid closed behind them, Skipper abruptly stopped kissing Faith's ear. Whimpering, he struggled to free himself from her arms. When he turned his head, she saw his eyes. They were bulging again.

"He's terrified," Faith said as the panel doors to TESA's central core parted. "He wasn't a moment ago, but he is now."

"Strange surroundings," Andrew said matter-of-factly. "It'll all be over soon."

Faith sucked in a breath as she realized that Andrew didn't give a damn about her precious pet. He had no interest in why Skipper would fear a place where he had spent so little time. Faith thought about the moments when Skipper arrived. He'd been overjoyed to see her. But should he have been? From his perspective, Faith had just been with him back in Cody.

"Set the dog down," Andrew said, gesturing at the translocation container in the center of the chamber.

Faith pulled Skipper closer. "He's so scared—"

"He's already dead," Andrew said. "His feelings mean nothing."

Tears sprang to Faith's eyes as she hugged Skipper more tightly.

"Set him down." Andrew commanded. "Now."

Faith pressed her face into Skipper's neck. "I'm so sorry," she whispered. "I'm so sorry." She placed the dog in the chamber. His pleading eyes met hers as she pulled away. A moment later, he was gone.

"Victory!" Andrew cried as soon as Skipper disappeared. "Perfection!" He hugged Faith and kissed both cheeks. Still stunned by what had just transpired, she didn't respond. He shook her shoulders. "Do you know what this means?" Faith stared at him as tears welled in her eyes. She watched the delight vanish from his face. The look of disgust that replaced it made her tears spill over.

"You're being ridiculous," Andrew said as Faith's shoulders began to shake. He dropped his hands, turned on his heels, and rushed back into the control chamber. Faith heard him speak angrily to Eric as she stood immobile, struggling to control her emotions. By the time she entered the control room, both Andrew and Eric were gone. She stood alone in the semidarkness watching figures and digital messages crawl across the monitors.

Pull yourself together, she commanded herself. She took a breath and wiped her eyes on her sleeve. Andrew is right. You're being ridiculous. The experiment was a success. Everything went according to plan.

Except—no! They definitely hadn't planned to terrorize a dog. Skipper's eyes flashed into her mind's eye. Could she have misconstrued the look of panic in them?

Of course not! It was obvious Skipper was terrified. And the last thing he knew before he died was not that I loved him. The last thing he knew was that I sent him to his death.

Faith gulped air as her shoulders heaved. Wracked with guilt, she held her head in her hands and sobbed.

XX

"We may have a problem with Faith," Andrew said as he closed the door to his office.

Eric said nothing. If he were going to assign blame, he'd say whatever was going on was Andrew's fault. How could he have thought it was acceptable to engage in a fling with Faith? Not only was he her boss, he was nearly twice her age. Even if Faith had been the instigator, Andrew was the one who looked like a predator.

Of course, both lovebirds thought they had kept their affair a secret. They didn't know that Eric's suspicions had germinated the day they showed up together for the meeting Andrew had moved to the afternoon. Since then, more evidence accumulated, mostly in the form of shared winks and smiles, or in intimate conversations suddenly truncated when Eric appeared. Eric tried to convince himself that he was adding unsubstantiated meaning to their familiarity until the day he walked by the kitchen at just the right moment to catch them in an embrace so steamy it rivaled the espresso maker. At that point, all Eric could do was hope that Sonia didn't know. She would not, to say the least, be amused. Eric decided that silence was his best hope for forestalling overt conflict in the IDES Lab.

"I don't want to replace Faith," Andrew said. "She's done a fabulous job for the last two months. It's her emotional health I'm worried about."

That makes us even, Eric thought. I'm worried about yours. All he could do was hope they'd make it through phase three without any meltdowns. Could they survive as a team for nine more months?

"She's been great to work with," Eric said. "And her dog was a perfect subject. So what's the problem?"

"She thinks we should scratch phase three."

"Really?" This came as a surprise to Eric. Phase two had gone so well. Faith had seemed happy to see her dog again.

"She's got a laundry list of reasons."

"Like what?" Eric asked.

"He could bring a virus or catch one while he's here. He won't be able to tolerate the food. The transport could kill him. What it boils down to is that she's scared."

"Have you explained everything to her? Does she understand that the risks are minimal, but we're taking precautions anyway?"

"She understands. She's still scared. She thought we terrorized her dog."

"She may be right. The only mitigating factor was that it was over fast," Eric said.

Andrew glared at him. "Don't even think about siding with her," he said. "I'm counting on you to calm her down."

"Is she still here?" Eric asked. "You want me to talk to her now?"

"No, she went home," Andrew said. "Let her cool off. Tomorrow is soon enough."

XXI

John Reynolds looked at his watch as he pulled into his parking spot. Good. Traffic had been heavy, but he still had plenty of time to check his email and phone messages before his meeting with Jeff Goldman, the producer of the History Channel's documentary about Julius Caesar inspired by John's best-selling book, *What Would Julius Caesar Do?* To accommodate John's teaching schedule, Jeff had moved the production schedule to coincide with summer break. In response, John wanted to be punctual for every appointment.

John stepped out of the car, reached behind the driver's seat, and pulled out his cane by its brass eagle-head handle. He could manage without the cane, of course, but he had long admitted that getting around was easier with it than without it. It had sentimental value, too. John had carried it for three years now, ever since his students at the Intercollegiate Center for Classical Studies in Rome presented it to him a few weeks into his year as professor in residence.

He had just finished showing them around the Largo Argentina, his favorite archaeological site in the city. His students surrounding him, he finished up the tour in the *curia* of Pompey's Theater, standing right where Julius Caesar spoke his last words on the Ides of March, 44 BCE.

He was about to describe the scene when Brian, a Yale student, stepped forward.

"Hail, Caesar!" he said. As the other students cheered, he held the cane out to John.

Surprised, John nonetheless grasped it. "You aren't trying to make me king, are you?" he said.

His students laughed.

"We would have gotten you a crown if we had that in mind," Brian said. "We just thought this would go well with your bow ties," he went on. "All you need now is a top hat and Ginger Rogers."

Brian's tactfulness touched John. He had walked with a significant limp since he was a child. Two years in traction had failed to completely erase the effects of Legg-Calvé-Perthes disease. At the beginning of that year in Rome, John bought a cheap pine walking stick at the Porta Portese flea market so he could keep up with his students on field trips. After they gave him the lacquered hardwood cane, he carried it everywhere, even when he wasn't on a field trip. It looked much better with his suits and bow ties than a rough-hewn pine staff, and it didn't give him splinters. Whenever John caught sight of himself in a mirror, he was even mildly tempted to acquire spats and a top hat.

Ginger Rogers was a different matter. After a disastrous marriage, John found he could not ignore the stirrings he first felt while confined in bed back in Texas. Neither would he indulge them, so he took a personal vow of abstinence. Had he been born twenty years later, perhaps such a drastic step would not have been necessary. As it was, he preferred to remain silent about his sexual orientation, to lead a life of social singularity, and to ignore the curious whispers of students and colleagues.

John had always thought it ironic that he owed his career to the twenty-two months he spent tethered to a pair of twenty-pound bags of gravel as a child. It was like a sentence in a Victorian penitentiary, and yet his time spent solitary and horizontal was one of the most defining periods of his life. Yes, he was forced to forsake his budding baseball career, but he consoled himself with the Midland Public Library, where his mother ruled as head librarian. She refreshed John's stack of books every day, and she paid close attention to what interested him. As long as it wasn't sports, the boy soon realized.

"You'll have time enough for that after you're back on your feet," his mother explained.

John discerned the truth early on, though his parents did their best to shield him from their fears. They were afraid their son would never walk again.

The young orthopedist who saw John every month in Dallas spoke a little more optimistically about his prognosis. Dr. Cummins was a baseball fan. He kept a ball autographed by the entire 1962 New York Yankees team in a glass box on his desk.

"No one can promise that you'll play ball again," he said, "but no one can say you won't, either."

I will do it, John told himself. No one can stop me.

"In the meantime, you've got a different game to play," Dr. Cummins said. "Your doctors, your parents, we're all on your team. We play our positions—you've got to play yours."

John's position was in a wheeled bed that could be moved from room to room. When he needed to take a bath or use the toilet, an adult carried him. Otherwise, the special bed and the boy were a unit.

During the entire twenty-two months of his sentence, John sneaked out of the bed only once. He was in his usual spot in the family room. His mother had answered the front door, and his father was mowing the lawn. The first game in the World Series was about to begin, and the television—an older model with no remote control device—was tuned to a program teaching viewers how to paint watercolors of cloudy skies.

Ten feet couldn't hurt, right? John would dart across the room and be back in bed in no time. It took forever to get the boots off—they were attached to the ropes that were tied to the weighted bags. Finally barefoot, John could hear his mother still chatting with Mrs. Munger at the door, and the roar of the lawnmower told him that his father was still occupied outside.

Swinging his skinny legs over the side of the bed, John stood up. Or at least that's what he planned to do. Instead, he collapsed into a heap on the rug.

Jeez! What's going on? He had been able to walk when he first took to the bed, and he had no idea the power had vanished during the months he'd lain immobile.

John's legs buckled again on his second attempt. Undaunted, he struggled again to his feet. Pain arced through his pelvis and shot down his legs as he clung to the end of the bed for support. Tears sprang to his eyes, and he squelched a scream.

I can't walk!

Dr. Cummins had told John that he'd have to learn how to walk again, but the words had made no sense. Babies could walk. John was ten years old, going on eleven. He wouldn't need to relearn. He would simply never forget. Only now—

Gritting his teeth, the boy tried another step. Swallowing another cry, he crumpled once again to the floor. He lay there a moment, shocked and confused. Maybe his parents were right after all.

No! I will walk. And by golly, I'll run, too.

John knew the ballgame had already begun. On his elbows, he dragged himself across the living room floor. He changed the channel on the television console and hauled himself back into bed.

John's parents never asked how the art program had morphed into a baseball game, and he never told them about his trip across the carpet. He never forgot it, though. He still wondered on occasion what that one act of disobedience had cost. His right hip never healed properly, leaving him with a permanent limp and the prospect of osteoarthritis. Had a game of baseball killed his own baseball dreams?

Eleanor Reynolds was a whiz at choosing books that would fascinate a ten-year-old who could read like a college junior. One day, she brought home a slim paperback called *The Decipherment of Linear B*. The small volume was a surprise. At the time, John had been devouring fat non-fiction best sellers like *The Territorial Imperative* and *The Naked Ape*. The new book's diminutive size drew the boy's attention, if only because it didn't seem very important—more like a pamphlet. He opened it, chancing upon a page near the front that displayed a chart of strange letters.

"That random page," John had said many times over his career, "set the course for the rest of my life."

John's mother, quick to respond to an interest that her son could pursue even if he were confined to a wheelchair, brought home all the books she could find about odd alphabets, ancient writing systems, and cryptography.

"Johnny's teaching himself Greek," she told her friends.

They just smiled and nodded, but when she mentioned it to the rector at St. Mary's, he brought John a New Testament with Greek and English on facing pages the next time he stopped by the house on a pastoral visit.

Before his convalescence was over, John had begun to teach himself Latin. By then, the superstars of the ancient world had supplanted his favorite baseball heroes. Even so, he never gave up his plan to play baseball as soon as his legs would cooperate. But, during his final appointment in Dallas—after he had endured three months of physical therapy and learned how to walk again—Dr. Cummins pointed to the baseball in the glass box on his desk.

"See all those autographs?" he asked.

"Mickey Mantle, Yogi Berra, Roger Maris, Whitey Ford—"

Dr. Cummins smiled and nodded. "They're all there, but there's something you've got to remember."

Lifting the glass, Dr. Cummins took the ball from its cradle and placed it in John's hands.

"It's just an old ball with ink marks on it."

John stared at the ball. What was Dr. Cummins talking about? The Yankees won the World Series in 1962. They were the World Champions—

"It's a treasure because of fans like us," Dr. Cummins said.

Fans like us. As young as he was, John knew what Dr. Cummins's words meant. He could walk, but his right hip was stiff. Worse, his legs were no longer the same length. He would never play big league ball.

John left the doctor's office carrying the baseball in its glass case.

"It's yours to care for until you pass it on to another true fan," Dr. Cummins told the boy. "We're the ones who keep the glory alive."

The doctor's words, intended merely to be comforting, instead gave John new resolve. All the zeal he had had for playing baseball now went into his new passion for ancient languages, history, and culture. He still loved the game, but his new lineup of heroes included Pericles, Themistocles, and Alexander the Great. At the top of the list was Julius Caesar.

"I became not only a student of ancient Greece and Rome," John would tell anyone who asked about the autographed baseball on his desk. "I became a fan. As a teacher of the classics, I'm one of those who keep the glory alive."

XXII

John smiled inwardly as he rode the elevator to the second floor. He loved how he had lived up to his signature statement about his mission in life. *What Would Julius Caesar Do?* had succeeded beyond his dreams in introducing a whole new generation to the wonders of ancient history. This television interpretation would expand that achievement exponentially.

I may well need a new dream, he thought as he stepped off the elevator and headed to his mailbox in the classics department office. What are some new ways I can keep the glory alive?

John's mailbox was stuffed. You'd think summer vacation would slow things down, he thought as he pulled out a stack of phone messages and letters and two packages that obviously held books. Or maybe it made sense. Summer was when people tried to finish all the projects they didn't have time for the rest of the year.

In his office, John started sifting. He still had half an hour before Jeff would arrive.

The first book package was from Wiley & Sons. Inside was a high-school history text written by a professor he knew at Bryn Mawr. As he had expected, there was a request for an endorsement tucked inside. No problem. He knew he'd be able to give it a nice blurb. He turned his attention to the second package, a padded envelope from Random House. Inside was a blue volume labeled "Advance Reader Copy."

Out of Place and Out of Time: My Quest for Truth, Beauty, and the Meaning of Life

The title meant nothing to John, but then his eyes dropped to the author's name.

Philippa Kenyon Sykes.

John let the book fall to his desk as though it had suddenly turned into a hot potato. There was no way he'd read the book, much less write kind words about it. It was awkward, though. Random House was his publisher, too. His editor would not be pleased when he refused to support a colleague.

Except Pippa wasn't a colleague, John thought as he stared at the book. Hadn't been since back in the seventies, when she scuttled her reputation with a hard turn into the twilight zone. Once she started pontificating about out-of-place artifacts, ancient aliens, and telekinesis, the academic world immediately backed way off. If Random House wanted someone to endorse this new book, they'd have better luck asking Erich von Däniken.

John felt a twinge of guilt as he set Pippa's book on the edge of his desk. He thought back to the day he met her at the annual meeting of the American Archaeological Association in 1972. Pippa gave a talk about the Temple of Aphrodite in Knidos. She was a superstar back then, still aglow from all the attention that came her way when she discovered the temple that had eluded archaeology's most renowned luminaries. Heinrich Schliemann himself had searched and failed to find it.

An eager undergraduate at the time, John had made his way through the crowd to shake her hand after her talk.

"I'm honored to meet you, Mrs. Sykes," he'd said.

"I'm not a Mrs.," she'd replied, "but nice to meet you, too."

There was nothing more to their interaction. He hadn't thought about the woman much since *Gifts of Hermes* made her a successful author but ended her academic career. It was sad that her strange metamorphosis into a popular celebrity had so thoroughly tarnished all her earlier achievements.

Now with only a few minutes before Jeff arrived, John turned his attention to the telephone messages. They were all the mundane housekeeping kind except one.

"Caller: Andrew Danicek," the note read. "Please call back. 626-555-3134."

Andrew Danicek. Of course John recognized the name, but why was a Nobel-winning physicist contacting a USC classics professor? Maybe it was just someone with the same name. Whoever it was, John would definitely be dialing the number on the note as soon as Jeff Goldman left.

◉◉◉

The meeting with Jeff went even better than John had hoped.

"*What Would Julius Caesar Do?* will be Pandora Productions' flagship project this year," he said. "Which means we now have a budget that can begin to do the subject justice. So I need you to think big, John. What would you create if money were no object?"

The conversation blossomed from there. By the time Jeff left, John was flying high on the producer's descriptions of which A-list actors they might tap and what wonders could be brought to the screen with the help of computer-generated graphics and cutting-edge special effects.

"We're going to bring Julius Caesar back to life," Jeff said before he left. "He'll be so real, our viewers will swear they met him."

Still exhilarated from the meeting, John called Andrew Danicek. The next day, he drove to Pasadena to meet the man at his lab on Raymond Street. After John signed a multi-page nondisclosure agreement with the Illingsworth Corporation, Andrew told him the truth about the new project of which he was now a part. Still floating on a cloud of incredulity as he drove to his house in the Hollywood Hills, John recalled Jeff Goldman's parting words to him.

"He'll be so real, our viewers will swear they met him."

What would you say, Mr. Goldman, if you knew your consultant really had?

XXIII

JULY 8, 1998
THE IDES LAB

E ric arrived around ten, not because he was being lazy, but because he'd just spent two hours with the contractor at Snyder Diamond Appliances picking out sinks and toilets.

He locked his bike to the stand next to the fire hydrant. As he headed up the steps, he noticed two cigarette butts on the top one.

Who the hell has been smoking out here? he wondered. He'd been very diligent about informing every visitor and workman about the IDES Lab's strict policy of no smoking inside and within fifty feet outside. And now that the air filtration system was about to be installed, he wanted to be extra-sure he had full compliance.

Inside, he headed for the kitchen, where he found Andrew eating an apple.

"Glad you're here," Andrew said. "John Reynolds just called. We

119

need to talk."

Eric followed Andrew into his office, where he shut the door. Interesting, Eric thought. This must be something he doesn't want Faith to hear about. Not that he really had to worry. Faith had pretty much kept to her lab ever since TESA succeeded in transporting her dog. More accurately, she had retreated to her private domain ever since her fling with Andrew came to a sudden end. Judging from appearances—mostly Faith's red, puffy eyes—this occurred the day after the dog episode. Eric never knew for sure who had dumped whom, but if pressed, he would have bet on Andrew. He'd been shocked enough when his mentor had initiated the relationship with his new hire. Andrew had long had a reputation as a bit of a ladies' man, but he was also known for courtesy and discretion. His behavior toward Faith had shown neither. For reasons he couldn't understand, Andrew seemed to have turned from a considerate admirer of women into a predatory skirt chaser.

As though she thought Eric had been complicit in Andrew's bad behavior, Faith now kept her distance from both men. Fortunately, and to Faith's credit, she maintained a high level of professionalism. They didn't need to be friends to get their work done, but Eric found the freeze in the IDES Lab depressing. It was so damned unnecessary.

"John wants to add his colleague to the team," Andrew said. "Elizabeth Palmer. Here's her CV."

He pushed a folder across his desk toward Eric.

"I'm inclined to agree that she'd be a good addition," Andrew said. "I really like the idea of having both a man and a woman who can speak Latin. As John pointed out, it increases our odds of connecting effectively."

Eric opened the folder. A photograph of a nice-looking brunette was clipped to the corner of the résumé inside. Not bad, Eric thought, for someone closing in on forty.

"Is she married?" Eric asked. He immediately regretted his question as Andrew arched an eyebrow at him and grinned.

"That's not what I meant," Eric said, but of course he couldn't say what actually had inspired his question. He was worried about what Andrew might do if another attractive woman joined the team. It might help if she at least sported a wedding ring.

"Her husband is a numismatist. He owns a coin dealership in Beverly Hills."

"Interesting," Eric said.

Andrew nodded. "Elizabeth and John will both be here tomorrow at eleven."

Typical, Eric thought as he left Andrew's office. *He let me think I was helping him evaluate his options when he had already made a unilateral decision.*

XXIV

A little past two on August 13, 1998, Las Vegas vanished in Cassandra's rearview mirror as she headed south on Interstate 15. It was the worst possible time to hit the highway in an old Volkswagen with no air conditioning, but it didn't matter. She would cherish the moment forever. At last, she was leaving sun-bleached Gomorrah for the shady groves of academe.

If all went well, in ten days Cassandra would be a junior in USC's classics program, with Professor Elizabeth R. Palmer, Ph.D. as her adviser. A few hurdles remained, but she was confident that her training and the Hunt Foundation's money guarantee would propel her through the last shreds of red tape.

Cassandra left Carefree Canyon Trailer Resort behind the wheel of her mom's trusty VW, Jeremiah. In its place, ready to drop her stepfather's jaw the next time he stopped by for a cash infusion, sat a much newer white Toyota.

"How would you like to handle your car allowance?" the secretary at the Ivy and Adrienne Hunt Foundation had asked.

Car allowance?

It was the first Cassandra had heard of it, but she wasn't entirely surprised. Ms. Jacqueline Stork had already taken care of paying her tuition at USC. She had also wired the first installments of her stipend and housing allowance into Cassandra's checking account, along with an extra $5,000 for "relocation expenses."

"Why don't I just wire the money to your checking account, dear?" Ms. Stork said when Cassandra failed to come up with a better answer. And just like that, she had another eight grand to spend on "something safe and economical."

"Ordinarily, we pay for vehicles and housing directly," Ms. Stork said, "but Mr. Hunt has instructed me to waive our usual procedures in your case. He said you were a bit more—" she hesitated. "More mature than our usual grant recipients."

Cassandra decided to take that as a compliment, though she wondered what word Alex had really used to describe her. It was just one more thing to wonder about Alex Hunt. She was still having trouble believing that he was really making all her dreams come true—no strings attached. But scary as free money felt, nothing would have her turning back.

The car allowance scored Cassandra the first car she had ever owned that was less than a decade old. The seven-year-old Toyota was no showpiece, but as she was driving it to Carefree Canyon for the first time, she felt a pang of guilt that it was so much newer and nicer than Jeremiah. Cassandra had lived with her mother for the past twenty-six years. Margot swore she was thrilled that her daughter was heading off to chase her dreams, but she was also getting left behind in a dingy old mobile home with a rattletrap car. Then it dawned on Cassandra that Malcolm couldn't talk Mom out of a car she didn't own. Margot put up a valiant fuss, but she still signed Jeremiah over to Cassandra. *Voilà!*

Cassandra now owned two cars, and there was no reason not to leave the one with air conditioning for Mom to enjoy. If things worked out, maybe someday Cassandra could buy a house and do the same thing. In the meantime, she didn't care that her magic carpet was hotter than a pizza oven. She rolled down all the windows, cranked up the crappy radio, and silently thanked Malcolm for teaching her how to drive a stick shift.

XXV

AUGUST 16, 1998
BEVERLY HILLS, CALIFORNIA

S imone was feeding the birds when the doorbell rang. Cléopâtre was squawking so loudly, she barely heard it. She walked through the dining room as quickly as she could.

Arthritis. *Quelle maladie terrible!*

Simone paused to take a quick look at herself in the mirror over the sideboard. Not bad, considering she'd been gardening all morning. She patted a stray hair back into place and crossed the living room.

Qui pourrait-il être? Simone wasn't expecting anyone. Gunther, her next-door neighbor who always gave her a hand when she needed a new tenant, had said the ad for the guest house wouldn't appear in the paper until the next day. She peered through the peephole. A young blond woman she had never seen before stood on the porch.

She didn't look like a Jehovah's Witness or a home invader, so Simone opened the door.

"Hello," the young woman said. "I'm interested in the house."

"The house?"

"Your sign. Is the house still available?"

Oh! Simone leaned around her visitor. Sure enough, a sign rose from the flower bed under the tulip tree. Gunther had been more efficient than Simone expected.

"It's a small guest house in the back," she said. "For one person only."

Simone paused and looked the young woman up and down. *Très jolie.* Beautiful, in fact. An actress, perhaps, or more likely a waitress with high hopes.

"One quiet person."

"I'm very quiet," the woman said, smiling. "I'm a full-time student at USC. My only music source is a Walkman with headphones."

A college student? *Intéressant.*

"What are you studying?"

"Latin and Greek."

"*Zut alors!*" Simone almost laughed. Fifty years in the entertainment industry had taught her a lot about sizing people up, but this girl had fooled her completely.

"*Ah! Nous pouvons parler en français!*"

Mon dieu! And she spoke French, too!

Before Cassandra left that afternoon, Simone asked her to pull the "For Rent" sign out of the petunia bed.

"I'd be happy to," Cassandra said. "*Avec plaisir!*"

Simone smiled. She was happy, too, though she knew that Gunther would give her grief for not running a background check on her new tenant. The more Simone talked with Cassandra—in French!—the more her spirits lifted. The young woman was well spoken, well read, and well mannered. If she turned out to be a fraud or a deadbeat,

Simone would deal with it. In the meantime, real French conversation was salve to her lonely soul, and she was going to relish every moment of it.

Simone led the way into the small garage and unlocked the padlock on the side door. The two women stepped inside.

"*Ooh, la la!*" Cassandra said after Simone flipped on the light. "That is one amazing car."

"This was Boxcar's baby," Simone said, resting a hand on the shiny red hood of the vintage Corvette. "My husband's pride and joy. I don't drive it much—I'm more of a taxi girl—but I make a point of keeping it in good condition. Boxcar always did."

"Boxcar was his real name?"

"It's not what he was christened," Simone said, "but it is what happens when parents who live next to the train tracks name their baby Balthazar." She smiled. "From the time he could talk, he was Boxcar. When he turned eighteen, he made it legal."

⊚⊚⊚

Cassandra called her mom that night.

"It's perfect," she said. "One big room, but Simone—the landlady—put in three bookcases to fill the gap left by the last tenant's grand piano. Creates kind of a bedroom area."

"Sounds cute," Margot said. "Where is it?"

"I'll put it this way. My new ZIP code is 90210."

A pause. Cassandra smiled as she imagined her mother's silent "Wow."

"You can afford Beverly Hills?" Margot asked.

"Yes, thanks to you."

"*Moi?*"

"*Mais oui!* In exchange for a couple of afternoon French conversation sessions a week, Simone knocked the rent down. And she's great, Mom! She's originally from Marseilles but grew up in New York. She was a Radio City Rockette until she met her husband, and he got a job building sets for *Ben-Hur*. His team won an Academy Award, and that meant he could pretty much write his own ticket in Hollywood for a while. And then they got into training birds for films, and Simone still has two lovebirds, two budgies, and a big blue macaw named Cléopâtre—" God, she was rambling. "Anyway, I'm moving in tomorrow."

"It sounds wonderful, sweetheart," Mom said. "Just remember that parrots can draw blood when they bite."

Cassandra laughed. "I'll keep that in mind, Mom."

XXVI

Elizabeth Palmer was not likely to forget the day she met Cassandra Fleury. She even remembered the date: August 21, 1998. It was Elizabeth's first day back on campus in nearly a month. Knowing that it would be her last chance for serious IDES Project preparation before classes started, she'd spent the last three weeks rereading every word Julius Caesar ever wrote. She'd read it all before, of course, but it was a whole new experience now that she would be meeting the man in person. She also began brushing up on spoken Latin, something she had never considered particularly important before.

When she walked into the classics department office in Taper Hall, she noticed a young woman with long blond hair sitting in one of the chairs next to the mailboxes. She's a real knockout, Elizabeth thought. Not everyone is born to wear black leather miniskirts and clingy sweaters, but this girl is definitely one of the lucky few.

A search was on for a new department secretary. Was this young woman here for an interview? Elizabeth wondered. If so, she had certainly chosen a gutsy outfit. Elizabeth pulled the stack of mail from her pigeonhole and headed to her office. She didn't give the girl another thought until about ten minutes later, when there was a soft knock on her office door.

Elizabeth glanced at her watch. 10:00 o'clock on the dot. Good, she thought, my new advisee is right on time. Elizabeth had been curious about this new transfer student, a young woman from Las Vegas with an unusual background.

"Cassandra Fleury has been studying Latin and Greek since she was fourteen under the tutelage of Dennis Martinelli, who was my roommate at Holy Cross," John Reynolds had explained.

"What's he doing in Vegas?" Elizabeth asked.

"He taught at Georgetown until ten or so years ago," John said. "Long story, but he moved to Las Vegas to teach high-school Latin."

Odd career path, Elizabeth thought, but John was already telling her more about the student.

"She's coming to us as a junior from the University of Nevada. She was a history major there, but Denny says her Latin and Greek are both strong. Says she's the best student he's ever had."

"Come in!" Elizabeth called in response to the knock.

The door swung open, and in walked the blonde she had observed in the department office.

"Oh!" Elizabeth said before she could stop herself.

"*Salve!*" the young woman said and continued in Latin. "My name is Cassandra Fleury. I am pleased to make your acquaintance, Professor Palmer."

Elizabeth tried to mask her surprise. "*Salve!*" she repeated. "Please come on in and have a seat."

"Thank you," Cassandra said. She sat down in the chair across from Elizabeth and set her handbag on the floor. She shot Elizabeth a quizzical look. "I'm sorry. I wasn't sure whether I was supposed to speak Latin."

"It's perfectly okay," Elizabeth said, "but to tell you the truth, we don't do it much around here—unless we're putting on a play or a reading—" She paused. "You spoke Latin with your teacher?"

"Always," Cassandra said. "He expected it from day one."

"What about reading and writing?" Elizabeth asked.

"Oh, that, too," Cassandra said. "And he's big on memorization. *Arma virumque cano*—"

Elizabeth laughed. "I'm sure you're going to have no trouble with our placement tests."

Elizabeth hoped she sounded sincere, though she had her doubts.

Cassandra took the tests that afternoon, sitting at the small work table in Elizabeth's office. Elizabeth glanced at her every so often, wondering what had led a girl from Las Vegas—with looks like hers—to study ancient languages on her own. There was also her relationship with Dennis Martinelli to consider. Was it purely an academic one?

When Cassandra was finished, Elizabeth scanned her work. Within five minutes, it was obvious that Cassandra would have no trouble with upper-division classes. She had translated selections from Plato, Euripides, Caesar, and Horace flawlessly. If Elizabeth hadn't been sitting three feet from her the whole time she was writing, she might have suspected the young woman of cheating.

Yes, Elizabeth was guilty of profiling, and it had started back in the department office. In her experience, girls who look like Cassandra Fleury took screen tests, not proficiency exams in Greek and Latin. And if they did somehow end up studying classics, they slid by on their looks.

Not in Cassandra's case. Her translations were letter-perfect, and her Latin composition arguably equal to Elizabeth's own. Before the week was over, Elizabeth had revised her condescending opinion of her new advisee's spoken Latin.

When Cassandra greeted her in Latin, Elizabeth assumed she'd learned a few phrases back in high school from a teacher attempting to make Latin seem a little less "dead." The truth was, as everyone in the department soon learned, Cassandra could converse in classical Latin as easily as she could speak English and French.

About a week after she first appeared at Elizabeth's office door, John Reynolds asked whether he might take over as her adviser.

"Sure, if you think it's best," Elizabeth said, "but why?"

Elizabeth had her suspicions, of course. John was USC's celebrity classicist. Now that *What Would Julius Caesar Do?* was on its way to becoming a miniseries, he'd become the "go-to guy" whenever national media needed an expert on the ancient world.

"Word is beginning to spread about Cassandra's unusual linguistic abilities," John said. "Nothing may come of it, of course, but if something does, I might be able to assist her with the media."

Elizabeth thought John's real motive might have more to do with his fear of losing the limelight, but she didn't really mind giving up an advisee. Her fall semester was looking extraordinarily busy. In addition to the IDES project, her regular teaching load, and a couple of publishing deadlines, her husband had an important coin auction coming up in January. But even if she had no obligation to keep an eye on Cassandra, Elizabeth planned to do just that. Cassandra was not only new to California and USC, she was five years older and far more mature than most college juniors. Her startling good looks made her a standout in any setting, while her Las Vegas background and unusual academic career made her unique among classics majors. There might be times a young woman like her would appreciate a friendly feminine ear.

XXVII

John invited Elizabeth into his office after a Friday faculty meeting.
"What do you think about proposing that we add Cassandra to the IDES team?" he asked after he'd closed the door. "The better I get to know her, the more I think she'd be a valuable addition."

"As long as you're not suggesting I give her my spot," Elizabeth said.

"Absolutely not," John said, taken aback at this response. "If you agree—and only if you agree—I'll ask Andrew to expand the team."

"He probably won't do it," Elizabeth said.

"All I can do is ask," John said. "Are you on board with that?"

Elizabeth shrugged. "What do we have to lose?" she said. "I like Cassandra, and her spoken Latin is better than ours."

John nodded, relieved that Elizabeth had agreed so easily. He wouldn't have to make a case for Cassandra's looks, which he considered almost as valuable as her language skills.

Even though Elizabeth liked his proposal, John knew it was likely to be a tough sell at the IDES Lab. Eric and Andrew had both expressed their concerns about enlarging the IDES team when Elizabeth was added. Faith went one step further and called it "unbelievably reckless." By suggesting the addition of yet another academic, John knew he was flirting with her permanent enmity.

The following Tuesday morning, John climbed the steps to the IDES Lab. As Andrew had told him over the phone, a new door had been installed. It was bright blue, matching the new blue-and-white-striped awning above it. John pressed the button on the new intercom next to it.

"Hi, Dr. Reynolds," a man's voice said. "Please watch the door. It will swing toward you."

John moved aside as the heavy metal door swung outward. He stepped into a stark foyer, where a shaggy-haired young man wearing a headset and a *Doctor Who* T-shirt sat on a tall stool behind a counter. Behind him, an array of monitors displayed exterior camera feeds.

John smiled. "You must be Jerry." Andrew had also told John about the new receptionist, a Caltech graduate student. He knew only the IDES Project cover story and was not permitted past the airlock.

"Pleased to meet you," Jerry said. "I think I've met everyone except Dr. Palmer now."

"She'll be here next week," John said.

"Dr. Danicek is expecting you," Jerry said. "I'll buzz you through."

John passed through the double doors released by Jerry's electronic command. The high-pitched hum of TESA surrounded him as he entered a small room where two painters were at work. Near a second pair of doors, he leaned his cane against the wall and sat down on a small metal bench. He slipped off his loafers and set them on a shelf next to some Oxfords and a pair of running shoes. A pair of Teva sandals occupied a shelf of their own—Faith's no doubt. Rising, John took a hanger from the coat rack, shrugged off his jacket, and hung it with the others.

A whoosh of warm pressurized air ruffled his hair as the second set of doors slid open. John stepped into the carefully controlled climate of the common room.

"John! So glad you're here punctually! I'd like to make our meeting quick if we can—I've got a phone conference in half an hour."

Andrew Danicek rose from his chair at the head of the folding table. Eric Barza sat on his right. Faith Hopper, her lean body clad in a form-fitting warm-up suit, stood clear at the other end. She shot John a quick glance, but she didn't say a word as she pulled out a chair and sat down.

"Hi, John," Eric said.

Leaning his cane against the table, John set his briefcase down and took a seat across from Eric. For a fleeting moment, he wished he hadn't called a formal meeting. Maybe it would have been better if he had simply telephoned Andrew after all—

"You're the only item on the agenda today," Andrew said.

"And I have only one proposal for discussion," John said. He looked at each of his colleagues' faces in turn. Andrew and Eric returned his gaze. Faith picked at a fingernail and looked at her watch.

"I would like to propose adding another member to the IDES team."

"I'm against it." Faith's response was instantaneous. She turned to Andrew. "We've been through this before. We already expanded the group to include *two* classicists." Looking back at John, she said, "You had your chance. You chose Elizabeth."

"Let him finish." Andrew said. Faith shoved her chair back and folded her arms across her chest.

At least she's predictable, John thought. "Elizabeth was unable to attend today's meeting, but I've discussed the matter with her," he said. "She agrees that the effectiveness of the IDES team would be greatly enhanced by the addition of one of our students." Opening his briefcase, John extracted three paper-clipped packets. He passed them around. He and Elizabeth had agreed that the best strategy would be to let Cassandra's *curriculum vitae* speak for itself. John waited while his colleagues scanned the pages, noting their response as they arrived at the last sheet—an enlarged copy of Cassandra's campus head shot.

John looked down at his own copy of the photograph. While it was a fair likeness, he was glad it did not do full justice to Cassandra's beauty. Her linguistic abilities were reason enough that she should be invited to join the IDES team. Her looks, like her hospitality experience, were merely an added bonus.

"Do you think she'll survive a background check?" Danicek asked when he finished reading.

"I think the odds are good," John said. "Until a few months ago, she worked at a major casino in Las Vegas."

"Fantastic," Faith said bitingly. "A keno runner is just what this team lacks."

"Ms. Fleury paid for college by working as a cocktail waitress," John said, trying not to sound defensive. "Anyone who works in a Vegas casino has been checked out thoroughly by the police."

"I like that she's fluent in Latin," Andrew said, looking again at Cassandra's photo. "An amazing skill for someone her age. How much logistical reorganization would an extra person require, Eric?"

"We'd have to add another bed, but Faith and Elizabeth's room is big enough."

"Easy for you to say," Faith said. "You're not the one who'd be sleeping in a goddamn bunkhouse."

Eric shifted uncomfortably in his seat but continued. "No problem with the dining room—the table can seat eight easily. So can the van. And there's plenty of room in here for another work station."

"I've already outlined the medical hazards we're facing," Faith said. "Every additional person raises the risk of—"

"Why don't we see what the background check turns up?" Andrew said. "John, can you give Eric what he needs to get that started?"

"Of course," John said. This was going considerably more smoothly than he had dared hope.

"What part of 'dangerous' don't you understand?" Faith said.

"I hear you," Andrew said. "We'll make a final decision when we have the results from Gleason & Gleason. If she can't pass the preliminary background check, it's all moot."

"And there's always the possibility that Cassandra will decline the invitation," John said, but only for Faith's benefit. It was hardly likely that an undergraduate would turn down such a rare and prestigious opportunity.

Before he left the IDES Lab, John stopped by Andrew's office.

"Thanks for giving Cassandra a chance," John said after Andrew closed the door. "I know it's difficult to reorganize at this late date—"

"John, she's perfect!" Andrew said. "I can't discuss everything in front of Faith, but an attractive young woman who can converse easily in Latin greatly increases our odds of success. We've discussed the possibility that Caesar is gay. Whether he is or not, an attractive young woman will come across as nonthreatening. Cassandra's hospitality experience is another plus. Elizabeth would have sufficed, but Cassandra takes us to a whole new level. It's like we had a friendly German shepherd, and now we have an adorable puppy." He chuckled. "A Caesar magnet, you might say."

"My thoughts exactly," John said, even though he cringed a little at the same time. At least Elizabeth hadn't been around to hear the dog metaphor.

"I'll deal with Faith," Andrew continued. "It's her job to hammer us on safety issues, but if Cassandra is all you've promised, she's worth any potential risk she might present."

John smiled. "I look forward to introducing you."

XXVIII

The day Cassandra drove to Pasadena for her interview with Andrew Danicek and the rest of the IDES team, she wondered for the millionth time why she was being considered for addition to such a high-powered roster. John Reynolds and Elizabeth Palmer were both experts in their fields, and Andrew Danicek had a freaking Nobel Prize. What could she, a mere undergraduate from Las Vegas, possibly add to such a lineup? Cassandra tried not to think about the only thing that made sense—that she would be fetching coffee or maybe posing for publicity photos. She also wondered whether she had made the right decision about what to wear. If this were Las Vegas, she'd wear a black dress and three-inch heels. Because this was definitely not Las Vegas, she'd opted for slacks and a sweater. The blazer she threw on made the whole outfit one notch more formal than what she usually wore to class. All she could do was hope that it would evoke a favorable impression in an environment that was completely alien to her.

As she pulled into the small parking lot at the address she'd been given, Cassandra was reassured to see John Reynolds's blue Saab already parked in a handicapped spot. Elizabeth's Jaguar was right next to it. A white van and a black Mercedes occupied the only other parking spaces, so Cassandra backed out and parked on the street. As she walked back to the building, a young guy with a beard stepped outside through a large blue door. He paused on the top step.

"Hi, I'm Eric," he called as she got out. "You're Cassandra, right?"

"That's me," she said. "Here for a meeting with—"

"Andrew Danicek," Eric finished. "He asked me to meet you. Welcome to the IDES Lab."

Cassandra smiled. Eric blushed just enough that Cassandra could see it through his beard.

She climbed the concrete steps. Eric held the door open, and Cassandra stepped into a lobby where another young guy stood behind a tall counter.

"Welcome," he said. "I'll buzz you through."

Two wide yellow doors to the left of the counter slid open with a whoosh.

"Controlled atmosphere," Eric said. "This is the airlock."

The doors slid closed behind them. The faint hum that Cassandra had noticed in the foyer was now louder. Eric sat down on a metal bench. He motioned to Cassandra to do the same.

"We leave our shoes in here," he said, pointing to some shelves where several other pairs of shoes were already lined up." They rose, stocking-footed. Eric handed Cassandra a hanger, and she hung her blazer on a rack next to a couple of others. There went her one extra statement of formality. But Eric was wearing jeans, so maybe it wouldn't matter.

When Eric placed his hand on a small panel next to a pair of doors at the other end of the airlock, they parted instantly with another whoosh. Warm air surrounded them as they entered a large room. The hum was a vibrating drone now.

Everything was still partially under construction, Cassandra realized as she took in the unpainted drywall and bare concrete floor. She glanced up. Amid a constellation of recessed lights, she noted an equal number of "eye in the sky" cameras. While they were something she was accustomed to seeing in Las Vegas casinos, she was a little surprised to see so many in a science lab. Was Dr. Danicek afraid members of the IDES team might steal the artifacts they were supposed to be evaluating?

The windowless room was empty except for a folding table surrounded by six folding chairs. John Reynolds sat at one end of the table, and Elizabeth Palmer was next to him. They both smiled and stood up when they saw Cassandra. Near the end of the table, a thirty-something woman with short red hair glanced up but did not smile or rise. Before Cassandra could say a word, a door on the far side of the room burst open.

A tall, slender man with angular features and combed-back silver hair strode to the table.

Andrew Danicek.

Cassandra recognized him immediately from the cover of TIME and all the other media exposure the man had enjoyed ever since he won a Nobel Prize. He was wearing pressed gray slacks and a black sweatshirt with an image of Marilyn Monroe on the front. That was a surprise, but Cassandra silently breathed a sigh of relief. She didn't need to worry about her wardrobe choices anymore.

Dr. Danicek motioned for everyone to take a seat. He introduced the red-haired woman as Faith Hopper, a medical doctor. She grunted something Cassandra couldn't catch.

"And you've already met Eric," Danicek continued. "My assistant."

"I'm food and beverage manager, too," Eric said. "Would you like some espresso?"

Food and beverage manager? Seriously?

Apparently so, because when Cassandra agreed to a cappuccino, Eric jumped up and opened another door. Cassandra could see a sink and a counter top in the room beyond.

"We're so happy you're interested in joining our team, Miss Fleury," Dr. Danicek said. "I trust Dr. Reynolds has told you a little about our mission here at the IDES Lab."

Cassandra nodded. "I'm honored to be considered."

"Why don't you tell us a bit about yourself?" Dr. Danicek said.

Since this was the only question Cassandra had been able to imagine she might be asked, she was fairly well prepared to answer.

"As you already know," she began, "I am a native of Las Vegas."

Eric returned with her cappuccino and set it in front of her. The foam had a perfect little infinity symbol marked in it.

Such a cute geeky touch! Cassandra smiled at Eric as she thanked him. He blushed a second time as he took his seat.

Cassandra went on to describe her academic background, her work experience, and her current status as a junior at USC. "So," she concluded, "I'm not exactly a polymath, but I do think I possess an unusual combination of skills. Not that I ever needed to speak Latin in a Las Vegas casino."

Dr. Danicek laughed. "Your French, though. I bet that came in handy on occasion."

"*Mais oui,*" Cassandra said. "And it got me better shifts."

Everyone at the table smiled except the doctor. She glared at Andrew and remained silent.

Just then, the automatic doors to the airlock slid apart again. Two burly guys in coveralls pushed something on a big furniture dolly into the room.

"Oh, the hot tub," Dr. Danicek said. "I hope it's the right one this time."

Cassandra caught a glimpse as the men pushed the dolly past the table.

Yes, a hot tub. A molded fiberglass model big enough for a party.

She shot a glance at Reynolds. The look he returned told her not to ask questions.

The interview lasted for only a few more minutes. It was more like a conversation you'd have with a new neighbor than a serious interview, Cassandra thought. No tough questions, and everybody wore friendly but unrevealing smiles except the doctor. She seemed permanently pissed off.

Cassandra had just finished her coffee when, at Danicek's signal, Eric escorted her back into the airlock and, after she'd put her shoes and blazer back on, out into the parking lot. He accompanied her to her car.

"Why does the IDES Lab need a hot tub?" Cassandra asked as she unlocked her car's door.

Her question seemed to catch Eric off guard. "I can't answer that," he said after an awkward pause. "I wish I could, but as you already know, everyone on the IDES team has signed a strict nondisclosure agreement."

"So, I'll find out later if I'm lucky enough to make the cut."

Eric nodded.

"Wish me luck, then," Cassandra said, even though what she really wanted was answers. She had resigned herself to the possibility that she might have to fetch coffee or pose for photos, but a hot tub set off her sleaze alarm. What was the IDES Team really up to?

XXIX

The next morning, after a sleepless night, Eric decided to use a pay phone to call Cassandra. He didn't have any hard evidence that his personal landline was bugged, but he'd heard mysterious clicks and static enough times to think it might be.

Cassandra sounded surprised when she answered, but she recovered quickly.

"Of course I'd like to meet with you," she said when he broached the subject. "And thank you again for making me feel so welcome at the IDES Lab."

He gave her directions to a picnic area in Griffith Park. "It's right near the big locomotive at Travel Town," he said. Eric also suspected that he had been followed from time to time over the last few weeks. Even though it was only a hunch, he didn't want to take a chance on being overheard at a restaurant or a coffee shop.

If Cassandra thought Eric's suggested meeting place was odd, she didn't let on. And she was waiting when he arrived. He slid onto the bench across from her.

"Thanks for coming," he said. "I hope you didn't have any trouble with my directions."

"None," Cassandra said. "Although it is pretty chilly."

"This won't take long," Eric said. "I just wanted to let you know that the work at the IDES Lab could be dangerous. Nobody has told you that, and I don't think that's right."

He studied Cassandra's face from his side of the picnic table. "That's about all I can tell you—"

"What do you mean—dangerous?" Cassandra asked. "How is working with a bunch of ancient artifacts dangerous? What are they, radioactive?"

Eric looked at his hands. It was a reasonable question, but he couldn't answer it without breaking several important promises.

"No," he said. "Different kind of danger, but I'm not at liberty to explain."

"*Not at liberty.* What are you, a lawyer?"

"No. Just someone who has signed a heavy-duty nondisclosure agreement."

Cassandra stared at Eric from across the table. A brisk breeze blew her hair away from her face. She hugged her arms around herself.

"I'm freezing. Let's go sit in my car."

"I'm sorry you're cold," Eric said. "I wish I could explain more—"

"Me, too," Cassandra said. "Because all you've done is freak me out."

"I'm sorry."

"Are you?" Cassandra said. "And did you really make me drive all the way to Griffith Park just to tell me nothing?"

Well, yeah. That's exactly what Eric had done. The Illingsworth nondisclosure agreement, with all its serious penalties for revealing the slightest detail about the real goals of the IDES Project, had made him paranoid. He wasn't about to send an email. He'd been nervous enough talking with Cassandra on a pay phone.

Cassandra shivered as another chilly gust swept through the oak trees. "Here's the deal," she said, sliding to the end of the bench. "I'm cold, and I'm going to my car now." She stood up.

Eric stared at the table. This was not going well.

"You should come with me." She didn't say it in a mean way, Eric noticed, even though he deserved it. He'd made her drive twenty miles to hear nearly nothing.

"I don't bite."

That did it. Eric couldn't let Cassandra drive away thinking that she'd scared him. He wasn't the one who needed protecting—she was. He'd kept his mouth shut while Andrew inducted John Reynolds and Elizabeth Palmer onto the Ides Team without telling them the risks. Keeping two professors in the dark was bad enough, but Cassandra was an undergraduate in a new city. Eric's conscience would not allow him to let her join the inner circle without enough knowledge to make an informed decision. He stood up.

"Lead the way."

"How did you get here?" Cassandra asked when she was behind the wheel and Eric had folded himself into the passenger seat.

"Bus."

"Consider me your taxi home." Cassandra turned the key. "Or wherever else you'd like to go."

"Caltech," Eric said. He braced himself for whatever Cassandra was going to say next, but she kept her eyes on the road and her mouth shut. She's a very good driver, Eric thought, as Cassandra shifted smoothly through the old VW's gears. How many women her age know how to slip a clutch?

Somewhere between Glendale and Eagle Rock, it began to rain. By the time they reached Pasadena, the rain was pouring down so hard that the VW's wipers couldn't keep up.

"I guess it would be better if you took me home," Eric said.

"You're the navigator."

"This is it," he said after Cassandra turned left onto Catalina from California Boulevard. "This is fine." She pulled to a stop at the curb, and Eric opened the passenger door.

"Thanks for the ride," he said as he began to get out. Rain pelted his head.

"Aren't you going to invite me in?"

"You want to come in?" The words jumped out before Eric could stop them.

"Yes, thanks," Cassandra said as she pulled on the parking brake.

Eric's heart sped up. What if Danicek saw them? The likelihood was minuscule, but—Cassandra pulled the hood of her jacket up and opened her door. "Let's make a run for it," she said.

Together, they splashed across the sidewalk and up the steps of the bungalow Eric shared with two other postdocs. Thank goodness they weren't home. Jeff spent most of his time in his lab or at his girlfriend's place, and Sundar was at a conference in Houston.

Since the only pieces of furniture in the living room were an aging foosball table and an old beanbag chair, Eric knew he'd have to take Cassandra to his room. He led the way down the narrow hall and flipped on the light as he held the door open for her. He watched her eyes travel over his worldly possessions.

"Who sleeps on the floor?" she asked.

Damn. Eric wished he'd rolled up his sleeping bag.

"I do, sometimes," he said. He hoped that would be enough of an answer. He didn't like lying, but he didn't want to explain that sleeping on a bare floor was how he solved problems.

The habit got its start the August Eric turned thirteen. The judge had given him the choice of living with his father or his mother. Until then, he'd been bouncing between Mom's condo and Dad's row house every week. Now, after six years of ping-pong parenting, he could choose. He could continue his back-and-forth lifestyle or pick a permanent home.

There in the courtroom, Eric instantly decided he'd live with his father. Dad had always been his anchor, and he was definitely the better cook. His rambling three-story row house in west Philadelphia had always felt like a real home. Dad had a Newfoundland named Fletcher and a salt water fish tank. Dad came to see Eric's teachers at school, cooked hotcakes for Saturday breakfast, and liked to take Eric to the airport to watch planes take off.

Mom, on the other hand, always had plans. Maybe next year, they'd go to Yellowstone. Maybe next month, she'd buy Eric a bunk bed. Maybe next week, they'd take in a movie. In the meantime, Eric was lucky if he got a ride to the library or a new pair of socks. At Mom's place, a two-bedroom condo in the center of town, Eric did the cooking. This meant he developed great creativity in the kitchen, because Mom was a sporadic grocery shopper at best. By the time he was thirteen, Eric had invented such culinary delights as Cheetos quiche and Corn Chex alla carbonara.

"You don't have to make up your mind right now," the judge said. "Take your time, and let me know when you're ready." Eric was relieved, because he knew how bad his mother would feel if he blurted out right then that he wanted to live with Dad.

After court, Dad took Eric home. It was a Dad week. Soon, he thought, every week would be a Dad week. It was something to look forward to.

That night, Eric lay in bed staring at the ceiling fan turning above him. Choosing a parent wasn't as easy as he had thought. Maybe he should live with Mom, after all. Was it right to pick Dad because he had a bigger house and a dog? Dad was strict, and he made Eric do chores to earn his allowance. As he lay there, Eric remembered that he also looked forward to Mom weeks. Mom wasn't big on rules or curfews. He could play computer games or watch TV all he wanted, and she gave him as much spending money as she could afford, no strings attached.

Troubled by the choice facing him, Eric slipped out of his bed and pulled the bedspread off. Bundling it into his arms, he tiptoed to the front door. The door squeaked as he pulled it open, but he managed to escape onto the front porch and close the door behind him without rousing Dad or Fletcher.

Eric spread the bedspread on the porch floor and stretched out. Maybe here—not quite inside Dad's house, and not at Mom's place, either—he could think more clearly about his options. He fell asleep in the warm summer darkness.

He awoke to the sound of an early street sweeper. The instant his eyelids opened, Eric knew he'd live with his mother. Somehow, in the hours that he lay on the hardwood planks of his father's front porch, he realized that his choice wasn't about dogs or allowances. It wasn't even about him. It wasn't about Dad, who could take care of himself just fine. It was about Mom, who couldn't.

Eric never slept on the floor to solve scientific problems. The solutions to those always seem readily available, as easy to access as books on a library shelf. Moral and ethical issues, on the other hand, seem to hide somewhere just beyond his conscious reach. Sleeping on the floor didn't always coax them out of the shadows, but it was the best technique he'd come across. Today, Eric had awakened knowing that he had to warn Cassandra about the risks of becoming involved with the IDES Project.

Eric looked at his guest. Still standing near the door, Cassandra was scanning his room, taking in every detail.

"You're reading about Julius Caesar?" she asked.

"Um—yeah," Eric said.

Damn. Leaving Michael Grant's *Julius Caesar* on his nightstand was worse than forgetting to put away his sleeping bag.

Or was it? As Cassandra crossed the room and picked up the book,

Eric admitted to himself what he had spent all day trying to deny. The only way to warn Cassandra properly was to tell her everything.

"Are you a fan of Julius Caesar?" Cassandra asked. She sounded skeptical.

"Not until a year or two ago."

She looked up. Eric met her gaze. He couldn't get over how arresting her face was. It was beautiful, but it was also unique—unlike any face he had ever seen before. Her wide-set blue eyes stared at him over cheeks the color of peach ice cream. Her full lips were parted. Her jacket had fallen open, and Eric could see the pulse in her neck.

"I started reading as soon as I found out—"

"Found out what?"

Eric's heart pounded. This was it.

"As soon as I found out I was going to meet him."

Cassandra's eyes widened. Eric heard her suck in a breath.

"The IDES Project," he said. "It's not what they've told you. It's not about dating ancient artifacts. Or at least it's not *only* about that. There's a lot more."

He watched Cassandra think this over.

"Once you've signed the nondisclosure agreement, Danicek will tell you everything. But he should have told you before. You should know what you're really getting into, while you still have a chance to decide—"

"What else is there to know?" Cassandra asked.

"Julius Caesar. He's coming in March. He'll be here for four days."

Cassandra set the book back on the nightstand. She sat down on the edge of the bed.

"Julius Caesar. Coming here." Cassandra looked at Eric hard. She looked kind of angry. "You expect me to believe this."

"I know it sounds crazy, but, yeah, it's true." He looked back down at the floor.

This was not going well.

"It's ridiculous."

"I know it sounds crazy, but—"

"When Reynolds approached me about joining the project, he was pretty vague," Cassandra said. "And he told me the name was just a coincidence,'" she said. "But now I see it isn't. IDES. Cute."

"I tried to convince Danicek not to call it that," Eric said. "But he likes to keep Mrs. Illingsworth happy."

"Mrs. Illingsworth?"

"She holds the purse strings, and she loves the name. You'll meet her when you sign the NDA."

Cassandra said nothing.

"Well, now you know everything."

"Do I? Somehow, I feel as though I know less and less."

"I'd like to change that."

"You're now at liberty to talk?"

Eric felt his face warm, and he hoped his beard concealed it. "No. I'm breaking all the rules. I think the rules are wrong."

Cassandra looked directly into Eric's eyes. He stared back.

"I think you should know what you're getting into while you still have a choice about being involved. You can still decide whether—"

"You seriously think I'm going to pass up a chance to meet Julius Caesar?"

It was Eric's turn to be surprised.

"You believe me?"

"I don't know," she said. "I guess I'll have to wait and see, but if I drop out, I'll never know. I'm trapped."

God. That was exactly how Eric felt.

"It may be dangerous," he said.

"Dangerous how?"

"Too many ways to list, almost. Worst-case scenario, we might all cease to exist. Bringing Caesar here—or failing to get him back—might affect subsequent events."

"So it could be the Ides for all of us. Is that what you're saying?"

"Well, that probably won't happen. We've done extensive testing and modeling. We've already transported an inanimate object and a dog, and nothing detectable was altered in the present. The dog went back to the moment he was snatched from—fifteen seconds before a pickup truck smashed him flat."

"Lovely." She paused for a moment. "So you already actually believe this."

"It's not about belief. There's evidence."

Cassandra thought that over.

"And it has to be someone seconds away from death?"

"Not technically. All we have to know is location and time. As I said, all our modeling and testing has shown that we can't alter the future by interacting with the past. But as a precaution—in case something goes wrong and they don't get back—we limited our choices to subjects who were about to die violent, unexpected deaths—people who were in good shape physically but who didn't have any time left. We considered JFK and Martin Luther King, Jr."

Cassandra stood up. She slipped out of her jacket and draped it over the back of Eric's desk chair. He watched her fluff out her hair, slip off her boots, and stretch out on his bed. She folded her arms behind her head and lay back against the pillow.

For a second, Eric totally forgot what this beautiful woman was doing in his room. It was like a dream—a gorgeous creature lying on his bed, her voluptuous torso visible through a clingy tangerine-colored sweater. It had ridden up a little, exposing a narrow strip of skin over the top of her jeans.

"Why Caesar, then?" Cassandra asked. "Why not one of those other guys?"

Collecting himself, Eric pulled the desk chair around to face the bed and sat down. "Are you warm enough?" he asked.

Cassandra smiled. "I'm fine, thanks. Just wanted to get comfortable before I hear how you're going to mess with the universe. And maybe a little intel about your plans for that hot tub."

◉◉◉

On her way home, Cassandra almost smiled at her faulty assumptions about Eric. When the phone rang in her cottage in Beverly Hills early that morning, she'd been expecting her mother on the other end of the line. Everybody else she knew was far more likely to call her cell phone.

When Eric identified himself, she figured he would ask her out. When she agreed to meet him in Griffith Park, she thought he was just hitting on her in a super-nerdy way. She went only because she hoped to learn more about the other IDES team members, especially the unfriendly doctor.

Nothing had turned out as she expected. Eric had made no moves at all, even when she stretched out on his bed. He seemed genuinely worried about the IDES Project and how Dr. Danicek was treating her. It had to be impossible that she'd be meeting Julius Caesar in the flesh, but knowing the secret in advance was an incredible advantage.

"Danicek will be looking for your first reaction when he tells you," Eric had told her. "Now you can plan what that will be."

XXX

When Andrew Danicek first told Sonia Illingsworth that a young woman would be joining the IDES Project team, she was quietly delighted that her advice had apparently been taken. While she always refrained from meddling, she had felt compelled early on to share her views that a young female might well be the key to connecting with Caesar.

"I would like to meet her," she said.

"Of course," Andrew said. "That's why I called. I'm hosting a reception at the IDES Lab next week to welcome her. Are you free on the fourteenth?"

The following Wednesday, Hector pulled the Bentley into the handicapped spot in front of the lab. Everywhere else, Sonia refused to allow her chauffeur to use her late husband's old handicapped placard in order to park more conveniently. But here at the IDES Lab, space was limited, so the handicapped spot had become Sonia's.

Sonia pulled a compact from her handbag and checked her hair and makeup. She stepped out into a cool breeze and took Hector's arm. As he escorted her up the concrete stairs to the IDES Lab door, she

looked down to see that she had stepped on a cigarette butt. And—
¡Maldito sea!—two more on the next step.

Sonia Illingsworth, like her husband, despised smoking. Everyone
at the IDES Lab was aware of her views. Who, then, could be responsible for this disgusting litter, and disrespectful enough to leave it on
the front steps, where she was bound to see it? The doctor perhaps?
Sonia could believe it. The woman was not always polite enough to
Sonia and often openly insubordinate to Andrew. It would come as no
surprise to learn that, despite her outward interest in fitness, she had
a secret cigarette habit.

No me importa.

Sonia strove to shake off her irritation. She was not the sort to
micromanage. It was disappointing, though, that Andrew so often
lacked attention to detail.

The door opened.

Sonia turned to Hector. "I will be here at least two hours," she said.
"You do not need to sit here all that time."

"Thank you, ma'am," Hector said. "Please call if you require me
sooner."

Hector retreated down the stairs. Sonia stepped through the door
as a young man rounded the end of the reception desk.

"Mrs. Illingsworth! Welcome!"

"Good afternoon, Jerry," Sonia said. "Do you smoke?"

The young man's eager smile vanished. "No, ma'am," he said.

"Well, someone does. There are cigarette butts on the stairs."

"There were painters working here today, ma'am," Jerry said.
"Maybe one of them is responsible. I'll clean them up right after I buzz
you in."

Sonia nodded as she took off her gloves and moved toward the
slick yellow panels on the left side of the counter. At Jerry's command,
they slid apart. Sonia entered the airlock.

As she removed her scarf, Sonia saw that she must be the last to arrive. Five pairs of shoes were already occupying the shelves near the inner door, and an equal number of jackets already hung on the coat rack. Sonia smiled at the one pair of shoes she didn't recognize—stiletto heels with silver ankle straps.

¡Por fin! she thought. At last there's a real girl on the team! The doctor, with her socks and athletic shoes, had been a total disappointment in that department. Elizabeth Palmer was better, but she was a serious academic with a fondness for loafers. But these shoes! These were footwear that Sonia herself would have chosen—delicate, feminine, and above all, sexy. Sonia placed her own heels next to them with a sigh.

Ay, como quisiera—

But the memory of her husband cut her thoughts short.

"Wishing," Chip used to say, "never achieved a damn thing. If you want something, do something about it. If you can't, shut up."

There was so little she could do. It was bad enough that age robbed a woman of looks and grace, but even worse was that it silenced her.

¡Cállate, Soso!

That's what Chip would have said if she had whined.

You've been given the world, and you cry for the moon!

Forget the moon. All she wanted was the job this new girl had. She would have gladly given up the world to play hostess to Julius Caesar.

From the moment Sonia learned of Julius Caesar's visit, she had yearned to be among the first to greet him. Extending hospitality had always been her greatest pleasure. She could think of no higher privilege—or challenge!—than to make Julius Caesar feel welcome in a strange land. How Sonia had longed to hear Andrew tell the others, "I am pleased to announce that Sonia Illingsworth is joining the IDES team in a new capacity: Julius Caesar's personal attendant."

Of course, Sonia had the power to demand that she be given the role. Andrew would have swallowed his displeasure and granted the request. Sonia could not deny she was tempted. What held her back were the beliefs her late husband had held so dear.

Charles Orion Illingsworth, who had himself benefited so greatly from the encouragement of mentors and the confidence of investors, believed in seeking out the best and brightest minds, giving them the resources and funding their projects required, and then standing back and allowing them to work without interference.

"That's how I was treated," he used to say. "I was given everything I needed and left alone."

Chip's confidence in Andrew was unshakable. Sonia could not allow herself to be a meddler. And, truth be told, her credentials were shaky. Her only Latin came from four years with the nuns at Colegio Nuestra Señora de Sión, far too many years ago to be of use. And there was her age to consider. Sonia was sixty-eight, thirteen years older than Julius Caesar when he met his death on the Ides of March, 44 B.C. Even if she polished her Latin skills, she could no longer bring youth and beauty to the table.

But, oh, there was a day! Chip Illingsworth might not have been Julius Caesar, but Sonia would cherish the day she met him as long as she drew breath.

It was the height of the rainy season in San José, Costa Rica. Sonia was at her desk in the American Embassy, where she served as secretary to William Blankenhorn, the American ambassador. Charles Illingsworth, an American engineer and entrepreneur, was visiting from Panama, where he was in charge of a project to install his innovative new braking systems on the electric locomotives used on the Panama Canal. He and Mr. Blankenhorn had just returned from lunch at the country club. Sonia had met Mr. Illingsworth earlier that morning. With a tall stack of correspondence to catch up on, she hadn't given the man another thought once she confirmed the ambassador's lunch reservation and called the chauffeur. Mr. Illingsworth hadn't paid any attention to Sonia, either. He and Mr. Blankenhorn were too busy talking about what would happen if John Kennedy became the next American president.

But now, politics had taken a back seat to a mundane problem.

"Mr. Illingsworth's shoe is torn," Mr. Blankenhorn said. Sonia had already noticed. She stood up and walked around to the front of her desk.

¡Qué sorpresa!

Mr. Illingsworth was even taller than she thought. Her eyes lined up with his tie tack. She looked up. Mr. Illingsworth met her gaze with dancing hazel eyes.

"I'm afraid I have a reputation for being a klutz," he said. Sonia was unfamiliar with the word but had no trouble understanding it as Mr. Illingsworth continued. "I tripped on a drain grate at the country club." He lifted his left foot. The sole of his shoe hung down, revealing a foot wearing a brown sock. Mr. Illingsworth wiggled his toes.

Sonia would never be able to explain how she recognized it, but in the instant that her eyes fell on Mr. Illingsworth's toes, she knew that a fateful moment had arrived. It was a moment so transitory she might easily have missed it altogether. It was as if, in a downpour, one single raindrop was a diamond. All she had to do was to hold out her hand at the right time and place, and the diamond would fall—plop!—right into her palm. But if she missed or failed to notice, the diamond would be lost forever down a storm drain, with no one the wiser about what might have been.

Sonia raised her chin. She smiled as her eyes met the tall American's. She watched his cheeks redden.

"I'm so sorry," she said with a laugh. "It's just that—" she paused for a split second, but there was no going back now. "Your shoe reminds me of an alligator."

Sonia's comment hung in the air for a moment, long enough

for her to worry that she might have earned a reprimand from Ambassador Blankenhorn.

Even as she wondered what Mr. Blankenhorn was thinking, Sonia thanked whichever saint had guided her to choose her blue taffeta sheath that morning, and to style her hair in a French twist. She watched Mr. Illingsworth take it all in. Then he smiled.

"Maybe I should rip the other one," he said. "Then I'd have a *pair* of alligator shoes."

Their laughter harmonized as sweetly as a duet. The ambassador did not join in.

"Miss Figueres," he interrupted. "We do not have time to waste. Mr. Illingsworth needs new shoes."

"Yes, sir," Sonia said quickly. "I—"

"I'm so sorry to inconvenience you," Mr. Illingsworth said. "But I'm afraid this is the only pair I brought with me."

"It's no trouble at all, sir." Their eyes met again. As her heart rose into her throat, Sonia's mind began to whir. There was a shoe store less than a kilometer away, but the afternoon cloudburst had already begun. The man could not walk through a rain shower in stocking feet. Perhaps a courier could be dispatched to bring a selection of men's shoes to the embassy. No! Sonia had a better idea.

"I know an excellent *zapatero*," she said, quickly calculating in her head how long it would take a courier to travel out to Heredia, wait for the shoes, and return.

"Mr. Illingsworth's flight is at six," Mr. Blankenhorn said.

"Six-twenty." The words popped from Sonia's mouth just as Mr. Illingsworth said them, too. They both laughed again.

"That gives me about two hours before I should head to the airport," Mr. Illingsworth said. "Okay if I take up space here that long, Bill?"

"Of course," Mr. Blankenhorn said. "I've got to run, but—" Sonia watched the ambassador's eyes move between Mr. Illingsworth's and hers. "You're in good hands with Miss Figueres."

"I know," Mr. Illingsworth said.

Sonia was reaching for the telephone as he spoke. Warmth slithered down her spine. This was more than a spark. This fire was already burning.

By the time the courier returned with the repaired shoes, Mr. Illingsworth was "Chip," and his flight was no longer at 6:20. Sonia had rescheduled it for the next day. Two weeks later, Chip actually boarded a flight to Panama City. A year and countless more plane flights after that, Sonia Maria del Pilár Figueres Ulloa and Charles Orion Illingsworth were married in a ceremony that made the front page of *La Nación*.

With a sigh, Sonia squared her shoulders and placed her hand on the reader next to the red panels in front of her. The panels slid apart with a whoosh. The vibrating hum of TESA engulfed her as she stepped into the common area in her stocking feet.

XXXI

A n hour earlier, Cassandra had stepped into the common area at the IDES Lab for the second time. The only familiar thing was the incessant vibrating hum that immediately surrounded her. The bare concrete floor was now covered in gray-green carpet. The naked drywall had been painted a soft beige. In addition to the recessed lights in the ceiling, bronze wall sconces illuminated the room. The folding table where she had joined the team for her interview had been replaced with a large dark wood conference table, where her new colleagues now sat in upholstered armchairs.

What a transformation! Cassandra was still taking it all in as Andrew Danicek rose to greet her. As he crossed the room and she caught sight of his tuxedo, she breathed a sigh of relief. Her own black silk cocktail dress had been a good choice for this gathering. Just as before, she hadn't been sure about what to wear tonight and had fallen back on the rule of thumb her stepfather had drummed into her: When in doubt, always err on the side of formality.

"Miss Fleury! How lovely you look," Danicek said. Instead of extending a hand, he put his arm around Cassandra's shoulders.

"Please come join us. As you know, we have a bit of business to take care of before the festivities begin."

As Cassandra sat down in the chair Danicek pulled out for her, a thought occurred to her. The other team members had arrived before her, even though she had been fifteen minutes early. Had they been given a different arrival time? It was the only explanation that made sense. Here they all were, already seated. Her own entrance seemed almost like an interruption.

Whatever. Nothing could possibly be as bizarre as what Eric had told her the other day. She nodded hello to him, and he responded with a shy—or maybe nervous—smile. Elizabeth Palmer and John Reynolds both said hello, but Faith Hopper, the doctor, kept her eyes down and said nothing. Still prickly, Cassandra thought. Nothing she could do about it, though, so she shrugged it off and focused her attention on Danicek, who remained standing at the head of the table.

"Thank you for arriving promptly, Miss Fleury," he said, which made Cassandra suspect once again that she had been given a different arrival time from the others.

"First things first," Dr. Danicek said. He opened a manila folder and pushed a stack of papers toward Cassandra along with a ballpoint pen.

The nondisclosure agreement.

Cassandra had already read Dr. Reynolds' copy, so she immediately got to work initialing each page. After she signed page ten, she slid the papers back to Danicek. He pushed them over to Reynolds, who signed the last page as a witness. It was all done in less than five minutes. Once Danicek had the papers in hand, everyone at the table looked at him expectantly. This is it, Cassandra thought. The truth I'm not supposed to know.

"Now that you are a bona fide member of the IDES team," Danicek said, "I need to share a few more details about our work."

Cassandra shot Eric a quick glance, and their eyes locked. I've got this, she tried to communicate. Don't worry. Her stomach fluttered, though. Would she really be able to pull off convincing fake surprise?

"Your role in this experiment is crucial, Miss Fleury. Your fluency in Latin, combined with your experience in the hospitality industry, provide you with an ideal combination of skills."

"As you already know," Danicek went on, "we will be testing new technology that will revolutionize archaeology and a host of other disciplines. What you are about to find out is that the technology has power beyond the dating of inanimate artifacts."

Cassandra raised her eyes to meet Danicek's. He paused a moment. Her heart pounded.

Cut to the chase, she begged mentally.

Almost as if he had heard her thought, Danicek spoke again.

"The week you are in residence here, we will be hosting a visitor from ancient times. You will be meeting Julius Caesar."

Cassandra allowed her mouth to fall open. She stared into Danicek's eyes. She said nothing.

So Eric hadn't been kidding. TESA really was a time machine, and Danicek really was a mad scientist. And here she really was, wrapped up in the middle of something right up there with *Back to the Future*.

She stole a glance at Eric again. She would never be able to thank him enough for giving her the chance to prepare for this moment.

"I know it is difficult to comprehend," Danicek said. "You no doubt have many questions, and there will be time for you to ask all of them. Right now, do you have any thoughts?"

Cassandra stayed mute for a couple of beats. She let the tension tighten for a few more seconds.

"I do have questions," she said at last. "At least a million of them."

She ran a hand through her hair, then straightened her shoulders. "But right now, all I can think of is—" She paused again, then looked straight at Danicek. "I speak a dead language, and I'm going to meet someone who can actually correct my pronunciation?"

The question hung in the air. Oh, God, Cassandra thought. I should have thought of something more serious—

But just then, Danicek laughed. As if waiting for his cue, everyone else chuckled. Well, everyone except Faith.

"Each person here," Danicek said, "had a different response when he or she learned about Caesar's visit. Yours just might be my favorite. Instead of reacting immediately with concerns about safety, your mind jumped instantly to the heart of our challenge. Connecting with Julius Caesar—speaking with him, learning from him—that's why we're here. The talents you bring to the team increase our chances for success exponentially."

Danicek went on to explain how the classicists would work together to study Caesar, and to act as interpreters for the scientists. He described how the IDES Lab was equipped with dozens of video cameras, so that every minute of Caesar's stay would be recorded for analysis after he left. Cassandra stole a glance at the ceiling, where, as she had already noticed on her first visit to the lab, she could easily see at least six "eye in the sky" cameras right there in the common area. Danicek caught her.

"Yes, even in the areas outside Caesar's residence," he said. "But rest assured, there are none in staff restrooms or staff sleeping quarters."

Not completely reassuring, Cassandra thought, but after five years at the Monte Carlo, it wasn't unfamiliar, either. All she had to remember was that being in the IDES Lab was just like being in a casino. Always assume you're being watched.

"A couple more things," Danicek said. "First of all, you should know, as everyone here is already aware, that you do not need to worry that when Caesar returns to the past, he can do anything that will affect subsequent events. While to explain the mechanics of time would take far too long, you can most easily understand what we have learned by thinking of past time as solid ice. It is immutable. Think of the present as the surface of that ice, and of ourselves as skaters upon it."

Danicek paused. Cassandra watched Renolds and Palmer shift in their chairs. Faith crossed her arms and looked away.

They've heard this before, Cassandra thought. This is one of Danicek's pet stories.

It was also obviously part of her initiation, so she leaned forward. She didn't have to struggle to be interested. She just wanted Danicek to know she was paying serious attention.

"The future is like the air surrounding the skaters. Invisible. Uncoalesced." He paused again. "This is not a perfect metaphor. The most important thing to remember is that all the precautions we are taking with this experiment are just that: Precautions. The truth is, even if Caesar does not return to the Ides of March, nothing will change. He will still be assassinated because he already was assassinated. He will still die because he already died."

Danicek looked from face to face, stopping last on Cassandra's.

"Secondly, we must never forget that we are planning a kidnapping. Seizing and transporting a man without his permission is not something I take lightly, nor should any of us. To mitigate this action, we will be giving Caesar the opportunity to return immediately to the moment from which we excised him. If he does not wish to stay with us, we will send him back. The decision, however, must be reached within a hundred and fifteen seconds. If Caesar remains with us any longer than that, he will be forced to remain the full four days—until the next synch becomes available."

Danicek must have read the surprise on Cassandra's face. "Yes, my dear," he continued. "All our preparations may be for nothing more than a minute and a half in Caesar's presence. One of your most important roles in this experiment is to entice the man to accept our invitation to stay with us. It is not too soon for you to be thinking about this task."

The moment these words emerged from Danicek's mouth, Cassandra no longer had any questions about why she had been added to the IDES team. Everything was both crystal clear and very simple. She was bait.

Cassandra was still thinking about this latest revelation as Danicek wound up the meeting with a reminder about the IDES Project's cover story. "It is perfectly acceptable for you to tell anyone who's interested that we are testing new technology for dating ancient artifacts." Danicek paused and glanced at his watch. Then he nodded at Eric, who immediately jumped up and headed toward the kitchen. Everyone else rose and stepped aside when he returned with an armload of black fabric that turned out to be a tablecloth. Before ten minutes had passed, the conference table had been laden with a buffet fit for high rollers. Eric had just finished lighting the candles in the flower arrangement when the doors to the antechamber slid open, and a petite woman in a blue dress stepped into the room.

"Sonia!" Danicek said as he rose. "I'm so happy you could join us to welcome our new team member."

Mrs. Illingsworth must have been assigned a personal arrival time, too, Cassandra thought, as Danicek crossed the room and greeted her with a kiss on each cheek.

The old lady made a beeline for Cassandra. "*¡Bienvenida!*" she said, taking Cassandra's hand in both of her own. "I can't tell you how thrilled I am to meet you. If you need anything—anything at all— please call me. We have much work ahead, but right now—*¡Es hora de celebrar!*"

The spread Eric had laid out on the conference table was lavish and exotic, with exquisitely crafted hors d'ouevres and elegantly arranged seafood, including caviar. Cassandra had served caviar plenty of times back at the Monte Carlo, but this was the first time she had been on the receiving end. She wasn't sure she would like it—it was fish eggs, after all. But when Mrs. Illingsworth saw her hesitate, she loaded up a toast point and held it to Cassandra's lips. "It's Ossetra," she said, "just off the plane this afternoon. You simply must try it."

Still a little reluctant, Cassandra took a small bite. She let it sit on her tongue a moment, expecting salty fishiness. But no! The flavor was rich and buttery.

"Oh my God! It's delicious!" The words popped out before she could replace them with something more sophisticated.

Mrs. Illingsworth laughed and held up her champagne flute. "To new experiences," she said. "We're all so happy you're here, Cassandra."

As she looked from face to face, Cassandra saw that Mrs. Illingsworth's statement wasn't quite accurate. Four faces wore smiles as warm as her own, but one face sported an undeniable frown. Four out of five wasn't bad, though, she decided. Somehow, she'd figure out what was eating Faith Hopper. In the meantime, she wasn't going to let the doctor's sour mood spoil her own.

"To the IDES Project," Cassandra said, raising her own glass. "*Prosit!*"

XXXII

The following Tuesday afternoon, Elizabeth and Cassandra joined John Reynolds in his office at 4:00 o'clock.

"So glad you are joining us, Cassandra," John said. "Dr. Palmer and I have been meeting weekly since July, but now that we're getting closer and you're on board, we're going to step things up to twice a week."

Cassandra nodded. "Fine with me."

"The first thing we did after joining the IDES Team was to develop a reading list. I've made you a copy." He pushed a stapled stack of papers across his desk toward Cassandra. "Caesar, his contemporaries, all the later ancient sources, and modern commentary."

He watched Cassandra look over the list. It was a pretty formidable bibliography for anyone, and especially an undergraduate.

"I've already started on Caesar," Cassandra said, looking up. "I figured that was the obvious place to begin."

"Good thinking," Elizabeth said. "If you need any help with any of the other authors, just let me know."

Perfect, John thought. He would have offered himself, but he didn't want to come across as patronizing.

"Thank you," Cassandra said. "I've also already read your book, Dr. Reynolds. It's excellent. You really brought Caesar to life."

Interesting, John thought. Was Cassandra serious, or was she just a good diplomat? Either way, it was a brilliant move on her part to jump the gun with *What Would Julius Caesar Do?*

"I guess we'll find out how good a job I did," John said. "Or at least we will if we can get Caesar to talk. That's our biggest challenge. We're snatching this man completely away from all frames of reference. We have to be ready for the possibility that he will simply clam up."

"We've spent a lot of time thinking about that," Elizabeth said. "Conversation is the key."

"Any questions, Cassandra?" John said. "Nothing is too trivial, and nothing is silly."

"The hot tub," Cassandra said. "What's the deal with that?"

"It was Danicek's idea," John said. "There are no specific plans for it."

Cassandra seemed to relax a little. "I guess I see his point," she said. "A modern version of a Roman bath. Caesar will probably think it's weird, though."

"Caesar will find everything about the IDES Lab weird," Elizabeth said. "Including us."

"Yes, and it makes me wonder—" Cassandra paused. "We'll be cooped up in the IDES Lab for four days. No exercise? No fresh air?"

"There's the field trip," Elizabeth said. "The party at Sonia Illingsworth's house. That's fresh air, at least."

"It helps to think of Caesar's time in the present as equivalent to an academic conference," John said. "They last around four days, too. Nobody gets any exercise. Everybody stays in the hotel. It's really not that much time, once you consider all the meals."

Cassandra nodded. "As long as we can get him interested in talking with us."

"Exactly," Elizabeth said. "We think that being as well informed as possible on Caesar's life and times—especially the events right before the Ides of March—will help us—both to provide context and allow us to understand whatever he brings up. I want to ask Caesar about his Parthian campaign, for example. Things that are current events to him."

"Cleopatra," Cassandra said. "I'd love to know more about her."

"Excellent," John said. "So—Tuesdays and Thursdays at four. Will that work for you?"

Cassandra nodded. "*Erit perfectum*," she said.

XXXIII

Six days before Christmas, Cassandra backed out of Simone's drive-way onto Maple Street. As she struggled with Jeremiah's recalcitrant clutch, Simone appeared on her front porch.

"*Un moment*, Cassandra!" she called. "I almost forgot!"

A moment later, Simone was at the passenger-side window. Cassandra leaned across her laptop bag and cranked the window down. Simone thrust a foil-covered bottle decorated with curly pink ribbons toward her.

"Champagne for you and your mother," she said. "Happy holidays!"

As Cassandra drove away, she marveled once again how lucky she had been to find Simone Babcock and her tiny guest house. In its way, it was right up there with meeting Alex Hunt and getting into USC. As she headed east on the Santa Monica Freeway, Cassandra's spirits rose even higher. As the sprawl of Los Angeles disappeared in her rearview mirror, she thought about how much her life had changed over the last four months. By the time she reached Barstow, her car was no longer an antique Volkswagen with a tricky clutch. It was a golden chariot bearing a victorious conqueror back to Rome. It didn't matter that her only tangible spoils were a bottle of champagne and a few Hollywood trinkets. Cassandra Fleury, formerly of Carefree Canyon Trailer Resort and now of Beverly Hills, was returning to Las Vegas in triumph. She was not only a successful student at the University of Southern California, she was a member of the IDES team. Could life get any better?

A glorious desert sunset blazed as Cassandra neared the exit for Zzyzx Road.

Perfect timing.

Zzyzx Road was one of Cassandra's favorite stops on drives between Las Vegas and Los Angeles. Malcolm had introduced it to her on a trip to Disneyland when she was ten years old. Cassandra asked about the peculiar name, and Malcolm answered by driving her down to the derelict buildings at the end of the half-paved road. The sign answered Cassandra's question: Zzyzx Mineral Springs and Health Spa. But it wasn't the decaying buildings that enchanted her. What she liked was how easily civilization could be left behind. A few hundred yards down Zzyzx Road, Cassandra felt like she was on another planet, completely disconnected from the hectic buzz of regular life. It was a sensation she enjoyed, especially if she arrived in time for a desert sunset.

Pulling off the interstate, Cassandra bumped a few hundred yards down the sandy road, turned off the car, and got out. Leaning against the passenger door of the old VW, she watched the sun sink behind the mountains. She lingered until the first star appeared in the purple sky.

The evening star, which meant it wasn't a star at all, but Venus.

Even better for wishing on.

As Cassandra stood gazing into the sky, she couldn't help smiling. A year ago, she would have wished for—well, everything she now had, from the money to go to college to an address without a space number.

The only item on her longstanding list that still hadn't come her way was a real soul mate. Peter was a fraud, but somewhere out there—

Cassandra tried to imagine her perfect partner. Instead, Alex Hunt appeared in her mind's eye.

Alex Hunt? He was old enough to be her father, and he even acted like one. Without asking for anything in return, he had given Cassandra everything—

She wrapped her arms around herself in the gathering darkness. Looking skyward, she sent a plea to Venus that she knew no goddess, star, or planet could grant.

Give Alex Hunt his wife and daughter back.

And yet, Cassandra mused as she headed back to the highway, if Adrienne and Ivy hadn't died, none of her own dreams would have been realized. Alex Hunt wouldn't have come to Las Vegas on their birthday, and he wouldn't have established a scholarship fund. Dorian would have set Cassandra up with someone else that evening, and she would still be a Vegas call girl trying to save money. No French landlady, no lyric poetry class, no secret project—

God! Cassandra tried to turn her thoughts to something else. It made her crazy to think that time really might be a two-way street.

Cassandra spent the weekend distributing the Hollywood trinkets to friends. She had lunch with Tanya at a sandwich shop next door to her new Master Massage franchise at the Sunset Galleria.

Over crab and avocado croissants, Tanya demanded more details about how Cassandra's one and only tryst at Caesars Palace had resulted in immediate retirement. Without revealing her benefactor's name, Cassandra related all the incredible but oddly unjuicy details.

"I know you're messing with me about the sex, Cass," Tanya said after hearing the tale. "But your secret's safe with me."

It was probably pointless to try to set Tanya straight. If she had told Cassandra the same story, she would have felt messed with, too. Even so, Cassandra opened her mouth to try. Tanya spoke first.

"Dorian says you're a goddess."

Cassandra's mouth was still open, but no words emerged for a moment. "How could he?" she managed at last. "I flaked out after one date. I figured he'd be pissed forever."

"Nope." Tanya shook her head. "Evidently you made your client very, very happy."

In spite of Tanya's mistaken conclusions about what she had done to elicit rave reviews from Alex Hunt, Cassandra smiled. Tanya kept shaking her head.

"It took me nearly eight years to earn enough to pay for my franchise," she said. "You work one night, and *poof*—Cinderella. Dorian's right. You're a goddess."

"Beginner's luck, more like it," Cassandra said, "but you just reminded me. I'm going to a party in a couple of months, and I'm supposed to look like a Greek goddess. I'm hoping you might have a dress I can borrow."

Tanya laughed. "I'm sure it's not *my* kind of party, now that you've gone all collegiate high society, but I know exactly what you need. I'll get you a goddess dress from my friend Kelly. She's wardrobe mistress at Caesars. Short or long?"

"Definitely long." Cassandra wished she could tell her friend the truth about why she needed a goddess dress, but for now, Tanya's assumption that the party was a snooty academic shindig would have to stand. At least it wasn't exactly untrue. The gathering where she would be greeting Julius Caesar could definitely be described as exclusive.

"I am so glad Dorian isn't mad at me," Cassandra said. "I was worried I might never be welcome at Caesars again."

"He'd welcome you with open arms," Tanya said. "You don't have to worry about a thing."

Hooray! Caesars Palace wasn't off limits, which meant Cassandra could take Dr. Martinelli to dinner at his favorite restaurant. She was eager to thank him properly for all he had helped make possible.

XXXIV

"John sent me email about a month after you arrived at USC," Dennis Martinelli said over *brasato* at the Lupercal Café. "I printed it out for you." He pulled a folded sheet of paper from his breast pocket. Reaching across the table, he handed it to Cassandra. The candlelight was just bright enough for her to read the message.

I think she may well be the best student I've ever had, too. Thanks for sending her.

Dennis watched the "too" hit home. When Cassandra's eyes met his, he saw the tears standing in them.

"I'll never be able to thank you enough." Cassandra said.

"You've already thanked me enough."

This was no understatement. When Dennis arrived in Las Vegas shattered by his experience at Georgetown, finding a student like Cassandra had been a lifeline. Now, as he looked at the capable young woman she had become, he almost told her how worried he was.

His concern had begun when Cassandra first told him about the IDES Project. When men in positions of power invite young women—especially beautiful ones—to participate in their grand schemes, it's rarely to elevate them to an equal level of influence. At best, they want attractive cup bearers. At worst—he thought about Georgetown again.

He had seen such girls suffer there. Every year, Gregory Timmins would flatter the best-looking female freshman in his classes by inviting her to become his research assistant. His real goal, of course, was sexual conquest. Dennis was not alone among his colleagues in recognizing Timmins's abuse of power. He was, however, alone in trying to stop him.

In 1990, Danielle Minassian entered Georgetown as a freshman classics major and Dennis's advisee. She was both gifted and beautiful, a combination Timmins prized. When she showed up in Dennis's office breathless with excitement one day, he was not surprised to learn that the reason was that Professor Timmins had bestowed upon her "a wonderful honor." Nothing Dennis said could convince her to turn this offer down.

A month later, Danielle again sat in Dennis's office, this time with tears streaming down her face.

"I don't know what to do," she cried. "I want to die."

Glad to provide a safe haven, Dennis encouraged Danielle to tell him what had transpired between her and her teacher. As he tried to comfort the young woman, his anger at his colleague boiled over.

Dennis could no longer sit idly by as Timmins abused his position. He stood by Danielle as she went to the dean with her story. He stood by her as she faced an entire panel of university administrators who would have preferred she keep her mouth shut.

Danielle stuck by her story for five long weeks. Then, a few days before Christmas vacation, she appeared in Dennis's office with both her parents.

"I lied," she said. No tears now, just stony resolve.

"We are sorry our daughter caused all this trouble," Mr. Minassian said. "We are taking her home to Chicago."

"I am so sorry," Danielle said.

The family left, but Dennis's battle had only just begun.

Danielle's retraction gave Greg Timmins a formidable weapon. He trained it on Dennis, accusing him of ruining his reputation and trying to get him fired. The university, pleased to be out of the limelight for alleged tolerance of sexual abuse, sided with Timmins. By the end of the academic year, Dennis had tendered his own resignation. He could no longer teach in a place that defended a predator.

As he watched Cassandra Fleury grow into a beautiful woman, Dennis worried that she might someday be victimized in the same way Danielle had been. Her work as a cocktail waitress on the Strip had, he hoped, provided her with some worldly armor. But had it prepared her to fend off predators disguised as academics? Street wisdom alone might not be enough protection from this more camouflaged type of hunter.

"It's all been so perfect," Cassandra said, yanking him back from his thoughts. "I know the magic has to end one of these days, but—"

Should he share his worries? No. Better to leave her confidence intact. He straightened his shoulders and smiled across the table.

"Don't be such a Cassandra," he said.

"Oh my God! You haven't said that to me since—"

"Since you told me you would fail your Catullus test."

They both laughed. "And then I aced it," Cassandra said.

"Exactly. Prophecy is not your gift. Be thankful."

XXXV

JANUARY 6, 1999

"I spent all of Christmas vacation asking myself, 'Why me?'", Cassandra said. She was sitting across from Dr. Elizabeth Palmer in the USC faculty club. "Working with Dr. Danicek is such an honor."

Dr. Palmer smiled. "To be honest, I felt the same way."

"But you're a professor. I'm just a—"

"You're just a great Latinist," Elizabeth said. "Which is exactly what the IDES team needs."

"Dr. Palmer, I—"

"Please, call me Elizabeth. We're colleagues now." She took a sip of coffee. Before she could set her cup down, "Für Elise" emanated from under the table.

"I've got to take this," Elizabeth said. She pulled her phone out of her purse and checked the screen. "I'm sorry."

Cassandra nodded and took her own sip of coffee.

"Hugo just faxed in a change from *Horses of the Night*." Cassandra could hear the man's voice on the other end of the phone.

"He's too late, Hank," Elizabeth said. "The catalogue's already in production. I sent everything to the printer this morning."

"Shit. *Corrigendum*, then."

"I'll start a list," Elizabeth said.

"Have you asked Cassandra?"

Elizabeth glanced up. Cassandra tried to look like she hadn't heard.

"I was just about to."

Elizabeth signed off, tucked her phone back into her purse, and took another sip of coffee.

"That was my husband." She paused. "He owns a coin dealership."

Cassandra nodded. She had learned of Elizabeth's relationship with Hank Morgan not long after she arrived at USC. The celebrity numismatist, and often Elizabeth, too, were frequently featured on the society pages, usually in the company of movie stars and billionaires. Elizabeth didn't talk about it, though, so everything else Cassandra knew came from hallway gossip and one faded newspaper clipping stuck to a bulletin board next to the mailboxes in the classics department office.

The *Los Angeles Times* story included a photo of Elizabeth in a Cinderella dress. "The Collector Takes a New Bride," the headline read, making it sound like she'd joined a harem. Cassandra wondered what Elizabeth thought about it but didn't feel comfortable asking.

"Hank and I would like to invite you to our winter coin auction," Elizabeth said. "It's January twenty-third at the Beverly Wilshire. Dinner afterward at Scala d'Oro."

Did I hear right?

At a loss for words, Cassandra stared at her tiramisu. She'd been surprised enough when Elizabeth asked her to lunch at the faculty club. And now—an invitation to a Denarius coin auction? In addition to all the other gossip, she'd been hearing about these lavish affairs ever since she arrived at USC.

"They're the Oscars of coin collecting," Dr. Reynolds had told her. "Red carpet, designer gowns, paparazzi … the guest list is star-studded."

"I hope you're free," Elizabeth said. "Hank and I would love to see you there."

Cassandra hesitated. She had nothing to wear.

The goddess dress Tanya had promised hadn't arrived yet. Her black silk cocktail dress had been fine at the IDES Lab reception, but it didn't qualify as true "formal wear." The only items in her wardrobe that were even remotely deserving of that adjective were her high-school prom dress and a billowing fuchsia bridesmaid's dress with a lime green velvet bolero. And they weren't actually "in her wardrobe." They were hanging in her closet back at Carefree Canyon, along with her first tutu and the cowgirl outfit she had worn to Helldorado Days. Margot was too sentimental to give them away.

"I—I—"

"Please say yes. You'd be doing us a great favor."

"I'd love to come." Cassandra couldn't see how her presence would benefit her professor, but she wasn't about to turn down such an amazing invitation. Somewhere, somehow, she'd find a dress.

"Hank's clients are all business people, and some of them are a little rough around the edges. One of the reasons they like collecting coins and other antiquities is that it gives them a connection to culture and academia. If you're there—well, you exemplify what they're so eager for."

So that was it.

Cassandra felt her shoulders tighten as she realized she was being recruited for a familiar role: eye candy.

"When they find out you're a Latinist, you'll be the belle of the ball."

Oh, and brain candy, too.

That was an improvement, she decided.

"The only thing is—well—I'm not sure I have the right sort of thing—"

"To wear?"

Cassandra nodded. Elizabeth smiled.

"Not a problem. You and I are close enough in size. I've got a closetful of dresses and an excellent seamstress. All you have to do is come over to my house. Nia and I will take care of everything else."

"Thank you, Dr.—Elizabeth."

They agreed on a day and time as they finished their dessert.

"Oh, I almost forgot," Elizabeth said before they parted ways. "Bring shoes."

XXXVI

The following Saturday, Cassandra pulled to a halt on the flagstone driveway of 142 Bellingham Court in Brentwood.

"I'll leave the gate open for you," Elizabeth had said. "Pull right up to the front door."

The house was spectacular. With its Corinthian columns flanking an enormous porch, the Palmer-Morgan residence reminded Cassandra of the White House. Her old green Volkswagen looked like a cockroach on a wedding cake.

Elizabeth answered the door. Her dark hair was pulled back in a simple ponytail, and she wore a dark green velour warm-up suit.

Wow.

She looked at least a decade younger than she did on campus in her stodgy Brooks Brothers suits. She also looked smaller as she stood in the massive doorway.

Cassandra stepped into the foyer. An enormous crystal chandelier hung from a vaulted ceiling at least thirty feet high. Beneath it, a sweeping staircase curved upward behind a white marble nude on a black stone pedestal.

"Aphrodite of Lydia," Elizabeth said as she closed the front door and joined Cassandra.

"She's beautiful."

"She won't be here long, unfortunately. Hank's got a buyer in Dubai. I've had to get used to temporary antiquities—here today and gone tomorrow."

Elizabeth led the way up the grand staircase. The wall was adorned with framed fragments of Pompeian frescoes and Roman mosaics. More temporary antiquities? Cassandra wondered, but she decided it would be rude to ask. At the top of the stairs, marble sculptures, bronze statues, and ceramic vases stood on tables and pedestals lining the walls. It reminded Cassandra of somewhere—of course! The Palatine Suite at Caesars Palace, where she had dinner with Alex Hunt. Suddenly she felt like she had made a weird full circle. The architecture here was different, but it looked as though the same decorator had chosen the furnishings. Was it possible that Caesars Palace was one of Hank's clients?

"Ah, here's Nia!" Elizabeth said, interrupting Cassandra's thoughts. She turned to see a petite olive-skinned woman emerge through a door on the far side of the room. After a polite nod, Nia looked Cassandra up and down.

"I think you're right about the black Versace," Nia said to Elizabeth. She turned back toward Cassandra. "Did you bring shoes?"

Cassandra had splurged on a pair of Ferragamos the day before with money from her book allowance. She pulled them out of her shoulder bag. "I hope four-inch heels are okay," she said.

"They're perfect."

The dress was perfect, too. A strapless black silk sheath with a thigh-high slit on the right side, it was already almost the perfect length with Cassandra's heels. Nia was still measuring and pinning the hem when Elizabeth emerged from the bedroom carrying several flat velvet-covered cases. She set them on the table in front of the sofa, picked up the top one, and snapped it open.

"I thought you might like to see your jewelry for the evening." She held up a heavy gold necklace and moved toward Cassandra.

"It's a Gallic *torque*," she said. "Something Julius Caesar would recognize from his time north of the Alps."

It was beautiful, but it made Cassandra nervous. She was going to look ridiculous at the Beverly Wilshire climbing out of her ratty old Volkswagen in a designer dress.

I'll rent a car, she thought. No way am I going to embarrass Elizabeth or put up with snickers from parking valets.

She was still thinking about how to pay for a nice rental as she and Elizabeth walked back downstairs.

"Arrive here at three-thirty on January twenty-third with your hair and makeup done," Elizabeth said. "That will give us plenty of time to dress before we head over to the hotel. The limousine will get here around five o'clock."

A limo! Of course!

"We'll have bodyguards, too," Elizabeth added. "because of the jewelry."

This all made perfect sense. While Elizabeth might trust Cassandra with a Versace, there was no way she and Hank would allow their ancient valuables to travel without an escort.

XXXVII

When she arrived at the mansion on Bellingham Court, Cassandra glanced at herself in her rearview mirror. Damn, she looked good. Simone had done a fabulous job on her makeup, and her hair had never looked better. She was glad Simone had insisted she borrow her beaded Walborg evening purse.

"It's roomy enough for a camera," Simone said. "You simply *must* take photos."

I'll look like a star-struck tourist, Cassandra thought, but she placed a small camera in the bag anyway. *Semper parata!*

With Nia's assistance, Elizabeth and Cassandra were soon bedecked in their spectacular couture. The black Versace sheath was the perfect backdrop for her blond ringlets and the ancient gold neck ring. Elizabeth's green Vera Wang gown had a sleek reptilian sheen. Her emerald-studded bracelet and Pompeian necklace were the perfect accents. As they stood side by side in front of the huge mirrors in Elizabeth's dressing room, Cassandra had a hard time believing the experience was real. They looked better than the slickest ads in *Vogue*.

"One last thing," Elizabeth said. Nia stepped forward with a large velvet-covered box and raised the lid. Elizabeth lifted out a delicate wreath fashioned of feathery gold leaves.

"This is one piece that's not on loan," she said. "It came from the tomb of a Hellenistic princess." She placed it on her head, where it stood out brilliantly against her sable bob. "Hank gave it to me on our wedding day."

Whoa. How Hank must love her. Cassandra couldn't suppress the wave of envy that rippled through her.

"It's beyond gorgeous," she said.

"I'm so glad you'll be meeting my husband tonight," Elizabeth said. "And after all I've told him about you, Hank's looking forward to it, too."

Two beefy bodyguards waited at the foot of the grand staircase. Elizabeth introduced the older white one as Bill and the younger brown one as Marco. Both were wearing tuxedos. They reminded Cassandra of the brawn that often accompanies high rollers in Vegas casinos, and she recognized the bulges under their jackets. The ancient jewelry would be traveling with both muscle and heat.

The windows of the limo were heavily tinted, but Cassandra had a good view out the left side. When the chauffeur slowed in front of the Beverly Wilshire, Cassandra could see a crowd swarming around several men on the steps at the front entrance. Cameras flashed like fireworks.

"Nick Stratos," Elizabeth said. "He threatened to protest—looks like he's done it."

Cassandra leaned forward to get a closer look at the Oscar-winning actor as the limo inched by. She'd known about his crusade to get Greek antiquities returned to his homeland for years, but she'd never seen him in action.

"I think he does it for personal publicity, but the Pericles Medallion makes a dynamite pretext," Elizabeth said. "It never fails to get him in front of a camera."

The Pericles Medallion was the most notable item in the auction. The large gold coin had garnered headlines in the preceding weeks, mostly because it hadn't been on the market for nearly three hundred years, but also because it might fetch a record price.

As the limo crawled forward, Cassandra could hear a man's amplified voice. Even distorted by a megaphone and muffled by the limo's closed windows, Stratos's distinctive gravelly drawl was unmistakable

"Would Americans sit idly by if the Statue of Liberty was on sale in Athens?"

Shouts of "No!" rose from the crowd.

"Should Greece watch calmly while her national treasures are sold to the highest bidder?"

"No!" the crowd roared.

"Return the Pericles Medallion to its rightful home!"

As the crowd shouted its approval, Cassandra watched a team of Beverly Hills police officers and hotel security guards close in.

"Looks like they won't be there for long," she said.

"Long enough for Nick's purposes," Elizabeth said. "That crowd is ninety-five percent media."

She had a point. Nearly every person was carrying a camera, and at least a dozen boom microphones stuck up over the throng like speared squirrels.

The limo turned the corner and pulled under the hotel's porte-cochere. Bill sprang out and held the door for the two women.

Nick Stratos hadn't cornered *all* the media attention, Cassandra noted as she stepped onto a red carpet. Camera strobes flashed as she and Elizabeth covered the space between the driveway and the hotel entrance.

Inside the lobby, the red carpet led to a wide doorway. Next to it, two attractive young women in Grecian goddess gowns stood beside a glass table supported by a Corinthian capital. Cassandra guessed they were in charge of the guest list, but she and Elizabeth needed no credentials. They headed directly into a palatial ballroom, Marco and Bill close behind.

"Ah! My darling Lizzie!"

A man in a dinner jacket kissed Elizabeth on the cheek.

Hank Morgan.

"And this must be the lovely Cassandra Fleury." Hank took her right hand and raised it to his lips. "You are more beautiful than words could possibly convey."

"Thank you," Cassandra said, feeling color rise to her cheeks. "And thank you for inviting me."

"The pleasure is entirely mine." Hank looked directly into her eyes.

Cassandra had seen photographs of Hank in the newspaper, so she already knew about the square jaw and white-blond hair. What photographs had failed to capture were the intelligence and intensity of his eyes. Hank Morgan had a gaze that wouldn't let you go—as though his eyes were powerful magnets. Cassandra stared back at him until he turned to Elizabeth.

"Guests are beginning to arrive," he said.

Elizabeth nodded. "Come on, Cassandra. We'll find our seats, and then I'll come back to help Hank greet our guests." She picked up a slick publication from a table near the door. "The auction catalogue," she said. "So you can follow along."

Cassandra looked out over the huge room. Not far away, a pianist played Ravel on a white grand piano. Next to it stood a modestly draped replica of the Apollo Belvedere. As she watched, Cassandra could swear the statue's arm moved. Could it be? Yes, there was no doubt, she realized as she drew a little closer. This was no statue, but an actor painted white and standing very still.

"We have those in Las Vegas," Cassandra whispered to Elizabeth. "At the Venetian."

"No coincidence there," Elizabeth said. "Steve Tarantino—a business partner of Hank's—arranged for them. He owns shops at the Venetian and at Caesars Palace. There are two more of them somewhere—an Athena and a bronze charioteer."

Elizabeth and Cassandra headed toward the tiers of seating banked around a raised platform. Surrounded by gold stanchions linked with velvet-covered ropes, it reminded Cassandra a little of a prizefight ring.

Elizabeth led the way to seats on the second tier, halfway along the platform. Removing a card that read "Reserved" from one of the chairs, she motioned for Cassandra to be seated.

"I'll be back as soon as I've finished my hostess duties," Elizabeth said. "If you need anything, just let Marco know." Cassandra turned to see that Marco had taken a seat right behind her, one level up.

As she sat down, Cassandra watched Elizabeth glide back across the room with Bill in close pursuit. This is perfect, she thought. From here—the best seat in the house—she could see everything.

As Elizabeth had said, a living statue of Athena stood near a long table. At the other end, an actor coated in dark green metallic paint posed as the Charioteer of Delphi. Men and women in business suits staffed the table, assisting guests as they filled out forms. Registration for bidding, Cassandra guessed.

Through the doorway, more fabulously clad guests arrived steadily. Cassandra watched Hank and Elizabeth greet each one. Slowly, seats around her began to fill. An especially glamorous couple settled in a few seats away. The woman's dress was an elaborate red chiffon creation with a plunging neckline.

Simone would have loved this, Cassandra thought. She'd recognize every designer without a second glance. Even so, she couldn't bring herself to extract the camera from her evening purse. It just didn't seem polite—

Suddenly, another couple appeared beside the one already seated near Cassandra.

"Francesca! You look *marvelous!*"

"*Josephine!* So do you!" The two women exchanged air kisses as their perfumes wafted over Cassandra.

"Kevin, you've got to take pictures!" The woman named Josephine said. "Or maybe—"

She turned toward Cassandra. "Would you be so kind?" she asked. She pulled a small camera from her evening purse.

"Of course," Cassandra said.

The four friends leaned in and smiled. Cassandra captured them with a press of a finger.

"May we take your picture, too?" Josephine said. "You look *marvelous!*"

"Of course!"

With camera-happy seatmates, Cassandra now felt perfectly at ease pulling out her own camera. Simone would be thrilled, and her mother would enjoy the finery, too. So would her stepdad, come to think of it.

Cassandra had snapped photos of a dozen or so magnificently dressed attendees when she caught sight of a silver-haired man entering the room alone. Hank and Elizabeth greeted him warmly. Cassandra kept her eyes on him as he walked to the long registration table. Why did he seem so familiar?

When he turned and headed toward the seating area, Cassandra could see his face more clearly.

Could it be?

The man drew closer.

Yes! It was Alexander Hunt!

XXXVIII

Cassandra rose. Would Alex see her? She waved. The man squinted. Would he recognize her? She waved again.

His gaze still on her, the man reached the first tier of seats. All at once, his face broke into a huge grin. A moment later, he was at Cassandra's side.

"Why hello, Miss Fleury," Alex said. "We meet in the most remarkable places." He leaned forward and kissed her cheek.

"I didn't know you collected coins," Cassandra said.

"I didn't know you attended coin auctions." He looked her up and down. "In designer gowns."

"Elizabeth Palmer loaned me the dress. She's my professor at USC."

"I guess I should have put two and two together," Alex said, "but I don't know her as well as I know Hank. I've known him for over a decade. He sold me my first gold Caesar."

"Mr. Hunt, I—"

"Alex."

"I just want to thank you for everything you've done for me."

Alex smiled. "Looks like you've done quite a bit for yourself, too.

201

I'd like to hear more." He glanced at his watch. "The auction's about to begin, and I'm a bidder. I've got to take my seat. Will you do me the honor of joining me for dinner?"

Before Cassandra could answer, Elizabeth arrived on the scene.

"Alex!" she said. "You know Cassandra?"

"We're longtime friends," Alex said. "I'm her funny old uncle from Arkansas." He winked at Cassandra. "Would it be possible for the two of us to sit together at dinner?"

"Of course," Elizabeth said.

Alex moved to his seat in the front row, and Elizabeth turned to Cassandra. "Why didn't you tell me you know Alex Hunt?"

"I had no idea he'd be here. I didn't know he collected coins."

"How do you know him, exactly?"

"Old family friend." There was no way she would reveal the truth about her relationship with Alex, and the man himself had given her an alibi.

Elizabeth gazed at Cassandra, curiosity obvious in her eyes.

"So how does all this work?" Cassandra asked, changing the subject. Activity on center stage suggested that proceedings were about to commence. Reluctantly, Elizabeth gave up her Hunt probe and cooperated.

"The auctioneer—that's the man in the white dinner jacket over there—will follow the catalogue. Everything is listed in numbered lots. Most coins are sold separately, but not all. Some are grouped and sold as a unit."

Cassandra nodded.

"The bidders are all sitting in the first row. You can't really tell who the buyers are, because most of the bidders are agents for big-time buyers like the Getty here in L.A. and the Braithwaite in Chicago. Alex Hunt buys for himself, but he's unusu—*Oh!*"

Cassandra followed Elizabeth's gaze to the doorway. Hank was greeting a tall woman in an ankle-length silver fur coat. On each side of her, and equally hirsute, stood two tall, lanky dogs, one black and one gold.

"Philippa Kenyon Sykes," Elizabeth said before Cassandra could ask. "She's our guest of honor."

Cassandra noticed the slight distaste in Elizabeth's voice. If they didn't like her, why had they invited her? she wondered. But that was the deal with celebrities, she reminded herself. How many times had her stepdad told her that celebrities didn't need to be liked? What they needed was to be a valuable brand. Then they could be as spoiled as they wanted and still get invited to events like this.

"I was beginning to think she was a no-show," Elizabeth went on. "I should have realized she'd want to make an imperial entrance." She sighed. "I've got to go back and give her—and her ridiculous dogs—the royal treatment."

"Are they Afghans?" Cassandra asked.

"Salukis. Imported from Turkey. She claims their ancestors lived with the royal families of ancient Troy."

As Elizabeth crossed the ballroom, Cassandra watched Hank kiss the hand of the woman in fur.

Philippa drew every eye in the room as she strode to the seating area and commandeered four chairs to accommodate her canine entourage and her Snow Queen coat. Almost immediately, a crowd gathered around her, blocking any chance Cassandra had of a snapshot. Maybe later, she thought. Maybe at dinner.

Elizabeth still hadn't returned to her seat when the auctioneer removed a gavel from a little leather case and set it on a small table at the back of the platform. He nodded to a woman wearing a short blue-sequined cocktail dress. On that cue, she made a circuit of the inner circle, carrying the first coin on a tray covered with black velvet. After the bidders all had a chance to look, she circled through the upper ranks to give the spectators a peek. The coin was silver. Cassandra looked in the catalogue to learn more about it.

The coin was an Augustan *tetradrachm* from Roman Antioch, estimated to sell for about $1,600. It was among the least expensive items listed, Cassandra noted as she flipped through the catalogue.

"Is that the only silver coin?" Cassandra asked Elizabeth as she slid back into the seat beside her.

"There are a few others in lots," Elizabeth said, "but Hank is known for dealing in gold. To be included, a silver or bronze coin has to be particularly rare, historically significant, or beautiful. Everything is museum quality."

The auctioneer went into action. Cassandra tried, but she could detect no movement among the bidders. Even so, the price of the coin rose steadily until the gavel came down, and the *tetradrachm* was sold. Cassandra managed to hear that it brought $1,775, but the buyer remained a mystery.

The auction continued, but Cassandra lost track of it as a veritable fashion show swirled through the outer ranks. Every two minutes, another clotheshorse would sashay up to Elizabeth to exchange pleasantries. Cassandra hadn't gotten a shot of Philippa Kenyon Sykes, but she was doing a fabulous job of documenting a host of other fashion statements for Simone. No one minded in the least.

At last, the Pericles Medallion came up for bid, the coin Nick Stratos wanted Hank to surrender to the Greek government. The whole room fell silent. Everyone wanted to catch a glimpse as it made the rounds on the velvet-covered tray. When the auctioneer brought his gavel down at $690,000, the room emitted a collective murmur. Almost immediately, more than half the spectators stood up and began moving toward the doors.

The auction was over, but the bidders remained seated. It was time to pay up, and everything was handled by a phalanx of men in dark suits who moved efficiently from one buyer to the next. The proceedings were still underway when Bill tapped Elizabeth on the shoulder.

"Your car is ready, ma'am."

"Thank you," Elizabeth said. "Cassandra, it's time to go over to Scala d'Oro. Hank will meet us there."

XXXIX

There were still a few photographers waiting as the two women and their bodyguards navigated the red carpet and climbed into the limo.

"There'll be more photographers at the restaurant," Elizabeth said. "They're probably hoping for Nick Stratos, but they'll settle for Pippa Sykes."

It was a short drive, and Elizabeth was right. Several dozen celebrity-mad tourists, a handful of photographers, and a video cameraman from Channel 7 were lined up on the sidewalk in front of Scala d'Oro.

"The one in black is Michelle Pfeiffer," squealed one voice as Cassandra emerged from the limo. "No, I think it's Nicole Kidman," said another. "No wait, it's gotta be that English actress—"

Amazing what a great dress, a fancy car, and a bunch of flashing strobes can do for you, Cassandra thought. She knew she looked good, but without all the props, nobody would mistake her for a real movie queen. It made her think about a guy she once waited on back at the Monte Carlo. He looked like a young Tom Selleck. The fact that he looked nothing like the current Tom Selleck didn't stop a steady stream of fans from asking for his autograph. The guy went along with it and let them think the autographs he provided were the real deal. During a break in the parade, he winked at Cassandra. "Just like you," he said, "I find it works out best when you give people what they want." Cassandra hadn't liked his assumption, even though he gave her a generous tip when he left. She would never feel comfortable taking advantage of other people's mistakes, even if they were stupid ones.

Ignoring the proffered autograph books, Cassandra followed Elizabeth into the restaurant. Bill and Marco followed close behind.

The maître d' greeted Elizabeth by name and escorted everyone upstairs to an indoor garden resplendent with fresh flowers, ivy garlands, white trellises, and marble birdbaths. Beside the entrance stood a long table draped with a silver cloth. On it stood dozens of gold shopping bags with sparkly silver tissue flaring out of the tops.

"Be sure you get a gift bag before we leave," Elizabeth said. "They have lots of great stuff in them." She paused. "You'll also get a copy of Pippa's brand-new memoir, hot off the presses."

Cassandra easily detected the change in Elizabeth's voice when she referred to the book.

"Have you read it?" Cassandra asked.

"No," Elizabeth said quickly. She lowered her voice. "Reynolds got an advance copy a while back. I flipped through it, but I just can't afford to be associated with her ludicrous theories. We both declined to endorse it."

So why is Pippa here? Cassandra wondered. Before she could ask, Elizabeth spoke again.

"Hank noticed that her book release coincided with this coin auction. Inviting newsworthy VIPs improves our chances for good P.R. So here she is, and I have to admit she's already a big hit with our clients." She shrugged. "What I think of her scholarship really doesn't matter."

Together, they moved further into the room. The tables—at least thirty of them—glittered with silver and crystal. Each setting was marked with a hand-lettered place card.

"Hank and I will greet all the guests," said Elizabeth. "I'll just make sure you have a seat next to Alex Hunt, then you're on your own." She smiled. "Except for Marco, of course."

Elizabeth switched a couple of place cards, then went to the door to wait for Hank. Cassandra made her way to the bar, ordered a glass of white wine, and watched the room fill.

A waiter had just offered Cassandra a fancy canapé when she caught sight of Alex Hunt. He greeted Elizabeth and Hank, scanned the room, and made a beeline toward Cassandra as soon as their eyes met. Together, they sat down at their places.

"I'm famished," Alex said. "Auctions are hard work."

"Did it go well for you?" Cassandra asked, uncertain of the etiquette required for such a conversation.

Alex glanced around. "I'll tell you later," he said quietly. "Right now, I want to hear about college. Is it everything you hoped?"

"It certainly isn't what I expected," Cassandra said. "Like tonight, I mean. This is more like Las Vegas than my idea of undergraduate studies in ancient languages."

"It's more like Vegas than you know." Alex tilted his head toward the next table. "See that guy over there, the one next to the woman in purple?"

Trying not to be too obvious about it, Cassandra looked in the direction Alex indicated.

"That's Steve Tarantino," Alex said.

"Hank's partner?" She glanced at Tarantino again. He was about sixty. His hair was shiny black, but his wrinkles gave him away. He was drinking champagne and laughing at something the woman in purple was saying.

"Yes," Alex said. "You know about him?"

"I feel as though I ought to," Cassandra said. "Elizabeth told me he owns stores on the Strip."

"Yes, including the one at Caesars that sells jewelry made out of ancient coins. I guess I shouldn't be surprised that he and Hank have joined forces, but I wish I knew what else they were up to—"

He paused, then shook his head. "But enough about them. I want to know about you. What else isn't what you expected?"

"That's a long list," Cassandra said, smiling. "I think the biggest surprise has been Andrew Danicek."

"*The* Andrew Danicek? The Nobel laureate?" Alex couldn't hide the surprise in his voice. "You certainly are hobnobbing with celebrities! But what does physics have to do with Latin?"

Just then, a waiter presented the first course, a salad that looked like art and tasted like lobster. As they ate, Cassandra told Alex about her unexpected invitation to join the IDES team.

"I think that's the reason Hank and Elizabeth invited me tonight," she concluded. "She didn't invite anyone else from the department."

"She usually invites only one or two academics," Alex said. "You're the lucky one this time, which makes me extra-lucky."

Cassandra smiled. "I'm extra-lucky, too," she said.

Just then, a flamboyantly furry trio entered the room.

"Do you know Philippa Kenyon Sykes?" Cassandra asked.

"Hank introduced me, but I don't know her," Alex said. "Unless reading *Gifts of Hermes* counts. Everybody read it back in the—when was it? The seventies sometime. You couldn't go anywhere without hearing people discuss nutty theories about time warps and wormholes."

"My stepdad called it junk archaeology," Cassandra said. "He had a copy, but he told me not to bother with it."

"Your father was right," Alex said, "although she really did find a temple of Aphrodite in Turkey that other archaeologists had spent decades searching for. She was well respected until she went off the deep end with her theories about aliens and telekinesis." He paused and shook his head. "Sometimes money is a liability."

"What do you mean?"

"As I said, I don't know her. But I do know that she inherited a large piece of Kreger-Billitsch Steel. It's a lot easier to be an archaeologist when you don't have to scramble for grants. The trouble is, it's also easier to think you're brilliant when all you are is crazy."

They watched Pippa feed a couple of jumbo shrimp to her dogs.

"How does she get away with bringing dogs into a restaurant?" Cassandra asked.

"Simple," Alex said. "She feels entitled. It's an attitude more powerful than most people know." He leaned closer. "You're surrounded by it, Cassandra. Hank Morgan is a prime example."

As if in response to his name being mentioned, Hank Morgan appeared at their table. He pulled up a chair between Alex and Cassandra and sat down.

"Small world, Alex," he said. "I had no idea you knew one of my wife's students."

"Cassandra and I are old friends," Alex said. "It's been way too long since we've seen each other."

Cassandra could tell Hank was as curious as Elizabeth about how she knew his wealthy client, but Alex said nothing further. Cassandra certainly wasn't about to.

"Sad about Pippa," Hank said.

"Those pesky aliens bothering her again?" Alex said.

Cassandra suppressed a chuckle.

"I guess you didn't hear her news," Hank said. "She's got six months to live."

What? Cassandra stared at Hank.

"You'll be reading about it soon enough," he said. "She chose tonight to announce to the world that she has cancer. It's inoperable."

Cassandra looked across the room. Pippa was enthroned in an armchair, a Saluki sitting at attention on either side. A woman in a white gown approached her, a fat hardback in her hand. Pippa chatted with her before signing the book.

Lots of adjectives came to mind as Cassandra watched Pippa interact with her admirers, but "sick" wasn't one of them.

"You'd never guess by looking at her," Hank said.

Alex remained silent, and Cassandra had no idea what to say.

"Would you like to get her autograph, Ms. Fleury?" Hank asked.

"I guess so—"

"Go for it," Alex said. "You'll never have anoth—a better chance."

"I'll introduce you," Hank said. They rose and crossed the room. Hank paused at the gift bag table to pull a copy of Pippa's book from one of the bags. He handed it to Cassandra.

Out of Place and Out of Time

The title was printed in embossed gold letters on a blue background. Underneath, the subtitle read: *My Quest for Answers, Beauty, and the Meaning of Life.* The only image on the cover was a photograph of a large brick-colored boulder inscribed with Greek letters:

OY MONON TO ZHN ΑΛΛΑ TO EY ZHN

Cassandra recognized the quote immediately, Socrates by way of Plato:

Not merely to live, but to live well

"It's her memoir," Hank said. "Should be a very entertaining read."

He steered Cassandra to Philippa's chair, where the gold Saluki politely sniffed her hand.

"Pippa, I'd like to present Cassandra Fleury, a Latin scholar."

Pippa's hair was platinum, but her eyes were two black coals. They smoldered through the taut mask that too much plastic surgery had made of her face. Cassandra could almost feel Pippa's eyes traveling over her.

"So pleased to meet a fellow lover of the classics and great dresses," she said. "Versace, no?"

Cassandra nodded. "I—I'm a great admirer of your work—" she stammered. Not quite true, but what else could she say?

Pippa raised a scarlet-taloned hand.

"No, no, dear," she said. "Hank, explain to this young woman that if she wants a career in classics, she must never mention my name in the same sentence she uses the word 'admire.'" She turned back to Cassandra. "That is, if you want tenure. If you don't—then, thank you! So nice to meet you!"

Pippa reached for the book in Cassandra's hands.

"To whom shall I inscribe it?" she asked. "You? A boyfriend? Or perhaps to no one at all, so you can sell it on eBay?" She opened the book to the title page. "Prices for a signed Pippa Sykes book should skyrocket in six months or so."

"To me, please," Cassandra said, having no idea how to respond to anything else Pippa had said.

Pippa wrote inside the book with a fat black fountain pen. She blew on the ink to dry it, then closed the cover and handed it back.

"Enjoy, sweetheart," she said. "You classicists may not consider me 'up to code,' but my stories are a hell of a lot juicier than anything you'll find in Caesar."

Cassandra was just opening her mouth to say thank you when an older couple stepped in front of her.

"Gerald, you old bastard!" Pippa said as Cassandra moved back to join Hank. "And this must be the slut you dumped me for!"

"I'm glad you got to meet her," Hank said as they walked away. "She's one of a kind."

Cassandra nodded. No arguing with that.

"Thank you for introducing me, Mr. Morgan. And for the whole evening. It's been wonderful."

"It's Hank, and you're welcome. Until we meet again." As before, Hank kissed her hand.

Cassandra sat down next to Alex and set *Out of Place and Out of Time* on the table.

"Nice memento," Alex said. "Will you read it?"

"Maybe I should," Cassandra said. "Ms. Sykes claims she's more riveting than Julius Caesar."

"No doubt better than Shakespeare, too," Alex said.

"Are you going to read it?" Cassandra said.

"I doubt it," Alex said. "Not my cup of tea."

They both smiled, but Alex's face soon turned serious again. He leaned closer.

"The auction didn't go well tonight," he whispered. "Well over half the coins didn't sell, because no one met the reserve—the minimum selling price."

Cassandra was silent for a moment as she considered this unexpected information. Obviously, she hadn't paid enough attention. All the excitement about Nick Stratos and the Pericles Medallion had made the auction seem like a wild success.

"I thought I should mention it. Since you'll be seeing Elizabeth—"

"Thanks for telling me. I had no idea."

Alex kept his voice low. "A word to the wise, Cassandra. Between Andrew Danicek and Hank Morgan, you're swimming with some pretty big fish. You'll probably do just fine, but I want you to consider me your extra ace." Reaching into his breast pocket, he pulled out a silver card case and pressed a business card into Cassandra's hand. "I'm spending a fair amount of time in Asia these days on business, but you can always reach me at this phone number—anywhere in the world, toll free. If you need to, don't even hesitate."

Cassandra looked at the card. She'd felt a variety of emotions over the preceding months, but the only time she'd felt scared was right before Eric told her the truth about the IDES Project. What was threatening about Andrew Danicek and Hank Morgan? They had both treated her with courtesy and respect. Maybe her benefactor was just feeling paternal.

"You've already done so much," she said, slipping the card into Simone's evening purse. "You changed my life."

"Money's just a tool, Cassandra," Alex said. "It's not as powerful as most people think. If your life is different, it's you who changed it."

The sadness in Alex's voice was unmistakable. He's thinking about his wife and daughter, Cassandra thought. A loss like that would never let a man forget just how useless money can be.

"I leave for Macau tomorrow," Alex said. "If you'll excuse me, I've got a very early call."

Cassandra watched Alex retrieve his coat. Maybe someday, she thought, I'll think of something I can do to thank him properly.

◉◉◉

Elizabeth didn't say much on the way back to Brentwood. Grateful for Alex's revelation about the auction, Cassandra kept quiet, too. After their gowns were back on their padded hangers and their jewelry safely locked away, Elizabeth accompanied Cassandra to the front door.

"I hope you had a good time tonight, Cassandra," she said.

"I can't begin to describe how—"

"You made quite an impression on Hank." Elizabeth sounded like she was about to cry.

"I—thank you," Cassandra said. "I hope—"

"Good night."

Elizabeth didn't quite shut the door in her face, but almost.

XL

"Where are you?" Hank asked.

"My office."

"I expected you to be at home."

One word would have changed everything, Elizabeth thought. *Hoped* instead of *expected*. His tone was demanding, too—dictatorial even. Not that she wasn't used to it. Elizabeth had fallen in love with Hank because of his charm and his thoughtfulness, but that had dropped off precipitously over the last few months.

It's the strain of his job, she had told herself. Hank's clients were not only incredibly wealthy but also incredibly spoiled. Catering to their whims was both demeaning and exhausting. Add in the money pressures that had been building for nearly a year, and their desperate hope that the auction would solve everything—

"I needed to pick up a few things."

A total lie. After shedding her gown and sending Cassandra home, Elizabeth had needed to get out of the Brentwood palace, away from all the beautiful things she had once believed belonged to Hank.

What else would a girl from Carthage, Missouri, think? If people in Carthage had vases on their sideboards, you could safely assume they had bought them, inherited them, or received them as gifts. And if people in Carthage needed money, they borrowed it from churchgoing bankers, not shady characters who showed up at their house after dark. Elizabeth had been shocked to learn how few possessions Hank truly owned. The house was leased, and his cars? He didn't hold title to even one of them. And though Hank had led her to believe that the gold diadem he'd presented to her on their wedding day was his to give and hers to hold, she now had her doubts.

Smoke and mirrors.

The phrase often came to mind when Elizabeth thought about her life with Hank. These days, that cliché kept suggesting another: *Where there's smoke, there's fire.*

She had allowed herself to believe Hank's assurances that everything was fine. That all changed late one Sunday afternoon a few weeks ago when she opened their front door to three men she'd never seen before. They made an odd trio—two in dark suits and one in a tank top and running shorts—and they seemed to have appeared out of nowhere.

"We must speak with Mr. Morgan," the oldest man said, boldly looking Elizabeth up and down. "If you please." She couldn't place his accent, but she recognized the demanding tone.

"He's not at home," Elizabeth said. "May I tell him who called?"

The man muttered something in a language that might have been Russian. Immediately, the guy in running shorts darted around the side of the house.

"What—?" she blurted.

"Please tell your husband we were here," the man said. He handed Elizabeth a business card. She looked down at it and saw a telephone number, nothing more. When she looked up, she was blinded by a camera strobe. By the time her eyes had recovered, the guy in shorts had rejoined the others, and the three men were heading down the driveway to the automatic gate.

Which should have been closed, Elizabeth thought. Which she had watched swing shut behind Hank's Maserati just an hour earlier.

Back inside the house, Elizabeth allowed her heart rate to slow down before she called Hank. She told him about the three unexpected visitors and read him the telephone number from the business card. He didn't reply.

"Is everything all right?" she asked.

"Everything's fine," Hank said. His voice was a little too silky. "Don't worry your pretty little head about it."

That was the moment Elizabeth lost her powers of denial. For weeks, she'd ignored the ever-tightening knot in her stomach and ascribed her insomnia to the pressures of business and academia.

Hank's a gifted entrepreneur, she had reassured herself many times. He travels in circles you know nothing about.

But Elizabeth did know something about decent people, and those three visitors were not decent men. They were thugs.

There were other signs, too. Hank had begun using throwaway cell phones, changing numbers every few days. He brought in an electrician who worked for three days installing cameras inside the house and out. He hired a new bodyguard and tried to talk Elizabeth into buying a Doberman. Most ominous were his conversations with a Bulgarian named Radkov about some Galen manuscripts that were either fake or stolen. If Hank decided to represent them to buyers as legitimate, who knew where it might lead?

The auction was supposed to solve everything, bring in lots of much-needed cash.

"Don't worry," Hank said. "It's a sure thing. Just help me with the catalogue, and press releases, and the guest list. You're a genius at that sort of thing. Together, we're a dream team."

Elizabeth threw all her energy and connections into making the event a success. She even swallowed her disdain for Philippa Kenyon Sykes when Hank suggested they make her the guest of honor.

"She's got a new book coming out," Hank said. "Offer to let her launch it at the after-party."

Elizabeth didn't love the notion, but she did succeed in reaching Pippa's agent. Pippa called Hank herself to accept the invitation. Would Hank have felt less jubilant if he'd known Pippa would use the occasion to announce her impending death? Not likely, Elizabeth thought. Hank lived by the axiom that "any publicity is good publicity." He was probably disappointed that Nick Stratos hadn't tried to crash the auction instead of holding a short-lived demonstration on the sidewalk.

"Come home," Hank said.

Elizabeth hesitated.

"Lizzie, please." His voice broke a little. "I—I need you."

Hell. When Hank turned the sweetness on—and especially when he called her Lizzie—she couldn't deny she still loved the guy.

She thought back to their engagement party—the night Hank placed the gold laurel wreath on her head and announced to the world that he'd found his queen. Later that same evening, he knelt down before his soon-to-be mother-in-law.

"I want to thank you," he said, "for giving me my lovely Lizzie."

Reaching into his pocket, Hank pulled out a gold bracelet. From it dangled three charms: a tiny key and two small dog tags.

"The key represents a co-op on Central Park West," Hank said. "The tags are stand-ins for Victoria and Albert—two Corgi puppies who are very eager to meet you."

"Oh, Hank," Donna Palmer said when she recovered from her surprise. "How did you know?"

That clinched it for Elizabeth. Hank was not only wildly wealthy and terrifically smart, but also a good and decent man. He knew how to please Mother, because he had *listened* to her. He was paying attention all those times she said how much fun it would be to live in New York. He was listening when she oohed and ahed over Queen Elizabeth's dogs. He even remembered her saying that "puppies need their own friends."

Two corgis and a Manhattan pied-à-terre. An incredible gift from an incredible man. Elizabeth's heart swelled nearly to the bursting point that night. Sure, she and Hank had different ideas about some things. Money, for instance. When Elizabeth looked at $100,000, she saw it for exactly what it was—$100,000. But Hank saw it as a starting point, seed money that could yield him a million. While Elizabeth warmed to words like "nest egg" and "financial security," Hank's heart beat faster at "on the come" and "leverage." They would never share financial views, but weren't Hank's risk-taking and showmanship part of what she loved about him?

XLI

Hank murmured something into the phone, something more about needing her, and making things right.

But Elizabeth wasn't listening. She was remembering the first time she spoke with Hank. She was already familiar with his flashy career. Like every other regular reader of the *Los Angeles Times*, she knew he was the owner of Denarius, the ancient coin dealership on Rodeo Drive in Beverly Hills. She also knew he played polo, owned a racehorse or two, and often threw money into independent film projects. Most of the details had emerged during Hank's lengthy negotiations for a professional hockey team he had tried to purchase and move to southern California.

Hank had called Elizabeth out of the blue on a Monday in early December four years earlier. His voice sounded even sexier on the phone than it did on the *Tonight Show*.

"I'm expanding my coin business," he said. "I'm now handling antiquities."

"Ooh, tricky territory," Elizabeth said. "Are you sure you want to deal with all the lawsuits and diplomatic crises?"

Hank chuckled. "I'm just doing it for my coin clients. I'll only be handling pieces that are already in private collections. Most have been forever—or at least since Lord Elgin was shopping."

"Lord Elgin—that was my point."

Hank laughed. *A nice laugh.*

"Don't worry. No *metopes* from the Parthenon. We're talking vases, bronzes, and the odd bust or stele. Nice stuff, but nothing that will make anyone draw up battle lines."

At that precise moment, Elizabeth remembered another tidbit she'd noted in the *Times*: Hank Morgan's divorce had just been finalized. Elizabeth had just emerged from a failed marriage, too. She had recently declared herself both "out of the woods" and "back on the market." So far, all the declaration had done was to prompt her to categorize every man she met into one of two groups: "taken" or "free."

Had Hank Morgan reverted to "most eligible bachelor" status? It was often difficult to tell if a man was actually "free," and it wasn't the sort of thing you could come right out and ask. And anyway, a student was waiting outside her office door. Elizabeth shook off the daydreams.

"How can I help you, Mr. Morgan?" she asked.

"My friends call me Hank," he said. "I hope you will too, *Dr. Palmer.*"

"Elizabeth!" she couldn't help laughing, and Hank joined in. The shared laugh went on a little longer than the joke merited.

Some might call that chemistry…

"I'd like to hire some young classicists as interns," Hank said when the moment ended. "I'll be unveiling the program at the classics and archaeology convention next month in New York. I'm hosting a cocktail party, and you are my first invited guest."

Elizabeth went, of course.

By the time she reached the mezzanine level of the Marriott Marquis in Times Square, the party was already in full swing. The room wasn't quite large enough to hold the throng. She wasn't surprised.

Anyone generous enough to supply free booze to graduate students is always guaranteed excellent attendance. She wriggled her way into the Ziegfeld Room, where three bartenders were pouring nonstop.

As she continued on her slow path through the crowd, Elizabeth counted three more bars, all of them as busy as the first. In the middle of the room, a giant table had been transformed into a ziggurat of food. At the top, which was all she could see clearly, was a replica of the Trevi Fountain sculpted in ice.

"Elizabeth."

She turned to find herself face to face with a man no photograph could adequately capture. The packed room fell away the instant their eyes met. At that moment, Elizabeth became a believer in love at first sight. Her heart pounded as she relived the most electrifying experience of her life. Then, realizing she was still holding a phone in her hand, she shook off the memory and spoke.

"I'll be there as soon as I can."

XLII

After Hank Morgan bade farewell to the last guest at Scala d'Oro, he drove over to the coast and headed north. It was nearly two a.m., and the Pacific Coast Highway was deserted. He floored the Maserati and zoomed past Malibu.

The auction had been a disaster. Three of his biggest clients failed to appear, and neither the Getty nor the Braithwaite had made a single purchase, despite repeated displays of interest in a dozen major lots. Alex Hunt had been a disappointment, too, going against habit and purchasing just a single *aureus*. The only bright spot was the sale of the Pericles Medallion.

Distracted by the record price and Nick Stratos's demonstration, the press hadn't dug any deeper. *Thank God!* No one would know that Hank's commission was a pittance. He had to cut his fee drastically to land the consignment. It was the only way to generate enough buzz about the sale. Those other lots had to sell to make up the difference. And they didn't. Not enough of them.

God. This time, I really am screwed.

As he passed Decker Canyon, Hank slowed down. There was

no escaping his next move. He might as well go home and face it. He turned around at Nicholas Canyon Beach and headed back to Brentwood. When he pulled into the garage at Bellingham Court, the space usually occupied by Elizabeth's Jaguar was vacant.

Where is she? Hank pulled out his cell phone and called Elizabeth on his way through the breezeway.

By the time he heard Elizabeth's footsteps in the hallway, Hank had changed into his smoking jacket, poured himself an Armagnac, lit up a Davidoff, and was relaxing in his Maloof chair. He knew Elizabeth would find him. Unwinding in the wine cellar was his late-night ritual.

She walked around the chair to face him. No longer the fashion plate she had been earlier at the auction—God, she'd looked stunning—she now wore a hooded sweatshirt over faded jeans. Hank had once found Elizabeth's fondness for denim endearing, but tonight it annoyed him. You could take the girl out of Missouri, but a thousand designer gowns couldn't take Missouri out of the girl.

"The Radkov deal," he said. "I'm going to do it. There's no other way. I need the letter."

Elizabeth's face contorted, but Hank withheld sympathy. He could no longer shield her from the gravity of their situation.

"I thought we agreed—"

"The Braithwaite will close the deal immediately with your endorsement and my guarantee."

"Hank, we've been through all this. I won't lie. Without further evidence—"

"I'm not asking you to lie. You can get your evidence."

"How?"

"I don't know why we didn't think of it sooner. We'll test the Galen manuscripts at the IDES Lab. That will give you your second reference."

"No."

Hank took a puff of his cigar. Why was she refusing? If Danicek's technology was everything she had described—a precise method for dating artifacts—this was the perfect solution to their problem.

"You know I wouldn't ask if there were any other way—"

"I know. It's just that—I can't do it."

"All right. I'll call Danicek myself, and—"

"*No!*" Elizabeth's fierceness startled him. "Please—it's not what you think." She paused and her shoulders sagged. "I'll write the letter."

Surprised, Hank scrutinized his wife. A month earlier, he had tried every argument he could think of to persuade her to write a letter supporting the authenticity of the Galen manuscripts. She refused, adamant that she wouldn't put her career and reputation in jeopardy.

"I'll sell the Jaguar and the condo," she'd said back then. "You can have my jewelry and take my retirement account. Just don't ask me to lie."

She was offering Hank everything she owned, including the condo in Silver Lake where she had lived before they met. If it had been enough to solve their problems, Hank would have already asked her for it.

Instead, he'd borrowed money from the Bratva, something he wasn't about to admit. He hoped he could still make it work. If the auction could attract enough of a turnout and generate decent sales, it would solve their cash flow problems. Until then, so long as he made timely payments on the loan, Elizabeth didn't need to know about the grisly methods the Russian mob sometimes used to deal with deadbeats. Everything was fine. So when Radkov called the first time, Hank turned him down.

Now the Bulgarian was back. Obviously, he'd been unable to find another broker to represent his three Galen manuscripts. Radkov claimed they'd spent the last fifteen hundred years hidden away in a monastery in northern Greece, but he couldn't produce any acceptable evidence of their authenticity. Hank was fairly certain the manuscripts were genuine, but he also had little doubt they were stolen.

It was a tricky deal, but if Hank guaranteed title and Elizabeth endorsed their authenticity, the Braithwaite would bite. Hank was sure of it. He'd clear just short of a million, which would keep the Russians at bay long enough for him to get his finances in better shape. If the monks at Mount Athos or the Greek government demanded the manuscripts back—even if the Braithwaite called him on his guarantee—the deal still bought some time.

"I'm glad you'll write the letter," Hank said. "But now you've got me worried."

Elizabeth shot him a puzzled look. "Why?"

"The IDES project. Is everything all right?"

"Everything's perfectly fine," she said, dropping her head. "I'll write the letter in the morning."

"I'd still like to chat with Danicek," Hank said. "I'd like to know more about his technology."

"No!" She yanked her head up. "Hank, please. The IDES Project isn't about—I mean, it can't help us with the Radkov deal."

"Why?"

"I can't tell you that."

Well, well, Hank thought. Maybe that explains the invasive background check. He hadn't been happy when the investigator showed up at Denarius—too close for comfort. The nondisclosure agreements Elizabeth had described seemed excessive, too.

"Don't call Danicek," Elizabeth said.

What in hell was going on? But he realized that asking her directly was not going to yield the answers he sought. More subtle tactics would be necessary.

Hank stood up. "Don't worry your pretty head, sweet Lizzie." He pulled her close and kissed her forehead. "Let's go to bed, my darling."

XLIII

"Any chance you're free to grab a bite to eat this evening?"

Cassandra paused before answering. She had given Hank Morgan her telephone number at the coin auction, when he said he'd like to chat with her more about conversational Latin—someday. But a dinner invitation? Totally unexpected, and—did Elizabeth know about it? Was she going to be there, too? No way she would meet the man alone.

"What I mean," Hank said, as though he sensed her hesitation, "is that we'd like to talk a little business with you."

Business? What kind of business would a coin tycoon want to discuss with a college student?

"We'd also like to show you around Denarius," Hank went on. "My wife and I thought you might like to see our offices now that you've been to an auction."

Cassandra's shoulders relaxed. Of course Elizabeth would be there, too. What had she been thinking? She listened to Hank's directions to Orvieto, an Italian restaurant on Rodeo Drive in Beverly Hills.

"It's a few doors down from Denarius," Hank said before signing off. "See you around seven."

Cassandra was glad she had worn her black silk cocktail dress. The maître d' at Orvieto greeted her like she was a movie star. Under the stares of every other diner in the room, he guided Cassandra to the most conspicuously excellent table in the place, where Hank rose to greet her. Before she could say much more than hello, she was ensconced in an upholstered chair and offered a linen napkin. Almost immediately, the chef himself arrived to describe the evening's specials. A wine steward followed. He suggested an Umbrian red to go with their entrées. Elizabeth was nowhere to be seen.

"I'm so glad you could come," Hank said once all the attention subsided. His smile revealed his perfect teeth. Their snowy brilliance matched the starched white collar that rose above his V-neck pullover, setting off his flawless tan. His blue sweater was the exact color of his eyes. "My wife sends her apologies. She won't be able to join us tonight."

Cassandra's eyes met Hank's. Was he lying? Maybe Elizabeth knew nothing about this little get-together.

But that would be so stupid! Hank had to know that Cassandra would mention their meeting to Elizabeth. The two women chatted at USC on a near-daily basis. She shook off her suspicions.

"To Las Vegas," Hank said, raising his glass. "What a great place to call home."

"You really think so?" Cassandra asked.

"I do. All the best artists and architects are tapped to work there these days. It's like Athens in the Golden Age, when Pericles wowed the world by building the Parthenon. Academic snobs won't admit that Sin City could have culture, but it's actually creating it. It's where culture is being born, not just preserved. I love that."

Cassandra had never heard Las Vegas complimented so nicely before. People usually talked about card counting and prostitution.

"You worked at Caesars, right?" Hank asked.

What? Had Alex Hunt said something? Cassandra hoped Hank was just fishing.

"No. I worked at the Monte Carlo."

"Oh, I guess I thought it was Caesars because of your Latin," Hank said. "It's my favorite hotel on the Strip. It's a lot more fun than a museum, and it's got almost as much art. Frankly, I'd rather sit at Neptune's Bar with a glass of wine and look at a good reproduction of the Prima Porta Augustus than trudge through the Vatican Museums to see the real thing. I don't admit that to just anyone, by the way. Only to people who are cosmopolitan enough to give Las Vegas the credit it deserves."

He shot Cassandra a conspiratorial grin, and she couldn't help smiling back.

"Classicists! It always amazes me that they won't consider holding their annual meetings at Caesars. It's one of the most lavish tributes to ancient culture in the world, and they turn up their snobby noses and call it tacky. I would laugh if it weren't so pathetic."

"You think ancient Romans would like Las Vegas?"

"They would *love* Las Vegas," Hank replied, "except maybe for prudes like Cato the Elder."

Cassandra chuckled as she imagined what a dour old Roman censor would have to say about her skimpy waitress outfit.

"And now," Hank said as Cassandra's saltimbocca and his own osso buco arrived, "I will have many more opportunities to visit your fair city. Did you meet my new partner at the auction?"

"Steve Tarantino?" Cassandra asked. "No, but someone pointed him out to me."

"The Golden Age of Denarius is about to begin." Hank said, "I'll tell you more about it after dinner. But now, let's raise a toast."

Hank lifted his glass, and Cassandra touched hers to it, but she was confused. Alex Hunt had said the coin auction was a disaster. Had Hank solved his financial problems? If he had, it was great news.

For the rest of the meal, Hank regaled Cassandra with entertaining stories about well-heeled coin collectors, eccentric racehorse owners, and Hollywood film producers. It was easy for her to understand how Elizabeth had fallen in love. Hank Morgan was funny, smart, and educated. He had great taste, good looks, and traveled in the social stratosphere. If Alex hadn't told Cassandra the truth about the auction, she would have called Hank perfect.

After they finished their tartufo and espresso, Hank led the way up the street, where he unlocked a door next to a polished brass plate that read "DENARIVS."

"After you," he said, holding the door open. Cassandra stepped into a small but elegant vestibule with a cut stone floor. An amphora filled with red roses stood on a table under a painting of Aphrodite and Eros. On the right was an elevator, and on the left a staircase with a golden banister and marble steps. Hank led the way up the stairs.

The room they entered instantly reminded Cassandra of the stories Malcolm told about Oxford colleges and exclusive British men's clubs. The walls were paneled in polished mahogany. Bookcases filled with leather-bound tomes alternated with oil paintings of classical subjects. If the large window overlooking Rodeo Drive hadn't reminded Cassandra that she was in Beverly Hills, she could easily have imagined herself inside a Sherlock Holmes story.

"Right this way," Hank said. He motioned Cassandra through the double doors on the other side of the room. The chamber beyond was paneled on two sides in mirrors and marble. Hank offered her a tall chair at a counter covered in dark green velvet. Behind the counter, two Ionic columns framed a polished steel door that stood slightly ajar. Light leaked out from the vault beyond.

"Ready for some numismatics?" Hank asked with a smile.

He walked behind the counter and pulled the steel door further open, revealing the vault's golden interior. Floor to ceiling, its walls were lined with dozens of shiny numbered drawers. Hank slid one open. Extracting a small black box, he stepped back to the counter and opened it.

"Cassandra," he said, "I have a proposal for you." He opened the box and laid a silver coin on the velvet in front of her.

"I would like you to work for me."

Cassandra didn't know which was more surprising, the coin lying in front of her or Hank's offer of employment.

"Mr. Morgan, I'm flattered."

"I'm not a flatterer, Miss Fleury. I'm a businessman." Hank pointed at the coin. "This belongs to a collector in Zurich. Care to make a preliminary assessment?"

Cassandra looked at the man's profile on the coin, and the letters next to it.

"I have no idea what it's worth," she said. "But it's Roman. 'BRUT' is probably short for—" She paused. This came a little too close to a topic she would rather avoid. "Brutus," She said at last.

"Good work!" Hank turned the coin over.

Cassandra sucked in a breath when she saw the words and figures on the back.

"It's Brutus, all right," she said. No steering clear of it now, she thought as her heart rate increased. "This coin was struck to commemorate the Ides of March—Julius Caesar's assassination."

Hank smiled. "You're a natural," he said as he stowed the coin back in its box. "Danicek is lucky to have you."

What? First the Ides of March, and now Danicek's name? Was it just a coincidence, or—

"I hope you're being careful," Hank said. "You're working with some pretty powerful people, and the technology may be risky."

"What do you mean?"

"I've been doing my own research."

Cassandra said nothing as her mind whirled.

"TESA is untested," he continued.

TESA! He knows about TESA!

"I fear it is unsafe," he went on. "I don't want Elizabeth risking her life for a time-travel experiment."

"But she isn't!" Cassandra blurted.

Hank arched an eyebrow.

"I can't tell you everything, but all we're doing is dating ancient artifacts—"

Oh, God, who was she kidding? If Hank knows about TESA, he probably knows about—

"Cassandra, I know you've signed a nondisclosure agreement, but I've read my wife's. All it does is protect the technology. Somebody ought to be looking out for the people involved, too, don't you think?"

Cassandra's heart was still racing as Hank turned and walked back into the vault. Her thoughts jumped to what Eric had told her weeks before, when she first learned the truth about the IDES Project. Eric thought it could be dangerous, too. Since then, she'd often wondered about how risky it might be to meddle with the fabric of time. Danicek took great care—maybe too much care—reassuring the team. Maybe Hank was right to be concerned. She took a deep breath and willed her heart to slow down.

When Hank returned to the counter, he was carrying another box.

"I know about Julius Caesar's visit," he said. "Four days, beginning March 12th."

Cassandra's heart pounded again as she failed to keep her jaw from dropping. Hank knew everything. Elizabeth had obviously leaked the secrets they had all sworn to keep.

"Tell *no one*," Danicek had repeated like a mantra. The nondisclosure agreements spelled the penalties out in great detail. Apparently, even the personal liability clause hadn't been enough to keep Elizabeth's mouth shut.

"I'm worried about my wife," Hank continued. "And—now that I know you—I'm worried about you, too. I'm concerned that no one is looking out for your best interests." He paused. "I can be your advocate, if you'll let me. I deal with people like Danicek all the time. If you keep me up to speed about what's really going on inside the IDES Project, I can make sure your safety is a priority."

Cassandra struggled to compose herself as she considered Hank's words.

Keep calm. Let him talk. You can figure out later what to do about it.

Hank opened the small black box he'd carried from the vault.

"Here's an interesting one," he said, laying another coin on the green velvet. This one was small and brown. Cassandra couldn't make any sense of the corroded relief on its surface.

"May I?" she asked, reaching to turn it over.

"Of course." But the other side was no more revealing.

"I give up," she said, unsure whether she wanted to keep playing this game.

"It's an obol," Hank said. "In its day, it was like a nickel, and I'm afraid it hasn't appreciated as much as you might expect in two thousand years. It's worth only about five bucks." He flipped the coin expertly with his thumb, sending it end over end and catching it in his left hand. "It came from the grave of a noble Roman. His family wanted to make sure he wouldn't get stuck on the wrong side of the River Styx."

"A coin for the ferryman."

"Exactly." Hank grasped Cassandra's hand. Placing the obol in her palm, he curled her fingers around it. "Keep it," he said. "And think about my offer. And, after the IDES Project is over, I want you to join the Denarius team."

"Thank you," Cassandra said. "But—"

"Just think about it. I'll call you tomorrow.

XLIV

"Hank knows about Julius Caesar."

Cassandra watched her professor's face. This time, Elizabeth failed to conceal her dismay. She'd almost succeeded when Cassandra told her about dinner with Hank at Orvieto, and Cassandra had played along. But now Elizabeth was fighting tears and losing.

"I'm sorry, but—" Cassandra hesitated. She hated tattletales.

"I'm the one who should be apologizing," Elizabeth interrupted. She pulled a tissue from the box on her desk and dabbed at her eyes. "I'm sorry you're in the middle of this."

"What happened?" Cassandra asked.

Elizabeth did not answer immediately. Instead, she shifted a pile of papers from one side of her desk to the other. Then she took a sip of whatever was in the mug next to her computer monitor.

"I told him," she said at last. "I didn't mean to—I mean—I didn't want to." She sighed. "Sit down, Cassandra. You deserve an explanation."

Cassandra slid into the chair across from her professor.

"Hank thought the IDES Project could help him date some manuscripts," Elizabeth said. "Not surprising, really, since that's been our cover story all along. He wanted to call Danicek. I told him not to—that it wouldn't help. He kept after me, and—oh, hell—"

Elizabeth reached for another tissue and blew her nose into it. "I was upset. I said too much." She wiped her eyes. "Way too much."

"Did you know he was going to talk to me about it?" Cassandra asked.

"No. He promised me he wouldn't tell a soul."

"Maybe he hasn't."

Elizabeth stared at Cassandra. "What do you mean?"

"Well, he did tell me, but I already knew. Maybe he hasn't told anyone else."

"We can hope, I guess. Oh, Cassandra, I'm so sorry. I've been under a lot of pressure, and—" She paused. "I won't blame you if you tell Danicek."

Cassandra looked down at her hands. There was no question that telling Danicek was the responsible thing to do. Reporting any breach of IDES Project security was mandated in their NDAs.

But what would happen if she squealed? At worst, Elizabeth's leak could halt the whole project. Or maybe Danicek would kick Elizabeth off the project. But what if Danicek decided to expel Cassandra, too? There was no way she was going to risk losing her chance to meet Julius Caesar.

"Will Hank tell anyone else?" Cassandra asked.

Elizabeth shrugged. "Up until now, I would have said absolutely not. He was thrilled I was involved in a groundbreaking project with such a renowned man. I can't believe he'd do anything to jeopardize that, but now—" She dropped her head.

"He's worried about you," Cassandra said.

Elizabeth looked up, her eyes bright with tears. "What? Why?"

"He thinks TESA is dangerous. He thinks there are protections in place for the technology, but not for us—for you."

"He never said anything about that to me."

"Maybe he didn't want to scare you. Maybe—" Cassandra paused. Maybe she was talking too much.

"I had no idea," Elizabeth said. This time, she let the tears roll.

Both women were silent for a moment.

"I don't see any reason to tell Danicek," Cassandra said at last. Her heart was racing. She couldn't believe those words had just come out of her mouth.

Elizabeth blinked at her.

"Caesar's arriving in two weeks," Cassandra went on. "Everything's going well. The last thing I want to do is cause a problem." Her heart was pounding. She took a breath and tried to slow it down.

Elizabeth squared her shoulders. "I'm sure you're right," she said, "Hank's probably just worried about me. I'm sorry he chose such a poor way of dealing with it. Thank you for telling me."

As she left Elizabeth's office, the word "Rubicon" popped into Cassandra's head.

It's from all the Caesar cramming I've been doing, she told herself. Except I'm not provoking a civil war or anything close to it. All I'm doing is keeping an unpleasant disruption from scuttling the IDES Project.

As she drove home, she thought about the old coin Hank had given her.

She'd already crossed her Rubicon. All she could hope was that she wouldn't need boat fare across the Styx.

XLV

Andrew Danicek stubbed out his cigarette in an empty Starbucks cup as he pulled into the parking lot at the IDES Lab. As dismayed as he was that his smoking habit was now firmly re-established in his life, he was also grateful that it soothed his headaches. Aside from his deck at home, his car was the only place he could light up without announcing his addiction to his colleagues or breaking the no-smoking mandate in the IDES Lab. He had smoked a few times outside on the IDES Lab steps, but he knew he'd be caught if he kept it up.

I'll visit my doctor as soon as phase three is complete, he promised himself. As much as he wanted to ascribe the pain behind his forehead to fatigue and stress, he couldn't completely convince himself that there might not be some other issue. But right now, smoking helped, and he wasn't going to deny himself the relief, even if it did make his car reek. A shot or two of single malt was the other secret weapon in his self-medication arsenal. Fortunately, that was something he could consume without detection in the privacy of his office.

Alone inside the lab, Andrew surveyed the common area. He

allowed a feeling of pride to expand within him as he recalled what this space had looked like the first time he set foot in it more than two years before. Everything had turned out just as he had imagined, and some things were even better. The kitchen, for example. Eric had equipped it with the skill of a first-rate restaurateur. Andrew was glad he'd configured it so the laundry appliances would fit. The original plan had been to put them in Faith's lab, but it was so much better to have them on neutral turf. Eric had also done a masterful job on the dining room. With its crystal chandelier, Persian carpet, mahogany sideboard and dining table, paneled wainscoting, and textured wallpaper, the room looked at least as elegant as the Athenaeum.

Andrew moved down the hall, entered Caesar's residence, and flipped the light switch next to the door. The living room was instantly bathed in the warm light of a bronze chandelier and two table lamps on end tables flanking the sofa. The fireplace was a perfect touch, Andrew thought as he glanced around the room, but he also liked the cut Berber carpeting and carefully chosen works of abstract art. The room was large enough to accommodate the entire team, but it still had a warm and cozy feel. As he looked around the living room, he was glad he had heeded the classicists' advice and not attempted to create a replica of a Roman house.

"Better to succeed perfectly at creating a space that we—the hosts— find welcoming and luxurious," John Reynolds had said. "A replica with even the slightest error will seem odd—and possibly even offensive—to Caesar."

"I agree," Elizabeth Palmer added. "We would end up with something like the Getty Villa—accurate in many respects, but with electric lights, elevators, and chlorinated pools. Far weirder for Caesar than something completely unfamiliar. I think modern beds are better than Roman ones, anyway."

Andrew stepped into the bedroom, where an inviting queen-size four-poster with a gauzy canopy was the centerpiece. He moved on through to the bathroom, where the hot tub occupied the far corner. Andrew was especially proud of the mosaic surrounding the spa. The seascape with jumping dolphins had been his idea. The facing wall had a glass shower stall and a marble countertop with cabinets underneath and a raised ceramic sink. The toilet was in a chamber of its own.

All perfect, Andrew thought, as he left Caesar's apartment and made his way to Faith's domain. He rarely entered when she was there.

Sad that things were so tense between them, he thought. Their relationship had started out so well, he never dreamed that she would turn out to be such a virago. And who could possibly have guessed that at the same time, she could be such a mouse? No matter how many times Andrew explained his theory of chronodiology and all the supporting evidence he had accumulated with TESA, she remained terrified of what she saw as the extreme potential for disease.

At least Faith had maintained strict professionalism in every other way. She kept her lab meticulously organized, and the operating theater, outfitted under her direction, rivaled a research hospital's.

Andrew walked through his own office to his private suite. He had napped on the bed there, but he'd never spent a full night. Back when his relationship with Faith was still blossoming, Andrew had told her how much he was looking forward to sharing the suite with her during Caesar's visit. If he had known then just how emotionally damaged she was, he would never have breathed a word. Andrew hated regrets, but when it came to Faith, he had a few.

With a sigh, Andrew walked back into the hall. As he headed to the common area, the airlock doors slid apart. Eric and Faith emerged together.

Without a word, the doctor headed to her lab.

"Breakfast sandwiches," Eric said, nodding down to the large cardboard box he was holding. "From Mi Piace."

He headed toward the kitchen.

Andrew retired to his office and closed the door. He pulled a bottle of Glenmorangie from the lower left-hand drawer of his desk. He poured a hefty slug into his Marilyn Monroe coffee mug, leaned back in his chair, and drank.

XLVI

Eric set the box of breakfast sandwiches on the kitchen counter and flipped on the espresso machine. He glanced at his watch. Good. He still had plenty of time to get everything set up for breakfast. This was the last meeting of the whole team before phase three officially began tomorrow, when everybody would take up residence. He hoped the croissants and paninis from Mi Piace would meet with everyone's approval. He knew it was Faith's favorite local restaurant, but he had long since given up hope that he could do anything to soften her attitude. Such a shame. She had arrived with such open enthusiasm, but the dog experiment, the end of her fling with Andrew, and her perpetually ignored concerns about safety had completely shut her down. Here they were, embarking on a world-changing experiment, and she was counting the days until it was over.

Who am I kidding? Eric asked himself as he carried plates and silverware into the dining room. I'm counting the days, too. The ever-enlarging pit in his stomach was impossible to ignore. Not only had he been forced to rush to prepare for Caesar's visit, Eric also knew that Andrew's theories needed more testing. It didn't help Eric's peace of mind that a new paper by Karl Gustafson had appeared in the latest issue of *Clepsydra*. Gustafson headed up the only team working overtly in chronodiology, and his theories contradicted Andrew's in several fundamental ways. If Gustafson was correct, Faith did have every reason to be terrified by Andrew's refusal to take health concerns more seriously. While Eric sided with Andrew publicly, he also thought that taking a few more precautions couldn't hurt.

Like canceling the party at Sonia's house. It was an obvious risk on so many levels! Faith had long since given up yelling at Andrew about it, because the more she railed, the more firmly he dug his feet in. Eric had tried quiet reason, but that hadn't worked, either. He had considered appealing directly to Sonia but decided against it. He was way too worried about Andrew's mental state. Going behind his back might damage their relationship beyond repair.

So the party was still on. At least it was limited to two hours, Eric thought. Plenty could happen in a window that size, but at least Sonia's house was only two miles from the IDES Lab. And he'd thought everything through, minute by minute. By having the party, they also had Sonia's good will and cooperation. Remember that, Eric told himself. If it weren't for the party, we'd have Sonia to deal with as a full-fledged member of the IDES Team.

Eric had just finished setting the table when Cassandra arrived.

"Anything I can do to help?" she said.

"No," Eric said. "Everything's just about ready." At least Cassandra is easy to get along with, he thought. And, thank God, Andrew hasn't hit on her. There was a time when that thought never would have crossed his mind, but his behavior with Faith had put Eric on high alert. While Andrew's wives and previous girlfriends had all been within ten years of his own age, Faith was nearly thirty years younger. Eric hoped against hope that Andrew wouldn't push things even further and try to seduce someone young enough to be his granddaughter.

"Here's a question, though," Eric said. "The sheets arrived. Should I wash them before I put them on all the beds?"

"I would," Cassandra said. "There could be stuff on them from the manufacturing process. Where are they? Want me to get them started?"

Once again, Eric gave silent thanks that Cassandra was a team player.

XLVII

When Elizabeth saw that the only available parking space at the IDES Lab was the handicapped one, she backed the Jag back out onto Raymond Avenue and found a spot along the curb. After John found out the hard way that the handicapped space belonged exclusively to Sonia Illingsworth, he'd spread the word. Since Sonia enjoyed dropping in unannounced, everything went more smoothly if that spot was always available.

This might have been irritating another day, but nothing could dampen Elizabeth's ebullient mood as she pulled her briefcase out of the passenger seat and headed back up the street. After months of stress punctuated by moments of panic, her life was back on track. Things had taken a major turn for the better after she wrote the endorsement letter that Hank used to get the Braithwaite Museum to buy the Galen manuscripts. Sure, she had misgivings about it, but the transaction had proceeded smoothly. Her worries subsided even more as, money problems solved, Hank had reverted to his old, wonderful self. He was fun to be around again, and he'd even started cooking again. Just this morning, in a surprise to recognize the significance of the last formal meeting at the IDES Lab before the team took up residence, he'd made her breakfast in bed. Strawberry blintzes, her favorite. She hadn't bothered telling him that breakfast would be provided at the lab. Today, she would enjoy the privilege of indulging in a second breakfast. What was wrong with acting like a hobbit once in a while?

The first person Elizabeth saw when she stepped out of the airlock was Cassandra. She was distributing silverware and napkins around the conference table.

What a remarkable person she is, Elizabeth thought. If I found out someone on the team had been loose-lipped about Julius Caesar, I probably would have gone running to Andrew immediately. Cassandra thought things through and decided against following the rules. That took not only intelligence but maturity.

"Hi, Elizabeth," Cassandra said when she saw her. "How are you?"

Elizabeth felt like hugging her student-cum-colleague, but she knew Cassandra wouldn't understand her euphoric mood. Someday, she told herself, I'm going to find a way to reward her appropriately. Without Cassandra, I wouldn't be here right now.

"I'm excited," Elizabeth said. "This is really happening."

Their eyes met.

"Thank you," Elizabeth said quietly.

"We're in this together," Cassandra said. "I wouldn't want to be here without you."

XLVIII

Andrew Danicek waited for Eric and Cassandra to finish clearing the table after breakfast, then called the meeting to order a few minutes after ten o'clock. Standing at the head of the conference table, he looked from face to face. For better or for worse, this was the team that would welcome Julius Caesar to the twentieth century. If things hadn't gone as smoothly as he might have hoped, they had at least progressed to the point where he was confident of success.

"Let's begin with parking," Andrew said. "As you well know, there are not enough spaces here at the lab to accommodate everyone's vehicles, and parking overnight on Pasadena streets is illegal. I'm leaving my car at home in my garage. I'll take a taxi in the morning." He paused. "One space is reserved for the IDES Lab van, and one for Faith's car. She will be providing redundancy for the van when we go off site. That leaves one regular spot and the handicapped space."

"I'll be on my bike as usual," Eric said.

"My husband will drop me off," Elizabeth said. "No parking space necessary."

"I'm leaving my car at home," John said. "Car service will get me here. I don't want my car sitting outside for a week anyway."

"My car lives outside all the time," Cassandra said, "so if there is a space available, I'd like to use it."

"Fine," Andrew said, "and that still leaves the handicapped space for Sonia if she needs it, although I have made it clear that her interaction with Caesar will be limited to the time he spends at her house. She won't be permitted past the common area."

Andrew looked at his agenda.

"A reminder," he said, "that 'Cèsar Spinoza' is Caesar's code name whenever we are in the presence of people outside the IDES Team. The only time we may need it is when we're at Sonia's house and interacting with members of her staff."

Everyone nodded.

"And if they ask what language he's speaking—"

"An unusual dialect of Catalan," John said. "He's visiting from Andorra."

"And then change the subject," Elizabeth added. "Say nothing about our guest unless absolutely necessary."

"Which shouldn't be difficult," Cassandra said. "Sonia's staff is used to entertaining VIPs from all over the world. They shouldn't find Caesar anything out of the ordinary."

Andrew smiled as he heard all of his own words parroted back at him. "Glad that's all clear," he said. "Anything to discuss about clothing?"

This had been a much-discussed topic at earlier meetings, but at this one, his question elicited only shrugs and more nods.

"Excellent," Andrew said. "I'll turn things over to you now, John. Anything to add or share?"

John shook his head "Unless someone wants some last-minute help with Latin phrases, we're all set."

Andrew worked his way down the rest of his list, making sure everyone was in agreement about schedules and responsibilities.

"If there are no more questions or issues to discuss, I will adjourn," he said at last. "Until tomorrow, when our project enters its final phase."

XLIX

It was still dark when Cassandra slid out of bed and tiptoed to the bathroom. She didn't want to wake Elizabeth or Faith, although she wondered whether they were even asleep. Cassandra hadn't dozed off for more than an hour, all told. Who could sleep when the next day's activities included meeting Julius Caesar?

Hoping she wasn't making too much noise, Cassandra went ahead and showered. Best to leave the bathroom available for the others. She liked the idea of heading to the kitchen for a cup of coffee before anyone else was up.

Except Eric. It would be fine with Cassandra if Eric were already there. He'd become a good friend over the last few months. Andrew Danicek could be a bit unpredictable, but Eric was someone she could count on. Plus, he made really good cappuccino.

By the time Cassandra stepped back into the room she shared with Faith and Elizabeth, both women were awake, and the overhead light was on. Elizabeth was standing at the sink, peering into the mirror, and brushing her hair.

"Good morning," Elizabeth said. "Did you sleep well?"

"About as well as a kid on Christmas Eve," Cassandra said. "How about you?"

"Same," Elizabeth said.

Faith rolled over in her bed, her face to the wall. She said nothing.

Cassandra and Elizabeth both shrugged. "I'm through with the shower," Cassandra said. Elizabeth headed into the bathroom.

Twenty minutes later, Cassandra headed down the hall and emerged into the common area. She was happy with how she looked. The dress that Tanya had borrowed for her from Caesars Palace was perfect, a long flowing white gown with a crossover bodice and gold trim. She'd piled her hair on top of her head. It didn't look particularly Roman, but she'd read enough ancient poetry to know about the erotic signal embedded in "letting your hair down." Without any way of knowing what Caesar's first impression might be, she figured it was best to be on the modest side.

"Whoa! You look spectacular!" Eric said when she stepped into the kitchen. He almost dropped the saucer he was holding.

"Thanks, Eric," Cassandra said. "Let's hope I've made the right decisions."

While Eric made her coffee, Cassandra decided it was a very good sign that her outfit had almost made Eric drop a dish. Guys were guys, she was willing to bet, in any century.

L

Faith stayed in bed while Elizabeth showered and dressed. As Faith hoped, she had the room to herself while there was still plenty of time before she had to join the team for Caesar's arrival.

Everyone else had worried endlessly about what to wear. Faith refused. What was the point in trying to anticipate the reactions of an ancient Roman? And who cared what he thought, anyway? No matter what they wore, they'd look like aliens to him. Since she couldn't possibly predict how Julius Caesar would react, Faith quietly decided she would wear what she pleased.

Faith sat up to watch Elizabeth leave the room wearing a skirt and blazer. That seemed like a much more reasonable outfit than Cassandra's stupid *Clash of the Titans* dress. Did she seriously think Julius Caesar would find a polyester Halloween costume familiar or reassuring? He just as easily might write it off as tacky, or even an insult.

Faith sighed and got out of bed. What kept her mood hopeful was that there was always the chance that things wouldn't go as planned. The best possible scenario was that Julius Caesar would fail to appear.

Too bad things had gone so smoothly with Skipper. Even though locating Caesar was far more challenging, she had little doubt that Eric and Andrew had succeeded. Caesar's instantaneous appearance might be surprising, but it wouldn't be unexpected.

What Faith hung her real hopes on was that Caesar might decide he wanted to go back immediately. Andrew claimed that he wouldn't hold Caesar against his will. All Caesar had to do was reject the invitation to stay for four days, and *poof!* He'd be gone, and that meant Faith could quit the project and disappear, too.

Twenty minutes later, she headed to the common area wearing black slacks and a bulky purple pullover. She knew Andrew would disapprove, even though he really should be grateful. She had almost decided on orange Lycra exercise pants and a hot pink sports bra.

As planned, Eric had set out a breakfast buffet on the conference table in the common area. Nobody was eating much or saying much, though, just glancing between the clock and the day's schedule.

At 8:30, Cassandra headed into the TESA complex, where Andrew and Eric were already in countdown mode. That left Faith alone with John and Elizabeth for another fifteen silent minutes. Faith thought about having a second cup of coffee but decided she was wired enough without another jolt of caffeine.

At 8:45, Faith stood up first. With John and Elizabeth right behind her, she headed into the TESA complex and took a left turn into the observation room.

Andrew and Cassandra were already on screen, both standing in TESA's central core. They made an odd couple, Faith thought. Andrew was in his tuxedo and Cassandra in her goddess getup. Caesar was in for a bizarre first impression.

John and Elizabeth each took a chair in front of the large main monitor. Faith remained standing. She was too nervous to do anything but pace a little.

"Hello, everyone." Eric's voice came through on the speakers. "Andrew, can you hear me?"

"Yes," Andrew replied. "Excellent sound quality."

"We're set, then," Eric said. "I'm beginning the countdown."

On a smaller monitor to the right of the big one, Faith watched the green digits decrease. 15, 14, 13...

She glanced at her companions. Both were riveted to the big screen. It doesn't matter what you've been told, she thought. Nothing can prepare you for a creature materializing out of thin air. I'll be amazed if you don't scream.

But Elizabeth didn't make a sound when Julius Caesar appeared, and John only gasped. Faith sucked in a breath of her own when she saw him. Damned if TESA hadn't latched on to the right guy. Now the only question was, for how long? She could still hope his visit would be over in a flash.

Caesar stood facing Cassandra. For a long moment, he just stared. Cassandra raised her arms a little, her hands outstretched toward him.

"*Ave*, Caesar," she said. "The people of America bid you welcome," she continued in Latin.

Caesar leaned toward her a little. He dropped his head. Then, before Cassandra had a chance to say another word, he cleared his throat with a loud hacking sound. With all eyes on him, Caesar spat on the floor, right at Cassandra's feet.

"Whoa!" "Oh!" "What the hell?" John, Elizabeth, and Faith emitted simultaneous shocked responses. John and Elizabeth looked at each other, but Faith kept her eyes on the monitor. Because—was she seeing things? No! The guy was falling! Faith didn't wait to see Caesar collapse completely. She was already out the door and heading across the control room.

"Let them out!" She yelled at Eric as she ran into the hall. "I'm going around to meet them in the residence!"

By the time Faith made it to the living room in the residence,

Andrew and Cassandra were dragging Caesar toward the sofa. If Caesar had passed out, he was conscious now. Faith saw him struggling. She ran to help, and the three of them managed to get Caesar safely ensconced on the sofa. By then, Eric, John, and Elizabeth had all entered the room.

Christ, Faith thought. This was not the welcome anyone had imagined, and they had tried to think of everything. Like—she rushed to the small cabinet next to the fireplace and pulled its top drawer open. She pulled out the stethoscope and blood pressure monitor she had placed there. Rushing back to Caesar, she set the tools next to him and pulled her medical pen light out of her pants pocket.

Sorry, old man, she thought, but I've got to see what's happening with you.

She shined the pen light into each eye. Good. No blown pupils, and both were the same size. She grabbed the stethoscope, hoping Caesar would continue to cooperate enough for her to listen to his heart. With everybody else hovering near, and after all that had happened, she was not surprised that Caesar's heart was pounding madly. Amazing, though, she thought, that outwardly he looks so calm. Almost like a learned skill.

Caesar even tolerated the blood pressure cuff. His numbers were a little high, but nothing out of the ordinary for a fifty-five-year-old. There were plenty of other tests she'd like to run, but at least these basic assessments suggested that Caesar was okay for the moment.

Faith's own heart rate began to slow as she sat back on the sofa. She scanned the worried faces around her, all staring at Caesar.

And then it dawned on her. In all the excitement, they had missed a vital deadline. It was now too late to send Caesar back. Whether he liked it or not, he was stuck in the IDES Lab for the next four days.

Shit, Faith thought, that means two awful things. First, we really did kidnap him. Second, it's all my fault.

LI

Cassandra lay in bed that night, exhausted but sleepless. Nothing had gone as planned, from the moment Caesar hocked a loogie at her feet to—oh, everything. She had never had the chance to offer Caesar the chance to go home, and things got worse from there. When he collapsed, she thought he was dying. Even after he recovered, she had to be on guard in case he had another attack. The whole team had worried about possible epileptic seizures, but who knew what else might be wrong with him or what damage time travel might have done?

The medical concerns were more than enough to keep Cassandra awake, but they weren't the only things making her thoughts churn. She had tried her best all day to get past the spitting incident and connect with Caesar. But no matter what she said, he wouldn't respond with more than an occasional monosyllable. She gave up trying during dinner, after Eric served the barbecued ribs.

"These are roast pork," she said, "with a savory sauce."

"*Tace*," Caesar said.

Cassandra could have translated the word mentally as "Be quiet," but Caesar's tone made it a clear "Shut up." Elizabeth and John's surprised reactions reinforced her interpretation. Caesar had definitely spoken to her like she was a child, or even an irritating dog.

So Cassandra did shut up, because what else could she do? She wasn't softening Caesar up by talking—she was only pissing him off.

They all ate in silence after that.

Andrew was the only person who seemed to interest Caesar in the least. Cassandra would have been as happy to act as interpreter as Andrew was to talk, but Caesar stayed mum. He just watched Andrew's every move. It reminded Cassandra of the white tigers at the Mirage in Las Vegas. They'd ignore all the visitors but keep their eyes riveted on the zookeepers, especially when feeding time approached. Caesar might not be interested in conversation, but Cassandra was pretty sure he was curious about the power structure inside the IDES Lab. It impressed her that, without asking any questions, he seemed to have figured out that Andrew was the boss.

And what did Caesar think of her? She couldn't get her mind off the spitting thing. Was it an act of intentional rudeness? If not, then what? She'd probably never know, but as hard as she tried to shake the memory out of her mind, the more persistently it nagged her.

Oh, hell. Who am I kidding? She might not know exactly what spitting meant in Republican Rome, but she had no doubt that Caesar thought she was a servant.

No, a slave! Here she had spent six months studying and practicing and planning, all to be regarded as a minion.

Cassandra knew that Faith was counting the minutes until the IDES Project was over. Now, Cassandra thought, I am, too. I'm a big, fat failure, and I've got three more days of frustration ahead of me. She reached for the travel alarm clock on her nightstand. Five a.m. Two hours until her shift with Caesar started, but there was no point in staying in bed. As quietly as she could, she slipped from under the covers and headed into the bathroom.

LII

I n the room he shared with John Reynolds, Eric dragged himself out of bed at five. He hadn't slept well, anyway. Today was field trip day.

As he let a hot shower pelt his head, Eric forced himself to be thankful that the first day of Caesar's visit had not been a total disaster. TESA had popped out her first human exactly as expected, and his own transformation from research scientist to food-and-beverage manager had also been glitch-free. The meals had arrived on time, and Eric had presented them, if not with the finesse of a five-star restaurateur, at least with all the skills he'd learned working summers at his uncle's sandwich shop in Philadelphia. A few secrets he'd picked up working one semester at the MIT Faculty Club came in handy, too. If today's events turned out even half as well as last night's baked Alaska, Eric would be thrilled.

He toweled off, combed his hair and beard, and slipped into corduroys and a button-down shirt. All was quiet as he headed through the residence. Good. Caesar must still be asleep. Faith was on duty until seven, when Cassandra would take over. Unless Caesar woke up early, breakfast service would begin at 8:30. That gave Eric plenty of time to set the table, prepare the food, and tweak the schedule if it needed it. With luck, he might also get to enjoy a private cup of coffee.

Light was pouring from the kitchen into the still-dark dining room when Eric stepped in from the hall. Someone else was up early. He stuck his head around the corner.

"Cassandra! I didn't expect to see you until—"

Cassandra turned from where she'd been fumbling with the espresso machine. "I couldn't sleep. How do you turn this thing on?"

"Let me do it," Eric said. "It'll take a few minutes to warm up."

"I'll set the table," Cassandra said. "The usual?"

"Yeah. Napkins are in the top drawer of the sideboard. Silverware's still in the dishwasher."

Eric watched Cassandra turn and walk into the dining room.

God, she was beautiful. Her long hair hung in golden curls down her back. He wondered whether Caesar had thought she was a goddess. The word came into Eric's own head the first time he met her, and it still did, pretty much every time she came into view. Even this morning, when it was obvious Cassandra was unhappy.

Eric poured filtered water into the Gaggia, switched it on, and walked into the dining room. Cassandra was sitting at the far end of the table, folding napkins.

"Are you changing your clothes before your shift begins?"

Cassandra looked up. She was as gorgeous as ever, but dark circles under her eyes betrayed fatigue, or maybe stress.

"No." One word, but she managed to give it a full charge of defensiveness.

Uh, oh. What's going on?

Cassandra was dressed in faded jeans and a University of Nevada hoodie. That didn't match with the plan. Cassandra had said she'd wear her long dress again today.

"Are you happy with how things are going?" Eric asked.

Cassandra kept her head down. "Seriously?" she said. "Of course, I'm not happy. And as long as I'm not happy, I'm damn well going to be comfortable."

"But you and Danicek—"

"As you're well aware, Danicek left my clothing decisions up to me," Cassandra said. "I know I said I'd wear—*God damn it.*" She looked up. Tears stood in her eyes, and two escaped down her cheeks. "I'm sorry, Eric. I know I shouldn't be so upset. It's just that Caesar is so—" She paused. "Oh, hell. It's not Caesar. It's me. I'm a failure. I haven't succeeded in getting a word out of Caesar. He hates me."

Eric wasn't sure Caesar hated Cassandra, but the man had definitely made a point of shocking her. Everyone saw him spit on the floor right at her feet. He hadn't done anything quite so unexpected since, but he hadn't cooperated either. In fact, he'd spoken so little that they might as well have transported a statue.

Except—he wasn't a statue. He was a real, breathing person. Not only that, he was *Julius Freaking Caesar*, and the team only had him for four—no, make that three—more days. There was no time to waste. It wasn't like they could invite Caesar back when he was in a better mood.

"Well, there's still time—" Eric said, tentatively. "Maybe things will be different today."

Cassandra dragged a sleeve across her eyes and glared at him.

Damn. He should have kept his mouth shut. Eric had always stuck to the science and logistics side of things on the IDES Project. He never poked his nose into what the classicists were working on. Now that Caesar was here, his job was to attend to everybody's food and beverage needs, maintain the schedule, and keep everything tidy. Except for monitoring TESA and assisting Faith with her tests, Eric wouldn't clock back in as a full-time scientist until Saturday at four, when Caesar would go back to—*scratch that thought.*

That's what Eric hated about the IDES Project. They had to

transport someone who was about to meet a violent end. True, they had snatched Caesar away from his impending death. But he had to go back, and they had to keep him in the dark about the horror that awaited him. Otherwise he might take evasive action.

What would happen if Julius Caesar escaped death on the Ides of March, 44 BCE? Science couldn't answer the question yet. Danicek's theory was that the past would be unaffected because of retrocausality. Put in its simplest terms, everything has already happened, and there's no way to change it. But even though all their tests appeared to support this theory, it was still just a theory.

Eric turned his attention back to Cassandra. She was still glaring at him.

"I didn't mean to criticize," he said. "Caesar's behavior is not your fault."

Cassandra's eyes bored into Eric's. How many women are beautiful even when they're exhausted, pissed off, and crying? Cassandra was lovely in spite of those things, even with those runny smears of mascara.

She said nothing. She just went back to folding napkins. Eric retreated into the kitchen, where the Gaggia was beginning its steam locomotive imitation. He turned on the coffee grinder, and within four minutes, he was back in the dining room with two double espressos. He set one down next to Cassandra's left elbow.

"Thank you," she said, her smudge-rimmed eyes locking with Eric's for an instant before she looked away. "It's just what I needed." She took a sip. "What time is it?"

"Five-thirty or so."

"Good. I have plenty of time to change."

What? Eric didn't quite believe his ears.

"You're right," Cassandra said. "I've got work to do. I can't waste time whining."

Relief washed over Eric. "You're the one who can get him to open up, Cassandra," he blurted. "I know you can do it. With your Latin and your—"

He cut himself off. And—*damn it*—he blushed. Would it show through his beard?

"My *what?*"

Her attitude was back.

"Your knowledge of his world," Eric finished lamely.

Cassandra arched an eyebrow at him, but she also smiled.

"Nice save, geek boy," she said.

LIII

Julius Caesar awakened with a start, briefly disoriented by the unfamiliar room, the ghostly light, and the enormous pillowed bed. No way he could continue thinking this was a dream. The strange land into which he had been snatched the day before still surrounded him.

Shaking off the remnants of sleep, Caesar glanced around the room. From the moment he had arrived, a guard had been at his side. Duckhead, the bearded lad, Cassandra, the dark-haired woman—one of them always remained, even when the others departed. They tried to pass it off as ordinary courtesy, but Caesar recognized custodians when he saw them.

So where?—

Then his eyes found her. Cassandra was nestled in a large cushioned *sella*, her head down, her knees drawn up. Dozing, Caesar surmised. Good. Perhaps he would have a few moments of peace before she awoke and began a fresh barrage of questions and commentary. The young woman seemed to have a fear of silence, a need to fill every lacuna with words and more words. But she was no doubt under orders. Duckhead was in charge here. It was likely he who abhorred

271

uncluttered conversation.

Caesar stretched, enjoying the smooth fabric of the bedding against his skin. It was very fine, something he could not say about the bed itself. When he first sank into its enormous expanse, he had feared he would suffocate in its softness. He had lain awake for hours, fearing sleep. Exhaustion eventually overcame his unease, and now—who could have foreseen it?—he felt more rested than he had in months. He wondered how to make a plan when he did not know what lay ahead. Caesar had little doubt that Duckhead and his underlings had every minute scheduled—they were like ants in this regard—but what were those plans? They obviously were not going to reveal them.

Caesar sighed. Nor would I if our roles were reversed, he thought. Never reveal a schedule to a prisoner. Avoid regular routines whenever possible. Practice unpredictability in your dealings with captives. Schedules and habits invariably provide prisoners with their best opportunities for escape.

Not that Caesar intended to break free of this place, at least not yet. He had no inkling of what lay beyond its walls. So far, he had not seen even one window or *impluvium*, though he had seen doors leading to—what? He had no way of knowing. There was no reason to consider a solo escape anything but supreme folly. Like a dolphin fleeing the ocean.

For now, Caesar needed power within these walls. Simple to imagine, much more difficult to achieve. He had little leverage, after all. He did not know where he was and could not speak the local tongue. Worse, he was unarmed.

Quid agam?

Still pondering what to do, Caesar looked at the signet ring on his forefinger. His captors had acquiesced quickly when he refused to part with it. Did that merely mean that they planned to slip it from his lifeless finger later? Not a pleasant prospect, but there were other possibilities. Perhaps he possessed more influence than he had heretofore realized with these kidnappers.

Kidnappers. Yes, that's what they were, even if they claimed to be hosts, wielded no weapons, and demanded no ransom. They were fundamentally no different from the Anatolian thugs who had held Caesar hostage for thirty-eight days back when he was still a young man. Why hadn't he recalled those brutes sooner? Caesar wondered, but the answer was obvious. Those were unapologetic pirates, not odd barbarians posing as admirers. Caesar thought back to a summer long ago, when a windless day had becalmed the ship bearing him to Rhodes. Anchored almost unnecessarily, the ship languished in the still waters just off the west coast of Pharmacusa.

Frustrated by the unexpected doldrums, Caesar tried to interest himself in reading a discourse by Plato, but without success. He was moping on the afterdeck when Aelius appeared. Like Caesar, Aelius was headed to Rhodes to study with Archelaus.

"Cheer up," Aelius said. "The wind is sure to rise soon."

"I'd be happier to have joined the crew going ashore," Caesar said. He dropped his scroll into his basket and rose to join Aelius at the rail. Together, they watched the oars of the longboat rise up and splash down as it crossed the quiet harbor.

"They're just stocking up on water while they have the chance," Aelius said. "There's nothing else of value on this godforsaken chunk of rock."

It was true that Pharmacusa was tiny and nearly devoid of trees. No one would call it a garden spot, Caesar thought, but was it possible that his comrade did not know of the island's claim to worldwide fame?

"It has an iron mine," Caesar said. "It has Rhondas."

Aelius spun around, a look of surprise on his face.

"Truth?"

Caesar nodded but said nothing, allowing his friend to ponder the tantalizing proximity of one of the world's most admired blacksmiths. A Rhondas knife was a status symbol every Roman youth coveted, and few possessed. Caesar knew that Aelius, who had a growing reputation back home for tactical fighting, would forever regret being so near the Rhondas smithy without at least attempting to acquire a blade.

"His workshop is near the town, half a mile inland," Caesar said. "If we had a boat, we could make the return journey easily by sundown." He held a finger in the air. "The wind is unlikely to rise until after that."

"We don't have a boat," Aelius said.

Caesar leaned over the railing. "What about the service dinghy?" He gestured toward the small rowboat bobbing alongside the ship. "Of course, we could be caught—"

The two young men looked at each other, then burst into laughter. Yes, appropriating the service dinghy and leaving the ship without the captain's approval would be, for most passengers, a serious crime. But for them, a pair of Roman nobles who outranked him so considerably on land? The worst the captain could do would be to frown or heave a disgruntled sigh. A joke to tell when they were back home showing off their enviable knives.

"Cimbro!" Caesar called. He turned back to Aelius. "My manservant will stay on the beach and watch the boat."

Not more than ten minutes later, Caesar was gliding across the harbor's glassy surface with Aelius, Cimbro, and a surprised deckhand pressed into service as an oarsman. Either no one saw them leave the ship, or no one raised an alarm.

Perfect.

The tiny dinghy was still several hundred yards off Pharmacusa's western shore when Caesar saw the longboat from the ship, men clustered near it.

"We can't beach there," Aelius said. "If they see us, we'll never make it to Rhondas."

Aelius was right, but where else could they land? Scanning the coastline, Caesar could see nothing but sheer rocky cliffs. He shaded his eyes and squinted. They didn't need much, just a—wait! What was that, just to the south of the sandy strand where the longboat was beached?

"There's a cove!" Caesar cried. "Oarsman! Veer half south!"

As they drew nearer, the little cove proved to be most suitable, with an easy access free of rocks. Better yet, an escarpment hid it completely from the big beach and the coastal village. Caesar could see the switchbacks of a path cut into the rock face beyond the beach. The path vanished over the crest to the east.

"The path to Rhondas," he said, pointing.

Again, everything was perfect.

As the boat neared the shore, a small ship came into view behind a rock outcropping.

"We are not alone," Aelius said.

"It's listing, and its mast is broken," Caesar said. "It's an abandoned wreck. Nothing to concern us."

The dinghy touched the shore, the slaves jumped out, and soon Aelius and Caesar stepped onto the warm sand. Now for a leisurely stroll to the blacksmith—

But of course that did not happen. No sooner had Cimbro and the deckhand stowed the oars than the four of them were surrounded. Caesar would never forget the sight of Aelius with his hair yanked back and a rough black blade pressed against his throat.

Pirates!

Caesar should not have been surprised. The shipwreck was an obvious clue. In addition, their own captain and the crew had been keeping an eye out for pirates ever since they had sighted Ikaria. The days since had passed with nary a threat, but raiders were a known threat in these waters. Caesar should never have allowed the allure of the Rhondas's smithy to distract him.

By Tartarus, this is my fault, Caesar thought as he stared into Aelius's terrified eyes.

"Take me," Caesar said. "I'm worth more."

"Are you worth twenty talents?" the ruffian barked. "In silver?"

"Twenty?" Caesar laughed. "Who do you think I am?"

The pirate lowered the blade at Aelius's throat ever so slightly. The two men stared at each other. The pirate blinked first.

"Who are you?"

"Someone worth thirty talents," Caesar said. "Far more than enough to replace your rotting barge." He heard Aelius suck in a breath and saw his eyes widen. "No, let me correct that. Forty talents might begin to reflect my value. You could buy a fleet."

Now Caesar had the attention of the entire band of ruffians. Aelius was breathing hard, and Cimbro had begun to weep.

"I shall remain with you," Caesar said, "until—" He locked eyes with Aelius. "Until my comrade returns with the required funds."

Maintaining an air of carefree superiority, Caesar slowly raised his right hand to his chin, making sure the pirate chief could easily see the large gold signet ring on his forefinger. Together with his patrician haircut, close shave, ornate bronze belt buckle, and gold *fibula*, it made an impressive statement of Roman rank and privilege.

Caesar's stratagem worked.

"Seize him!" the pirate shouted. He released Aelius as two of his henchmen rushed forward to grab Caesar by the arms.

"Wait!" Caesar commanded. "For my comrade to raise my ransom, he must bear my ring."

The man holding his left arm released it long enough for Caesar to slip the signet ring off his right forefinger. He held it out to Aelius. Still stunned, he nevertheless grasped the ring and slipped it onto his own finger. Neither the pirate chief nor any of his men made a move to take it from him.

He holds my future in his hand, Caesar thought as he watched Aelius and the deckhand walk back toward the dinghy. I am nothing but a nameless prisoner until he returns, and a dead one if he does not.

Weeks of squalor lay ahead. But it wasn't the filth or poor food that made Caesar's stay on Pharmacusa so difficult. More challenging by far was wondering whether Aelius would return with the ransom or send help in his place. It was no small task to amass a small fortune so far from Rome, even with the power of Caesar's name and ring behind the request. He knew as he watched the dinghy pull away that the back of Aelius's head might well be the last bit of Roman he'd ever see.

"Show me to my quarters," Caesar said to the pirate chief as soon as Aelius was out of sight. "If I am pleased, I will consider slitting your throat when the time comes—instead of crucifying you."

Caesar waited, enjoying the look of startled uncertainty in his eyes. Then he laughed, loud and long. Before he stopped, the pirate joined in. "What is your name?" Caesar asked.

"Atta," he said, still smiling.

"Keep me happy, Atta," Caesar said.

Atta showed Caesar to what had surely been his own bivouac, a crude construction of pine branches and goatskins set into a rocky cleft. The other pirates slept without cover near the cook fire.

"This will have to suffice," Caesar said. "Leave us."

Atta obeyed without hesitation. He returned an hour later to invite Cimbro and Caesar to join the band around the cook fire for the evening meal.

"No," Caesar said. "I shall dine here, with my man."

Again, Atta acquiesced. He turned to leave.

"One more thing," Caesar said. The pirate paused and turned his head. "We need a toilet."

An hour later, two of the younger thugs arrived bearing dinner and shovels. As Caesar and Cimbro sat in front of their shelter to eat, they railed against their leader and dug a latrine.

This was somewhat surprising. Why did they not rail at Caesar, whose turds they would soon be forced to bury?

Seize the advantage, Caesar told himself.

Beginning that night, Caesar returned the best morsels of his meals to the lads who delivered them. A woodcock or a strip of venison, supplied on a daily basis, soon earned him more loyalty from Atta's errand boys than their leader enjoyed. Within a week, Cimbro and Caesar could easily have escaped from the pirates' enclave. But what would escape gain them? Without a ship, they could not leave the island. With neither silver nor arms, they might as well enjoy the pirates' hospitality.

"Never forget that we are pigs here," Caesar said when he observed Cimbro fraternizing with the pirates. "What does a pig think, a week before the feast day? 'Oh, how much my masters love me! They give me cream to drink and apples to eat!' Always consider the motives of men who can decide your fate."

A man can learn much from captivity. Stuck on that island, with no assurance of ransom, Caesar knew his life depended on his ability to radiate confidence. The pirates could never know his fears. For five long weeks, they saw only a self-assured nobleman with the resources of empire at his fingertips.

Caesar's servant, too, saw only the carefree visage of a young man of privilege. Cimbro could afford to cry if he felt like it. He was responsible only for Caesar's person. But Caesar bore what felt like all of Rome on his shoulders. He would slit his own throat before he would allow his servant or those brigands so much as see tears in his eyes. He knew that his cocky arrogance was all that could save him from an ignominious death on the island of Pharmacusa.

By the end of the fifth week, when autumnal breezes signaled a change of seasons, Caesar wondered if his swaggering façade would hold. Then, on a clear day with a strong wind from the north, Aelius returned, not in a dinghy but aboard a Bithynian ship, with a detachment of Nicomedian soldiers and the ransom to secure Caesar's release.

Caesar presented the silver to Atta himself.

"Your spoils," he said, proffering the leather bags with a theatrical bow. "With thanks for your peerless hospitality."

Not even a pirate could misinterpret the sarcasm. Caesar laughed as he straightened up, glad that he still had the audacity. "You shall see me again," he said. "When I return to slaughter the lot of you."

Caesar laughed again, though mirth had left him weeks before. He had languished in that wretched place long enough. What he wanted at that moment was a civilized meal, a shave, and conversation in Latin with someone other than his slave. Vengeance would come later. No one held Julius Caesar captive for a month and lived to boast of it.

Shaking off the memories, Caesar tilted his head to look at Cassandra sleeping in the corner. She was no pirate, but things would be so much simpler if she were. Whoever these people are, Caesar thought, and however obsequious they sound, they still hold the power to decide my fate.

As he yawned, Caesar heard Cassandra stir in her chair. A moment later, she was at his side, looking down at him with her bottomless azure eyes.

Venus.

"*Salve,*" she said.

No, not Venus. Just a strange, mortal woman who happened to look like a goddess.

LIV

John Reynolds woke up in a cold sweat. As he shifted his body, the sheets clung to him like seaweed. Christ. He was soaked.

Field trip day.

Faith had coined the term. She had opposed taking Caesar outside the IDES Lab from the beginning. She lobbied Andrew constantly to cancel the excursion. Just yesterday, John had overheard an emotional argument in Andrew's office. The door wasn't quite closed.

"Don't you see that the risk is far greater than any possible benefit?" Faith's voice was shrill.

"*God fucking damn it*, Andrew!" she went on. "What does it take with you? The guy already had an episode. You want him to keel over and die at Sonia's? What do we do then?"

John couldn't hear Andrew's reply, or even if he made one. It didn't matter. A couple of minutes later, Faith threw the office door open, slammed it behind her, and stormed into her lab.

If he hadn't seen this sort of thing before, John would have been more upset. Fortunately, Faith's professionalism always seemed to prevail over her geyser-like emotions. Once she blew off steam, the

calm, skilled, rational side of her would take over. When she wasn't
being Old Faithful, John could easily understand why Andrew had
her on the team.

Still, John didn't like that Faith had managed to seduce the entire
IDES team into calling the excursion to Sonia Illingsworth's cocktail
party a "field trip." At least no one else called it "your little field trip."
Faith saved that phrase for Andrew, from whom it rarely failed to evoke
some tiny sign of irritation, even if it was only a lowered eyebrow.

Childish it might be, but here John was, unable to think of the
day as anything but "field trip day." Faith's concerns about Caesar's
health had also succeeded in making his stomach boil, and he had no
doubt it was the fears she had sown in his mind that had dampened
his bedsheets.

A quick shower helped a little. Soon, John was on his way through
the common area to Caesar's residence, his cane clicking along beside
his soundless stocking feet. At least he was wearing his own clothes.
The idea that the men wear togas to engage with Caesar had fortunately
been discarded almost as soon as Andrew suggested it. Never mind
the skills of his tailor.

"Albert is a costume designer by training," Andrew had said. "He's
creating the toga Caesar will wear to Sonia's dinner party. He would
be happy to make authentic Roman garb for the rest of us, too."

John had cringed at the word "costume." He had loathed costumes
ever since he outgrew trick-or-treating on Halloween.

"It will be challenging enough to interact with Julius Caesar in any
meaningful way," he'd said immediately. "Wearing unfamiliar clothing
will add to our unease. In addition, there is no way to ensure that
whatever outfits a modern tailor designs won't look odd in some way
to our guest. Better to be comfortable in our own apparel than to risk
wardrobe mistakes that could further distance us from Caesar."

Elizabeth chimed in immediately.

"I agree with John," she said. "In the same way that we welcome Caesar to this modern dwelling instead of to a replica of a Roman house, we should greet him wearing our own clothes. We're welcoming him to our world. It's better to explain ourselves than to pretend to be his contemporaries."

"I'm not dressing up like a Roman, and that's final," Faith said. "I don't care what the rest of you do."

"I think I should wear a long dress," Cassandra said. "I won't feel uncomfortable—I'm used to them. And I think the first person Caesar sees when he arrives should not startle him. I'll pin my hair up, too. Unlike a man, I can look ancient and modern at the same time."

John looked at his beautiful advisee, pleased that she was speaking up. This was only her second IDES Project meeting, after all, and certain members of the team had not been particularly welcoming. Well, make that one member. Faith had been only barely civil to Cassandra when she arrived, and she was showing no signs of thaw.

Andrew, on the other hand, was warming with each passing moment. John watched him gaze at Cassandra as she spoke, a smile on his face. Andrew had already told him how impressed he was. Her latest contribution to the conversation seemed to have elevated his opinion of her at least another notch.

"It's settled, then," Andrew said. "We will each choose our own wardrobes. As you decide what to wear, keep Caesar in mind. While we can't know precisely what he will think about modern dress, we can at least be restrained with our choices."

So far, the wardrobe issue hadn't caused any problems. Cassandra looked lovely in her floor-length gown, her blond hair twisted high on her head. There was no question that Caesar found everyone else's clothing peculiar, but at least everyone had erred on the side of modesty. He bet Faith looked the most outlandish to Caesar in her black jeans and purple turtleneck. Her short red hair probably seemed even stranger to him than her clothes. Sculpted into a spiky style with pointy sideburns, it might be the height of hipness in AD 1999, but it had to look bizarre to a BC man.

As John pushed his way through the double doors separating the common area from Caesar's residence, the aroma of bacon and Hollandaise sauce wafted from the kitchen. He joined Andrew and Eric in the hallway next to the dining room.

"Good morning—" Andrew began, but just then, the door to Caesar's suite opened, and Cassandra stepped out.

"We're ready," she said. She held the door open. Caesar appeared, dressed in the toga that Albert the costume designer had made for him.

It was perfect. If John hadn't known it was a reproduction, he would have thought it was the toga Caesar had been wearing when he arrived.

"He wanted to wear the toga," Cassandra said. "I tried to talk him into the running suit—"

Caesar shot Cassandra a severe frown. She stopped talking.

"Let's have breakfast," Andrew said.

"Everything's ready," Eric said. "Andrew, can you give me a hand for a second?"

"Of course," Andrew said. He turned to Cassandra and Caesar. "Please go in. We'll be right there."

John opened the dining room door and stepped aside. Caesar entered the room first. Cassandra followed.

In the two seconds it took for John to join them at the table, the dominoes had already begun to fall.

Christ! How was it possible?

Instead of taking the seat he had occupied at dinner the night before, Caesar was sliding himself into Andrew's chair at the head of the table. John shot a questioning look at Cassandra. She shrugged slightly but said nothing.

John wasn't sure what to do. The team had spent most of an entire meeting deciding the dining room seating arrangement. It had never crossed their minds that Caesar would have his own ideas. Best to see how Andrew wants to handle things, John decided. He moved to the sideboard to wait and watch.

As John observed the scene, Caesar grasped the linen napkin folded on the plate in front of him. He unfurled it like a flag and, with exaggerated movements, placed it on his lap.

He was a quick study, John had to give him that. With only last night's dinner to instruct him, Caesar was preparing to eat in contemporary American style as though he had done it all his life. Maybe it shouldn't be too surprising that he had also decided that Andrew's position at the head of the table was worth commandeering.

Just then, Elizabeth appeared at the dining room door. Her eyes widened as she saw Caesar sitting at Andrew's place. She shot John a confused look and moved to his side just as Andrew entered the room, a tray of croissants and fruit in his hands.

Andrew stopped short the moment he saw Caesar sitting in his chair. John watched his eyes dart to Cassandra's, then his own. No one said a word.

Bending forward, Andrew set the tray he was carrying on the table in front of him.

"I see we have a change in the seating arrangement," he said as he straightened back up. "Whose idea was that?"

He looked at Cassandra. Cassandra looked at Caesar and waited.

Good God. Nothing had improved since dinner. She still couldn't speak without his permission.

Caesar nodded, ever so slightly.

"Caesar prefers this seat," she said.

"Very well, very well," Andrew said, a forced smile curling his lips. "In that case, I shall sit next to him." He motioned to the chair on his right. "Cassandra, will you please—?"

Cassandra began to rise.

"Stay where you are," Caesar said in Latin, his eyes trained directly on Andrew. He maintained the gaze as Cassandra sank back into her chair. Then, jabbing his right thumb in Andrew's direction, he turned toward her. "Tell him."

Cassandra translated, though John had little doubt Andrew had already understood.

"All right, all right," Andrew said, nervousness apparent in his voice. "Everyone else, sit—" he paused, almost as if he expected Caesar to issue another directive. "Sit where you please."

Andrew moved to the side of the table and took Caesar's original seat. John moved to Andrew's right. From there, they could easily see both Caesar and Cassandra across the table. Elizabeth sat down at Caesar's left. Good, John thought. At least they could exchange glances.

Everyone was seated when Eric appeared, a huge serving tray in his hands. It wobbled a bit when he saw the unexpected seating arrangement, but he held it steady long enough to set it on the sideboard. He distributed the eggs Benedict, then circled the table with a coffeepot. Still no one spoke.

After Eric sat down, Andrew cleared his throat. He opened his mouth to speak, but Caesar beat him to it.

"Let us eat," Caesar said. He picked up his spoon with his right hand. Everyone else picked up forks. Caesar set his spoon down.

"Tell me about this dark beverage," he said to Cassandra, pointing at his cup and saucer.

"We call it coffee," Cassandra told him. "A hot drink brewed from the dried berries of a tropical tree." She stirred several spoonfuls of sugar into Caesar's cup and added enough cream to lighten it. "If it does not please you, we have—"

Tea, John finished mentally, but Cassandra didn't get the chance to say the word aloud.

"Vah!" Caesar interrupted. His face contorted, and he directed a lethal stare toward—

John turned his head to see the source of Caesar's anger.

Faith filled the doorway. Her spiky red hair, backlit by the hallway lights, looked like a devil's nimbus. But John quickly saw that it wasn't her hair that made Caesar angry. It was her outfit. Faith was wearing a neon pink tank top and skintight orange Capris with a green stripe running down each thigh. *Christ.* How could she possibly have thought that spandex was a good idea?

"Faith—" Andrew began, but Caesar had pushed his chair back. He tossed his napkin on the table.

"Caesar will not dine in the company of—" he paused, either for effect or to decide on the right words. "This vulgar bitch," he finally finished. He turned to Cassandra. "Bitch," he repeated, a little louder. "Be sure to translate accurately."

Oh God. John couldn't help wondering how he would translate the word. Poor Cassandra, who was stuck with the task.

"Caesar—" Cassandra began, a little hesitantly. "Caesar says he can't eat with—"

John held his breath. Everyone stared at Cassandra, hanging on every word.

"He can't eat in the presence of a harlot."

The words hung in the air for a moment. John stole a look at Elizabeth and was surprised to see the beginnings of a smile working at the corners of her mouth.

"Faith!" Andrew broke the silence. "Please take your breakfast into the common room."

Everyone stared at Faith. Her jaw dropped, but no words emerged. She looked from Cassandra to Caesar and back, but John could read nothing in her gaze. Caesar was still standing when she swiveled 180 degrees on her yellow socks and disappeared down the hall.

Caesar sat back down and repositioned his napkin in his lap. With the air of a man who was performing for an audience, he raised his coffee cup to his lips and took a sip.

"Pleasant," he said. Then he picked up his fork with his left hand, passed it to his right, and began eating eggs Benedict as though he had done it a thousand times.

"Quick study" didn't even begin to describe him. How could he jump ahead two millennia and seem so at ease? It was nothing short of—well, something Julius Caesar might be capable of. Why should any of them be surprised?

The croissants were going around a second time when the light from the hallway was once again eclipsed by a figure at the door. Faith had returned.

This time, she was swathed in a long-sleeved, high-necked black dress that fell below her knees. Black stockings covered the distance to the floor. From the neck down, the effect was almost that of a nun's habit. Or the Grim Reaper.

Everyone stared at Faith, then every head turned toward Caesar. He didn't quite smile, but there was no mistaking the smug look of satisfaction that crossed his face. He waited a few seconds, then nodded in Andrew's direction.

Looking slightly unsure, Andrew dabbed at his lips with his napkin.

"Faith," he said. "Please join us."

Silently, Faith slid into the only unoccupied chair. Eric passed the croissants.

Despite her funereal garb, Faith's return seemed to lighten the mood. John was just beginning to think that everything might get back on track when Andrew cleared his throat and began to speak.

"We have a very special event planned for today," he began. He stopped and waited. Caesar nodded at Cassandra, who promptly translated. Andrew's face relaxed a little.

"You mentioned this last night at supper," Caesar said. "I believe you said something about a gathering at the home of your patroness."

"That is correct," Andrew replied when Cassandra had interpreted. "We have been planning for weeks."

Caesar listened to Cassandra. Then, pulling his napkin once more from his lap, he carefully folded it. Placing it next to his plate, he stretched both arms into the air. Everyone watched as he clasped them behind his head. He held that position a few moments before releasing his hands. He leaned forward.

No one else at the table moved. They were all just puppets now, and Caesar was the puppeteer.

"I appreciate your efforts," Caesar said. "I am sure you will all enjoy the festivities."

What? John locked eyes with Elizabeth. Had Caesar just implied what they all thought he had?

Cassandra translated accurately, and a similar questioning look appeared on Andrew's face. Then Caesar clinched it.

"I regret that I will not be attending," he said. "I shall remain here."

He rose from the table.

"Right now, I shall retire to my rooms." He turned and placed his hand on Cassandra's shoulder. "Cassandra alone will attend me."

LV

Once inside his room, Caesar moved to the sofa and sat down. As he watched Cassandra manipulate something on the wall near the door, he spread the folds of his toga wide on his left side. Even if Cassandra turned to look at him, he could push his fingers down between the cushions unseen.

The forked utensil he had stolen from last night's meal was still there, nestled down in the crevice between the pillows. Carefully, making sure no clink of metal called attention to his surreptitious thefts, he pushed the knife he had pilfered from the breakfast table downward to join the other implement.

Neither utensil was a satisfactory weapon, but either was better than none. The knife was especially maddening, with its rounded tip and dull blade. What use was a tool like that? It was just for show, Caesar decided as he watched his captors use the implement to spread softened butter and boiled fruit. Despite its ridiculous design, it was still a stout length of steel. It might be useless as a blade, but it could crush a larynx.

"Would you like to listen to some music?" Cassandra asked. She drew near and stood in front of Caesar.

"You play the harp?" he asked.

"No. We have a music machine."

"I will agree to it as long as we remain alone."

"We shall."

Caesar watched as Cassandra crossed the room to a cabinet. A moment later, the sound of a dozen unseen musicians surrounded them. How is this possible? Caesar wondered, but he did not voice the question.

"Come and sit with me," he said instead.

Cassandra turned from the cabinet and looked up at the ceiling. Caesar followed her gaze there but saw nothing save a few shiny black semispherical ornaments attached to the ceiling's smooth white surface. Ugly decorations, he thought, but so were many of the features of this strange domicile. Caesar was grateful for his experiences with other barbarian cultures. He knew it was pointless to argue about taste.

Cassandra sat down at the far end of the divan, careful to keep her distance from Caesar. How could he assure her that he was no threat to her virtue? The last thing he wanted was to touch this woman.

What Caesar most wanted was to arm himself, but that was proving difficult within these walls. The whore doctor might have some tools worth appropriating, but how? He could feign illness and hope to be taken to her surgery, but a stratagem like that was fraught with risk. Better to avoid the harpy and look elsewhere.

Caesar glanced at Cassandra again and recalled the shocking moment he arrived in this place. Too bad she wasn't really Venus. How much more pleasant that would have been, even if it meant that he had died.

Caesar sighed. There was no denying it. He was very much alive. With no available armaments in his immediate surroundings, he reached an obvious conclusion. He must seize the chance to venture beyond these windowless walls. Perhaps the home of Duckhead's patroness would offer better opportunities than this strange edifice. Even if it, too, failed to provide Caesar with any means of personal defense, he could at least expand his knowledge about the unfamiliar land in which he was now a prisoner. Knowledge never fails to augment power. He would strive for both. True, he appeared to have prevailed in the breakfast engagement, but he was still unarmed. He was still a captive. If he could not surmount those two obstacles, he might as well lie down, fold his arms across his chest, and bid the real Venus to lead him home to Elysium.

Caesar had never left his fate to hope. He was not about to begin now.

"I have decided," he said.

Instead of acknowledging his statement, Cassandra glanced at the ceiling. What an odd mannerism. Is she praying?

"I have decided that I will attend the gathering at the home of your master's patroness."

Instantly, Cassandra's eyes dropped to meet Caesar's.

"He is not my master," she said, "but he will be pleased with your decision."

Caesar watched Cassandra's eyes travel upward once again. This time, she was smiling.

LVI

*H*ooray!

The IDES Project was back on track. Cassandra grinned up into the eye-in-the-sky camera over her head. Field trip day could now move forward according to plan. Caesar had tried to throw his weight around at breakfast, but so what? He was agreeable now, and that was all that mattered. Everyone would go to Sonia's cocktail party, and all would be well.

If Cassandra had known then about the silverware between the couch cushions, she might not have felt so confident. And what if she had known about the lamp, too?

"It's difficult for me to believe that Caesar managed to grasp a burning light bulb in a full-palm grip without my seeing him," Cassandra said when Eric told her what the team in the communications room had witnessed while Cassandra had been fiddling with the sound system. "I'm not blind."

She had to concede, of course. Even without the video footage, Caesar's reddened palm was evidence enough that he had indeed burned himself on Cassandra's watch. Not only was Caesar sneaky, he was very good at being sneaky. He hadn't emitted so much as a squeak.

"I was opposed to all the cameras," she said. "Remember? They seemed like spying to me."

"But now?" Eric said.

"I'm glad Andrew insisted. They didn't stop Caesar from burning his hand, but at least we know about it."

"I wonder about what we *don't* know," Eric said.

"You think the cameras haven't captured everything important? Caesar has no way of knowing he's being taped—"

"No, I don't think he's trying to hide what he's doing when we aren't looking. It's just that the cameras can't see under tables. And there are always corners—hidden spots—no matter how many—"

"What we really need is a camera inside his head."

"That's you," Eric said. "Getting inside his head is your job."

So true. It was Cassandra's job, and she was still failing brilliantly at it. She would need to be on her toes at Sonia's house.

LVII

As she got ready for the party, Cassandra almost felt sorry for Faith. She didn't say a word as she applied two thick black stripes of eyeliner and a ruby coating to her lips. She was still wearing the somber outfit that had readmitted her to breakfast, now completed with calf-high black boots. It wasn't a bad ensemble, actually. If it had been any other color, she wouldn't have looked quite so much like a witch.

Cassandra chose another floor-length dress for the occasion, a gown that had come her way unexpectedly a few years earlier, when her stepfather had drafted her to be maid of honor for the daughter of some visiting acquaintances.

"Why me?" Cassandra had said. "I'm a total stranger."

"I know, I know," Malcolm said. "Just do it for me. The family doesn't know anyone in Las Vegas, but they want nice wedding photos. If you won't be the maid of honor, they'll have to use whatever witness the wedding chapel drums up."

The payoff was a designer dress. The shopping trip took three hours longer than the wedding itself, and the dress was nothing Cassandra would have chosen herself. Crafted of a few dozen yards of bright fuchsia chiffon, it boasted a lime green velvet bolero. The whole thing sparkled with rhinestones, seed pearls, and gold embroidery. Cassandra had always called it her "Fabergé egg dress." Her mother insisted that she keep it, but unless she was invited to a very fancy garden party or the Academy Awards, Cassandra knew she would never wear it again.

The moment Sonia Illingsworth said "a cocktail party in my library," the dress popped into Cassandra's head. Yes, it was a bit over the top, but Mrs. Illingsworth would probably approve. Better yet, Cassandra wouldn't have to go shopping. She sent an email to her mom. After delivering the expected "I told you so," Margot packed up the dress and mailed it to California.

When she was ready, Cassandra left Faith still fiddling with hair gel to join Elizabeth in Caesar's suite. At least the rest of the morning had gone smoothly, she thought as she rustled down the hall. After Caesar tired of listening to Beethoven, she had turned on the television. By the time Andrew entered the room thirty minutes later, Caesar was operating the remote control as though he'd been doing it for years.

"He's enjoying *The Price Is Right*," Cassandra said. She hesitated, waiting to see whether Caesar would scold her for speaking English. He didn't even give her a momentary glance. "He's been switching between that and *World Wide Wrestling*."

Andrew watched Caesar for a long moment. Cassandra was amazed, too, but she didn't say anything. What could anyone say? "Wow" wasn't enough, and "Holy shit" wasn't polite.

"Eric's about ready to serve a light lunch in the dining room," Andrew said a few moments later. "Do you think—?" He let the question hang unfinished.

Cassandra shrugged. "All I can do is ask."

As soon as she mentioned the noonday meal, Caesar handed Cassandra the remote and stood up.

"*I am yours to do with as you please,*" he said. Cassandra was pretty sure his smirk meant the exact opposite.

She translated for Andrew and watched as the two men locked eyes. A slight smile spread across Caesar's face. Andrew squared his shoulders and set his jaw. Two thousand years and six thousand miles collapsed into that quick interchange. Cassandra read what it meant as easily as she'd read every boy she'd known since kindergarten. Battle lines had just been drawn. Once again, because breakfast hadn't quite finished the job, Caesar was challenging Andrew's standing as alpha male in the IDES Lab.

Why did boys always think they had to answer such challenges? If Andrew had simply ignored Caesar, he might have held on to his better judgment. By engaging, Andrew acknowledged that he had something to lose and put himself at an unnecessary disadvantage. So stupid!

Cassandra always thought about Ridley Boone's tortoises when she saw men square off like this. Ridley was a retired ventriloquist who lived in a single-wide a couple of blocks away from her mother's at Carefree Canyon. His female tortoise laid eggs every year, and whenever they hatched, he'd let all the neighborhood kids come over to see the babies. The hatchlings weren't much bigger than a casino chip, but otherwise they looked exactly like their full-grown parents. Sometimes Ridley let Cassandra pick one up. She'd hold the baby carefully between her thumb and forefinger. Invariably, the tiny tortoise would stretch its neck forward and open its mouth in a tiny but ferocious snarl. It would paw the air with its little claws. So belligerent, and yet so powerless.

Wasn't that what Caesar was—defiant but actually helpless? Why was Andrew taking his taunts seriously? Why couldn't he just ignore them? The answer was simple, of course. *Boys!* Cassandra sighed. There wasn't anything she could do about testosterone.

Caesar gave everyone room to relax during lunch. He munched

his crab sandwich happily and afterward even admired Andrew's violin-playing skills. Later, he allowed Elizabeth and Cassandra to dress him in his bespoke toga. He chuckled at their ineptitude, but in a friendly sort of way, Cassandra decided. They were still fiddling when he waved them off.

"It will suffice," he said." He paused, patted Cassandra on the forearm, and added, "*Mea columba.*"

My dove!

Elizabeth smiled, but all Cassandra felt was instant suspicion. Who knew what Caesar might be plotting behind this amiable familiarity? Maybe nothing. All they could do was hope that Sonia's party would be a success.

LVIII

At precisely 3:35 p.m. on March 18, AD 1999, the IDES team stood as a unit on the concrete steps in front of the main door to the IDES Lab. Cassandra would later be able to swear to the time. Eric's schedule for the day was detailed to the minute, and everyone's watches had been synchronized after breakfast. If it was not precisely 3:35 p.m., it was very, very close.

The team boarded the white cargo van in the exact order Eric's schedule prescribed. Andrew took the front passenger's seat. Elizabeth and John climbed into the seats furthest back. Julius Caesar—with what Cassandra considered surprising equanimity—slid into the middle bench seat. She took the space next to him. Eric closed the door, then took his place at the wheel. Exactly as they had rehearsed. So far, so good.

Everyone watched as Faith climbed into her own car, a silver Nissan parked next to the van. Again, according to plan.

Everyone in the van fastened their seat belts.

"For your safety," Cassandra said to Caesar as she secured the strap across his lap. "The coach moves rapidly."

301

Caesar acquiesced. Cassandra noted his interest in the seat belt buckle, but he didn't attempt to unfasten it. Eric started the engine, backed out, and paused at the driveway, waiting for Faith.

A minute passed. Faith's car had yet to move. Cassandra swiveled her head around in time to see the Nissan's door open. Faith strode to Andrew's window.

"Battery's dead," Faith said. "I guess I should've checked it the last couple of days."

"I guess you should have," Andrew said. "Who'd have thought we'd need a backup for the backup?"

"I guess I'd better ride with you, after all," Faith said. "There's room."

"No. We need redundancy," Andrew said.

"Take my car," Cassandra said. "I've got the key right here." Fishing in her evening purse, she pulled out her key ring. "The battery should be fine, and it's got a full tank." Jeremiah was parked right next to Faith's car.

"Thank you for being prepared, Cassandra," Andrew said as he passed the key ring through the window. His insinuation was not lost on Faith, who knitted her brow in a tight scowl.

Cassandra heard her car start on the first try, but the engine stalled as Faith tried to back out of the parking space.

"Oh—I'm sorry," Cassandra said. "I didn't think to ask if she could drive a stick."

The gears ground a few more times. At last the green beetle lurched into line behind the white van.

"I'll consider that transmission my personal gift to science," Cassandra said. No one replied, but Eric winked at her in the rearview mirror. Good. Maybe she'd helped lighten the mood a little.

Or maybe not. She could also see a shiny film of perspiration glistening on Eric's forehead, though the van's air conditioning was working just fine. Cassandra glanced at Caesar. No sweat there. How could he remain so impassive in such unfamiliar surroundings? With a face like that, he should be playing high-stakes poker.

They were at least twenty minutes behind schedule when they arrived at the gates of Sonia Illingsworth's estate. Faith had stalled out at every stop sign and traffic light on the way to the house. She nearly slammed into a taco truck at the corner of Glenarm and Fair Oaks. By the time the two vehicles turned into Hedgehope Circle, Eric was sweating mightily. Andrew probably was, too.

Faith jerked to a stop at the curb in the cul-de-sac just past the gates, the agreed drop-off point for the backup car. Cassandra watched as she pulled herself out of the car, slammed the door, and stormed toward the van. Cassandra moved closer to Caesar and allowed Faith to slide in next to her. Faith pulled her skirt inside the van and slid the door shut with a bang.

A whirring sound drew everyone's attention as the massive wrought iron gates in front of the van parted and swung slowly open. Cassandra glanced at Caesar. She would have been happy to explain, but she knew better than to try without a specific request.

It's magic. That must be what he thought.

Unless—Cassandra couldn't shake the feeling that Caesar was just watching and biding his time. He reminded her of her mom's cat when there was a mouse in the house. Aphrodite was usually a very relaxed cat, but when she knew there was prey within reach, she became as alert as a sentry. If she'd possessed opposable thumbs, she would have whipped out a rasp and started sharpening her claws. *Watchful waiting*—that was the aura Caesar gave off. But what was he on the lookout for?

As soon as the gates opened, the van moved slowly up the flagstone drive. Through the side window, Cassandra could see the tall, vine-covered fence that ran alongside the road. Ahead, the formal rose garden had begun its springtime bloom. The hillside beyond it was a perfect green carpet studded with grand old oaks. At the top of the hill, the road fanned out into a flagged courtyard. On the left was a two-story edifice with a tile roof and six carved wood doors. The "carriage house," Mrs. Illingsworth called it, the kind with chauffeur's quarters upstairs. Straight ahead stood the Illingsworth homestead itself, a sand-colored Mediterranean palace with arched windows, colonnaded balconies, and an imposing front entrance flanked by carved Moorish columns. The door was open, and moving toward the van were two people: a tall man in a tux, and Sonia Illingsworth in a peach-colored gown. Something on her head glittered in the raking sunlight as she walked.

Faith jumped out of the van as soon as it stopped and took a few steps toward the house. Eric and Andrew followed. But when Cassandra stepped out, Faith stopped and turned.

"Hey, Cassandra! Catch!" she hissed.

Cassandra couldn't react fast enough to catch her keys, and they landed at Caesar's feet just as he emerged from the van. As Cassandra bent to retrieve them, she heard Faith sputtering angrily at Andrew.

"I'm done driving that piece of shit. Cassandra will have to get it back to the lab."

Andrew uttered a few mollifying phrases. Cassandra took a deep breath and stood up. Rise above it, she told herself, but the admonition didn't work.

"Goddamn fucking bitch," she muttered under her breath.

"*Quid?*" Caesar asked. Before Cassandra thought about what she was doing, she translated what she'd just said.

Instantly aghast, she stared into Caesar's face. He stared back, but his eyes were twinkling. Then he laughed. He *really* laughed, and Cassandra realized with surprise that it was the first time he'd done so since he'd arrived. He'd laughed for effect plenty of times, but this was the first time a genuine laugh had emanated from Caesar's own belly.

It made Cassandra laugh, too. Everyone else looked at them in surprise.

"It's nothing," Cassandra said, still giggling. "I'm just glad we're here, and I guess Caesar is, too. But *shh*. Here's our hostess."

LIX

Her guests were a little late, but at first Sonia attached no significance to it. She was putting the finishing touches on her orchid arrangements. She wondered whether Julius Caesar had ever seen an orchid. Certainly not a New World variety, she thought, and even Asian orchids must have been a rare sight in ancient Rome. She let her thoughts wander further. What would Caesar think of a toucan, or a monkey with a prehensile tail—creatures that had delighted Sonia as a child in Costa Rica?

It was nearly four-thirty when the IDES team arrived, almost half an hour later than scheduled. Sonia had just begun to worry when she saw the gates begin to open on the security monitor. She pulled on her shawl and stepped out onto the front porch. Her heart beat faster when she caught sight of the white van rounding the curve beside her rose garden. It is finally happening, she thought. Julius Caesar is arriving at my house. Her second thought was about Chip, of course. If only her husband could be standing at her side.

But Sonia did not have time for reflection. As she crossed the flagstones, Faith Hopper burst from the van's side door. Sonia, hoping for Cassandra or Caesar at that moment, was disappointed to see the doctor. She simply did not warm to the woman. Faith was intelligent, of course, and very capable, but Sonia could never understand women who felt they must compete with men. Women had their own power. Faith reminded her of the female engineers who had worked for Illingsworth back in the seventies. How those rare birds had struggled!

Faith's clothing was also a minor surprise: a dark dress and black boots. At least it was a dress, she thought. Sonia watched the woman pull a leather satchel from the van and sling it over her shoulder.

The front passenger door opened, and Andrew Danicek stepped out. He was wearing a black tuxedo and black patent leather shoes.

Eric Barza, who had been driving the van, rushed to the passenger door. He was wearing khaki slacks and a navy blue sport coat. While it was a less elegant ensemble that Andrew's, it was the most formal outfit Sonia had ever seen Eric wear before. Even at the reception to welcome Cassandra, he had been wearing jeans.

Just then, Cassandra Fleury emerged through the side door, resplendent in a bright pink gown with a green top. At least there was one woman on the team who knew how to dress. Just then, Sonia glimpsed a flutter of white fabric. She drew a breath as Julius Caesar stepped from the van. Both he and Cassandra immediately bent down in response to something Faith did. When they straightened up, Cassandra stepped aside. There he was, the man himself, magnificent in his toga. Caesar looked toward Sonia, then raised his eyes to the sky.

As she walked toward him, Sonia looked up, too. She paused, and for a moment, they stared together at a passenger jet flying overhead, its long white contrail stretching out behind it. Sonia lowered her eyes again. Caesar lowered his a few seconds later and met Sonia's gaze as she drew closer. His eyes were dark, just as ancient authors described them. At that moment, at the same moment that Sonia's heart was beating like a drum, the fact that Caesar's eyes matched her expectation was comforting. She reached both hands toward him. With no change of expression, Caesar stretched his own hands forward and closed them around hers.

At Caesar's touch, a rush of emotions swept through Sonia. It surprised her that his hands were soft. She had been expecting the rough and battle-hardened hands of a warrior. But the Caesar she was meeting was the statesman, not the soldier. She struggled to imagine Caesar at a single point in time. Until she met him in the flesh, she had imagined the legend, not the man. He was Pontifex Maximus, consul, general, student, boy, a man who wished to be king—everything rolled into one. But standing before her, he was only one of these: Rome's first citizen, a pampered aristocrat. Of course his hands were soft! But his eyes told a different story. As they gazed directly into her own, Sonia saw evidence of those earlier Caesars—strength and cunning. She saw pain, too, and exhaustion. Caesar was nine years her junior, but Sonia recognized world-weariness when she saw it.

"*Hail, Caesar*," Sonia said in Latin. "*Welcome to my home.*" Between Cassandra's tutelage and her own Spanish accent, Sonia had mastered this greeting well. Although Caesar did not smile, his eyes seemed to brighten a little. Moving to his right side, Sonia slipped her arm under his. She detected no uneasiness. Caesar seemed perfectly at ease with her fingers resting on his forearm under the folds of his toga. Followed by the other IDES Team members, they crossed the courtyard and entered the house as planned.

In the foyer, Caesar and Sonia paused in front of a niche that held a small bronze statue of Hercules. Hector had placed an orchid arrangement at its feet. Caesar looked at Hercules, then dropped his eyes to the purple flowers. The orchids held his interest longer than the sculpture. He said nothing.

They progressed to the library, where Hector and Graciela were waiting with refreshments in front of the fireplace. Hector provided each guest with a flute of champagne. Andrew had planned to make a toast, but Caesar immediately drank from his glass. Everyone else followed his example. Cassandra said something in Latin to Caesar. Caesar replied with a phrase that Sonia took to be an affirmation.

"Caesar would be pleased to see your artworks," Cassandra said.

Sonia took Caesar's arm. Together, they made their way around the library with Cassandra close behind.

"Hannibal," Sonia said as they paused in front of the French oil painting she had chosen to display especially for Caesar's visit. Caesar nodded, but Sonia saw his attention drift, first to the flowers on the window sill and then to the window itself.

Sonia did not find it surprising that Caesar was more interested in his immediate surroundings than a painting of an historic event. If she suddenly found herself in ancient Rome, she realized, she would find the details of everyday life far more fascinating than a painting or a statue. Regret washed over her as she wished she had realized this before wasting time trying to interest Caesar in objects that bored him.

In spite of Sonia's regrets, they continued their perambulation as planned. Caesar cooperated but said nothing. Sonia thought she detected a tiny smile as Caesar regarded her etching of Cincinnatus, but she still had to admit that her idea of an "art tour" was completely ineffective as a means of sparking conversation with this complicated man.

Although she understood why she had been asked to remove her painting of Cleopatra with her asp and her replica of the Prima Porta Augustus, Sonia almost wished she had left them for Caesar to see. Showing him Rome's future might have kindled some response. Instead, by the time they had circled the room and arrived again in front of Graciela and her tray of bite-sized empanadas, Caesar yawned.

Sonia did not know whether an overt yawn was considered rude in Caesar's world, but it conveyed his feelings to her clearly. Caesar found her tedious. Her heart sank as she watched him lean toward Cassandra and whisper a few words.

"He needs to use the restroom," Cassandra said.

"Of course," Sonia said. "Please follow Hector."

Elizabeth took Sonia's place at Caesar's right hand, according to established plan. The two women were his designated restroom escorts.

Sonia watched them disappear through the archway that lead back to the foyer and on to the guest washroom. Then she turned her attention to Graciela and the next course of appetizers.

LX

Cassandra motioned to Elizabeth, who took Caesar's arm when Sonia stepped aside.

They followed Hector back down the hall and past the front door. The butler opened a dark paneled door and ushered them into a sitting room furnished with a velvet chaise lounge and a vanity table in front of a lighted mirror.

"The bathroom is in the chamber beyond," he said. "If you need anything, just pull this cord." He pointed to a tasseled silk rope hanging out of a hole in the ceiling.

Hector retired, leaving the three standing in the sitting room. Cassandra was about to open the door to the bathroom when Caesar spoke.

"I feel a little dizzy," he said. "I would like some water on my face."

Dizzy! Oh, no, she thought. Maybe he's really sick. Maybe she should call Faith—but Caesar read her mind.

"I do not wish to submit to the attentions of the harpy doctor," he said firmly. "A little cold water is all I require."

"All right," Cassandra said, and he opened the bathroom door.

The bathroom was a large, white-tiled room with French doors leading onto one of the stone porches on the front of the house. The toilet was in a separate chamber, as was a large glassed-in shower. An oversize shell-shaped sink stood on a pedestal against one wall. Cassandra pulled a hand towel from the gold rack next to it and held it under the tap.

"Is he all right?" Elizabeth asked quietly.

"I think he's fine," Cassandra whispered back.

"I guess I'm just still worried after—well, earlier."

"Me, too," Cassandra said, turning back to Caesar.

He had moved to the French doors. He was gazing down the hill toward the rose garden they'd seen when they arrived.

"Put this on your forehead," Cassandra said, holding out the damp towel. "Perhaps it will help."

"I want to walk in the garden," said Caesar, ignoring it. "Fresh air is what I need."

"You will walk later with our hostess," Cassandra said.

"I wish to walk now." Caesar put his hand on the handle. He pushed down, and the door swung open. Before Cassandra could do anything to stop him, he had stepped out onto the terrace.

"Maybe I'd better call Andrew and the others," Elizabeth whispered.

"No," Cassandra said. "What harm can a little breather do? He's been cooped up for two days. Just tell them we'll be a little longer than we thought. Constipation."

"I don't know—"

"Oh, come on. Five minutes won't hurt."

Elizabeth caved. Cassandra joined Caesar on the terrace. He was sucking in deep breaths of cool air, and his color had already improved. When Elizabeth returned, Cassandra shut the door behind her.

"Let us walk among the roses," said Caesar, pointing down the hill. The garden was farther away than Cassandra liked.

"We must return in a little while," she said.

"A little while," Caesar repeated, and he started down the steps. Elizabeth and Cassandra followed. They were definitely breaking all the rules. On the other hand, Caesar seemed to be enjoying himself immensely. Cassandra figured she'd give him five minutes.

They followed a path bordered by dainty white flowers and soon arrived at an arched trellis covered in a honeysuckle vine. Passing through it, they found themselves surrounded by roses. Cassandra worked to keep up with Caesar, who was moving quickly down the garden path. Suddenly he stopped and pressed his face into a large yellow rose.

"Ah," he said. "Your roses are large and ungainly, but they smell as sweet as any Roman's."

Cassandra smiled at what Sonia would think about having her prize blooms described as "large and ungainly." She turned to laugh about it with Elizabeth.

Elizabeth had stopped dead twenty feet behind them. "What's the matter?" Cassandra called, but Elizabeth was staring toward the driveway. Cassandra followed her gaze. She was watching two men.

One of the men was Sonia's security guard. Cassandra had been keeping her eye out for him when they left the house, hoping she wouldn't have to explain their presence outside. She wasn't surprised to see him now. But who was the other guy? He was big, and he was wearing a black jacket. Cassandra couldn't see his face.

Suddenly, the big guy lunged at the guard. As the men struggled, Cassandra saw what had transfixed Elizabeth. The big guy was Bill, one of the bodyguards who had escorted them to Hank's coin auction. What the hell was he doing here?

"Run back to the house!" Cassandra shouted as the men continued to fight. "Call for help!" Elizabeth hesitated a moment, then kicked off her heels and ran. As she sprinted up the hill to the house, Cassandra saw Bill slam the guard on the head with the butt of a big black hand-gun. He crumpled to the ground in a lifeless heap.

Damn. This was worse than she thought. Bill had seen them, and there was no way they could outrun him to the house. Cassandra had no idea what his intentions were, but the guy had a gun.

"Come on," she said to Caesar, grabbing his arm. "If we stay here, we shall be killed."

Cassandra kicked off her shoes and gathered up her dress. Together they ran down to the end of the rose garden. Cassandra looked over her shoulder as they leapt over a stone bench onto the lawn. Bill was behind them, but he wasn't moving very fast. He was holding what looked like a cell phone or a walkie-talkie to his ear.

Cassandra had no idea where they were headed or what they would do. They half ran, half slid down the slick grass. The Illingsworth sprinkler system must have been working overtime. Caesar tripped and slid ten feet on his rump, but he managed to regain his footing and keep moving. Cassandra slipped, too, but Caesar grabbed her before she hit the ground.

At the bottom of the hill, the two were met by the tall, vine-covered perimeter fence. If we get past the fence, Cassandra thought, we'll be on the street. If we get to the street, we can get to my car. If we get to my car, we can get back to the lab. Praise God for Faith's bitchiness, she thought. She had her car keys in her pocket.

"We must get through this," Cassandra said to Caesar, but she needn't have bothered. He was already on his hands and knees, and soon he'd flattened himself on the ground. Shredding his toga as he moved, he slithered under the fence in a spot where the runoff from the sprinklers had created a depression.

"Lie down," Cassandra heard him call from the other side. "I shall pull you."

She lay down and stretched her arms under the fence. Caesar

grabbed them and yanked. Cassandra heard her dress tear as she slid through, and a sharp pain ripped down her thigh. It was still only a moment before she was standing up in the gutter on Hedgehope Circle. Her car was less than fifty feet away.

"Come on!" She grabbed Caesar's arm again, and they ran to the cul-de-sac together. She fumbled for her keys and opened the passenger door.

"Get in!" Cassandra ordered. "We will go home." Caesar obeyed, and Cassandra slammed his door. She rushed around the front of the car, unlocked her side, and slid into the driver's seat. She shoved the key into the ignition and prayed silently. Start, start. And please oh please, don't let Faith have destroyed the transmission.

The engine fired right up, and Cassandra shifted into first gear with no trouble at all. She looked up as she released the emergency brake. Damn. Bill was on the street in front of them. And then she saw something even more troubling. It was a gray Trailblazer with darkened windows, and she realized with a start that she'd seen it before. It had been parked on Raymond Avenue yesterday when she slipped out for some fresh air. Now it was coming straight at them from around the corner.

"Get the hell out of here" was all Cassandra could think. She floored Jeremiah and pulled a tight U-turn in front of the Trailblazer. She made it to the corner and turned left onto Orange Grove Boulevard without stopping. It was an insane thing to do, but miraculously there was no opposing traffic. Just get to the lab, she was thinking, just get to the lab. She glanced into the rearview mirror as she approached California Boulevard. The gray Trailblazer was on her bumper.

LXI

Hank Morgan looked at his watch for the thousandth time. It was now ninety minutes past the time Marco and Bill should have arrived with Julius Caesar and the two extra operatives. He had the cash to pay them—$20,000 in unmarked hundreds—in a briefcase that was now resting on the stained recliner next to the front door.

It should have been so easy. But somehow, in spite of a performance bonus if they got Caesar to the house before five o'clock—two former Navy SEALs backed up by two experienced bodyguards had failed to snatch an old man from a garden party.

Marco texted the bad news to Hank's throwaway cell phone at 5:20. "Junco has flown. Pursuit in progress. Stand by."

"Keep me posted," Hank texted back. He was trapped and powerless inside the disgusting house that had seemed like such a brilliant choice when he selected it. Bill's girlfriend's grandfather had just been carted off to a nursing home, leaving the house unoccupied but not yet listed for sale. In addition, the dump was only a few miles from both the IDES Lab and the Illingsworth estate. Set back from the street, it was nearly invisible behind a dense hedge of overgrown prickly pear cactus. A long decaying driveway led to an unattached single-car garage at the back of the lot. The house was the perfect hideout until you had to sit inside alone for three hours.

Hank thought about his grandmother, who had set him on the path that had led circuitously to this very spot. There was a time when he had wished she had lived to see the accomplishments of her cherished grandson. Now Hank was glad she would never know about his latest deeds.

Ten days after Hank turned thirteen in Huntington Beach, California, Nana skied into a tree in Steamboat Springs, Colorado. Several hours and a helicopter ride later, doctors declared her brain less responsive than a cauliflower. Hank's father and his two aunts traveled from separate corners of the continent to converge on the University of Colorado Hospital in Denver. There, they clashed for three days over whether the electricity powering Diana Longstreet Morgan's ventilator should be turned off. On the fourth day, Diana ended the battle by dying.

The three-way skirmish among Diana Morgan's children grew into a ten-year war over her estate, but one provision in her will was executed almost immediately. Hank, her sole grandchild, got her father's coin collection.

Nana Morgan had already promised Hank the collection when he turned twenty-one or graduated from college, whichever came first. She fully anticipated being alive to make the presentation. She was only sixty-two—and still skiing—when interaction with a mature ponderosa altered her expectations.

Because Nana had done such an outstanding job of convincing Hank that managing "a prestigious asset with unlimited potential" required diligent study, the boy had talked his father into letting him cash out three savings bonds when he was nine years old. With the proceeds—a whopping $342.87—Hank ordered three Indian head pennies, a couple of buffalo nickels, and a standing Liberty half dollar from a catalogue he'd bought at a local hobby store.

The day Nana died, the collection Hank had begun four years earlier was worth about $12,000. The day after she died, Hank removed a Revolutionary War half penny, his best Morgan silver dollar, and two nice Indian head pennies from the safe Nana had given him for his tenth birthday. When his mother dropped him off at Carrefour Middle School, Hank waited until her blue Cadillac had disappeared around the corner onto Bolsa. Then he walked out to McFadden and caught a public bus to Los Angeles.

One transfer later, he got off at Union Station. From there, it was a half-mile walk to the corner of Fifth and Hill, where he arrived at Kleinman Brothers, a coin dealership he had dealt with only by telephone and mail up to now.

"I want to buy a silver *denarius*," Hank said, when a man in a black suit walked out in response to a bell that rang when he walked through the door. "Gaius Postumius, 74 BC. Draped bust of Diana right, wearing hair tied into knot, bow and quiver over shoulder. 'C. Postumi' *in exergue*, hunting dog running right, spear below."

The man smiled. "How do you do?" he said. He extended his hand, and Hank shook it. "I am Joel Kleinman. And who might you be?"

"Hank Morgan. Do you have that coin?"

Hank rode back to Huntington Beach with the exact coin he had found in the Kleinman Brothers catalogue. Joel tried to steer him toward something with "more potential" but gave up when Hank refused to budge. The boy traded three of his coins for the *denarius*. Joel threw in a bronze *as* from Sicily and a ride to the bus station, but Hank knew Kleinman Brothers had still come out ahead. This was one time he didn't care.

Hank also didn't care when he was grounded for two weeks for going to Los Angeles without permission. One of the weeks would be taken up with the trip to Colorado for Nana's funeral, and being grounded didn't matter, anyway. Hank was skilled at sneaking away from home undetected, and the only reason his parents had found out about his field trip to Kleinman Brothers was that the school had called his mother when he didn't show up for class. Hank wasn't a habitual truant. There wouldn't be a weekend free before he returned from Nana's funeral. He'd had no choice but to play hooky.

As if in preparation for the battle over all her possessions, Nana's three children squabbled over whether her casket should be open at her funeral in Colorado Springs.

"Absolutely not," Hank's father said. But his two sisters won out, and the undertakers went to work on Nana's poor flattened face.

"Our family will not take part in barbaric activities like 'visitations,'" Dad said, but at the funeral, Hank joined the long procession of people who wanted to bid Diana Morgan a final farewell. Not only was she a generous local philanthropist, she was a well-respected dachshund breeder. If dogs had been permitted inside the First Congregational Church, the ranks of mourners might well have doubled.

"Let him go," Hank's mother hissed when Dad tried to hold him back. "He's old enough to decide for himself."

When he arrived at the casket's side, Hank reached in, grasped Nana's right hand, and opened her fingers. As it happened, a reporter from the *Colorado Springs Gazette* was watching.

After the ceremony, the reporter caught up with Hank while he was waiting with his family for the limousine to the cemetery.

"What did you put into Mrs. Morgan's hand?" the reporter asked.

"A silver *denarius*," Hank said.

"Why?"

"She needed a coin for the ferryman."

The next day, the story about Diana Morgan's funeral was flanked by a second piece about her grandson, Henry Hadrian Morgan III. Having stuck to the family like a tick through the graveside ceremony and the reception following at the Air Force Academy, the reporter had gleaned details about Hank's close relationship with Nana and the interest in coin collecting she had nurtured. She learned how the boy had pored over coin catalogues and disobeyed his parents to acquire the perfect parting gift—an ancient *denarius* bearing the likeness not only of the goddess Diana, but also of a dog. Before the week was out, the story had appeared not only on the front page of the *Colorado Springs Gazette*, but also—via wire services—in newspapers across the country. The *Stars and Stripes* ran it, too, meaning that it was read in places as far-flung as Hellenikon and Subic Bay.

It was the first time Hank made international headlines, but it would not be the last. At twenty-seven, he was named one of *Trend* magazine's most eligible bachelors. A decade later, his portrait graced the cover of *Time*.

Hank was now in his mid-forties. He hadn't made any fresh headlines since January, which was fine with him. Denarius's winter coin auction had promised to be his most lucrative ever. To observers, it looked like a runaway success. The Pericles Medallion alone sold for $698,000, the most ever paid for a single coin at auction. Nick Stratos's protest had only added to the event's buzz. So had the flamboyant appearance of Philippa Kenyon Sykes, who announced to the press corps on hand at the auction that she was dying of bile duct cancer.

It should have solved everything. Instead, here Hank was, standing at the cracked window of a rubbish-filled bungalow in Highland Park, peeking out onto Bertha Street through the dusty slats of a decrepit Venetian blind. The room was freezing in spite of the pathetic efforts of a small electric heater. Hank had turned it down to "low" after it tripped a circuit breaker, but even on "high," it had made hardly any difference to the ambient temperature.

On the other hand, maybe it was a good thing that the house was cold. It smelled awful, and heat would only make it stink even more. The stench wasn't bad enough to make Hank start looking for a corpse, but it was nonetheless depressing to be forced to sit—hour after hour— in a closed space that reeked of rotting garbage, old cigarette smoke, and diesel fuel. But it would all be worth it, he reminded himself, when Julius Caesar arrived.

LXII

C assandra glanced in her rearview mirror.

Damn! What did these guys want? It had to be Caesar, but why? She couldn't answer that question. All she knew was that she had to get Caesar back to the lab.

She made a right onto California Boulevard, again without stopping. The Trailblazer stuck to Jeremiah's tail like a trailer. Suddenly she knew she couldn't drive directly to the IDES Lab. She had no cell phone to alert the security guard there, and she could never get Caesar to safety without his assistance. Since help didn't seem to be arriving from the crew at the Illingsworth house—where were they, anyway?—She was on her own. I'll go up Pasadena Avenue, she thought. Maybe I can lose the Trailblazer by getting on the freeway.

At the last possible second, Cassandra swerved into the left lane, cutting off a Volvo station wagon full of kids. The driver slammed on her brakes and honked as Cassandra made a left turn. Narrowly avoiding an oncoming city bus, she floored the accelerator and headed north. There was no way the Trailblazer could have made that turn behind me, she thought, as she approached the entrance to Interstate

210. But as she merged left onto the ramp, there it was, right behind her. *Damn!*

Then Cassandra remembered something she'd noticed on her first visit to the IDES lab. It wasn't legal, and it was dangerous, but it was possible to jump several lanes to get on a flyover that joined a west-bound freeway, instead of staying in the lanes that headed north.

"Hold on!" Cassandra yelled at Caesar. Poor guy. He might be an asshole, but he didn't deserve this. Jamming the gas pedal to the floor, she swerved hard to the right, jerking the car at a near ninety-degree angle across four lanes of traffic and several rows of raised reflectors. As Jeremiah joined the traffic on the ramp curving upward to the west-bound lanes, Cassandra saw the Trailblazer below them, still speeding north. Hooray! she cheered silently, but her relief was short-lived.

The Trailblazer screeched to a halt, and Cassandra saw it start to back up. As she merged with the traffic heading west, it appeared once again in her rearview mirror. Damn. Her pursuers were experienced and fast, and she was just a stupid chick in an old VW.

Cassandra was beginning to lose heart. She glanced at Caesar. His face was ashen, and he was holding onto the sides of his seat in a death grip. They're not going to catch me, Cassandra told herself. She gritted her teeth and swerved onto the exit ramp that had just appeared on her right.

The ramp ascended to a stoplight. It was red, but Cassandra ignored it and made a tire-screeching left turn onto a two-lane road. It went over the freeway, where an intersection with a traffic light would have allowed her to get back on heading westbound. Too soon—they'll see me, she thought, and she blew through a yellow light. Her plan now was to try to lose them on some smaller roads, but the one she was on ended half a block beyond. Despite a red light, she made a left turn in front of a motorcycle that nearly T-boned Jeremiah in the intersection. She sped east, but her best efforts were in vain. The Trailblazer was closing in on them. The Colorado Street Bridge was right ahead, the one the locals call Suicide Bridge. How apt, Cassandra thought grimly.

I'm not leading them onto that bridge, Cassandra thought. Even though the side rails looked formidable, she had visions of her little car lying hundreds of feet below on the bottom of the Arroyo Seco, cracked open like a roadkill armadillo. There was no way she was going to take the chance of becoming airborne.

Just as she was beginning to believe that Suicide Bridge was inevitable, Cassandra saw one last chance to avoid it. Without slowing down, she made a left turn from the far right lane. It was her scariest move yet. A panel truck coming off the bridge braked, swerved, and smashed into the barrier on the side of the road. Horrified, Cassandra stomped on the gas pedal and careened under the freeway and up a single-lane, one-way road. She couldn't see the Trailblazer, but she knew it wouldn't be long before it caught up.

A hundred yards past the freeway, Cassandra slammed on the brakes. It was time for another illegal turn, this time a hairpin switchback. She hoped she could complete it before the Trailblazer closed the gap. It's my last chance, God, she prayed silently. I'll do anything you want if you get us out of this alive.

Jeremiah's tires squealed as the car spun nearly a full circle. They were headed south now, and a thick hedge blocked their view of the road they'd just been on. Cassandra wished she could see what the Trailblazer was doing, but took comfort in the thought that if she couldn't see it, the bad guys couldn't see her, either. If things were going as she hoped, their pursuers were speeding northward toward the Rose Bowl. As for Cassandra, she was back on a freeway entrance ramp. Having made an insane but complete circle, she was getting back on the freeway at almost exactly the same place she'd gotten off.

Cassandra merged into the right lane, all the while glancing into the rearview mirror. She couldn't see the Trailblazer. She turned her head. Nothing. She moved to the left lane and drove as fast as the traffic would allow. Had she lost them? She couldn't be sure. Not knowing what else to do, she kept driving.

The Trailblazer still hadn't materialized in the mirror when they reached a major interchange. Cassandra decided to head south, partly because she thought it made sense to change roads from time to time, and partly because it was the route she'd be taking if she were headed home to Beverly Hills. By the time she reached the next big intersection, she'd made a decision.

I'll go to Simone's, she thought. I can't stay long, but if she's home, I'll get her to help me. If she's not home, Caesar and I can at least go inside my place and clean up a little.

Cassandra's dress was shredded, and her leg was bleeding. Caesar had a big scratch on his cheek, and he was probably in shock. He hadn't said a word the whole time they'd been careening around the Arroyo Seco. Cassandra couldn't imagine what he'd been feeling.

"Are you all right?" she asked, looking once more in the rearview mirror.

"I am alive," Caesar replied quietly.

Cassandra looked over at him and was surprised to find him smiling. His eyes were even twinkling. Damn! How could that be?

"I apologize for the speed," she said. "I'm sorry for the unpleasantness."

"You are hardly to blame," Caesar said, "and you are a champion with your chariot."

Stunned, Cassandra found herself smiling, too, and her shoulders relaxed for the first time. She glanced in the mirror again as she exited the freeway onto Los Feliz Boulevard. The gray Trailblazer was nowhere to be seen.

LXIII

"I had planned to return home," Cassandra said, "but I do not believe it is safe. Instead I shall take you to my home, where we can refresh ourselves and plan our next move."

"I never considered that prison 'home,'" replied Caesar, "and I thank you for not returning me there. I am pleased to see more of your country, and I am grateful that I have such an accomplished attendant to guide me."

Cassandra shot Caesar a sidelong glance, wondering why he was flattering her. And suddenly it dawned on her that this was all his fault. If he hadn't tricked her into taking him into the bathroom, insisted on walking in the garden—damn! He'd done it again. He'd turned the tables, far more thoroughly than before.

"You are—you are—" Cassandra began.

"I am what?" She could hear the smile in Caesar's voice.

"You are incorrigible."

Caesar laughed, the same way that he had earlier, a real laugh. Cassandra looked at him. His face was muddy and bleeding, his toga was wet and torn. And still he laughed, as though this were all a big joke.

"You laugh?" she asked. "You laugh when we are in mortal danger?"

"Sometimes that is the best time to laugh," Caesar said.

Cassandra turned right onto Western and dropped down to Sunset Boulevard. That'll shut him up, she thought, and she was right. Caesar rode silently, spellbound by the billboards, the buildings, the people, the traffic, the noise. Cassandra was glad he didn't ask any questions, because how do you explain Hollywood to an ancient Roman?

It was after six when they pulled into Simone's driveway. The light was on in her kitchen. Cassandra eased herself out from behind the steering wheel—her injured leg was starting to get stiff—and limped around to the passenger door. She was helping Caesar get out when Simone burst through her kitchen door.

"Cassandra! What's happened?" She rushed around the car and grabbed Caesar's other arm. "Your friend is bleeding! You've been hurt! Come inside! Come inside!"

They crossed the driveway, and Simone held the door open while Cassandra ushered Caesar into her kitchen. Simone pulled a chair out for him at the Formica table next to the window.

"Sit down," Simone said. "I'll get the first aid kit, and then we'll take a look at those cuts."

Cassandra hesitated. She had always resisted accepting help from others, but she knew she couldn't handle this situation alone. As she watched Simone bustle around her kitchen assembling first aid supplies, she knew she'd have to tell her what was up, and she didn't have the energy to concoct fiction. Simone was going to hear the unvarnished truth. Cassandra hoped to God she'd know what to do with it.

Caesar, meanwhile, was transfixed by Simone's blue macaw, who was, as always, reigning over the kitchen from her perch next to the table.

"I have never seen such a bird as this," he said, stretching his hand toward her beak. "Is it a living creature or a fabricated work of art?"

As if she understood, Cléopâtre bit down hard on Caesar's forefinger. He yelped and jumped back.

Cassandra couldn't help laughing. "She is real," she said. "Her name is Cleopatra."

"She has a personality to match her namesake," said Caesar, shaking his hand. Cassandra grasped it and checked his finger.

"You're lucky she did not draw blood."

Simone stopped rummaging through a drawer to stare at them.

"What language are you speaking?" she asked. "It sounds a little like Italian, but—"

"It's Latin," Cassandra said, realizing that the time for explanations had arrived. Simone looked at her in amazement.

"Latin?" she cried. "*Mon dieu*, Cassandra! Who is this man, the Pope?"

"I wish he were," Cassandra said. "That would be easier to believe than the truth. Your turn to sit down, Simone."

But Simone wouldn't sit. "Start talking, Cassandra," she commanded as she daubed Caesar's cheek with a cotton ball. "Whatever it is you've got to tell me, I'm all ears."

After telling Caesar why she was about to launch into a lengthy monologue, Cassandra told Simone everything. Every once in a while, another shocked "*Mon dieu*" escaped from her lips, especially when she realized whose wounds she was dressing. She kept staring at him and shaking her head, but she didn't interrupt until Cassandra had finished the whole crazy story. Caesar sat patiently, too, and by the time Cassandra was done, all his cuts and scratches had been cleaned and dressed with antiseptic ointment.

Simone picked up a pair of scissors and turned to Cassandra. "Your turn, *chérie*," she said. "Let's see that leg." Carefully, Simone cut away the shredded remains of her pantyhose, peeling the nylon gently out of the long scrape that ran the length of her left thigh.

"Now tell me again what you were saying about good guys and bad guys," Simone said as she cleaned Cassandra's wound. "I want to make sure I'm straight on that part."

"Oh, God! I'm not sure I know anymore. Until all this happened, I was sure that the good guys are Dr. Danicek and the rest of the 'in' group—Eric Barza, John Reynolds, Elizabeth Palmer, Faith Hopper. The bad guys are the ones who chased me here. Both of them work for Hank Morgan, so I think he put them up to it. But I've got to get Caesar back to Danicek, because—ow!"

"Sorry. This is a fairly nasty scrape."

"Because if he doesn't go back to his own time—"

"I know, I know, I got that part. History could change. But here's what I'm wondering. You said that the big guy—Marco in the black jacket—you said he was inside Sonia's estate when you saw him hit a guard. What I'm wondering is—who let him in? Unless he was as torn up as you are, he didn't crawl under the fence."

"No, he wasn't torn up," Cassandra said slowly. "And the gate was closed."

"How does it open?"

"Eric opened it with a remote when we arrived. But there's no way he could be involved. Maybe there's a way to control the gate from the house, but that would mean—oh my God—Sonia?" Cassandra was shocked at herself for assuming she knew so much, when the facts proved so little.

"See what I mean about good guys and bad guys? You could be right about whom you've trusted, but you could also be dead wrong. This whole thing could be far larger and far more complex than you've been told."

Christ. Simone was right. Cassandra couldn't believe Eric might be a turncoat, but what about Sonia, or even Elizabeth? Maybe Elizabeth and Hank had hatched a plan together. He was her husband, after all, and he could just as easily be her partner in crime. And speaking of partners, what was it Hank had said about Steve Tarantino? *The golden age of Denarius is about to begin.* He hadn't been upset at all when Cassandra refused his job offer. Could it be he didn't need her because he'd come up with a better plan—a plot to kidnap Julius Caesar and hold him for ransom? Oh, God. Cassandra's head was spinning.

"My point is this," Simone said calmly. "Until you're sure what's going on, you're better off staying invisible. Caesar doesn't have to go back right this minute, and I think you both would benefit from some time away from the frenzy."

"I'm pretty sure I can trust Danicek and Eric," Cassandra said, desperate for some truth to cling to. "They brought Caesar here, and they're the only ones who can get him back. I think I should call the lab."

"Has it occurred to you that they might be thinking you're a 'bad guy' right now? Think about it."

As Cassandra stared at Simone, tears welled up in her eyes before she could stop them. How had things gone so wrong? Would she get all the blame? She buried her face in her hands and tried to stifle a sob.

"Buck up, Cassandra. Just remember, if you do change history, you'll probably never be born to be held accountable. It could be the perfect crime."

God, she was as bad as Caesar, laughing in the face of calamity. Simone patted Cassandra on the shoulder and reached for a box of Kleenex on the windowsill.

"But seriously, *chérie*," she said, holding out a tissue, "you're the one holding all the aces. You've got Caesar, and if I were you, I wouldn't give him up until I could see a bit more of the big picture. A little time will buy a little clarity, and that will help you know what to do."

"But I've screwed everything up. It was stupid of me to come here.

Now you're in danger, too." Cassandra blotted her eyes with the Kleenex and was shocked to see how much dirt came off her face in the process.

"You did just fine coming here, but obviously you can't stay. It won't take any of them—good guys *and* bad guys—very long to start looking for you in obvious places, like where you live. So here's what you're going to do. As quickly as you can, you're going to wash up and change your clothes. I'll find our friend here something cleaner and less conspicuous to wear. Then we're going to move Boxcar's Corvette out of the garage and put your car in its place. There's some old canvas in there, and a bunch of old scenery and boxes. We'll cover your car up, make it look like it's just a pile of old junk. Then you and Caesar here will take the 'Vette—it's got a full tank of gas, and it was tuned up just last week—and hit the road. Okay?"

"What?" Cassandra asked, wiping her nose. "You're going to trust me with Boxcar's baby?"

"*Merde!* I'm doing much more than that," Simone cried, jumping up from the table. "If what you've told me is true, I'm trusting you to save human civilization!"

She was smiling, but fresh tears sprang to Cassandra's eyes. "Why should you trust me with anything?"

"*Zut alors!* Trust is all we've got in this world! How do you know the sun will come up in the morning? You don't *know*. You *trust*, and the more you trust, the closer you are to walking on water! So stop blubbering! You're taking the car, and you're taking Caesar, and you're going to a hotel. A big, nice hotel, like the Beverly Wilshire. A place where you can vanish easily, call room service, and stay off the street at least until morning. Things will look much clearer then, I guarantee it. I've got three hundred dollars in cash you can take. Have you got any money?"

Cassandra stood up and wiped her eyes. "I left my purse back at the Illingsworth mansion. I don't have my driver's license or cell phone.

But I've got a hundred bucks or so at my place. And I should grab my laptop. And my—" Simone's suggestion made a sort of crazy sense, although the thought of the Beverly Wilshire Hotel made Cassandra shudder. It was where she'd first met Hank, after all. She'd go somewhere else. Los Angeles had no shortage of nice hotels. And she could call Danicek later, when he was back at the lab—

"Just get going," said Simone, jolting Cassandra from her thoughts. "We don't have all night. You go change while I search through Boxcar's stuff for some clothes for Caesar. They're nothing like the same size, but I'll find something."

"Stay here," Cassandra said to Caesar, praying that he wouldn't vanish while their backs were turned. "When I return, we shall embark on another adventure."

LXIV

Cassandra's apartment looked strange in its ordinariness, every-thing exactly as she had left it back when she was a normal college student. The air was stale, and she left the front door ajar as she went into the bathroom. She stripped down to her underwear as she moved. Thanks to Simone, her leg was feeling considerably better. Grabbing a face towel from the rack next to the sink, she wet it under the faucet and gave herself a quick once-over. No time for a shower.

Five minutes later, Cassandra was back in Simone's kitchen wearing dark brown corduroys, a black pullover, and her favorite footwear, a pair of tooled leather cowboy boots. She was carrying her laptop computer, a hairbrush, a black leather jacket, and a USC baseball cap she thought Caesar might like. Caesar, thank God, was still sitting at the Formica table, taking a big bite out of a chicken leg. A glass of red wine was sitting in front of him.

Cassandra had just set her computer on the table when Simone bustled back into the room holding up a pair of black sweat pants. She had some other clothes thrown over her shoulder, something plaid stuffed under her right arm, and a row of safety pins between her lips.

"I've done my best," she managed to say through clenched teeth. "Cassandra, explain that it's time to change."

Caesar rose agreeably when Cassandra told him what they wanted to do. The two women removed the remains of his toga right there in the kitchen. He was wearing a wool tunic underneath, and Cassandra helped Simone pull it over his head. *Voilà!* There stood Julius Caesar, stark naked on the linoleum. Cassandra studiously avoided looking at him, but Cléopâtre emitted a loud wolf whistle.

They all laughed, and Caesar said, "The bird is most definitely well-named. Cleopatra herself uttered similar cries of rapture when my assets were revealed to her."

What a conceited ass, Cassandra thought, and she told Simone what Caesar had said.

"So typical," Simone replied through the pins. "The less they've got, the more they crow about it."

Cassandra chuckled, and Caesar demanded a translation.

"She says she would whistle, too," Cassandra told him, "but she has pins in her mouth." She glanced at Simone, but if she was aware of Cassandra's strategic misinterpretation, she didn't show it.

When Cassandra held a pair of plaid boxer shorts open, Caesar obligingly stepped in. They were several sizes too large, but Simone cinched them around his waist and secured them with a safety pin.

"Fortunately, he's not a buttless wonder," she said as she reached for the sweat pants. "They should stay up."

"She says you have quite a handsome behind," Cassandra said in Latin. Caesar glanced at Simone and smiled. Flattery will get you everywhere, Cassandra said to herself. And she had to admit she was feeling better. Maybe things could still work out.

It took Simone three safety pins to alter the sweat pants sufficiently, and a black knit turtleneck covered up the tucks and bunches. She finished his ensemble off by helping him into a purple Universal Studios hooded sweatshirt, and when he was all dressed, Cassandra placed the red baseball cap on his head.

"He looks like a hillbilly tourist," Simone said, "but it'll have to do."

Caesar was still wearing the leather sandals he'd had on all afternoon. Simone stuffed a pair of suede moccasins and some heavy wool socks into a plastic shopping bag. "Take these in case his feet get cold," she said. "And I'll put what's left of his toga in another bag—can't leave any evidence behind. But right now, go move the cars. The keys to the Corvette are on that hook by the door. The light in the garage is on the left-hand wall."

Leaving her computer on the kitchen table, Cassandra went outside and backed Jeremiah out onto the street. The garage door was unlocked. She pulled it up, flipped on the light, and immediately saw that Simone hadn't been kidding. There was junk stacked everywhere, and the only available walking space was an aisle down the left-hand side, exactly wide enough for her to open the driver's door of the Corvette. She slid behind the steering wheel.

The car started on the first try. Nervously, Cassandra engaged the clutch and made a tentative attempt to shift into reverse. She'd heard stories about the touchiness of expensive sports cars, and, even though she had no audience, she had no desire to reprise Faith's performance of earlier in the afternoon.

Cassandra needn't have worried. The clutch was responsive and smooth, and she eased the car into reverse without a sound. She backed slowly out of the garage onto the street, stopped, shifted smoothly into first gear, and pulled next to the curb.

It'll be fun to drive this thing, she thought, as she set the emergency brake and turned off the engine. She was still amazed that Simone was trusting her with Boxcar's pride and joy. It was a macho-mobile, the ultimate '70s dream car, an irreplaceable classic. And Simone kept it in mint condition, from its sleek red paint job and shiny spoked wheels to its immaculate leather upholstery and fancy dashboard full of lighted dials and gauges. At least it won't look out of place at a snazzy hotel. Cassandra thought with a smile. Valets will be jumping over each other to park this thing.

Jeremiah fit nicely into the space left by the Corvette. Cassandra was just beginning to pull a canvas tarp she'd found on a shelf at the back of the garage over its roof when Simone appeared.

"There's some more canvas in that loft space," she said, pointing upward. "Hold the ladder for me."

By the time they were done, Cassandra's car was completely obscured under a heap of old canvas and burlap, two old scenery flats, three rolled-up carpets, and a full-sized mattress. As a finishing touch, they stacked a bunch of old paint cans and sawhorses in front of it.

"If I hadn't seen your car with my own eyes," Simone said, "I'd never know it was there."

She turned off the garage light, and Cassandra pulled the door down. Simone locked it and slipped a padlock through the hasp. Snapping it shut, she said, "I just don't know what I've done with the key to this lock. Haven't been able to find it for months." She chuckled. "That should buy a few extra minutes!"

When they were back in Simone's kitchen, Cassandra saw how dusty both of them had gotten from the car-concealing escapade. "Just brush yourself off," Simone said. "We're running out of time."

"Are you really going to be okay?" Cassandra asked, "When those goons get here?" She suddenly had visions of Bill taking a crowbar to her garage door. What would prevent him from doing the same thing to Simone?

"I'll be fine, *chérie*," Simone replied. "You can't believe how well I play the hare-brained biddy. I suddenly get extremely hard of hearing, and I keep mixing up my soap opera characters with real people. I'll have something burning in the oven, and the bathtub will be overflowing. Oh, and I don't speak so good ze English—"

Cassandra smiled at the thought of Simone playing the witless crone. She had no doubt her landlady would be good at it.

"But seriously, Cassandra," Simone continued, "I will tell them you were here—alone as far as I could tell, but I wasn't paying much attention. It's safer for both of us if I mix a little truth into the lie. I'll be telling them what they want to hear—that you were here and that you left again. And I really don't know where you're going. You aren't going to tell me." She stuffed Caesar's dirty toga and tunic into a garbage bag.

"They may ransack your apartment, Cassandra, but I'll do my best to be helpful enough to keep them from busting doors." She tied the bag shut. "And if need be, I'll call the cops. Anything to keep them from looking in the garage."

Cassandra looked at Simone with new respect. "You're amazing," she said. "How will I ever be able to repay you for your help?"

"We're in this together now, *chérie*, like it or not. I just wish Boxcar were here to enjoy the excitement, too. He would have—but this is no time to be gabbling. You've got to get out of here."

Handing her the bag containing Caesar's toga, Simone said, "You left your dirty dress in your apartment, right? That's okay, that's okay. You were never in my house, but you did stay for half an hour in yours. Or maybe it was longer—how can an old lady keep these things straight?" She was getting her story down, and Cassandra had no doubt she'd be perfect by the time she needed to use it.

Before five minutes had elapsed, Caesar and Cassandra were ensconced in Boxcar's 'Vette, and a bottle of red wine was tucked behind the passenger's seat. Cassandra's computer was on the floor behind her, along with her leather jacket, her hairbrush, and the bags containing Caesar's old clothes and spare shoes. Cassandra had four hundred dollars in cash in her front right pocket, along with Simone's telephone number written on a slip of paper. "Call between ten and

eleven," she said. "We can compare notes and decide what to do next."
As an afterthought, she also gave Cassandra an email address. "I don't
have a computer," she explained, "but I'll go to the library and check
my messages if I don't hear from you by noon."

"And here's a *Thomas Guide*," Simone added, thrusting a Los Angeles
road atlas through the window, "and there are more maps in the glove
box. The car's registration is in there, too, and there should be some
spare change in the ashtray. Oh, and wait!" She rushed back into the
house.

"You can't possibly leave without this," she said when she returned.
She pressed a small object into Cassandra's hand and gave her shoulder
a parting squeeze. And then she was gone, her last *"Adieu!"* hanging
in the air behind her.

When Cassandra opened her hand, she saw that she was holding
a corkscrew.

LXV

Cassandra handed the corkscrew to Caesar and shifted into first gear. He examined it as they headed south on Maple Street, but he didn't ask any questions. At Wilshire Boulevard, Cassandra knew that by turning right, she could be at the Beverly Wilshire Hotel in a matter of minutes. Simone's suggestion has some merit, she thought, trying to talk herself into going there. In half an hour, she and Caesar could be "invisible," as Simone had put it, with the red wine.

But could they, really? Boxcar's Corvette might give her instant rapport with the parking valets, but fancy hotels look askance at odd couples paying cash. Cassandra had no credit card, and even if she did, would it really be safe to use it? She had no ID, either. Since she couldn't leave Caesar in the car, she'd be checking in anonymously with a strange-looking foreign dude in baggy old sweat pants. The desk clerk would call the manager, and the manager would ask a bunch of prying questions. Even if they were lucky enough to rent a room, they'd create a lasting impression. If anyone came around asking about them, they'd be far too memorable. There's no way, Cassandra thought. We're going someplace else. She had no idea where, but instead of turning right onto Wilshire, she turned left.

"Where are we going?" Caesar asked, and Cassandra decided he deserved a decent answer. He'd been remarkably compliant for the last couple of hours.

"I am not certain," she replied honestly, "but we must stay somewhere safe tonight. My home is not safe."

"Is that place really your home? That woman is not your mother," Caesar said. Cassandra was turning south on La Cienega now, but she still didn't know where they were going.

"I am a student here," she said. "My mother lives in another city, as far from here as Rome is from the Rubicon."

"Why can't we go there?" asked Caesar. "If the road is good, this chariot can certainly cover the distance quickly."

Cassandra looked at Caesar while she waited for the light to change at Pico. What had Simone said about trust? Did it really let you walk on water? If it did, then Caesar must have crossed the Rubicon on foot. How could a man who had first seen an automobile only hours before have the confidence to suggest a 250-mile journey beginning at sundown? And how could he possibly trust a woman he barely knew?

"How can you trust me?" she asked as the light turned green. He'll probably just laugh, she thought, but she was wrong.

"How can you trust me?" Caesar asked in reply, and Cassandra looked at him in surprise. She was the one with the steering wheel, after all. She was in charge. She had the money, the voice, the contacts. She was the one who needed to be trusted, not him. He was at her mercy.

Or was he? Hadn't this man created this entire crazy situation? Hadn't he orchestrated the whole thing, from feigning dizziness to dragging Cassandra under a fence? Maybe she had the steering wheel, but Caesar had found a way to pull all her strings. And now he was as much as telling her he couldn't be trusted.

Damn! It was the one thing the IDES team should have known. If there was anything history had recorded accurately about Julius Caesar, it was that he couldn't be trusted.

"No! I don't trust you!" Cassandra blurted. Caesar laughed as she went on. "I don't trust you at all. You have done nothing but manipulate people since you arrived, and you have never once thought about anyone but yourself."

Caesar's laugh enveloped her again as she turned left onto the ramp to the Santa Monica Freeway.

"I know you were snatched from your world without warning, but have you no decency?"

Again Caesar laughed. Angry, Cassandra stepped on the gas. The freeway was uncharacteristically free of traffic, and by the time she had shifted into fourth gear, the speedometer was hovering over eighty. It worked. Caesar stopped laughing.

"You want to know what we shall do now? Well, too bad. You will just have to sit there and wonder, because if I tell you, the next thing I know, something else will go wrong. I will tell you this much, though. If you think this city is big and bright—well, you have not seen anything yet."

Yes, Caesar had done it again. He planted a notion and let Cassandra run with it. Suddenly she knew exactly where they were going. They were headed to a place where she didn't need a credit card, and she didn't need ID. They were headed to a place where a couple like Cassandra and Caesar would raise no eyebrows, a place where hotel clerks ask no questions and their guests tell no lies. Damned if they weren't headed for Las Vegas, and when she realized she'd made up her mind, Cassandra slowed down. She didn't want to risk having to explain her odd passenger and her lack of driver's license to the California Highway Patrol.

It was six o'clock. If she could avoid getting pulled over by a cop, and if there were no accidents or traffic jams, they could be in Vegas by eleven.

I hope I can figure out how to put gas in this thing, Cassandra muttered to herself, and her mind was instantly awhirl. I need a new schedule, she thought as her stomach twisted into a tight knot. Eric's schedule had covered every minute until eight o'clock. If things hadn't gone so horribly awry, they'd still be following his detailed instructions, still shepherding Caesar from library to garden, and then back to the IDES Lab.

I've got to email Danicek, Cassandra thought next. She wanted to mitigate her new "bad guy" status, but she didn't feel capable of explaining herself over the phone. Email couldn't talk back, didn't allow interruptions. If she managed to compose a message with just the right tone, maybe she could redeem herself along with making arrangements for Caesar's safe return.

But how could she possibly explain Las Vegas? Wouldn't Danicek deem a 500-mile detour an unnecessary risk? He'd been worried about the distance between the IDES Lab and Sonia's house, after all. Now here Cassandra was, doing sixty on Interstate 10 in a red Corvette with Julius Caesar riding shotgun. Was she out of her mind?

But what else could she do? She couldn't go back to the lab, and now that she had Vegas on her mind, no place else seemed quite as safe. She longed for the strength she'd gain from familiar turf. The Monte Carlo was reeling her in, and she had no desire to try to resist the tractor beam of her old Nevada home.

The irony of the situation was not lost on Cassandra. Of all the ridiculous places to take Julius Caesar, wasn't Las Vegas the absolute worst? It probably made Hank Morgan's schemes, whatever they might be, seem positively reasonable. Damn. More impossible stuff to try to explain to Danicek. Help! She screamed to herself silently. This is more than I can handle!

But who could help her? Who in all the world? Cassandra had already tapped Simone, already exposed her to danger. Calling her mother was out of the question, and Dr. Martinelli was no good, either. She needed someone who couldn't be hurt, someone with resources equal to Hank's. She needed someone rich and strong.

"I need Alex Hunt," Cassandra said out loud. "If the chicken king can't help us, nobody can." Caesar looked at her questioningly, but when she wasn't forthcoming with a translation, he fell back to watching the highway ahead. Cassandra retreated into her thoughts, hoping desperately that she had Alex's telephone number in her computer case. Her date book was stuck in the side compartment, and she kept business cards in a zippered pocket inside the cover. Had she put Alex's card there after the coin auction?

Cassandra pulled off the freeway in Covina, after she caught sight of a shopping mall with fast-food restaurants dotting the parking lot. She wanted a telephone she could use while keeping an eye on Caesar, and she found one between a Starbucks and a bagel shop.

Cassandra heaved a sigh of relief when she found that she had indeed stashed the chicken tycoon's business card in her date book. After explaining to Caesar as well as she could, she climbed out of the car and walked over to the telephone booth. She punched in the long string of numbers on Alex's card. "Call me anytime," he had said, and Cassandra wondered whether she'd be waking him up in Macau.

Alex was wide awake in Taipei. "Where are you?" he asked.

"Covina. In a parking lot next to the San Bernardino Freeway," she said. "I need your help."

"Nothing like cutting right to the chase, sweetheart. How can your funny old uncle be of service?"

Cassandra hadn't rehearsed what to say to Alex, hadn't even thought about how much to reveal about her unusual cargo. She'd already committed a major security breach by telling all to Simone, and she found herself balking at doing it again. The effect of her sudden attack of conscience was that she stammered and stuttered until Alex cut in.

"Cassandra," he said, "I have no idea what you're trying to tell me, but it's obvious that you're scared. Is someone trying to hurt you?"

"I think it's Hank Morgan," was all she could manage in reply.

Alex was silent a moment. "Are you in immediate danger?"

"No. Some goons in a gray SUV chased me around Pasadena, but I managed to lose them. Now I'm on my way to Las Vegas. Nobody's following me at the moment."

There was another pause on the other end of the line, and Cassandra waited for Alex to ask her for the details. She was still debating whether to tell him about Caesar when he spoke again.

"I don't know whether this has anything to do with what you're mixed up in, but Hank Morgan called me a couple of weeks ago. He tried to sell me on a plan to get hold of technology being funded by the Illingsworth—"

"That's it!" Cassandra blurted. "That's the IDES Project! What I told you at the auction was just a cover story. Hank made Elizabeth tell him the truth, and now I think he's trying to, trying to—kidnap Julius Caesar!"

"What?"

"I know it sounds crazy, but it's true! You've got to help me!" There was nothing left for Cassandra to do but to tell him the rest of the story. She kept her eye on Caesar as she talked. He had obviously seized the opportunity her absence provided to indulge his curiosity. First, the headlights flashed off and on, and a minute later, the radio antenna slowly rose and receded. Good thing I removed the keys from the ignition, she thought, and she hoped he wouldn't discover the hand brake until she got off the phone.

"I'm looking at him right now," Cassandra concluded. "He's real, and I'm scared, and I don't know what to do anymore." Her voice trailed off, and she couldn't tell whether she'd just sealed her fate or secured assistance. Alex's silence was unnerving, but just as Cassandra was beginning to regret calling him, he spoke.

"You're on your way to Vegas in a car no one will recognize?"

"Yes." She told him about Boxcar's baby as she watched the dome light flicker off and on inside it.

"Well, keep going. As soon as we hang up, get back on the road. Go directly to Caesars, and give the doorman—don't get out of your car—my name at the front entrance. Once you do that, you'll be taken care of. They'll take your car, show you to a suite, and give you whatever you need. I mean it—food, clothes, whatever."

"But—"

"Shh. Let me finish. I'll send my security chief—her name is Rachel Tan—to meet you in a few hours or tomorrow morning at the latest. She'll look after both of you. And I'll get there, too, but it'll take me a while. As I said, I'm in Taipei."

"But Danicek's got to know, and John Reynolds—"

"I'll take care of them. Give me their numbers. Don't call them or anybody else. Don't send email."

Cassandra explained how she'd left things with Simone, and Alex said he'd take care of her, too, and provide security at her house. He was even dispatching a car to watch Cassandra's mother's place, just in case somebody had the bright idea to check her old home for leads.

"I wouldn't be quite as worried if it weren't for Steve Tarantino," Alex said. "He's got plenty of money and plenty of juice. Paired with a determined sonofabitch like Hank, you've got a dangerous combination."

When she hung up, Cassandra felt a strange mixture of relief and terror wash over her. She'd broken her promise to Danicek yet again, and she'd enlisted the aid of a powerful man she hardly knew. Her actions had progressed far beyond the realm of anything she could ever defend as responsible, but at the same time, they made a sort of crazy sense. Simone had been right when she questioned whether Cassandra's knowledge was sufficient to judge who was "good" and who was "bad." All she could do was cling to the belief that whatever else happened, Caesar had to return to 44 BC on the evening of March twentieth, no later than seven o'clock.

As Cassandra stepped off the curb, a young man passed in front of her carrying a little cardboard tray with two tall paper cups wedged into it. Starbucks was open, even though the bagel store next to it was locked and dark. We've got a long trip, she thought, and even though a jolt of caffeine was probably the last thing she needed, she decided to get one anyway.

Cassandra returned to the Corvette just as Caesar's hand was reaching for the emergency brake.

"*No!*" she commanded with vehemence that surprised both of them. "*It is a brake, and we are on a slope!*" Amazingly, Caesar obeyed her without resistance, and she told him that if she could trust him not to destroy their vehicle in her absence, she was going to procure something to drink. Returning to Starbucks, she ordered two large caffe lattes. As an afterthought, she asked the clerk to throw a handful of chocolate truffles into a bag. Back in the driver's seat, she handed her haul to Caesar. She could tell he was fascinated by the bag and the cups. She pulled back onto Interstate 10, explaining as she drove that the little hole in the cup's plastic lid was there to drink through.

"Drinking in a chariot is a novel experience for me," Caesar commented. "But of course this vehicle is not really a chariot but a litter. A fast litter on wheels."

Once again, Cassandra was amazed that Caesar didn't ask questions, especially since she knew his curiosity was alive and well. Wasn't he baffled as to how the car moved without horses? Shouldn't a man from a world of pottery have a few questions about paper bags and plastic lids?

"Haven't you wondered what propels this litter?" Cassandra asked, and even as the words passed her lips, she suddenly understood the source of Caesar's apparent lack of curiosity. Asking questions not only reveals ignorance, but also places the asker firmly in a subservient position. Caesar had no lack of inquisitiveness. He just had an overweening desire to be in charge.

"If you wish to explain the intricacies of your country's machinery, I shall be pleased to listen," said Caesar, "but in fact, the most important thing is that it moves like the wind, and that you are a competent pilot." He reached into the paper bag and pulled out a truffle. "And you have selected delectable morsels to eat, too," he added.

"You had better save me some," Cassandra said, and they drove on into the night, heading north on Interstate 15 over Cajon Pass and down into the Mojave Desert.

LXVI

Cassandra hadn't planned to exit the highway at Zzyzx Road, but somewhere in the dark past Barstow, a big tanker truck pulled in front of the Corvette from the slow lane without warning. It wasn't a big deal—at least not for people accustomed to internal combustion engines, rubber tires, and brake shoes. A bit of a screech, that was all. Then Cassandra changed lanes, and the journey continued.

She stole a look at Caesar after she passed the truck. He was staring straight ahead, as he had been on most of the journey. But now something was different about the set of his jaw. Cassandra glanced down. Caesar was gripping the sides of his bucket seat so hard his knuckles had turned white.

Fear. Caesar couldn't admit to it. Cassandra was more certain of that than of anything else she had learned about the man in six months of intensive study. But just because you can't admit something, it doesn't mean you don't feel it. She'd been pissed at the guy ever since he spat at her feet, but seeing his clenched jaw and white knuckles—she knew what they meant more clearly and indisputably than if he had told her.

Caesar's fear dissolved Cassandra's anger. She was almost sorry to see it go, because, as her resentment ebbed, in its place rose something far more difficult to manage: empathy. She couldn't permit herself to call it pity—didn't even want to admit it might be compassion. She couldn't let her guard down, not with this guy. But no resolve could prevent her from thinking about what it must be like for a person to have so many points of reference suddenly snatched away. Yes, the man was a rude control freak, but he had also been whisked to an utterly foreign time and place without his permission.

She glanced at her passenger again. This time he caught her looking, and their eyes met. Cassandra turned her gaze back on the road. She'd already given up any hope of getting Caesar to fill in historical gaps or solve ancient mysteries. Now she wondered whether she'd ever even have a normal conversation with him—on any topic.

Forget all that, she commanded herself. All that matters is getting Caesar back to the IDES Lab in time to go back to—she stole another look. Caesar was staring straight ahead again.

God. In two days, he'd be dead. Except that wasn't true. Julius Caesar was already dead. He'd been dead for over two thousand years, and nothing could change it.

"Don't forget," Danicek had said. "Time travel is a Gordian knot, and TESA can cut through only part of it. Expect to be disoriented, and hold fast to the unalterable truth that Julius Caesar has already died. Withholding information is not cruelty, but rather compassionate etiquette. Be happy that we are giving him four extra days of life."

Whether those days were worth living was a separate question. Would a wild tiger accept an offer of four extra days if it had to spend them pacing in a cage? As another wave of empathy rippled through Cassandra, the sign for Zzyzx Road appeared in her headlights. She moved to the right lane. A moment later, she and Caesar were bumping down the narrow road into the darkness. As soon as the road curved behind a hill, she pulled the Corvette to a stop.

Cassandra killed the engine and headlights, opened the door, and hoisted herself up and out of the low-slung car. Her right leg was still stiff and sore, but she limped a few feet into the chilly desert night and paused next to a clump of saltbush. She wrapped her arms around herself, grateful that she'd grabbed her leather jacket on her way out of the guest house. Behind her, a door slammed. She listened to Caesar's footsteps as he crunched through the crusty sand. He stopped when he reached her side.

They stood there together in the dark stillness. A tiny sliver of moon had risen on the eastern horizon, and the stars, free of urban competition, blazed in a diamond canopy across the cloudless sky. This is what Cassandra loved—the pristine splendor of wilderness. It always made her feel infinitesimally tiny and unfathomably huge at the same time. *Nothing and everything.*

She listened to Caesar breathe next to her in the silence. The man was not a phantom, and he wasn't two thousand years old. He wasn't *imperator, dictator,* or *pontifex maximus,* either. In twentieth-century terms, he was a fifty-five-year-old tourist in gray sweatpants, a Universal Studios sweatshirt, and a USC baseball cap. By far the most important thing about him was that he was alive.

"The Great Bear."

Cassandra turned her head at Caesar's words.

"At last, a familiar friend."

As she gazed at his profile, starlight glistened on a tear. It stole down Caesar's cheek.

Cassandra's heart took an extra beat. She couldn't resist the feeling now—couldn't deny that she felt sorry for the man. She raised her right hand. Softly—tentatively—she patted his upper arm.

Instantly, Caesar's left arm shot around her shoulder. He pulled her close, his grip almost—but not quite—painful. Cassandra's heart crashed against her ribcage.

Oh my God! What have I done? What does he think? What is he going to do? I should never have left the highway—

Wild thoughts were still tumbling through her brain when Caesar abruptly let go.

"I appreciate the quiet," Caesar said, "but we still have a journey ahead. Let us continue."

Damn! He still thought he was in charge. How had she let herself pity this guy?

LXVII

C aesars Palace. Caesar was looking straight at the big marquee, but Cassandra didn't ask him how it made him feel. He wouldn't answer even if she had, so what was the point?

While she waited for a taxi to disgorge a fat family in cargo shorts and matching Grand Canyon T-shirts, Cassandra glanced at Julius Caesar. He had shifted his gaze from the marquee to the fat family. The father's shirt was a couple of sizes too small, and his shorts were waging a losing skirmish with his paunch. Turning his back to the Corvette, he bent over to pick up his sports bag. The shorts retreated. Cassandra cringed. She had never seen it mentioned in ancient texts, but she was willing to bet that showing crack is tacky in any century.

On the other hand, one might think the same thing about spitting, and one might be wrong. Cassandra still wasn't sure why Caesar had spat on the floor right in front of her when she had just greeted him with the words she had worked so hard to hone into a warm and perfect welcome. Even though she had braced herself for unexpected—and possibly inexplicable—behavior, she couldn't prevent the feeling of offense that immediately seized her. It was a natural response to an act that—to twentieth-century sensibilities—seemed like intentional rudeness.

Later, Cassandra wondered about other possible motives. Caesar had, after all, just been yanked from the Ides of March, 44 BC, and plunked down not only two thousand years later but also six thousand miles from Rome. Nausea was one plausible side effect, even though Danicek had told her that Skipper hadn't displayed any symptoms of it when he was transported. Yes, Skipper was a dog, but all the dogs Cassandra had ever known threw up regularly, often with no apparent cause. If time travel caused queasiness, surely it would have induced it in a cocker spaniel.

Cassandra still didn't know how to interpret Caesar's response to her well-rehearsed and painstakingly planned salutation. Her fellow team members could speculate all they wanted about reasons ancient Romans might expectorate in public, but unless Caesar himself decided to explain, it would remain an annoying mystery.

Whatever Caesar's motive for his possibly rude act, Cassandra wished he could have spent his full four days in the modern world without being treated to a view of Mr. Grand Canyon's grand canyon. If things had gone as planned, it never would have happened. Instead, they would be relaxing right now in the IDES Lab's living room after a leisurely dinner of lobster Thermidor, beef Wellington, and a raspberry chocolate ganache tart. Maybe sipping Chartreuse, maybe listening to Danicek on the violin. Caesar's visit to the present was supposed to be as untraumatic as possible. How many times had Danicek stressed that? It was the one thing he and Faith agreed on, and Cassandra knew it was her job to help. She wasn't completely thrilled about her "hostess" role, but for the sake of science and knowledge, she was ready to do her part.

Instead, here she was in Las Vegas, hoping that Alex Hunt had succeeded in setting up a temporary hideaway. A few hours should be long enough to figure out how to get Caesar back to the IDES Lab before it was too late. Cassandra needed a break from looking over her shoulder.

That thought made her look over her left shoulder, even though she hadn't seen the gray Trailblazer since she managed to ditch it near the Rose Bowl. Nobody besides Alex and Simone knew that she was driving the Corvette. Simone—a talented liar—had vowed to release false information if confronted. Cassandra had no choice but to trust Alex. All evidence suggested that he was a good guy, but she had met him only twice. The first time was right here at Caesars Palace.

The taxi pulled away. Taking advantage of the momentary vacuum and the Corvette's horsepower, Cassandra zipped the car into a spot at the curb under the porte-cochere. She reached for the door handle, but before she could do anything with it, black suits sent both windows into full eclipse. Caesar shot Cassandra an ever-so-slightly uneasy look. Thank God, she thought. A bit of human frailty makes him considerably more likable.

"As I told you—" Cassandra began, although she was well aware that her earlier explanation in Latin had done a poor job of preparing him for the spectacle swirling around him. How do you explain the Las Vegas Strip to a man who lives by lamplight? And what if the man acts like he doesn't want to know, anyway?

Both doors swung open before she could finish her sentence.

"Good evening, Miss Fleury and Mr. Spinoza," the suit on Cassandra's side said. "Welcome to Caesars."

LXVIII

Caesar's ears perked up when he heard the word "Caesars." He had been listening to his hosts (*captors* would, of course, be the more accurate word) converse for two days now, and he had learned far more than he permitted them to realize. "SEE-ZAR" was what they called him—that had been simple to resolve. At first, he thought it was a moniker they had invented, but as he listened to them chatter among themselves, he gradually realized it was a bastardization of his *cognomen*. Caesar could now recognize a few other words, too, including "yah" and "nah" and "o-kei." These are the simple words in any language—agreement and disagreement form the basis of human conversation. He had been concentrating on nouns—food words were the easiest—when the events of this afternoon abruptly changed his priorities. Deciphering a foreign tongue is a worthy pastime for a prisoner, as long as the prisoner never takes one eye off escape.

Listening to a new language had also allowed Caesar to concentrate on issues other than life or death. His first thought—after he realized that he was no longer listening to Quintus Pollio's whiny drawl in the *curia Pompei*—was that he was dead. The woman shimmering before

361

him was Venus, ready to welcome him at last into the pantheon. Then he slipped and staggered—fell forward. Venus and a man in strange dress grabbed him by the arms—prevented him from striking the floor. A slick lead-colored floor that seemed to be made of glass. Caesar gasped for breath, regained his balance. His left knee throbbed, and the dull ache in his right back molar persisted.

Could this be immortality? Apparently, apotheosis was not the pain reliever Caesar had always assumed it would be.

Dangerous phenomena, assumptions. The woman had looked like Venus. She still did, from the neck up. If she had never changed her clothes or opened her mouth, Caesar might well have continued to believe she was a goddess.

The moment Cassandra spoke, his suspicion that he was still dwelling in mortal realms gained strength. It was not, however, her words that made Caesar doubt her divinity. She uttered them in intelligible—if oddly Gallic-sounding—Latin. Her message was acceptable, too, although not precisely what Caesar would have expected if he had just taken a ferry ride to the far side of the Styx. He had always thought of death as a confrontation with the unknown. He could accept the possibility that a sore joint and a toothache might survive the crossover—perhaps even persist in Sisyphean perpetuity.

Pain, perhaps, but not fear. Death cannot conquer life without killing fear in the process. That is how Caesar knew that this creature was an attractive but obvious fraud. She radiated fear as perceptibly as the sun gives off heat.

And it wasn't even the angry fear of a cornered dog. No bared teeth on this girl, only the quivering lips of a decidedly mortal female. Her voice carried a tremor when she spoke.

"Hail, Caesar. The people of America bid you welcome."

Here was a second clue that Caesar might yet be a mortal. He had never heard of "America," but it could well be an island west of the

Hesperides. Or perhaps a country to the east—beyond the silk people?

Then again, perhaps "America" was a region of the underworld, undocumented in the realms of light. Perhaps Caesar was dead after all. He was still reconsidering this possibility when the man in dark breeches barked a command at Cassandra in a brutish tongue.

By Pollux! In spite of her golden hair, lapis eyes, and gossamer gown, the woman was a slave. And not only a slave, but the property of a man clearly less culturally advanced than the rubes of northern Britain. That, combined with a fresh stab of pain in Caesar's knee, convinced him—for the moment, at least—to abandon the last shred of hope that he had entered eternity. Where he was and how he had gotten there, he had no clue, but that only heightened the importance of the tenets he had lived his life by. If you are lost and unarmed, take stock of your surroundings. Find order in the chaos. Maintain unfailing vigilance. Seek opportunity, and seize it when it appears. All the rules add up to one basic goal: *Gain control.*

LXIX

C aesar did not like admitting it, but he had pegged Cassandra wrong. She was not a slave. What, exactly, her relationship with Duckhead was, he still had not construed. The man was clearly her superior in some respects, but he was not her father, and he was not her husband. Most importantly, he was not her owner. The woman had autonomy.

Of primary value to Caesar was that Cassandra spoke Latin. That skill was obviously a rarity in this country, and now that he had escaped Duckhead's compound, an interpreter was vital. While he could decipher some words on walls and buildings, the vernacular was completely foreign. His best guess so far was that he had somehow been transported to an unfamiliar region of Africa. That explained the expanse of desert he had just crossed in the swift horseless vehicle. It could also explain the enormous black pyramid and illuminated Sphinx not too far from where he was at this moment. It might even explain the huge wall with torches spelling out his name.

Cassandra had dutifully relayed Duckhead's message that Caesar had supposedly traveled through time—two thousand years into the future. If true, it offered easy rationalization for the self-propelling machines, flameless torches, absence of animals, and ghastly smells. On the other hand, it was just the sort of story Caesar himself might tell a prisoner to confuse and disorient him. For now, he planned to stick with his working belief that physical distance was the only thing separating him from Rome. It would take more than a tall barbarian with oiled hair to convince Caesar that he had also journeyed across twenty centuries.

The men in black costume escorted Caesar and Cassandra into a small chamber with a marble floor and reflective walls. They were clearer than a mountain tarn on a calm day, and they were vertical. Dressed as he was in the soft elastic garments that Cassandra and her elderly friend had insisted upon, not to mention the ridiculous hat, it took Caesar a moment to realize that he was looking at a reflection of his own person. He did his best not to stare, looking instead at Cassandra. Their eyes met in the glass. Caesar held her gaze. She looked away when the doors of the chamber—pushed by an invisible hand—slid closed. The chamber vibrated, and red characters appeared on a small black panel next to the door. No one spoke until the doors parted, revealing an entirely different vista from the one they had closed on. One more explanation to elicit from Cassandra, but it was getting progressively more challenging to extract information without asking direct questions. In the meantime, Caesar permitted the scene that met his eyes to turn his lips up in a smile.

LXX

Beginning at a tender age, Cassandra had learned that many of Las Vegas's most fabulous wonders lay behind closed doors. Thanks to her stepfather, who had a hobby of attaching himself to whales and trust fund babies, she got quite a few peeks inside spectacular hotel accommodations and uber-exclusive venues up and down the Strip. Once, Malcolm even wangled an invitation to a bat mitzvah where the guests got to ride in a chariot pulled by two white tigers. But even with a host of fantastic images stored away in her memory banks, Cassandra had to apply conscious effort to keep her jaw in place the first time—as Alex Hunt's guest—she stepped into the Palatine Suite.

Now, eight months later, she watched the smile spread across Caesar's face as he took in the courtyard ringed with gold-crowned columns of purple porphyry. In the center, a golden Neptune sat on a throne of fanciful shells, a trident in his hand and a frolicking hippocampus at his feet. Water spilled over the statue into a reflecting pond tiled with a glittering mosaic of whimsical undersea creatures. Six enormous red-figured amphorae flanked the fountain, each one boasting a splendid arrangement of fresh flowers. The scent of roses and gardenias wafted over them.

She was still watching Caesar take in his surroundings when an Italianate Adonis in a tux appeared in an archway to their right. Cassandra recognized him. The night she was here with Alex Hunt, this guy had served the wine.

"Welcome to the Palatine, Mr. Spinoza," the man said, nodding at him with a practiced touch of deference. "Welcome *back*, Miss Fleury." He gave her the same nod, but Cassandra couldn't help noticing that his tone changed ever so slightly. She knew why, too, and she bristled.

It wasn't fair! All Alex and Cassandra had done was to share a Chateaubriand and a bottle of pinot noir. It didn't matter. She'd known even then that up and down the Strip, she'd forever be branded a—

"I am Baldassare," the butler went on, "here to attend your every wish. I would be pleased to acquaint you with the premises. Our Japanese chef is preparing a repast in the drawing room for your refreshment."

The drawing room. Cassandra shook off her irritation. She had loved being invited into the drawing room the last time she was here. It made her feel like she was dining with royalty.

And that's exactly what I'm doing tonight, she told herself. If having Julius Caesar for your date doesn't give you regal status, nothing could. She straightened her shoulders and lifted her chin. If this piece of Eurotrash was going to yank her chain with condescending inflection, she'd raise him one, and not only with her nose.

"We'll freshen up first," Cassandra said. "You are dismissed."

Surprised, Baldassare raised an eyebrow and opened his mouth. Then he closed it again, ducked his head at each of them, turned on his well-polished heels, and vanished through the archway.

When Cassandra turned to Caesar, he was staring at her. She could see thoughts moving behind his eyes, but she knew it was pointless to ask what he was thinking. She hadn't learned as much as she had wanted about him in the last twenty-four hours, but he'd made one thing abundantly clear: Caesar didn't like questions—in either direction.

"This way." Cassandra pointed toward the archway on the other side of the colonnade. Together they walked into a wide hall that wouldn't have looked much out of place in the Vatican Museum. Paintings and statuary lined the walls, punctuated by more awe-inspiring flower arrangements. Bypassing the sumptuously decorated living room and library on the right and left, Cassandra steered Caesar farther down the hall. Alex had given her an exhaustive tour of all 15,000 square feet during her last visit, but she wasn't in a mood to show Caesar the beauty salon, screening room, billiards room, solarium, cigar lounge, or even the indoor swimming pool. Even though she'd cleaned herself up a little back at her place, the scrape on her right thigh needed more attention. No doubt Caesar would appreciate a chance to wash up, too. The thick white terrycloth robes Cassandra knew were waiting in the bathrooms were just what both of them needed. If the medicine cabinets weren't stocked with first aid supplies, Baldassare could be summoned to remedy the problem.

Caesar followed Cassandra into the first bedroom suite. The lights were already on, and Pachelbel was emanating softly from unseen speakers. A fire flickered invitingly in the ornately carved stone fireplace. An elaborately draped canopy shaded a huge four-poster bed piled high with pillows on top of a puffy white duvet. Caesar caught up with Cassandra at the entrance to the bathroom. He grabbed her wrist.

"You have hidden much from me."

Cassandra pulled her hand away and turned to face him.

"I have hidden nothing," she said. "You have chosen not to learn."

"*Macte!*" Caesar smiled.

What? Cassandra stared at his smile. Had he really just said "touché?" To *her*? And his grin looked genuinely friendly—completely unlike any expression she'd seen on his face before.

"You can wash in here," Cassandra said. A smile spread on her face as she pulled a robe from the closet by the door. Was it possible this interchange was the beginning of a real conversation?

"Change into this if you like," she said.

"I do like," Caesar said, looking directly into her eyes.

On the long marble counter between the sinks, a gold tray held an astonishing variety of high-end toiletries along with brushes, combs, a razor, a curling iron, a flat iron, and a hair dryer. Cassandra peeled the wrapper off a bar of soap and unscrewed the lid on a bottle of after-shave lotion. Danicek had been in charge of demonstrating bathroom technology for Caesar back at the IDES Lab. She hoped to God that Caesar had paid enough attention. Just to be sure he could at least use the sink, she turned the faucets on and off.

"If you need me, I shall be in the room across the hall." Cassandra left before Caesar could say anything in reply.

LXXI

As he listened to Cassandra cross the bedroom and close the door behind her, Caesar examined himself in the enormous reflective wall above the basins. The garments Cassandra and Birdwoman had dressed him in were hideous, but the fabric was amazing. Softer than the finest wool, it stretched like bread dough and then shrank back to its original shape. In addition, the tunic had been dyed a deeper purple than the richest Tyrian. These people were barbarians, but they possessed some enviable crafts.

Caesar removed the ridiculous duck-billed hat—nothing at all appealing about *that*—and set it on the counter next to the tray of flasks and tools. For the thousandth time since his abrupt arrival in this country, he tried to piece together the puzzle of what had happened. Was this strange sequence of events what old Spurinna had been yammering about?

"Be careful—the Ides are come," the *haruspex* had said, with the irritating vagueness so typical of augury. Earlier, Calpurnia had begged Caesar to stay home, but of course it was only her madness talking. Terentia and the other maids claimed she was now a mouthpiece for the gods, but if Caesar stayed home every time Calpurnia voiced her fears, he would spend his life in bed.

Still, he could not suppress a twinge of unease when three more such warnings fell on his ears. They were all equally vague, but they came from sources completely disconnected from his wife and the *haruspex*. Caesar was not one to bend like a reed in the face of imagined threats, but he was well aware that the direction of a breeze often foretells the path of a powerful wind. He respected the importance of tiny whispers and small synchronicities. The challenge—and what Caesar considered his greatest talent—lay in recognizing which subtle indicators deserved attention and which should be ignored. Whether he could have avoided this baffling and inconvenient trip, he might never know. He could not deny that he had been warned.

Caesar leaned forward and gazed at his own face—at once so familiar and so alien. He had never observed it in such great detail under such brilliant lights. *By Pollux*, the lamps and mirrors are fabulous here, he thought. So are the razors, for that matter. Caesar had never had a shave closer than the one Duckhead gave him back at his compound. Perhaps Cassandra could be drafted for the task in the morning.

Cassandra. Who—and *what*—was she? At Duckhead's compound and later at the villa of his patroness, she acted like a servant. At the house they escaped to, Birdwoman treated her like a daughter. Here in this palace, Cassandra was clearly queen. It all added up to a sharp gray fin on the surface of the sea. Dolphin, monster, or something else entirely? Without knowing what lurked beneath, one could only guess.

Once again, Caesar considered the question of time travel. Perhaps Duckhead was not lying when he claimed that he transported him to the distant future. It did not mean that Duckhead had actually achieved the impossible—merely that he thought he had. He *believed* he was telling the truth, and his colleagues seemed equally convinced.

If Duckhead were mistaken, it made little difference in practical terms. Fiercely held convictions—regardless of fact—were like religion. What did it matter whether Olympus truly housed the pantheon? As long as the gods flourished in the minds of believers, their power was indisputable.

Pah! It was all moot. Caesar could no more assess Duckhead's claims than he could be certain what year it was or in what country he stood. All he could do was what he had been doing since he arrived: watch, wait, and build strength.

That thought made Caesar reach into the pouch sewn into the front of the purple tunic. He had lacked sufficient time to be selective back in Birdwoman's kitchen, but he had still managed to palm something just after the two women had finished clothing him.

Caesar examined his prize under the bright lights. It was a short, pointed knife, sharpened to a fine edge on one side. Its smooth black handle fit snugly in his palm. He smiled. It had taken him well over twenty-four hours, but he had achieved the first goal he set for himself after he arrived in this alien place.

He had a weapon that could kill.

LXXII

C assandra turned in front of the full-length mirrors in the dressing area. The scrape running down her right thigh wasn't as deep as it had looked back at Simone's house. It was still painful, but the shower had cleaned it up nicely—no need for a new bandage. She slipped into a thick terrycloth robe and cinched it around her waist. A pair of plush slippers looked inviting, but luxuriant wool carpet felt too good on her bare feet to bother. Piling her hair on top of her head, she clipped it in place with a big gold butterfly clip she found among all the toiletries on the counter. That'll have to do, she told herself. Caesar had already been alone too long.

Even though he couldn't escape the Palatine Suite without battling his way past their two personal bodyguards and the entire security staff of Caesars Palace, Cassandra was still uneasy. She thought again about how Caesar had almost released the Corvette's parking brake while she ducked inside the Starbucks in West Covina. Thank God she'd left the car in gear and taken the key. Not only was the guy smart and fearless, he was good at seizing small advantages. Like at breakfast, when Caesar turned the tables on all of them—

375

Holy crap! Her pulse sped up as Cassandra realized she'd left him alone for more than twenty minutes.

Her heart rate slowed when she spotted Caesar in the library they'd passed on their way to the bedroom suites. Clad in a white robe identical to hers, he was standing—his back toward her—in front of a large globe on a dark mahogany stand. Cassandra walked over and stood beside him.

"The world," she said. She was tempted to point to Italy—it was directly in front of them—but she resisted. Danicek had issued strict orders not to reveal certain details of Caesar's near future. Cassandra had already disobeyed far too many of Danicek's mandates to expect forgiveness, but she wasn't about to break the rule that might put the whole universe in jeopardy.

"Look at this," she said, mostly to draw Caesar's attention away from the spherical map of the world. She walked to the wall of floor-to-ceiling drapes and located the control panel at one end. She pressed a button. The curtains parted, sliding silently on an overhead track. In a moment, Caesar and Cassandra were standing over the glittering panorama of the Las Vegas Strip.

"My province," she said. "I had not expected to be able to show it to you, but the events of today—"

Cassandra paused to glance at her companion. Caesar, mesmerized by the neon extravaganza below him, did not return her gaze. That was okay. While he admired Vegas, Cassandra could admire him. He looked regal—or should she say imperial?—in his white robe. The Trojans baseball cap and purple sweatshirt had done too good a job of masking his aristocratic face and warrior's physique. She leaned a bit closer and breathed in. *Mmm.* He smelled great, if not as exotic as he had when he first materialized.

Caesar's scent was one of the most surprising features of his arrival, even if it wasn't the most important. Although the IDES team had made every effort to think of tiny details, what Caesar might smell like had never been discussed. If Cassandra had thought about it, she would have guessed he'd smell like sweat. Sure, Romans bathed, but wasn't extreme aversion to natural body odor a peculiarly American fetish? She'd heard French people laughing about it when she served them drinks at the Monte Carlo. She rarely let on that she could understand their conversations. It was far too entertaining to learn their unedited opinions about the United States.

It must have been the subliminal expectation that Caesar would smell like a ripe Frenchman that gave Cassandra's nose such a shock. All the while she and Danicek were trying to prevent their visitor from falling on his face, his aroma was wafting over her. The man smelled fantastic. She wondered what combination of spices and essential oils created a fragrance that evoked mass in a Catholic church and her stepfather's Yves Saint Laurent aftershave at the same time.

As she stood next to Caesar with all of Las Vegas at their feet, Cassandra couldn't deny that her attitude toward him had changed dramatically over the last several hours. Part of it was the conversation that had emerged while they were catching their breaths at Simone's house. She'd also been surprised by Caesar's willingness—enthusiasm, even—to put on Boxcar's clothes. And then there was their little detour down Zzyzx Road. Cassandra couldn't prevent her heart from warming when he called the Big Dipper a familiar friend.

She studied his chiseled profile—at once so classic and so contemporary in the white robe. He studied the view below him, and she wondered once again how he could keep himself from asking questions. Cassandra had a thousand of them.

"What are you thinking?" she asked.

He turned to face her. "You have so many questions."

"Have you none?" she asked.

"Yet another."

Cassandra sighed and shrugged. Caesar smiled.

"I do have one question. I hope you have an answer."

"I hope so, too."

What would this one question be, when he must have so many?

"Is there something to eat?"

LXXIII

Andrew Danicek lit a cigarette from the stub of his last. That made eight in the last hour. If ever there was an excuse for chain smoking, Julius Caesar's abduction had to be it.

He took a long drag on the new Marlboro.

Julius Caesar was gone. The worst possible scenario, except perhaps the one he was trapped in right now. Smoking in his office at the IDES Lab, completely incapable of doing anything to change—or even mitigate—what had happened at the Illingsworth estate three hours earlier. All he could do was wait and hope, the two activities he most detested.

As Andrew knocked ash off the end of his cigarette, his phone buzzed.

He grabbed the phone and checked its screen.

Restricted number.

Damn. He held the phone to his ear.

"Hello."

"Dr. Andrew Danicek?"

"Yes. Who is this?"

"Alexander Hunt. I'm calling to arrange the return of—your guest."

"Who are you?"

"As I just said, I'm Alex Hunt. I need to know—"

"Where are you?"

"Slow down. I need to know—"

"I need to know some things, too. If you are indeed holding—my guest—I need to know your location. I can arrange for transport—"

"I'll be making the arrangements, Dr. Danicek. All you need to do is sit tight."

Sit tight? Was he hearing right? Who was this yahoo, anyway?

"I'm in charge here, Mr.—whoever you are. If there are arrangements to be made, I will make them."

Silence.

"Are you there?" Andrew asked.

"Yes. I will require—"

Andrew's anger got the better of him. "What is this, some kind of fucking ransom demand?"

Silence.

"Hello?" he said. "Are you there?"

Silence.

He yanked the phone from his ear and looked at the screen.

Call ended.

The guy had hung up. Andrew looked incredulously at the cell phone in his hand. Had he really just blown his one and only chance to salvage the IDES Project?

God damn it.

He slammed the phone down on the table and slumped into his chair. He couldn't even call back.

Andrew had just taken a drag on a fresh cigarette when his phone sprang to life again.

"Hello?"

"This is Alex Hunt. Is this a better time to talk about how we're going to get Julius Caesar back to the Ides of March?"

It would be a far better time to rip you a new bunghole.

Andrew managed to refrain from sharing this thought aloud. As frustrated as he was, his only chance for getting his experiment back on track was to play ball with this bastard.

"Thank you for calling back," he said.

"You're welcome. Now, please tell me the location of the airstrip nearest to the IDES Lab."

LXXIV

Elizabeth Palmer would have poured herself something with vodka in it if any had been available. As it was, she nursed an aging cup of coffee on the sofa in the IDES Lab common room. Andrew was in his office. John and Eric were in the TESA complex trying—pretending was probably the more accurate word—to figure out Julius Caesar's whereabouts.

Not that vodka would help. There was no escaping her unforgivable role in Julius Caesar's disappearance.

Amazingly enough, Andrew was all too willing to let her off the hook. He thought Cassandra was the weak link, even though Elizabeth had come totally clean.

"Cassandra is not to blame," she insisted to John and Andrew. "It's all totally my fault."

Which wasn't really true. It was Hank's fault. She'd known the awful second she saw Bill at Sonia's house. There was only one possible explanation. Her husband was trying to kidnap Julius Caesar.

Dear God. Elizabeth regretted that she had revealed the truth about the IDES Project to Hank, but who knew he would plot to hijack it?

Sure, they had money problems, but she never dreamed they were bad enough to set Hank on a hardcore crime spree. They'd been married for two years, and they'd dated for a year before that. Wasn't that enough time to get to know what a man was made of? Apparently not.

Damn it. This *was* her fault. She was the one who had broken the NDA.

She looked at her cell phone again. 8:30. Still no word from Hank, and apparently no one else in the IDES Lab had heard any news about Julius Caesar. Except for the constant drone of TESA, the place was silent. Elizabeth's work station was just across the room, but no amount of will power could drag her from her spot on the sofa. Until something happened to break the curse, she felt as paralyzed as if she'd caught a glimpse of Medusa.

Elizabeth's phone buzzed, reanimating her momentarily. Hank? No, only the pool man, calling to remind her once again that he hadn't been paid.

She had just tucked the phone back into the side pocket of her bag when Andrew Danicek burst into the room through the door on the west side.

"Have you heard from Hank?"

Elizabeth wished she had. She'd told Andrew what she'd seen at Sonia's house and how her husband had to be behind it, but that was all she knew. Without details, it wasn't much help. Elizabeth shook her head. "I would have told you."

"Okay, yes. Okay." Danicek crossed the room. "We got a call from an Alexander Hunt."

"Alex Hunt?" She couldn't help repeating the name.

"You know him?"

Elizabeth stood up and met Danicek's stare.

"Of course I know him. He's one of Hank's biggest clients."

"He's got Julius Caesar."

"Oh—that doesn't make sense."

The Arkansas chicken king had more money than God. Why would he get wrapped up in a kidnapping plot? Then again, most people thought Hank had riches to burn. Appearances were not reliable indicators of solvency, as Elizabeth had learned all too well.

"Is there anything I can do?" she asked.

Just then, the door to the TESA complex opened, raising the noise level. Eric held it open for John Reynolds, then closed it behind both of them.

"I have news," Danicek said when the two men had joined them. "Julius Caesar will be arriving at the IDES Lab the day after tomorrow at two o'clock."

LXXV

Caesar stood at the wall of glass, his arms folded across his chest. Cassandra had invited him to watch the youth in the scarlet robe prepare the food on the counter behind him, but the only thing that interested Caesar about the process was the long sharp knife the raven-haired lad was using to bone fish. It was a better weapon by far than the item in the pocket of his robe, but he had no way to get it without overt force. A shame Almond-Eyes was not the only person in the room. Caesar would have seized the knife before the boy even realized his intent.

Cassandra's presence, however, demanded a different approach. At the very least, Caesar had to appear civilized. Over dinner, he planned to do better than that. As he looked down once again at the stunning display of fire and light below him, he reaffirmed his goal of winning Cassandra's friendship. Without her as an ally, Caesar could not hope to achieve control.

Caesar could not help regretting his impulsive behavior when he first arrived at Duckhead's compound. If he had not spat upon the floor at Cassandra's feet, his task this evening would be ever so much easier.

If only she had looked less like a goddess and behaved less like a slave. If only Caesar hadn't just been blindsided with a lightning-fast journey to strange surroundings. He had felt duped when the woman he thought was Venus opened her mouth.

Rarely had Caesar's presumptions been so inaccurate. If he had known how high the price would be for his little power play, he would have suppressed his urge to expectorate. By spitting, then remaining silent and taking pleasure in Cassandra's shocked disgust, he had effectively forced her to despise him.

As he watched gigantic water fountains lit as if by daylight burst high above the pools below him, an image jumped before Caesar's mind's eye. On a spring evening not so long ago, Caesar had stood—just as he did now—next to a beautiful young woman in front of heavy drapes. In response to a subtle gesture, those other drapes had parted. Just as tonight, an astounding landscape had met his eyes. Reflected in the lapping waters of the Nile and a polished malachite foredeck, a huge orange sun hung heavy on the western horizon. Bathed in its raking fiery rays stood those mythic monuments, the great pyramids of Giza.

With her usual attention to logistics, Cleopatra had timed Caesar's first view of Egypt's legendary wonders to the second, along with every other detail. As the sun descended, the music of flutes floated to his ears. Had she even orchestrated the gentle breeze that carried the fragrance of frankincense to his nostrils? With Cleopatra, it was foolish to assume such feats were impossible. If she was not a goddess, she came closer than any mortal Caesar had ever met.

Once again, he contemplated the conundrum that was Cassandra. She, too, had opened drapes with apparent magic and displayed a landscape even more astonishing than the skyline of Giza at sunset. She, too, was beautiful—some might say more lovely than the Egyptian queen. But that only proved how unimportant mere physical appearance is. A lovely facade is like honey—a tempting topping. If the cake underneath is spoiled, honey cannot save it.

Cassandra's face might evoke comparisons to Venus, but the illusion vanished as soon as she spoke. Cleopatra, on the other hand, not only looked and dressed the part, she conversed and ruled as though she were truly divine. At every port along the Nile—even those without temples—grateful subjects waited in joyous throngs, all carrying gifts, all singing paeans to Isis incarnate. Even in Rome, she was greeted as a goddess. As surprised as Caesar was at first, his incredulity rapidly morphed into envy. To be sure, he had secured ample respect for his military prowess, but the prestige gained from battlefield victories paled next to the religious fervor Cleopatra so easily inspired.

Caesar once again strove to assess Cassandra. She was no goddess, but perhaps it was unfair to measure her qualities against Cleopatra's. He thought back to their journey across the desert. Cassandra piloted the horseless vehicle with the skill of a master. She might have shown deference to Duckhead, but when it was time for her to escape the ambush at the dinner party, she dived under a fence without a second thought. Caesar tried and failed to picture Cleopatra scrambling under thorny shrubbery on her belly. Cassandra not only followed Caesar's lead, she didn't cry out when sharp branches ripped a gash in her thigh. Her garments hanging in shreds and blood streaming down her leg, she had leapt into the driver's seat, evaded their pursuers, and forged a new plan of action on the fly.

Caesar stole another glance at Cassandra. As servile and fearful as she seemed in some situations, she possessed traits a warrior would be glad to boast in others. By basing assumptions about her on his own culture, Caesar had made egregious errors.

As he watched the lights dance across Cassandra's profile, Caesar pondered his predicament. He did not know enough to categorize his companion properly. His earlier suppositions had damaged his chances of gaining her good will. From now on, he told himself, he would stand firm. Goddess, slave, Amazon, noblewoman—no matter how tempting, he would resist applying a label.

If I arrive at a point, he told himself, where I feel unsure about how to proceed, I will ask myself a simple question: What would you do if this were Cleopatra?

As Caesar settled on this plan, he felt himself relax. No woman in the history of the world has ever taken offense at being treated like a queen.

LXXVI

Her peripheral vision still on Caesar, Cassandra watched the Japanese chef put the finishing touches on a magnificent platter of sushi and sashimi. The result was one of the most beautiful works of food art she had ever seen. This impression was no doubt enhanced by the fact that she hadn't eaten anything except a Starbucks truffle since she and Caesar left Simone's kitchen. Even then, she'd been far too anxious about their pursuers to eat anything more than a cracker and a sliver of cheese. Now, safe behind the walls and security staff of Caesars Palace, Cassandra felt perfectly capable of wolfing down the entire mountain of sushi all by herself. And maybe she'd have the chance. Who could tell how Julius Caesar would feel about rice and raw fish?

Cassandra sneaked a glance toward him. At the same instant, Caesar turned. Their eyes met, and Caesar smiled.

What is he up to now? she wondered. A smile on Caesar's face was nothing to be trusted.

"Shall we dine?" she asked.

"A question I am delighted to answer, my lady," Caesar said. "Indeed, let us dine."

My lady. Coupled with the smile, it was one more bit of discon-
certing new behavior.

Just then, Baldassare entered the room through the double doors
behind the bar. With overly self-conscious choreography, he arranged
candles, place mats, utensils, and glassware on the low table near the
wall of windows. When all was ready, the Japanese chef carried his
sushi Everest to the table.

"Supper is served," Baldassare said with a slight bow. Together,
Caesar and Cassandra moved to the low table. Careful to keep her robe
wrapped securely around her body, Cassandra lowered herself onto one
of the upholstered ottomans next to it. Caesar needed no invitation to
take the one beside her.

"What may I bring you to drink?" Baldassare said. "Chrysanthemum
Princess is our chef's recommended pairing—" He motioned toward
a green bottle in an ice bucket. "Of course, we have a full offering of
wine and spirits—"

"The sake will be fine," Cassandra said. Baldassare filled their
glasses and placed the bottle back in the silver bucket.

"That will be all for now," Cassandra said. "You may go."

Baldassare ducked his head, but she saw him wink as he did it.

Bastard. But Cassandra had more important things to worry about
than whether a cocky butler was "dissing" her.

"Cassandra."

She turned to find Caesar smiling again. "A beautiful name for a
beautiful princess."

Was he talking about her? Or was he referring to the original
Cassandra? Either way, she felt her defenses rise.

"Beauty aside, she was a tragic figure," Cassandra said, opting for
the latter interpretation.

Caesar nodded. "Foreknowledge is a curse if one is powerless to act on it."

Their eyes met. Cassandra sucked in a breath. Could it be? Was Julius Caesar engaging in genuine conversation with her?

"Do you agree?"

And asking for her opinion, no less.

"I do," she said. "I will confess, however, that I have always questioned whether Cassandra was genuinely powerless. While it must have been demoralizing that no one believed her predictions, she still had the power to act on her own."

"You speak as though you dislike your namesake."

"I was named for my great aunt, but it is true that I studied the original Cassandra from the time I learned of her existence."

When she was six years old, and Malcolm brought her *Cassandra of Troy* for her birthday.

"And you were disappointed?"

"Not when I was a child. But later, yes. I would have preferred her to be heroic, not merely tragic."

"You believe Cassandra could have saved Troy?"

"Perhaps not, but she could have done a lot more than shed tears and go insane."

Caesar laughed—another genuine laugh!—and Cassandra felt her pulse quicken. *Holy crap.* They were really talking.

"Would you like to taste our supper?" she asked, mostly to shift back into safer territory. She still couldn't trust this man, regardless of whether his attitude toward her had changed.

"I hunger," Caesar said, looking directly into her eyes. Feeling her cheeks warm, she looked down. He hadn't laid a hand on her, but his words felt as suggestive as if he had.

LXXVII

"I owe you an apology."

Startled, Cassandra looked up. Caesar's dark eyes burned into hers. She set down her chopsticks.

"What for?" she asked, but not because Caesar had behaved well. While she had no idea what he was sorry for, he had been making things more difficult than they needed to be ever since he arrived.

"Poor manners," Caesar said. "Spitting."

Cassandra almost smiled.

"I hope you will forgive me."

She considered his words. Was he truly sorry? Did he want something from her? Maybe it didn't matter. Apologizing was polite, and good manners were worth encouraging.

"I shall forgive you on one condition."

Caesar grinned. "Spoken like a warrior. Always try to improve your position."

"I'm no warrior. Please just tell me why you did it."

Caesar's gaze shifted into the distance. He took a sip of sake. He set his glass down next to Cassandra's. At last, he took a breath. "I did it because I could."

"What is that supposed to mean?"

"Think for a moment," Caesar said. "Before I committed that small act, what was I?"

"You were Caesar. Who else?"

"I was a prisoner."

Cassandra cringed inwardly. How many times had the IDES team discussed that very issue? Danicek had been the most adamant on the topic.

"If he does not wish to stay, we shall send him back immediately." It was Danicek's mantra in the weeks leading up to Caesar's arrival. But then, when Caesar actually arrived—

"Spitting was unexpected," Caesar said.

No argument there.

"I now regret it, because it has caused you to label me a boor."

It was Cassandra's turn to look into the distance. This didn't feel like a sincere apology.

She glanced at Caesar out of the corner of her eye.

Maybe it didn't matter if he was genuinely sorry. Spitting wasn't a crime, just bad manners in some societies. Apologizing was good manners.

"You are being polite. Why should I trust your sincerity?"

"You trusted my rudeness."

"I don't know whether you were truly being rude. I rather think you were not."

"No matter," Caesar said. "Apologies are polite."

"They can be insincere."

"Obviously, so can rudeness."

Cassandra locked eyes with Caesar. She was enjoying the verbal sparring—no denying it.

"So your rudeness—if indeed you were being rude—was insincere, but your apology is heartfelt?"

"You could say that." Caesar picked up a piece of California roll with his fingers. "The fish delicacy is excellent, but I am not accustomed to dining with sticks." He raised the sushi to his mouth. "I hope I cause no offense by eating with my fingers."

"You do not." Cassandra shook her head. "I still don't understand about the spitting."

Caesar set the sushi back down on his plate. He looked at her again. "Two days ago, without the slightest warning, I found myself suddenly alone and unarmed among strangers in an alien land. I thought I had—" He stopped himself. "You looked like—" He cut himself off again. "None of it matters save the fact that I was still alive. If a man breathes, he has power. His challenge is to muster it when he appears to have none."

A chill rippled through Cassandra's body as she listened to Caesar's words. This was Julius Caesar speaking—the real man, not a phantom or an actor. She was really, truly eating sushi with one of the most famous men in all of history—

"There is always something you can do."

Cassandra let his words sink in. He had a point. Everything was different after the catarrh hit the concrete.

"Has my apology been accepted?"

She was about to say yes when Caesar's words repeated themselves inside her head.

There is always something you can do.

Cassandra's mind jumped to a Saturday morning years ago, when she was in ninth grade. Standing in front of her mom's trailer, she waited for Lindsay Gallagher's mother to pick her up for swimming. As she stood on the gravel path, old Mrs. Wolfburger emerged from her single-wide with Howard on a leash. Howard was a white cockapoo. Cassandra sometimes took care of him when Mrs. Wolfburger went to visit her grandchildren in St. George.

"Good morning, Cassie!" Mrs. Wolfburger called.

Cassandra had taken two steps toward them when Brutus rounded the corner.

Brutus was an enormous Rottweiler that belonged to Mrs. Conn's crazy son. Whenever the crazy son went into rehab or prison, Mrs. Conn had to take care of Brutus. No one cared until the day Brutus grabbed Mr. Coletti's Lhasa Apso behind the ears and shook her until her neck snapped. After that, everybody signed a petition to ban Brutus from Carefree Canyon. But here he was.

As Cassandra watched in horror, the big black dog—rushing forward unimpeded on his self-retracting leash—lunged at Howard. The small dog jumped behind Mrs. Wolfburger, wrapping his own leash around her ankles. Brutus followed. Mrs. Wolfburger shrieked.

What can I do?

Desperately, Cassandra looked around as the perilous scenario unfolded in front of her. Mrs. Conn let go of Brutus's leash and stood immobile with her mouth hanging open. No one else was around. If she didn't act quickly, Mrs. Wolfburger would fall, and Brutus would kill Howard. The only thing within reach was a full garbage bag waiting on the curb for pickup. Cassandra grabbed it. Ripping it open as she ran, she dashed toward the snarling whirl of Rottweiler, old lady, and cockapoo. Aiming as well as she could into the melee, she hurled the contents of the bag.

This was one time Cassandra was glad she had postponed doing her chores until her mother threatened to ground her. The overly ripe contents of Aphrodite's litterbox fell squarely on Brutus's head. Howard managed to escape everything except some damp coffee grounds. Mrs. Wolfburger said later that eggshells and bacon grease in her hair had never been more welcome. Nobody was sorry that Mrs. Conn slipped on a cantaloupe rind and broke her wrist.

Cassandra looked at Caesar again. She recalled how, for months, she was the hero of Carefree Canyon.

"How's our champ today?"

"Hi, Supergirl!"

"Brains, beauty, *and* bravery—it isn't fair!"

The glory faded, but the feeling that she was something special lingered.

Now, as Cassandra thought about Caesar's small and unexpected act, her intervention of long ago seemed nothing more than obvious, necessary, and lucky. She just happened to be the person standing by a bag of garbage when action was required. And all the adulation afterward? It was just the gratitude people show when a person takes some initiative and the result is a good one. What if Mrs. Wolfburger or Howard had been killed by flying cat poop? Cassandra wouldn't have looked like such a genius then.

But Caesar's act was something different entirely. If he hadn't explained, Cassandra might never have realized it was an intentional power play. She had mistaken a brilliant tactic for indigestion, superstition, or ordinary impoliteness.

Still thinking, Cassandra reached across the table for another piece of salmon roll. It was farther away than she thought. She reached further. Before she could prevent it, the slick ottoman slipped from under her, propelling her toward the plates, glasses, and what was left of the tower of sushi. She narrowly missed falling on everything—and the glass table underneath—by dumping her entire body into Caesar's lap.

"Oof!" Caesar said. Laughing, he planted a kiss on the top of her head.

No! Clutching her robe, she struggled to get up.

Damn it. This was exactly what Cassandra needed to avoid. And something solid was digging into her back.

And—damn again. Now she was the one who had to apologize.

"I am sorry," Cassandra said, staring straight up into Caesar's dark eyes.

"Apology accepted."

She straightened up, adjusted her robe, and settled herself back on her ottoman.

"What is in your pocket?" she asked.

Caesar's right hand disappeared into the pocket of his robe. When he pulled it out, she saw the knife.

LXXVIII

How very inconvenient.

Caesar had just begun to worm his way into Cassandra's confidence, and now here he was—caught with a knife in his hand.

He considered his options as he watched her stare at it. Was she frightened? Angry? Probably both.

Slowly, Caesar loosened his grasp on the knife's handle. Leaning forward, he laid it gently on the table next to the eating sticks.

He heard Cassandra release a breath. Good. At least her fear had diminished. He watched her readjust her robe.

Modesty. Caesar liked it in a woman, even if it was just for show.

She reached for the knife. She picked it up.

"A kitchen knife," she said, turning it over in her hand.

"It belongs to your friend with the birds," Caesar said. "I borrowed it."

Cassandra was silent for a long moment. She set the knife back down on the table, just where Caesar had placed it. She kept her eyes on it.

"Perhaps I should have taken my wife's advice the other morning," Caesar said.

Cassandra jerked her head up and stared at him.

"After she gave up begging me to stay home, she begged me to take a dagger."

Caesar thought back to the morning of the Ides, when Calpurnia had worked herself into a state of hysteria. If she had been any other woman, he might have heeded her tears and frantic entreaties. But Calpurnia—was she an instrument of the gods, or was she merely insane? Caesar protected her from the eyes and ears of strangers because he would never know. What he did know is that she was far more likely to be called a witch than a prophetess.

"Why did you refuse?"

Caesar shrugged before replying with the obvious answer. "I am not a coward, and I am not a ruffian. I refuse to carry a weapon when I conduct state business."

"And yet—this knife. Why?"

Another question from Cassandra was a good sign, Caesar decided. She was no longer afraid, and she didn't seem angry. Curious, he could deal with.

"I am a hostage in a strange land, and you ask me why I feel a need to arm myself?"

Cassandra shook her head. "You weren't supposed to be a hostage. You were supposed to be our guest. All we wanted was to talk—to learn from you." She stared into Caesar's eyes. "You should have been offered the option of returning home immediately."

Caesar considered this revelation for a moment.

"I am a busy man," he said. "I depart for Parthia in a fortnight. You cannot imagine what a disruption this—this excursion has been."

Cassandra looked away. "You are right. I cannot imagine."

"Why was I not given the opportunity to return immediately?"

Cassandra hesitated. "Well—to begin with, you spat on the floor."

Caesar could not hold back a laugh. "That is your excuse for turning me into a prisoner?"

"Not entirely. You fell, remember? Our doctor feared you might be seriously ill."

"Ah, the fire-haired harpy. I am happy to blame that gorgon for my detainment." Caesar paused. "But why—after she had completed her ministrations—did you not offer to send me home? Why did you continue to hold me prisoner?"

"The chance to send you back was fleeting. During the—commotion—the opportunity passed. There was no point in offering you something we could no longer provide." Cassandra touched Caesar's arm. "You need not worry. We'll get you back—to the exact place and time where we found you. It will be as though nothing has happened. This will seem like a dream—"

"A nightmare, you mean."

As soon as the words escaped, Caesar regretted them. He looked at Cassandra's bowed head. "I jest, my dove. This will live in my memory as a grand adventure."

Cassandra looked up. As he gazed into her eyes, Caesar realized how close he had come to never living this moment. If he had been offered the opportunity to return to Rome moments after he arrived, he would have seized it. He would have missed all this. Whoever this woman was, she was no nightmare. Wherever he might be in time and place, calling it a "grand adventure" made him guilty of understatement.

What if he had indeed traveled to the future?

"Tell me what you know about me," Caesar said.

He watched Cassandra think before she answered.

"I have read your books." She looked at him. "I have read what others have written about you."

Caesar remained silent.

"I know you have married three times."

"Not true," he said. His eyes locked with Cassandra's. "Calpurnia is my fourth wife."

"You married Cossutia?"

"Indeed I did."

Interesting that she knows about Cossutia, Caesar thought, and he rather liked that she didn't know that he had married the girl. He had all but forgotten the whole awkward fiasco himself.

"You had a daughter," Cassandra said, a little hesitantly.

You had a daughter.

How could a simple past tense still cause him pain after all this time? It had been ten years since the terrible day Caesar learned of Julia's death.

As it always did when he was reminded of that awful day in Britain, the memory of roasted mullet overtook his senses. Caesar could almost taste the fish—almost feel the bone stuck between the two back molars on the right side of his mouth. The unrelenting dreary rain once again surrounded him—the reason he had retreated to his pavilion to consume his midday meal. The bone had just lodged itself when he heard hoof beats.

"Perfect timing," Caesar said to his *aide-de-camp.* "I shall greet the courier myself."

Not for a single second did Caesar question his assumption that the messenger carried intelligence from the north. For three days, he had awaited the intelligence he needed to advance his campaign against Cassivellaunus. No other messengers were due for at least a fortnight.

Rising, Caesar pulled his bronze stick pin from his tunic. From the day Julia had given it to him, he had never considered himself fully dressed without it.

"I had it made just for you," she said. "See the eagle?"

Sure enough, topping the pin was the intricately sculpted head of a tiny eagle.

The occasion was a party held three days before Julia married Pompey. Caesar gave his daughter a frivolous gift, too—an ivory comb carved in the shape of a crocodile.

"It's brilliant!" she exclaimed. "You know how I love everything Egyptian." She jumped up, rounded the table, and planted a kiss on Caesar's head—right on the spot he never allowed anyone to touch. "I love you."

Picking his teeth with the stick pin, Caesar stepped outside his tent. The courier had just dismounted.

He knew it then. Something was wrong. The courier, although astride a shaggy local mount, wore a Belgian tunic. Whatever message he bore had come from at least as far away as Transalpine Gaul, and that meant only one thing: news from Rome.

Back inside his pavilion, Caesar opened the letter. Rain pelted the sagging canvas over his head as he stared at the words informing him that Julia was dead. Alone in the damp gloom, he also learned of the child whose birth took her life. Three days later, the baby boy died, too.

In the morning, Caesar forced himself to dress and go about his duties. But in truth, he realized once again as his eyes met Cassandra's, he had never left that sodden tent. A part of him was still there—would always be there. Life had never been the same without—

"And a son," Cassandra said.

A son.

Caesar's attention snapped back to their conversation. To whom did Cassandra refer? It must be Cleopatra's child, even though Caesar had as yet not recognized him as his heir.

This made him wonder. Did Cassandra somehow know that he planned to acknowledge the boy after his return from Parthia? The only other possibility was that she had somehow managed to learn a different secret.

Either way, she was broaching a topic Caesar had no wish to pursue.

"You have been misinformed," he said. "I have no son."

Before Cassandra could respond, he went on. "What do you know of my conquest of Parthia?"

Cassandra chewed her lip, then shook her head.

"Nothing."

Just as Caesar had thought. She knew nothing because it hadn't happened yet. This was a pointless exercise. He raised his cup and took a sip of the clear sweet wine. Unless—he set the cup down slowly and looked at Cassandra again. One more question would set all this to rest.

"How will I meet my death?"

Cassandra looked away, but not before Caesar caught the look of distress on her face.

"Tell me, Cassandra." He touched her shoulder. "When will I die?"

Slowly, she turned back toward him. Her face had lost all its color.

"Don't ask me questions about your future."

"Why not? If I have indeed traveled forward in time, you must know—"

"No! I do not know! As you've said, I've been misinformed."

She held Caesar's gaze for a moment, then looked away.

"You are a very bad liar, Cassandra."

He studied her face as he contemplated his next challenge. Acquiring a knife was a simple task compared to convincing this young woman to divulge what she thought she knew about his future.

LXXIX

Cassandra stared at the knife on the table in front of Caesar. His right hand rested just inches from the handle.

He could grab that knife and slit her throat before she even knew what was happening. Strange, though, that she felt no instinctive fear. She had to remind herself that Caesar was a threat. Why wasn't her body sending all the usual signals? Why wasn't she scrambling to protect herself?

All at once, every hair on her neck and arms jumped to attention.

I'm not the one in danger here—Caesar is.

What if he tried to escape when she wasn't looking? Her eyes on Caesar's weapon, Cassandra imagined him confronting the security guards with a paring knife. They'd pull their guns. Neither sharp nor shiny—and nothing like a bow and arrow—the objects they brandished would give Caesar no clue of their long-range deadliness.

Stay calm, Cassandra, and think.

Her hand shook a little as she took a sip of sake.

No point in trying to explain the mechanics of handguns, she decided. It would only make him curious—put him at even greater risk. So far, he'd managed to pilfer only a kitchen knife. She shuddered at the thought of what might happen if he got hold of a revolver.

Somehow I've got to keep him safe until morning.

Caesar's life—and perhaps the lives of every person on the planet—was Cassandra's responsibility for the next fourteen hours. One way or another, she had to keep him securely contained, preferably without letting him know she was doing it.

Damn.

That meant Baldassare was right to think that she was back at Caesars Palace plying her trade. Alex Hunt hadn't saved her from being a prostitute. He'd merely delayed it. He may not have realized it while they enjoyed their chaste chateaubriand and platonic pinot noir, but Alex had set Cassandra on a path that had just brought her right back to the moment they met. Only now her assignment was much more difficult. She might have been nervous about her first date as a working girl, but she didn't have to worry about Alex. He was a guy who liked women, and they'd both known he was meeting her for sex.

But this! God, it was almost enough to make Cassandra lose her *nigiri*. She had fourteen hours to kill with a man she didn't understand, didn't much like, and—if you could believe ancient gossip—might be gay. Even though her instincts—and maybe the kiss he had just given her—told her he probably wasn't, he seemed more interested in stealing weapons than anything Cassandra could tempt him with.

At least they were in the Palatine Suite, she thought, a lavish pleasure palace with attendants at their beck and call. But then again—wasn't that awful, too? Of all the ridiculous places to take Julius Caesar, Caesars Palace topped the list. And it was not only silly, but perfect for making Danicek think she was a kidnapper. He could logically deduce that she'd planned this all along, or that she was in league with whoever had. Without any evidence to convince him otherwise, it was a theory that fit the facts perfectly.

Shaking off these thoughts as best she could, Cassandra looked at Caesar. He was playing with the salt and pepper shakers. Two tiny piles, one black, one white, were forming on the edge of his plate. He was bored, which meant she had to get her brain in gear.

She was still trying to figure out what to do next when Caesar abruptly pushed his ottoman back, rose to his feet, and rounded the half-wall of glass bricks behind them. Clutching her robe, Cassandra stood up, too. She caught up with Caesar just as he reached the archway to the kitchen.

Oh, no! More knives!

"My friend," Cassandra said, still racking her brain for ideas, "I would like to show you the rest of our domicile. There is so much more to see." She laid her hand on his shoulder. He had just grasped a cupboard door handle, but he let go.

"My friend? You surprise me." He chuckled and turned to face her.

"I think it is time we become friends," she said. "We need each other."

Caesar narrowed his eyes but said nothing.

"I would like to arrange entertainment," she said. "I think you will enjoy seeing a play about your—" She paused, struggling for words. "About your life."

Caesar raised an eyebrow.

"I will agree," Caesar said, "On one condition."

It was Cassandra's turn to say nothing. What would he demand? If it was sex, well, she'd already put that on her mental table...

"Tell me what you have planned for tomorrow."

"Oh!" she said. "Of course!"

But Christ! What should she tell him? How would he use the information? While she thought this, she kept what she hoped was a convincingly confident smile plastered on her face.

"We shall remain here," she said, "while preparations are made for our return to—to—"

"To your master's compound," Caesar finished.

Cassandra nodded. "So that you may return to Rome—as we promised."

Caesar frowned. Oh, no! Perhaps she should not have reminded him...

"I look forward to that," he said. "I have much to attend to."

Cassandra smiled. "In the meantime," she said, taking his arm, "I will arrange for the drama." She gestured back to the table. "While we wait, shall we see what our chef has prepared for dessert?"

LXXX

"How fares your leg?" Caesar asked. He and Cassandra had just finished eating a snow-like dessert that tasted vaguely of fruit and—vinegar, perhaps? The food in this land was beautiful, but the flavors all seemed tainted with coal or metal—as though Vulcan were the chef. The wine was good, at least. The servant had just refilled their small glasses with a strong sweet green variety that Cassandra said was made by priests in a mountain village north of Gaul.

Cassandra set down her glass and turned to meet Caesar's gaze. Her mouth hung slightly open. Good. He had caught her by surprise. Just what he hoped when he asked her a polite but personal question.

"Improved, thank you," she said. "The cut is long but not deep. How is your elbow?"

Even better, she seemed to have relaxed enough to ask Caesar a question. He could no longer avoid asking questions himself, which meant he could no longer bully Cassandra into conversation free of interrogatives. Perhaps it was time to show a little vulnerability, too.

He pushed up the sleeve of his robe to reveal the broad scrape on his left forearm and elbow. "Nothing worth mentioning," he said. "You fared far worse. I owe you an additional apology for that."

He watched Cassandra study his injury.

"You had no choice," Cassandra said. "If you had not dragged me under that fence, we would not be sitting here now."

Caesar pushed the sleeve of his robe higher. He watched Cassandra's eyes widen as he revealed the long, jagged scar on the outside of his bicep. He heard her take in a breath. Not surprising. There was no word for it but ugly.

Slowly, Cassandra reached out her forefinger and touched the scar. "I am glad your fresh wound is not serious—like this one must have been."

Caesar glanced at his arm. "That happened a long, long time ago."

Cassandra pulled her hand back. Her eyes met his, an obvious question hanging in them. He waited.

"How did it happen?"

Good. Another question. Things were definitely on the mend between them.

"I was just a boy."

Caesar glanced at the scar again as he thought about the crossroads at which he had just arrived. Should he tell this woman what had really happened on a summer day in his twelfth year? Or should he spin out the other tale, the story that had always served him so well?

Caesar let the events of that hot afternoon engulf him. It had always amazed him that they had remained so vivid. On the other hand, he supposed, it should not be surprising that the most defining moment in his early life had lingered with such intensity.

LXXXI

It was the third day of the games at Rufio's farm in the Sabine hills. The first two were taken up with archery and javelin contests next to the corrals. Caesar had already earned more points than any of the other boys, and today he would prove his superiority beyond all doubt. The hunting challenge was his favorite. Everyone else would return with a squirrel or a hare. Caesar was determined to bring back nothing less than a stag. Or at least evidence of a stag. A fine set of antlers would be perfect. He fingered the small knife under his tunic. Besides his short spear, it was his only weapon. He had no idea whether he could dehorn a buck with such a tiny blade, but that wasn't going to keep him from trying.

When Rufio sounded the horn, Caesar sprinted eastward. A spring fed a stream in the valley between two hills just beyond the next farm. He remembered it from the year before, when the boys had camped on its banks. The sun was just breaking over the ridge, but the day was already hot. He looked over his shoulder and chuckled to himself. The other boys were running en masse to the northwest, heading to the pond past the cypress grove.

Ha! Leave them to their muskrats! Shy deer wouldn't venture to an open lagoon, even in this heat. They'd keep to the shadows under the oaks on the hillside and drink at the hidden brook in the glen.

Instead of following the stream up the canyon, Caesar took the high trail on its southern bank. He moved silently from tree to tree, looking for a place to watch and wait for a thirsty deer. His best chance would be to strike from above.

As he made his way through a dense cluster of junipers, he heard the sound of twigs breaking in the ravine below him. He stopped. Slowly, carefully, he inched through the branches until he could look past the gravel slide on the side of the ravine to the creek below. His body still camouflaged by the trees, he stuck his head out and peered down.

Tatae!

That was no deer at the water's edge. It was Fronto crouching there, Rufio's horse's ass of an apprentice. What was that oaf doing here? Along with everyone else, Caesar had clearly heard Rufio tell him to clean the tack while the boys went hunting. But here he was fishing—

Or was he? Caesar eased himself forward a few more inches, careful to avoid making a sound. As he stared down, his mind struggled to make sense of the scene below him.

It was easy to see that whatever Fronto held in his right hand was alive. But what was it? It was too big to be a worm, and Caesar could see no fishing equipment, anyway. He edged forward another couple of inches and quietly bent a juniper branch aside.

Fronto turned and opened his hand just enough for Caesar to see the creature he held captive.

By Hercules, it was a salamander! Clearly, Fronto was not fishing. No sane person used a salamander for bait. So what, then?

Caesar watched as Fronto picked up a small river rock and rammed it savagely into the salamander's mouth. Grabbing another, he forced both stones down the small animal's throat as its body twisted and writhed.

When the salamander at last hung limp from his hand, Fronto flung it aside. Without hesitation, he reached into the leather pouch on his left hip and pulled out another hostage.

A toad!

Fronto had just picked up a stone when Caesar felt his left foot give way on the scree. He grabbed hold of a juniper branch, but it was too flimsy to prevent him from slipping. Before he could stop himself, he was skidding down the side of the canyon.

Startled by the sound, Fronto looked up. Caesar slid to a stop, up to his ankles in loose gravel. He watched the expression on the young man's face morph from surprise into anger. Fronto dropped the toad. Caesar watched his hand move toward the sheath on his right hip.

Caesar had never for a second doubted that he and Fronto would someday come to blows. He had detested the older youth from day one, when he caught him twisting a small boy's arm to the breaking point. The small boy turned out to be Quartus, Fronto's own younger brother. Fronto had released the lad as soon as he realized he'd been observed, but Caesar decided the tormentor deserved punishment.

At roughly half the older youth's size, Caesar knew that direct physical confrontation would be folly. He'd never beat the big bully at his own game, but stealth tactics were one of his specialties.

The night after Caesar caught Fronto torturing Quartus, he sneaked into Fronto's tent, stole his boots, urinated copiously into each, and returned them. The next morning, all the boys assembled for a forced march exercise into the hills.

"Wear your boots," Rufio had told them. "Sandals will not offer enough protection against the terrain and underbrush."

Caesar smiled inwardly when he saw that Fronto was wearing house sandals.

"Idiot!" Rufio said when he saw Fronto's footwear. "Why can you never follow the simplest of commands? Stay on the farm today and mend fences."

The next day, Caesar came across Quartus in one of the barns. He was huddled in a corner whimpering.

"What happened, boy?" Caesar said.

Reluctantly, Quartus revealed his feet. Both were red and blistered up to the ankles.

"Someone burned you?" Caesar said. "Who?"

But he already knew. "Your brother, am I correct?"

Sobbing, Quartus nodded. "He said I peed in his boots."

That did it. From now on, Caesar would leave no doubt in Fronto's twisted mind who his enemy was.

His next gambit was to make Fronto miss morning assembly by delivering him fake orders from Rufio. Fronto received Caesar's message with doubt but ended up following the bogus instructions to the letter. He got no dinner that night, which inspired Caesar to set up a similar trick with an accomplice two days later. Fronto fell for it again and got a whipping. Perfect! Caesar thought, but he didn't push his luck with a third attempt. Instead, he let four unbroken horses escape from the corral. As planned, Fronto got the blame along with another whipping. Caesar was on a roll, and he made sure the rumor mill informed Fronto who was responsible for each reversal of fortune.

As intended, these actions made Fronto Caesar's permanent and mortal enemy. This would have resulted in immediate repercussion had it not been for Caesar's standing among the other boys. For as long as he could remember, he had always been the leader of every group he joined. It didn't matter whether the other boys were bigger, smarter, or more skilled. It was as though Caesar was born with "DUX" inscribed on his forehead.

Or maybe it was because he was born with a caul. That's what his mother had told him ever since he was old enough to understand.

"When I pulled away that glistening veil," she said, "no blank-eyed infant stared back at me. You looked at me with the eyes and the understanding of a man."

Over the years, Aurelia often reminded Caesar of the important endowment she believed that scrap of amniotic sac foretold.

"You are destined for greatness," she'd say. "It is a wonderful gift and an even greater responsibility."

Whatever had bestowed Caesar's talent for influence upon him, he discovered early on that his natural role of man-in-charge could be greatly enhanced if he rewarded good behavior among his followers. Within two days of residence at Rufio's farm, and well before he aroused Fronto's hatred, Caesar had secured the undying loyalty of every one of his youthful colleagues. They all knew that keeping Caesar happy meant treats and privileges. Displeasing him meant—well, look at Fronto. By angering Caesar, he had earned the enmity not merely of a single adversary but of an entire young and fiercely faithful army.

Because he had planned to strike an animal from above, the one thing Caesar had in his favor as he stared down at Fronto was position. This was important, for in every other respect he was at a serious disadvantage. Fronto, at seventeen, had reached his full adult height and strength. Caesar hadn't sprouted a single facial hair. It was only his prodigious jumping ability that allowed him to mount a horse without assistance. Worse yet, Fronto wasn't limited by the rules of the hunting challenge. While Caesar carried only a short spear and a small dagger, Fronto had a long knife, a bow, and a full-length javelin.

And that's all Caesar could see. He knew Fronto usually carried a dagger concealed in his legging. Sometimes he carried two.

Wait. Let your adversary attack.

Later, when Caesar tried to relive the whole experience, he always had the feeling that someone or something spoke these words aloud.

This was only an illusion, of course. There was no one on that hillside to counsel him. Either a god spoke to him or his own thoughts were so strong that they sublimated into words.

Wait.

The voice was adamant, screaming in Caesar's head. His eyes locked on Fronto, he held his position on the rocky slope. He watched as the youth raised his javelin. Brandishing it as high as his head and snarling like a mad dog, Fronto scrambled up the slope.

Caesar crouched. Just as Fronto's arm moved to release the spear, Caesar flung himself forward, aiming low. The slope gave him just the advantage he needed. When his head barreled into Fronto's belly, the youth fell backward, winded and flailing. The javelin bounced away harmlessly. Both boys rolled down the hill and landed in a heap in the stream bed. Caesar scrambled to his feet while Fronto was still thrashing in the water and struggling to catch his breath.

"You—you bull's bollock!" Fronto managed to spit out. Caesar didn't bother with insults. This was no boys' game. Fronto had aimed his spear to kill. Caesar unsheathed his small knife.

That night, when he lay in his hammock and tried to piece together the frenzy of the following few moments, Caesar wondered when he knew he was going to kill Fronto. Was it when he first saw him torturing harmless animals in the spot where he expected to find worthwhile prey? Or was it when he saw the look on Fronto's face as he rushed up the hillside brandishing his spear? All Caesar knew for sure was that it was not when Fronto hurled a verbal insult at him. By then, the unfamiliar but unmistakable force of bloodlust had already overtaken him. By then, Fronto was already dead.

Fronto fought back, of course. Still pinned on his back in the stream, he managed to pull a short dagger from his right legging. Caesar was able to keep the blade from his torso, but could not prevent a long, deep cut on his left arm. Fronto managed a few more shallow stabs to Caesar's forearms and legs, but he never gained a true advantage. Caesar would never forget the moment his blade slipped into Fronto's throat. The spurt of blood, the sputtering gurgle, the smell of copper—all of it remained indelibly etched into his memory. It was not only his first kill. It was his first encounter with his own instinct, passion, and strength. All the powers he had been hoping to develop someday were already right there inside him. All it had taken to muster them was an adversary worthy of death. Simply put, the day he killed Fronto was the day Caesar became a warrior.

LXXXII

C aesar knew immediately what he would do now that Fronto was dead. Just as he had learned how to inspire loyalty among his friends and followers, he had long since perfected the art of bending the truth to guarantee an outcome he perceived to be advantageous. As he lay in the stream bed catching his breath, his mind was already fabricating the report he would take back to Rufio's farm.

Fronto had deserved to die. Even if he had not attacked Caesar unprovoked, he had tortured small children and harmless animals for sport. He was useless to Rufio and a danger to the other boys in camp. By killing him, Caesar had solved a burgeoning problem. Who could say how many injuries and deaths had been prevented by Fronto's demise? Now all Caesar had to do was to help everyone move forward without causing any additional trauma or distraction.

As he struggled to his feet, Caesar realized that his left arm was still bleeding profusely. Using his knife, he ripped strips from Fronto's tunic and—with one hand and his teeth—tied them as best he could around the wound. I must get back to camp, he realized as blood quickly turned the fabric crimson. He glanced at Fronto. For a second, he considered taking the dead lad's long knife but quickly thought the better of it. Possession of Fronto's weapon would require a story with more detail than Caesar wanted to provide.

"What happened to you?" Rufio demanded after Caesar had returned to camp and the cook had bandaged his arm. "Where have you been? You look like you've been at war."

"A lion," Caesar said. "A lion attacked me."

"*A lion?*" Caesar was a little startled by Rufio's incredulity, but he didn't back down.

"Yes, sir," he said. "A lion ambushed me while I was hunting for deer. She almost killed me."

Rufio shook his head. "I have never heard of lions in these hills."

Curses!

Caesar wished he had said "wolf." Too late now, though. "Lion" was his story, and he stuck to it.

Perhaps that decision was to be expected from a twelve-year-old, Caesar had thought many times since. Perhaps the fact that it was the wrong decision was the most important lesson he learned from the incident, even though it was not as immediate as the others. Caesar didn't fully realize that he should have told Rufio the truth until years later. Only then did he understand what his fabrication had cost not only him, but his entire family. Caesar's sister never married Rufio's oldest son as everyone in both families had always expected. Business relations between the families cooled. Rufio insisted that the mill he owned in partnership with Caesar's father be sold, even though it was profitable.

"A lion, you say?" Rufio said again. He peered down at the cuts on Caesar's legs. "*A lion?*" Rufio locked eyes with Caesar. "Are you *certain?*"

Caesar held Rufio's gaze. He swallowed. This was his chance. No, he should have said. It was Fronto. He attacked me unprovoked. I was only defending myself.

Caesar looked away first. "It was a lion. I swear."

Rufio never broached the subject again, but Caesar's reaffirmation that his wounds were the result of a lion attack forever altered their relationship. Caesar was never again invited to participate in the summer games at Rufio's farm.

If it did not impress Rufio, the lion made Caesar an instant hero among the other boys. "Hercules!" a few of them shouted, but Caesar silenced them.

"If I were Hercules, I would be wearing a lion skin," he said. "Instead, I am the loser in today's contest. You came back with quarry. I returned wounded and bleeding." Even at age twelve, Caesar couldn't quite bring himself to accept hero status based on a lie.

No one called him Hercules after that, but his claim to leadership among his comrades was even more firmly established. Hares and muskrats simply could not compete with a lion, even an imaginary one.

Fronto, of course, never returned to camp that day. He was still missing two days later. It wasn't until two slaves from the neighboring farm discovered human remains in the stream bed that everyone learned that Fronto was dead. Because animals had been at work on his body, it was Fronto's long knife that identified him.

Rufio must be just as relieved as I am that Fronto is no longer a problem, Caesar told himself when the news spread through camp. He's got to be grateful that he doesn't have to worry any more about what that stupid bully might do next. But later that day, when Caesar discovered Quartus howling in the barn, doubts rose in his mind.

"Why are you crying, boy?" Caesar demanded.

In between deep, heaving sobs, the child struggled to reply. "My brother is dead."

"He injured you. He was a torturer," Caesar said. How could Quartus feel such sorrow for a lad who had held his feet in boiling water?

"My brother is dead," Quartus wailed. "My brother is dead."

He could have killed you, Caesar thought to himself. I saved you. But there was obviously no way to drill any sense into the boy, so Caesar left the waif to his ridiculous tears.

At dinner, Rufio addressed the assembled boys. As he spoke of Fronto's violent end, tears streamed down his cheeks.

"I was proud to be his patron," Rufio said. "Losing Fronto is like losing a son."

What?

Caesar couldn't believe his ears. How could Rufio feel such grief over an idiot apprentice who had caused him nothing but trouble? The only explanation was that Rufio was stupid, too.

It was only much later, after losses mounted in his own life, that Caesar began to understand irrational grief. The image of a weeping Quartus rose in his mind's eye on that awful day in Egypt when a smooth-cheeked Ptolemy, older but no less naïve than Caesar had been that summer at Rufio's farm, expected him to rejoice at the sight of Pompey's severed head. Yes, Pompey was Caesar's nemesis, the foe he had sought to destroy for seven arduous years. That was a simple fact, obvious to the world. So obvious, in fact, that the young pharaoh had looked forward to reveling in Caesar's gratitude when he saw the savage evidence of his enemy's demise. Instead, like Quartus, Caesar wept.

Caesar had never told a soul the truth about the lion he summoned into existence that summer long ago. Keeping the secret had become the punishment he gradually realized he deserved. Still, he thought as he moved his eyes from the smooth pink ridge of the scar on his upper arm to meet Cassandra's gaze, here was a chance to set the record straight. There was no compelling reason to tell this woman about a lion that never existed. Why not let the story so long suppressed come forth? Caesar drew a breath.

"This was no minor wound," Cassandra said before he could speak.

"Indeed it was not." Caesar hesitated before continuing. "I could have died."

"What happened?" Caesar read genuine concern in Cassandra's eyes.

He let his breath out slowly. He knew, as clearly as he had known when he reaffirmed his story to Rufio all those summers ago, that there would be no going back once his next words emerged.

"A lion attacked me."

"A *lion?*"

By Jupiter, she sounded just like Rufio. Caesar's reply was automatic. "Yes. A lion attacked me in the Sabine hills when I was hunting for deer."

LXXXIII

Baldassare had cued up the movie on the DVD player by the time Caesar and Cassandra took their seats in the screening room. Cassandra was glad Caesar had already been introduced to television, but he still sidled up to the screen and looked behind it. No questions, though. As the overture played, he took a seat next to Cassandra in the front row. He seemed mesmerized as the opening credits rolled. Good. As long as he was entertained, she was doing her job.

CLEOPATRA

Cassandra glanced at Caesar to see if the name registered. His face revealed nothing.

She had seen *Cleopatra* once before, at a film festival at UNLV featuring the "worst movies of all time." She didn't think the film deserved to be packaged with low-budget disasters like *Plan Nine from Outer Space*, but she did remember thinking that Elizabeth Taylor as Cleopatra was so unconvincing that Marilyn Monroe could have done a better job. And Rex Harrison as Julius Caesar? Cassandra kept expecting him to start singing, "I've grown accustomed to her face."

And now? All she could think of was the title of Dr. Reynolds' best seller, *What Would Julius Caesar Do?* She half-wished Reynolds could be here to see Caesar's response to 1963 Hollywood's reconstruction of his life and times.

Of course, Cassandra knew she was treading on extremely thin ice. One of Danicek's most repeated admonitions was to keep Caesar in the dark about what was going to happen when he got back to Rome. She knew that the movie in front of them included coverage of his death, and went on to show how Marc Antony succeeded him in Cleopatra's affections. Remote in hand, Cassandra planned to turn off the action as soon as it progressed beyond anything that—in Caesar's experience— hadn't already happened. Risky? Sure, but since the staff at Caesars Palace had been able to provide the DVD, she was now dying to see Caesar's reaction to 20th Century Fox's legendary cast of thousands.

Caesar watched the opening scenes—the aftermath of the Battle of Pharsalus—without reaction. Cassandra watched her companion closely during the scene where the young pharaoh Ptolemy shows Rex Harrison a big clay jar. Two slaves remove the lid, grasp the contents and pull upward. Only the forehead is revealed, but it's obviously a severed head. Rex Harrison's face registers a fleeting look of slight disgust.

Would Caesar recognize that this was supposed to illustrate the death of Pompey the Great, his archenemy in Rome's civil war? How had he really reacted when he learned that Pompey—who was also his former son-in-law, had been beheaded?

Cassandra couldn't ask. Not yet. She could only hope that an opportunity might present itself later. In the meantime, she switched her gaze back and forth between the screen and Caesar's profile. He looked slightly pained, she thought, but she couldn't be sure. Maybe he was disgusted. Perhaps he was baffled.

When Elizabeth Taylor rolled out of a rug, Cassandra no longer had to guess what Caesar was thinking.

"Oh," he said as she got to her feet and faced Rex Harrison. "So this is a comedy."

"No," Cassandra said. "It is intended to be the story of Cleopatra's career." She paused the DVD on a close-up of Elizabeth Taylor's face.

Caesar turned to stare at her. She saw thoughts moving behind his eyes. "I begin to understand," he said. "I did meet Cleopatra in Alexandria. She used stealth to travel through enemy lines to meet me in the palace there. But—" He shook his head and gestured toward Elizabeth Taylor. "I suppose there is no accounting for taste among dramaturges."

"What prompts such comment?" Cassandra asked, genuinely curious. Caesar hadn't said a thing about Rex Harrison, after all.

"The Egyptian queen looks nothing like this woman," he said. "In addition, Cleopatra is young."

It was Cassandra's turn to laugh. "Artistic license," she said. "Would you like to see more?"

"No."

Oh my God. Why had she asked? She'd had no chance to think about what to do next.

"So ... what does Cleopatra really look like?" Cassandra asked.

"She is a goddess," Caesar said. "Isis incarnate."

That did not answer her question, so she decided to try a different tack.

"Did she deliver herself to you rolled up in a carpet?"

"Oh ... I see now what your drama was attempting to portray," he said with a chuckle. "No, she did not conceal herself. She transformed herself."

What? Cassandra didn't ask the question, but she was sure her expression was easily readable.

"Cleopatra takes on other forms, both for stealth and to gather intelligence."

She stared at Caesar, hoping he would go on.

"When I first saw her, she stood before me in full pharaonic regalia, even though she had traveled into Alexandria in secret—to elude her brother's forces. The two were at war—did you know that?"

Cassandra nodded.

"Later, she told me that she had taken on the form of a coarse carpet for the journey. She liked the irony of appearing to be the kind of rug upon which men wipe their boots." Caesar smiled. "If there is one thing Cleopatra is not, it is a doormat."

Cassandra said nothing, fearing she might stop him from telling her more.

"She has been a raven and a cat, too," Caesar said. "And once, a crocodile."

Cassandra was still trying to process this information when Caesar slid forward in his seat. Cassandra rose to her feet along with him and stuck by his side as he headed for the door.

"Would you like to bathe?" she asked. The thought of Cleopatra as a crocodile must have given her the idea.

"Perhaps," Caesar said.

"Allow me to show you the baths," she said. "Then you can decide."

LXXXIV

They sat on the edge of the caldarium. The hot water felt good on Caesar's feet, and he would have loved to disrobe and immerse himself completely. Cassandra, however, had decided that the scrape on her leg was still too raw for bathing.

Or was she simply avoiding nudity? Whether it was because of her wound or her modesty, they sat there on the broad balcony, wrapped in their thick robes. The city blazed below them, as though the Milky Way had been harnessed and brought to Earth.

Caesar glanced at Cassandra. She was studying him.

"What are you thinking?" she asked.

Caesar smiled. "This is the most luxurious prison I have ever had the privilege of being detained in."

She hung her head.

"I jest, Cassandra." He touched her arm. "The truth is—" He paused. "I would like to know more about you."

She said nothing for a moment. Had he offended her?

She spoke at last, without looking at Caesar. "I was born here—in this city. My mother is a teacher."

"And your father?"

She paused to think a moment. She took a breath. "I never knew him."

Interesting.

"When I was young," she continued, "my mother told me my father was a god."

Very interesting.

"But I realized soon enough that she was lying."

"Why did your mother lie to you?"

"Out of embarrassment. My mother does not remember my father's name."

"How do you know this second story is not a lie?" he asked.

Startled, Cassandra stared at Caesar. Had she never asked herself that very question? Like a snake, one lie most often lives in a nest of others.

"It—it was difficult for her to reveal the truth. I have no reason to doubt her. And in any event, I will never know my father."

"Have you not ever wondered whether she was lying to protect someone?"

As if to ponder this, she looked down. "You mean—she knows who my father is but refuses to tell me?"

"It is possible, is it not?"

"No. If she knew, she would tell me."

"Perhaps." It was Caesar's turn to take a breath. "Or perhaps not, because to tell you the truth would cause you greater pain."

Cassandra said nothing as Caesar searched for words himself. He did not know her mother's story, but it gripped him as though it were his own. How many children have been told that they are the result of a shower of gold coins or a divine visitation? How many men live near children they have sired without enjoying the privilege of public paternity?

"Many things are possible," Cassandra said. "I choose to believe my mother's second story."

"Forgive me for questioning it."

She shrugged. "I have not suffered harm. I have had an adoptive father since I was a child."

Caesar gazed down at those fantastic lights, wondering if somewhere amid them, a man knew that this young woman was his daughter. Did he gaze at her in unrecognized silence and wish he could tell the world? Had he longed to hold her hand when she was small, to teach her, to protect her, to show his love? The pain of denied relationship is not searing agony. It is a dull ache that never recedes. It is an ever-present longing for what might have been.

LXXXV

Cassandra awoke before dawn. In the faint light from the hallway, she could see Caesar's face turned toward her on his pillow. He appeared to be sleeping deeply.

Cassandra had not begun the night on Caesar's bed. She had climbed into one in the room across the hall and tried her best to fall asleep. It was only after two hours of restlessness that she gave in to her fears that Caesar might try something unexpected. She tiptoed into his room and lay down on top of the covers on the far edge of his bed. Caesar had remained asleep. In a few minutes, she was sleeping, too.

She listened to his slow and rhythmic breathing. Even in the low light, she could see the large gold ring he wore on his right index finger. No matter how hard she and Elizabeth had tried to convince him to let them store it with his other belongings, Caesar had steadfastly refused.

Why? Cassandra wondered. Perhaps it was like ID to him. Perhaps it gave him a feeling of security to keep it on his finger. Or maybe he thought it was too valuable to entrust to strangers. She sighed. One more thing she would probably never know.

She thought about what she had told Caesar about her father. She hadn't lied, but she hadn't told the precise truth, either. Her mother never said, "Your father was a god." What she said was, "You're very special. Jesus is your father."

Yes, she meant Jesus as in Jesus Christ, and Cassandra grew up believing her. It was their secret, her mother said. Nobody else could know. In retrospect, Cassandra was grateful for that part of the story. It protected her from what would have been brutal teasing when she went to school.

Cassandra didn't like admitting it now, but when she was little, she loved believing Jesus was her dad. She felt protected and special when she went to school, and she didn't envy the kids with real fathers. She gave up on Santa Claus and the Easter Bunny in kindergarten, but not her paternity myth. She held onto it even after Malcolm became her stepdad.

Then one day in fifth grade, right before spring break, Cassandra's friend Kendra invited her to go to California with her family. Cassandra had been grounded, but she was sure that Mom would suspend her sentence in the face of such an amazing opportunity.

"Disneyland and the beach!" she said. "Isn't that awesome?"

"Yes," Mom said. "Too bad you can't go."

"Mom! Please!"

"No. Lying is the one thing I won't put up with."

"But Mom! All I did was—"

Well, it was actually pretty bad. Cassandra had told her mother she was having dinner at Kendra's when she really went bowling at the Showboat with two other kids her mom didn't like. When she got home, her mother was at the door.

"What did Kendra's mom serve for dinner?" she asked. "Meatloaf? Mac and cheese? *Croque monsieur?*" Mom always pulled out the French when she was really mad.

"Um—"

"Don't bother," Mom said. "I already know."

Cassandra switched tactics.

"Can't I be grounded after I get back?" she said. "For twice as long?"

"No," Mom said. "Lying has consequences."

At that, Cassandra stormed to her room, slammed the door, and threw herself onto her bed. How could Mom deny her this trip? It just wasn't fair. Okay, she had lied, but—

Cassandra sat up and wiped the angry tears from her eyes.

Lying has consequences.

She'd see about that.

Cassandra stomped back into the living room, where her mother was about to turn on the television.

"How come *you* get to lie?" she said. "How come *you* don't have any consequences?"

Surprised, Mom straightened up and looked at her.

"What are you talking about, Cassie?"

"Your daddy is in heaven," she said. "Your daddy is Jesus. Those are lies."

Mom's eyes widened in surprise. Cassandra watched her face crumple.

"Tell me the truth," she said, still angry. "Tell me why you lied to me."

Cassandra got only part of the story that day. All her mother would tell her was that she didn't know who her real father was, and she was sorry.

Over the years, Cassandra tried to pry more details out of her mom. She slowly realized that Mom wasn't hiding much. She really didn't know who Cassandra's biological father was. She'd made up the Jesus story because the truth was too embarrassing. What mother wants to reveal to her daughter that she is the result of a summer road trip from Montreal to Las Vegas?

Cassandra had forgiven her mom years ago, and until now, she had never told anyone. Why had she told Caesar? Was it because she knew his family thought it had a goddess in its family tree? That thought occurred to her now, but it hadn't then. Last night, she had simply felt comfortable.

Caesar stirred. Cassandra watched his eyes flutter open. A moment passed as they held each other's gaze.

"Like a shadow," he said with a smile, "you follow me everywhere."

"I apologize for sharing your bed without your knowledge," Cassandra said. "I did not want to wake you to ask your permission."

"There is a surfeit of beds in this domicile. I am curious why you chose the only occupied one."

There was no point in dodging the truth any longer. "It is my duty to stay with you. To protect you."

Caesar smiled. "As though I need a girl to defend me."

"Belittle me all you want. There is much you do not understand."

"You sound like Cleopatra."

Having no idea whether this was an insult or a compliment, Cassandra said nothing.

"No, you are not like her," he said at last. "I take it back."

"Is she truly able to take on the form of animals," Cassandra asked, "and a rug?"

Caesar laughed. "No. That is all horse bollocks."

It was Cassandra's turn to laugh. "Why did you tell me she could?"

"I was simply repeating the story she tells Egyptian peasants. Those idiots will believe anything. And now she has half of Rome believing it, too."

"And you thought I believed it."

"I was not certain," he said, "but you expressed no incredulity."

"I thought *you* believed it," Cassandra said. "I was being polite."

"We should dispense with politeness," Caesar said. "It only creates misunderstandings."

He had a point.

"So tell me about Cleopatra," Cassandra said. "Do you love her?"

Caesar emitted a sound halfway between a laugh and a groan.

"When I arrived in Egypt four years ago, I was war-weary and soul-scarred," he said. "When I saw her—when she arrived in Alexandria—" He paused. "It was like seeing a goddess. And it didn't stop there. She doesn't merely look like a goddess, she behaves as one. Everyone treats her like one—and so she really is—Isis incarnate."

Caesar sat up. "I was under her spell there in Egypt. The weeks I spent with her were enchanted—I was enchanted. We sailed up the Nile, and in every port of call—even the ones without temples—hordes of her adoring subjects gathered, bearing food and gifts and flowers and frankincense … They worshiped me like a god when I was with her."

Cassandra stayed quiet, afraid he might stop if she interjected a thought.

"I knew even then what she really wanted from me—an unbreakable tie with Rome." He turned toward her. "You know she has a son?"

"Caesarion," Cassandra said.

"The name attests to her ambitions."

"Is the child not yours?"

"I will never know for certain. If I acknowledge him as my son, the truth will not matter."

"Will you?"

Caesar shot her an impish smile. "You are Cassandra. You should tell me."

She forced a smile. "I am Cassandra, so what is the point? You would not believe—"

He took her hand. "Try me."

Cassandra wasn't sure what her face expressed as thoughts whirled in her head.

Nothing will unfold as you expect. In two days, you will be dead. Octavian, not Caesarion, will be your heir, and Cleopatra, still seeking power, will move on to her next conquest: Marc Antony.

Cassandra stared straight into Caesar's eyes, her mind still spinning. This conversation could not continue. Too much was at stake. Since she was fresh out of other ideas, she grabbed both lapels of his robe and pulled him toward her. Before he could protest, she kissed him on the mouth. When Caesar's brief surprise subsided, he responded. Two hours vanished in that intimate communication that requires no language other than the one all humans know, regardless of the era into which they are born.

They slept again. When Cassandra awoke, Caesar was nestled next to her. Gently, she disengaged herself from his sleeping body and covered him with a sheet. Silently, she slipped out into the hallway and crossed into the facing bedroom suite. Rachel Tan could be here any minute. Cassandra needed to be presentable.

LXXXVI

The clock by the bed read ten after six when Cassandra emerged from the bathroom, clad in a fresh robe. She peeked into the room she had shared with Caesar. He was still asleep, so she headed for the kitchen. She hoped her mood would benefit from a shot of caffeine.

The sun had just come up, its emerging rays mingling with the man-made glitter of the Strip. Vegas loses its magic at dawn. The neon spell is broken, leaving a wake of dirty bathrooms, empty wallets, and full ashtrays. Even the buildings wake up with halitosis and a headache.

As she gazed over the dying lights of Las Vegas Boulevard, Cassandra wished she had never noticed the words on Alex Hunt's wedding ring. She might still be a call girl, but at least she wouldn't be guilty of seducing a man for the sole purpose of returning him to the scene of his imminent murder.

If only she had never studied Latin, never heard of Catullus.

Her favorite lines sprang into her mind. As she stood there waiting for the coffee to brew, she spoke them aloud.

"*Odi et amo. Quare id faciam fortasse requiris.*"

"I hate and yet I love. How this can be, perhaps you wonder." God, how she wondered.

"*Nescio sed fieri*—" It was Caesar's voice. "I know naught but this—"

Cassandra turned to see him standing at the end of the counter, draped in a sheet.

"*Sentio et excrucior*," she said. "I feel these things, and I am tormented."

Drawing close, Caesar wrapped her in an embrace.

"Catullus," he said, kissing her forehead. "He was my friend once."

"I know." Cassandra pulled away and poured two mugs of coffee.

"Are you hungry?" she asked as she added cream and sugar. "If you are, I shall order food."

"Let us enjoy the dawn, Cassandra," Caesar replied. "There will be time enough later to eat."

Time enough. His words, spoken so lightly, brought tears to Cassandra's eyes. There was no time for anything. She hung her head as more tears flowed.

"Why do you weep? Have I hurt you?" Caesar asked.

"You have not," she said, but her voice broke.

"Then why?" There was genuine worry in his tone.

Cassandra looked up. "You have been treated badly. We should never have brought you here."

Caesar raised his cup and drank. Setting it down carefully, he spoke slowly, deliberately.

"You, Cassandra, have not treated me badly."

Caesar walked to the sofa and sat down with his back toward her. She stared at the nape of his neck.

Drawing a deep breath, she walked around the sofa and knelt in front of him. She took his hands in her own.

"If it were my choice, I would keep you here."

Caesar smiled and stroked her hair. "I have obligations I cannot ignore."

Cassandra nodded as tears once again stood in her eyes.

"You fear for me," Caesar said. "You believe you know what lies in store for me in Rome. What is it?"

Cassandra spoke before thinking. "I cannot tell you."

"You could if you wanted to. You had no trouble kidnapping me, bringing me here against my will, and then forcing yourself upon me."

"What?" She couldn't believe her ears. Is this what he had been thinking the whole time?

Caesar laughed. "You disagree?"

Cassandra was too stunned to say anything.

"You saved me from abductors intent on my murder and transported me to safety. We fell in love."

Not exactly how she would put it, but better.

"Either way," Caesar said, "If I wrote the words, they would become the history of what happened."

His dark eyes pierced into hers. "Cassandra, have you never learned that the most dangerous thing in the world is that which you *think* you know? History—the words that seek to preserve the past—is nothing but a fortress built of smoke. It may look like solid truth, but the tiniest arrow passes easily through its walls."

Cassandra stared into his unblinking eyes as she realized he was right. Much—maybe even most—of what we accepted as fact about Caesar was extrapolation, whole cloth fabricated by historians to unite the bare shreds of primary source material. Ancient history was really nothing more than a house of cards, a fragile construct of best guesses.

"I myself," Caesar continued, "have tried to preserve events with words. But words can never trap the complete truth, no matter how skilled the author. A written account is only a footprint. It reveals only an impression of the occurrences it seeks to immortalize."

He hesitated, then continued. "Sometimes I think poets do the best job of preserving the past. In three short words, a man like Catullus can evoke the ardor of passion. In an entire book, I never once captured the heat of battle."

"Your books are still studied by those who seek to master the art of war," Cassandra said.

Caesar smiled. He sat back, and Cassandra pulled herself up beside him. The sheet had fallen off his shoulders, revealing the horrible scar he had sustained fighting off a lion.

"You need something more to wear," she said. "Guests will be arriving soon."

"There is something else you should always remember about history," he said. He raised a finger to touch the scar on his shoulder. "People lie."

Cassandra said nothing, and Caesar continued. "I did not like the truth about this wound," he said. "I made up a better story."

"So I was right to be surprised when you told me it was caused by a lion," Cassandra said.

Caesar nodded. "But in the end, you still accepted it as truth."

She shrugged. "Who was I to question you?"

"A youth injured me. I killed him."

"Why should I believe you now?" she asked. "I prefer the lion story."

Caesar laughed. "You have made my point, Cassandra."

"I know," she said. "You are not to be trusted. But right now, I hope I can trust you to stay here while I get you something more to wear."

LXXXVII

Caesar had not moved when Cassandra returned with a fresh robe. She helped him put it on, and they both sat back down on the sofa.

"We both need more clothing," Cassandra said. "We cannot go out in public like this." She reached for the telephone on the end table next to her and tapped "0" on the keypad. A nasal male voice with a stilted British accent answered immediately. She explained her request.

By the time she hung up, Cassandra had made two appointments. A tailor would arrive later to provide a wardrobe for Caesar, and a "personal shopper" from the Forum Shops would "pop in" to do the same for her. Replacing the receiver, she turned to explain.

"Will you show me your city once we are clothed?" Caesar asked before she could say a word.

"I plan to," she said, even though she did not have the power to make any promises. "But right now, I am hungry." She picked up the phone again and ordered breakfast.

Cassandra had just turned on the TV when three chimes announced that someone was at the door. She opened it to find a woman standing in front of her, flanked by two men in dark suits.

"I am Rachel Tan," the woman said. Dressed in a maroon business suit, she was a head shorter than Cassandra but weighed at least twenty pounds more. Her straight dark hair, streaked with gray, was cut in an angular bob. She had to be close to sixty, a surprise. In her mind's eye, Alex's security chief had looked more like Catwoman, not a Chinese grandmother.

Cassandra shook her hand and stood aside. "Where is Mr. Spinoza?" she asked. Wondering whether she knew Caesar's real identity, Cassandra gestured toward the living room. "We are about to have breakfast. Have you eaten?"

Rachel said nothing, just motioned to her two sidekicks. They each picked up two large metal-clad cases, adding to the backpacks each one was wearing.

"Where can we set up?" Rachel asked. Cassandra showed them to the formal dining room. Furnished with a long table, eight chairs, and a counter that ran the length of one wall, it seemed like a perfect command center.

"We'll make it work," Rachel said.

"Can you tell me what's going on?" Cassandra asked. "With Hank Morgan, I mean."

"I'll be briefing you as soon as Mr. Hunt arrives," she said. "Ms. Fleury, I must ask you," she said. "Did anyone—anyone at all—recognize you when you arrived in Las Vegas?"

"No," Cassandra replied. "At least no one I was aware of."

"Good," Rachel said.

"No, wait!" she said, suddenly remembering the obvious. "Our butler—Baldassare—recognized me. I met him briefly when I was at Caesars a few months ago."

"Anyone else?" Rachel asked. Cassandra shook her head. Rachel went back to unpacking a computer.

"I'll be with Mr. Spinoza if you need anything," Cassandra said.

When she joined him in the living room, Caesar was channel surfing with the remote.

"Who are those people?" he asked, without moving his eyes from the screen.

"They are here to ensure your safe return to Rome," Cassandra said. She was about to explain more when the door chimes sounded again. A sumptuous breakfast buffet soon appeared on the bar. She was about to invite Caesar to have something to eat when—more chimes. The Palatine Suite was beginning to feel like Grand Central Station.

Alex Hunt stood at the door alone. He was dressed casually in a pale blue cashmere pullover and khaki slacks.

LXXXVIII

Alex could easily have let himself in, but he chose instead to knock on the door of the Palatine Suite. He knew Rachel had already arrived, but there was much he didn't know. And it was still difficult to believe he was about to meet Julius Caesar.

As he stood there waiting for someone to answer the door, he thought about the night he first met Cassandra, which had ended in this very place. It was amazing that their date had happened at all. He'd told his casino host over and over that he wasn't interested in his offers to provide female companionship. Alex had grown up Baptist, after all. Escorts—or whatever you want to call them—just weren't his style. Never had been.

But Alex was drained that afternoon, and—as always on that awful anniversary—consumed with grief. Dorian was doing his darnedest to cheer him up. Alex gave in just to get Dorian to leave him alone. He never planned to keep the date his host set up for him. But when the time came, he dutifully dressed and headed to Cleopatra's Barge. The good Baptist boy that still lived inside him didn't want his casino host penalized for his client's poor behavior. Meeting Cassandra seemed like the lesser sin.

Alex told Dorian later how much he had enjoyed Cassandra's company. He let him believe that their rendezvous had turned out just the way he expected. What would have been the point of telling him otherwise? He wouldn't have believed that the girl he'd procured for Alex surprised him with a Latin translation and distracted him from his grief with her academic dreams. Cassandra was just what he'd needed that night. At a time he had felt so utterly powerless, she was someone Alex could help.

When Cassandra opened the door, Alex was glad he had decided on courtesy. She was wearing a hotel bathrobe.

"I'm so glad you're here," she said. She sounded genuinely relieved, but she still looked worried. And perhaps embarrassed, Alex thought, as he watched her draw the robe more tightly around her body and cinch the sash.

Then she pulled the door farther open, and Alex stepped into the atrium.

"Ms. Tan is setting up in the dining room," Cassandra said, apparently unaware that Alex already knew. He and Rachel had been in constant contact ever since Cassandra's phone call.

"I—thank you for helping me. I didn't know where else to turn," Cassandra continued.

"I'm glad you called," Alex said. "We'll get everything taken care of."

She shot him a doubtful look.

"Where is—Mr. Spinoza?" Alex asked.

"He's watching a stock car race on TV." Cassandra gestured toward the archway on her left.

Alex was still processing this statement when Cassandra went on.

"What's going on with Danicek?" she asked. "Does he know where we are? Is everything okay?"

"Yes, he's up to speed on everything—helped me plan it all, as a matter of fact. We'll leave tomorrow morning, and we'll get to the lab with plenty of time to spare. Don't worry. Mr. Spinoza will make his return flight, guaranteed."

"Mr. Spinoza," Cassandra repeated. "I'm glad we're using his code name."

"Danicek insisted," Alex said. "It's one thing we agreed on completely." He lowered his voice. "You and I are the only ones here who know the truth about our guest's identity. All our security staff knows is that he's a VIP under threat of abduction, and that getting him to Pasadena on time is vital."

Just then, Rachel appeared in the atrium.

"Hello, Mr. Hunt," she said. "Is this a good time for a general briefing?"

"First I want to meet my guest," Alex said. "Cassandra was just about to do the introductions."

"Very well, sir," Rachel said. "I'm ready when you are." She disappeared again.

Alex turned to Cassandra. "This is all still so difficult for me to believe."

"I'm afraid it won't get any easier," she said. Alex followed her through the archway.

As soon as they entered the room, Caesar turned his gaze toward them and stood up. He wore a robe identical to Cassandra's, which surprised Alex even though it shouldn't have. As he moved closer, he extended his right hand. Such an ordinary gesture, but it caught Alex off guard. Did ancient Romans really shake hands just like us? If they didn't, Caesar was certainly a fast learner. Alex shook his hand, appreciating his firm grasp.

"I am very pleased to meet you," Alex said, not knowing a proper greeting in Latin.

"*Salve*," Caesar said, which was reassuring.

Cassandra said something in Latin. Caesar looked at Alex, smiled, and replied. Cassandra smiled, too.

"Caesar meets Alexander," she translated. "Obviously, I have not traveled into the future, but the past." Cassandra paused and looked into Alex's eyes. "Did you get that?" she asked. "He's comparing you to Alexander the Great."

Alex nodded and felt his face warm.

"Tell him I am truly honored," Alex said when he finally found the words. "Meeting the world's most renowned general is the greatest moment of my life."

The conversation would have continued if Rachel hadn't appeared in the archway to the atrium.

"Sooner would be preferable to later, sir," she said. "We need your input on a few things."

"We'll be right there," Alex said, and Rachel vanished again. He turned again to Caesar.

"We shall return shortly," he said. "Once we have taken care of the details of tomorrow's journey, the day will be ours to enjoy."

Cassandra translated. Caesar sat back down on the sofa and picked up the TV remote. Could this possibly be a real ancient Roman? Or was this all an elaborate prank with Alex as gullible victim? This wasn't the first time he'd wondered, but it made no difference. He was in the game to the end, or as long as Cassandra needed him.

She spoke a few more words to Caesar, and they left him to his car race.

LXXXIX

"You were right about Hank Morgan," Alex said as he and Cassandra walked down the hall. "He and Tarantino have been trying to abduct Caesar."

"But why?"

"A couple of possibilities. They may want him to identify the location of ancient treasures they can sell through Denarius. More likely is that they'll demand the technology itself in exchange for Caesar, then sell it to someone with deep pockets, like Microsoft or the U.S. government."

"How do you know all this?"

"Elizabeth. She told Danicek about Hank right after you and Caesar disappeared. If Hank's heavies hadn't blown out all the tires on the IDES van, Danicek would have come after you immediately. By the time he got the keys to one of Sonia's cars, you were long gone."

"Is Elizabeth in on the plot?"

"Danicek thinks she's clean, but I'm not so sure. She certainly knew things she should have revealed a long time ago. On the other hand, she's been trying to find out more about Hank's schemes—and passing anything she learns on to us. Everything she's told us has panned out."

Cassandra was silent for a moment. "Should I call Danicek?" she asked.

"Only if you want to talk to a pissed-off scientist," Alex said.

Cassandra frowned.

"Don't worry," Alex said. "We got things worked out. But when I called him the first time, he accused me of being a kidnapper and demanded Caesar's immediate return—made some nasty threats. So I hung up. When I called back, he was a little more polite. I don't blame him for being upset, but the good doctor should have known better than to annoy the one person who could get his runaway experiment back."

Cassandra dropped her head, clearly still upset.

"Don't worry," Alex said again. "We'll get Mr. Spinoza to Pasadena in time for his return trip." He paused and lowered his voice to a whisper. "And if you're wondering what I get out of the deal, I have already been paid in full. I've shaken hands with Julius Caesar."

Cassandra looked up with a half-smile. She sighed and straightened her shoulders, and together they headed into Rachel's command center.

Alex took his place at the head of the table and invited Cassandra to sit on his right. Rachel and the two guards remained standing.

Mostly for Cassandra's benefit but also to inform the guards, Rachel outlined the next day's travel plans. Alex already knew everything but the small details.

"If Morgan and Tarantino don't know our whereabouts now," Rachel said in conclusion, "they will momentarily." She looked at Cassandra. "Miss Fleury, your picture just appeared in today's security alert, which means it's available to every casino on the Strip."

"How do you know they're looking for us in Las Vegas?" Cassandra asked. "We came in an unrecognizable car, and we haven't left the suite since we arrived."

"They've been looking everywhere," Rachel said, "and they know you used to work on the Strip. Tarantino has access to casino security intelligence. We have no choice but to assume they've made all the connections."

Cassandra shot Alex a worried glance.

"It'll be all right," he said. "As long as we're here, we're backed up completely by Caesars security. Ms. Tan is assembling everything we need for a safe trip to California."

"Operation Spinoza is now underway," Rachel said. "It is up to each one of us to ensure its success."

As they rose from the table, Alex turned to Cassandra.

"For now, we just have to sit tight," he said.

"That's more of a challenge than you might guess," Cassandra said.

Together, they walked back to the atrium. Cassandra hung back as Alex continued toward the living room.

"Is everything all right?" he asked. "Are you okay?"

Cassandra nodded, but Alex could tell something was bothering her.

"Do you remember the last time we were here together?" she asked.

"Of course," he said. "Why?"

"When I drove off to Los Angeles last summer," she said, "I thought I was leaving my old life behind. I believed you'd saved me." She paused. "I still believed it when I was invited to join the IDES Project—and when I saw you at the coin auction." She looked away, shaking her head. "But in the end, here I am—full circle. The butler knew it as soon as I walked in." She looked directly into his eyes. "I am that girl you met in the bar, only this time—I really am."

They both stood silent for a moment.

"It was my choice," Cassandra said. "Entirely my choice."

Afraid of saying the wrong thing, Alex said nothing.

"It was how I kept him safe last night," Cassandra said, and she explained about the knife Caesar stole, and how frightened she was when she realized he wouldn't fear a gun.

"And it wasn't just that," she said. "I mean—we kidnapped him. The longer I spend with him, the worse I feel about that—that we kidnapped him and we're sending him back to—well, you know—and not telling him. I know it's supposed to be a fancy science experiment, but what it really is—is awful and cruel and—" Cassandra covered her eyes with both hands. Alex put a hand on her shoulder.

She dropped her hands, and Alex saw the tears standing in her eyes. "I just wish I didn't care," she said.

"About what people think?" Alex asked. "I can assure you, I will do my best to—"

"No. I wish I didn't care about Julius Caesar."

Cassandra didn't give Alex a chance to say anything else. She turned and led the way back into the living room.

"Where is Caesar?" Alex asked. He wasn't on the sofa where they had left him.

"Maybe he's in the bathroom," Cassandra said.

"So—we wait?" Alex asked.

"No, we have to find him," she said. "It's too dangerous to leave him alone, and he might need my help."

She led the way to a bedroom. A door on the opposite side stood ajar, and Alex could hear water running.

XC

They crossed the room, and Cassandra pushed the door open. Caesar was sitting naked in an empty bathtub. Water from the tap splashed over his back.

"Ah, Cassandra," Caesar said. "Perhaps you can make this caldarium hold its water."

Cassandra entered the room, knelt at the side of the tub, and flipped the gold lever that controlled the drain. The tub immediately began to fill.

"I was able to make the water run hot, but the secret of stopping the drain eluded me," Caesar said. "Thank you, my dove." He laid his wet hand briefly on her cheek.

She stood up.

"I hope you are not leaving again," Caesar said. "Tell Alexander I would like to talk."

Cassandra relayed the message to Alex, who didn't seem awkward at all as he entered the room and took a seat on a velvet-covered footstool. Cassandra sat down on the end of its matching chaise. An odd gathering in an unlikely place, she thought, but everybody seemed comfortable enough with the arrangement.

"I must tell Caesar again how honored I am to meet him," Alex said. "Does he know that his reputation has done nothing but grow over the last two thousand years? Does he know that his books are still read, still admired? Does he know we still have a month named after him, that we still mark our days by his calendar? Does he know that his achievements are more widely revered than those of Alexander the Great?"

Cassandra translated. Caesar splashed water over his head and face and took his time in composing a reply.

"No," he said at last. "I did not know. And until now, I did not completely believe that I had traveled to the future. I seemed to be in a dream, a phantasmagoria beyond reason. But you, Alexander, speak with authority, and you, Alexander, I shall believe."

Cassandra could have found Caesar's words unflattering. Hadn't she already made it utterly clear that he had traveled to the future, and that his writings were still studied? Did her words hold no weight because she was a girl?

It would have been easy to label Caesar a chauvinist for his refusal to accept her declarations, but when she thought about it later, Cassandra decided that would have been an error. Caesar had been asked, in effect, to swallow a buffalo whole, and it should have come as no surprise that he couldn't accomplish the deed until the beast was reduced into edible portions. Danicek and the rest of the IDES team had done the tenderizing, the cooking, the cutting up. Alex had come along at just the right moment to serve the feast.

And Alex was exactly Caesar's kind of guy. It was a wonderful coincidence that they were almost identical in age, and that they both took pride in their fitness and appearance. She had thought Andrew Danicek and Caesar had hit it off well, but their rapport was nothing compared to what blossomed between the two veteran soldiers.

"I have enjoyed my stay in your country," Caesar said, reclining in the tub and looking at Alex. "Cassandra has been an excellent companion. What I thought might be a sojourn in a prison cell has turned out instead to be a first-rate adventure."

"Do you have questions about our world, our society?" Alex asked when Cassandra had rendered Caesar's comments.

"I have refrained from posing queries," replied Caesar when she translated. "I have always found it more useful—and more accurate—to observe. I trust my own senses over other people's opinions." He paused thoughtfully. "I have observed a godless society with a dearth of animals, too many old fat people and women with cropped hair, and an endless supply of machines. Is there something more I should know?"

When Cassandra translated, Alex laughed. "Your observations are accurate," he said. "And the truth is, I am the one with questions. The stories that survive about you are glorious, but they are tantalizing in their missing pieces. It would please me greatly if you would simply talk about your life."

"I always look on my own past as my stepping stone to the future," said Caesar. "In every other respect it is useless, and I marvel at how many men wallow in it, allowing it to suck them down into a mire of regret and inactivity.

"And yet, I have gained much from studying the past of others, especially the histories of those men who triumphed over seemingly insurmountable obstacles, who succeeded in ways no one before them ever dreamed. Alexander. I saw a likeness of him once when I was in Spain, and I wept at the sight of it. He lived a life scarcely more than half the length of mine, and yet he conquered the whole world."

"The story of your visit to Alexander's statue lives to this day," Cassandra said after she had rendered Caesar's words for Alex. "Historians have debated the truth of the anecdote for centuries."

"They need argue no more," said Caesar with a sad chuckle. "It is the truth. Caesar wept before Alexander. And if the truth be known, it is because of him that I shall be marching on Parthia before the month is out."

Alex and Cassandra shared a glance, but Caesar didn't pose any awkward questions.

"Did you know I have had four wives?" he asked instead. "Four wives and not a single son."

"Am I correct that you had a daughter?" Alex asked when Cassandra had translated.

"Yes, I had a daughter," Caesar replied. "She died."

The sadness in Caesar's voice made her hesitate, but as Cassandra turned toward Alex to translate, she realized he had already understood.

"I ask not because I wish to open a wound," Alex said, "but because I, too, lost my only child. My daughter and my wife both perished the same day."

Cassandra had a hard time speaking as she thought about the terrible tragedies both men had faced.

"I—It's just that I'm so sorry," she stammered.

Alex patted her knee. "I just wanted Caesar to know that he and I share a similar bereavement."

Cassandra translated, and Caesar looked directly at Alex as he replied.

"Time is always cruel, but never more ruthless than when it colludes with death to seize a child while its parent still lives."

They fell into a silence that lasted until Alex asked a question that changed the subject.

"The injury to your shoulder—it happened in battle?"

Cassandra translated, but Caesar did not reply immediately. "I was a boy," he said at last. "I was hunting for deer in the Sabine hills when a lion attacked me."

"*A lion?*" Alex reacted exactly as Cassandra had, and his tone alone was enough for Caesar to understand.

"Is it so difficult to believe?" Caesar asked.

"Tell Caesar I was not responding in disbelief," Alex said. "I was thinking about how different our world would be if he had died as a child."

Caesar smiled when he heard Alex's explanation. "I am honored by your words, Alexander," he said. Then he pulled himself to his feet.

"The water has cooled too much for comfort," he said as he stood there naked in front of them. "I am amazed that this caldarium, for all its shiny splendor, lacks a hypocaust."

XCI

"What's a hypocaust?" Alex asked when Cassandra told him why Caesar had leapt from the bath so suddenly.

"It's an ancient water heater," she replied as she held a robe open for Caesar. "The baths had raised floors, and heat was forced under them from a central oven. Like radiant heating."

Caesar indicated that he would like a shave. Cassandra led the way to the adjoining room, where Caesar took a seat at the counter in front of the mirror. Cassandra looked at all three of their reflected faces. Caesar and Alex both looked content, as though this tableau were the most ordinary thing in the world. Cassandra lathered Caesar up with some expensive-looking Italian shaving cream and shaved his whiskers with an equally high-end razor.

Although she was afraid the interruption might destroy the progress of their conversation, she was happily wrong. As soon as he sat down in front of the mirror, Caesar said, "I wish to speak of the Egyptian queen."

Cassandra ran the razor over his cheek, wondering what Caesar would divulge.

"Would that I had never succumbed to Cleopatra's wiles," he said. "It appears now that I shall pay in perpetuity."

"She is in Rome now," he went on, "with her son, the boy she calls Caesarion. Cassandra has told me you know of him."

Alex nodded after Cassandra translated.

"I believe he is my son. It would be better for Rome if he were not. I have not yet decided whether to recognize him as my heir. What would you do in such a circumstance, Alexander?"

What a question! How would Alex answer? Did he know he was supposed to keep Caesar in the dark about his immediate future? Alex said nothing for at least a minute.

"If I believed he was my child," he said at last, "I would claim him. I would want my son to know his father."

Cassandra translated accurately, even though she could easily have altered Alex's message. What difference did it make? Caesar would never have the chance to act on Alex's advice. Even so, she knew she needed to redirect this conversation, in case it went further into areas they needed to avoid.

Cassandra was certain that Alex was interested in how Caesar waged war. "Caesar is the reason I loved Latin in high school," he'd told her the night of the coin auction. "When I was in Vietnam, I often thought about what might have happened if he'd been our general. I think we would have emerged victorious, or, as Caesar did in Britain, we would have withdrawn before committing ourselves too deeply to a war we weren't willing to win."

"Alexander is now a private citizen," she said to Caesar, "but he was a commander in one of our country's recent wars." It was enough. Caesar, distracted by her words from his question about Caesarion, brightened instantly, and fresh conversation flowed.

For the first time, Cassandra was truly grateful to Dr. Martinelli for guiding her through Caesar's *Commentaries*. She knew all the words for siege towers and winter quarters and artillery and materiel, knowledge that served her well as long as the men spoke of Caesar's campaigns. It was another story, however, when Alex attempted to explain his own military career. How do you say "helicopter" in Latin? It's a Greek word, of course, but "spiral wing" doesn't carry sufficient meaning for someone who preceded the Wright brothers by a couple of millennia.

"It's all right," Alex said when in desperation Cassandra suggested getting a pad and pencil. "Tomorrow is soon enough. Tomorrow, Caesar will be traveling in a 'spiral wing!'"

"Of all the machines I have seen in your world," said Caesar when Cassandra had translated, "this one will interest me the most. I am eager to see a flying chariot."

Caesar was even more delighted to find that their transportation plans for tomorrow also included a "fixed wing," which is how Cassandra described an airplane. He's got guts, she thought, but maybe she shouldn't have been surprised. She knew he was a lover of speed, a man who'd astonished his enemies by traveling a hundred miles a day with only horseflesh underneath him. It was no wonder he'd enjoyed the stock car race so much.

They talked, or, more accurately, Alex and Caesar talked, about all things military until the tailor arrived. Caesar was intrigued by the thought of fighting battles from the air, but Alex defended his view that, in the final analysis, victory remained elusive without the infantry.

"No matter how many birds of war fly overhead, it is the foot soldier who claims the triumph," he said. "You, Caesar, set a standard that has never been eclipsed. Not only did you fight and win against hideous odds in engagements like Alesia, you wrote about them. Your pen has proved to be even mightier than your sword."

"Alesia," Caesar said. "It was indeed a battle for the ages." As he recounted how he had prevailed over an enemy that outnumbered his own forces five to one, Cassandra was seized with the nagging thought that there had to be more to the story than this one man's recollection. Would the Gallic leader recall events the same way? She had the uneasy feeling that if Vercingetorix related his own version of what transpired on that hillside, it would be difficult to believe he was talking about the same battle.

It was both distressing and enlightening to realize that history, even when reported by an eyewitness, is not the same thing as the past itself. At most, it is an impressionist painting. It conveys an image of real events, but it is blurred by swirls and daubs of opinion and agenda. Everything Caesar told them, Cassandra already knew from his *Commentaries*. Having codified his memories in writing, he stuck with his official rendition. Cassandra supposed this should have encouraged her to trust his veracity, but instead she was reminded of politicians on TV. They get their story straight, and then stick like barnacles to their "talking points." If they're as good at the game as Caesar was, no interviewer can ever pierce the veneer.

But Alex didn't seem to notice or mind that Caesar was using the conversation to reinforce his prestige. He was happy to play the part of awe-struck admirer and dish out praise whenever it was his turn to talk. By the time Rachel entered with the tailor, Caesar had been thoroughly deified.

In his wake, the tailor left three sets of underwear, three pairs of socks and shoes, a striped sports shirt, a purple cashmere V-neck pullover, a brown suede jacket, a white dress shirt, and a purple bow tie with a matching silk cummerbund. Caesar also tried on a pair of khaki trousers and a black tuxedo that needed some minor alteration to fit perfectly. The tailor promised to return them within the hour.

Cassandra was amazed that Caesar was so willing to don such restrictive and barbaric garments, but he liked Alex and seemed to be enjoying himself. He'd also heard about their plans for the evening, and Cassandra was right. He loved the idea of rolling dice for money, and the opportunity to leave the confines of the suite—if only to go to one other room—pleased him even more.

The "personal shopper" from the Forum Shops arrived just as the tailor left. Cassandra had assumed that she'd retire to one of the bedrooms to decide on her wardrobe privately, but the shopper, whose name was Angel, had different ideas. She was a Vegas type Cassandra remembered all too well from her casino days, a lady who had—when younger—likely pursued the career path Cassandra had embarked on when Alex changed her plans. Obviously paid on commission, she was a pro at sniffing out whose money was at stake and how to maximize its flow in her direction.

Cassandra could have refused, but instead the two men got to watch her parade in front of them in everything from a silk negligee to a sequined silk evening gown. It didn't make her feel exactly proud of herself, but she couldn't think of a better way to keep Caesar's mind off stealing knives or attempting to escape.

Cassandra ended up keeping everything Angel brought except a red nylon raincoat and matching hat.

"It makes you look like a fire hydrant," Alex said, but it was his only negative comment. She ended up with a complete new wardrobe, including shoes, underwear, a tourmaline necklace with matching earrings, and a calfskin coat. There wasn't a price tag in sight, but Alex didn't seem bothered in the least. He was the one saying, "Go for it!"

XCII

While Caesar dozed on the living room sofa after lunch, Alex beckoned to Cassandra from the balcony off the library. She stepped out into a cool breeze to join him.

"I have given what you told me some thought," he said. "I wish I could promise you that everything will be all right."

Cassandra gazed into his eyes, wondering what he meant.

"It won't be. You've done something vital—maybe even heroic—but few people will ever know. And not only that, they'll believe the worst about you."

Cassandra said nothing. Her shoulders sagged as she realized he was talking about Caesar and her.

"You will be all right."

"But didn't you just tell me—?"

"I said *everything* won't be all right. But *you* will be."

She sighed. "I don't understand."

"When I was in Vietnam," Alex said, "I did something that got me court martialed."

Cassandra said nothing.

"Only one other person still alive knows the truth," Alex continued. "There were a few others, but—"

"And you're going to tell me?" Cassandra asked. "Why?"

"Because I think you'll understand. Because I think it might help—"

He looked at her, a question in his eyes.

"I'd like to hear," she said.

Alex looked out over the city and began his story. "When I was in Vietnam, I took a helicopter one night without authorization. I used it to pick up three Vietnamese children and their father an hour before their village was bombed. When I returned to base, I was arrested. Later, I was court martialed. Although I escaped conviction, I received a dishonorable discharge."

"But you saved four people," she said, "so why—?"

"Officially, they were the enemy," he said. "But in reality the man I rescued worked undercover for the American cause. His intelligence had saved hundreds of American lives, including my own. To save him without revealing his role and risking more lives, someone had to be the fall guy." His eyes locked with Cassandra's. "The few who knew the truth applauded my actions even as they prosecuted me. To the public—and even to my family—I was a traitor."

Cassandra gazed out over the Strip as she pondered Alex's words.

"You are a hero, Cassandra."

"I am a traitor."

"Andrew Danicek might think so, but—"

She looked Alex square in the eyes. "I do not care what Andrew Danicek thinks. I care what Julius Caesar thinks."

"Caesar does not think you are a traitor," Alex said. "He cares for you."

"And I care for him," she said. "I didn't want to, but I do." Tears jumped to her eyes.

Alex held out his arms. Cassandra fell into them and sobbed against his chest. She couldn't be sure, but she thought Alex was weeping, too.

When at last she pulled away, Cassandra glanced back into the living room. Caesar was still dozing on the sofa. She had to pull herself together before he woke up. There was nothing to be gained by shedding tears in front of him.

Cassandra wiped her eyes and forced herself to think about the moment at hand. Time was flying, but there was still plenty left. As she thought about their evening plans, an idea sprang into her head.

"Do you think it would be possible," she asked, "to invite my tutor to join us tonight? Next to you, I can think of no other person more deserving of a chance to meet Julius Caesar."

After Alex made arrangements for Dr. Martinelli to join them for the evening, they taught Caesar how to shoot craps on the coffee table in the living room. He loved the large, translucent red dice the concierge supplied, partly, Cassandra thought, because they had "CAESARS" stamped on one side. He asked if he could take a set back with him to Rome.

"Unfortunately," she said, "that will be impossible. You can take only the items you arrived with. Your signet ring, your toga, your shoes."

"So you have said," Caesar said, and he didn't pursue the subject. Cassandra was both relieved and unnerved. He seemed a little too acquiescent.

At five o'clock, they changed into their high-roller clothes, and a little later the champagne and caviar arrived. As she loaded up a toast point and took a bite, Cassandra was immediately transported to the first time she'd tasted expensive fish eggs. It was back at the IDES Project lab, at the small reception Danicek hosted to welcome her to the team. Too bad he'll never trust me again, she thought. There was no way that he would ever think of her as anything but a traitor, especially now that she had added her former teacher to the growing list of people who knew the truth about the IDES Project. Cassandra was on her own, with only Alex's helicopter story to bolster her nerve.

XCIII

The call came in at three o'clock, just after Dennis Martinelli had returned home after helping his mother get settled in her new room at a convalescent hospital on East Tropicana. It was a relief to see her health and spirits improving. Worrying about Cassandra Fleury was enough of a burden. John Reynolds had called two more times, but Dennis knew less than he did. Almost as troubling as Cassandra's disappearance was John's reluctance to tell Dennis what was really going on at the IDES Lab.

"Mr. Dennis Martinelli?" A woman's voice asked. When Dennis acknowledged that she had reached the right person, she continued. "Ms. Cassandra Fleury has requested the honor of your presence this evening at Caesars Palace."

While Dennis was, quite naturally, surprised by the unexpected invitation and this unfamiliar woman's formal manner, he replied that it would be his pleasure to accept. But coming as it did after John's phone calls, the invitation worried him, too. He couldn't begin to guess what the evening held in store.

"It is a formal affair," the woman said, which sent Dennis to his spare closet in search of his ancient tux. Unable to find all the required accessories or the right shirt, he settled instead on a navy blue blazer and gray slacks. Formal by most Vegas standards, at least.

At precisely 4:30, three sharp raps called Dennis to his front door, where, just as the woman had explained over the phone, two men in black suits greeted him and escorted him to a huge black SUV driven by a third dark-suited gentleman.

Cassandra Fleury, exactly what have you gotten yourself into?

The black SUV delivered Dennis and his two escorts to a door deep in the bowels of the Caesars Palace parking garage. They rode up several levels in an industrial elevator, walked several hundred yards down a service corridor, and then took another lift to a floor high in a tower. Dennis soon found himself facing Neptune and a frolicking hippocampus in a lavish replica of a Roman atrium.

Pulling out the handkerchief he was glad he had remembered to tuck into his pocket, Dennis wiped a few beads of nervous sweat from his brow. What scenario awaited him?

He was still wondering when Cassandra appeared in an archway to his right. Dressed in a sparkling silver evening gown, she looked like a creature from a fashion magazine.

"Dr. Martinelli!" she said, smiling as she glided to his side. "I can't tell you how happy I am that you are here."

"Thank you for inviting me," Dennis said, "but—"

"Before you meet everyone," she interrupted. "I must tell you something." She lowered her voice to a whisper. "The truth about the IDES project."

And as they stood there surrounded by faux Roman grandeur, Dennis learned the identity of the evening's guest of honor.

Could it be true? He stared at his beautiful student. What she was telling him was utterly beyond belief. And yet, he thought, there's no reason for her to lie, and it's unlikely she would have been fooled by an actor. No actor could fool me, either, he told himself. If this Julius Caesar is a fake, he'll have to be the best fake in history.

Dennis gave his forehead a final blot, stuffed his handkerchief back into his pocket, and followed Cassandra through the archway.

XCIV

The entourage descended several floors. When the doors slid apart, the aroma of expensive tobacco surrounded them. The two guards preceded them into the hall, conducted a quick security check, and led the group down an elegant corridor paneled in marble and mahogany. A concierge stepped from behind a tall desk as they approached the end. Welcoming them with smiling politeness, he held a heavy set of double doors open.

The room they entered was nothing like the public casino downstairs. This salon, with its opulent decor and spectacular view of the Strip, boasted a much more rarefied atmosphere. It was used exclusively for private parties, Alex had told Cassandra, and tonight he was the host. They could have had the room to themselves, but because Alex wanted to give Caesar a taste of real Las Vegas nightlife, he had arranged with the manager to invite thirty or so hand-selected guests.

"I don't know any of them personally, and they think the casino is 'comping' them," he told Cassandra. "We can mingle without attracting any attention, and Caesar can enjoy the feeling of a larger party." Together they agreed that if they found a need to introduce Caesar to anyone, they'd use the story that he was visiting from Andorra, and that he spoke only a local dialect of Catalan. Just to make sure they weren't met with any surprises, Alex had instructed the manager to invite only all-American monoglots, the kind who expect the rest of the world to speak English. Given the dossiers casinos keep on their high-rolling customers, Cassandra was confident that they wouldn't be confronted by anyone with multi-lingual capabilities. In addition, they'd all be enjoying a magnificent feast, drinking free booze, smoking free cigars, and gambling. They'd be far too self-absorbed to give a damn about anyone but themselves.

Even so, Cassandra had been nervous about leaving the penthouse with Caesar. Alex knew what had happened at the Illingsworth estate, but he was confident that Hank Morgan and Steve Tarantino were no match for him, his team, and his juice.

"Andrew Danicek may be a genius, but his security measures are amateur," Alex had said. "Mine are not."

But Hank Morgan didn't seem like an amateur, and Steve Tarantino had a lot of juice in Las Vegas, too. What if they had more influence with Caesars Palace than Alex? All Cassandra could do was hope the good guys would win.

When Caesar realized that he could converse easily with Dr. Martinelli, conversation flowed between the two men. At first, Cassandra was concerned that two men speaking Latin might arouse curiosity among other guests, but no one paid either of them any attention at all.

Cassandra chatted with Alex as she caught bits and pieces of Caesar's comments about the challenges facing the Roman Republic. It was exactly the sort of conversation John Reynolds and Elizabeth Palmer had hoped for.

The two men had moved on to writing and grammar when a waiter appeared at Caesar's side with a humidor. Caesar shot Cassandra a questioning look, but Alex came to his rescue before his uncertainty became apparent. With Cassandra's help, he suggested that Caesar wait until they had retired upstairs to try his first puff.

"You set it on fire to use it," Cassandra warned in Latin. "It takes some practice." Alex tucked three cigars into his breast pocket. "We'll enjoy them later," he said, and instructed the waiter to bring a round of vintage port.

At the craps table, Cassandra stayed at Caesar's side. She had taught him about placing bets, but he needed her to interpret his desires to the croupier. At first, Cassandra wasn't sure he could remember everything she'd told him about points and pass lines, but it wasn't long before she had no doubt he understood the game perfectly. He grinned when it was his turn to shoot.

Caesar's smile was prophetic. Fifteen minutes later, he was still rolling, and as word rippled over the salon that the shooter was "hot," the crowd around their table grew. When Cassandra looked up five minutes later, the entire room had gathered to watch and bet, including Alex and Dr. Martinelli. The air was thick with smoke and excitement, and the stacks of chips on the table represented a tycoon's salary. Caesar's run lasted well over half an hour, and when at last he "crapped out," every larynx in the room emitted a simultaneous groan.

"Good work, my friend!" said Alex, slapping Caesar on the back and gesturing toward his towering piles of chips. "You paid for the party!"

Not long afterward, Alex suggested they retire to the suite. "We can speak more freely there," he said, "and we have a long day ahead of us tomorrow."

Again they found themselves reflected in the mirrored walls of the elevator. Cassandra gazed at Caesar. The craps game had distracted her for a moment, but now, all she could think about was that he'd be facing his murderers in less than twenty-four hours. Alex, as though he knew what Cassandra was thinking, squeezed her shoulder.

"The night is still young," he said softly.

When they had returned to the suite, Alex invited Caesar, Dr. Martinelli, and Cassandra to sit down on the sofa facing the window. Alex sank into a chair. Reaching inside his jacket, he extracted the three cigars and laid them on the coffee table.

"Cassandra," he said, "I hope you won't label me sexist for assuming that you don't smoke cigars. If I'm wrong, you can have mine. Either way, I have something else for you, a memento of the evening."

Reaching once more into his breast pocket, Alex opened his hand. There, covering most of his palm, was a gold coin.

"This is for you."

The coin was large, at least twice the size of a silver dollar. Cassandra picked it up. It was thick and heavy. An image of Augustus was embossed in the center. Above, "Caesars Palace" and "Las Vegas" below in raised letters. She turned the coin over to find the profiles of two boxers with raised gloves. "Haycock-Flores," the letters spelled out, "December 17, 1997.

"It's solid gold," Alex said. "Six ounces. It represents some of the winnings Caesar rolled for me."

Caesar, who had been busy removing his shoes, leaned over to take a look. Cassandra handed him the coin and translated what Alex had told her.

"Men get tobacco, and ladies get gold," she added with a laugh. Dr. Martinelli inspected the coin, too. "Haycock-Flores," he said. "That was a fight for the record books."

"I wish I had been there," Alex said. "Cassandra, I'm sure the coin is worth more than its weight in gold. Save it for a rainy day."

Caesar would have preferred a gold coin, too. There was no convincing him that a cigar was a pleasure. Every puff made him hack and cough, and, while he liked the smell of tobacco when it wasn't burning, he hated it when it was. It wasn't long before Alex set his cigar down.

"I am going to bed," he said. "We have a long day ahead of us tomorrow. I hope you will forgive me for retiring early."

As soon as Alex stood up, Dr. Martinelli was on his feet, too.

"This has been the most memorable experience of my life," he said. "I thank you, Cassandra and Alex, for including me."

He turned toward Caesar and spoke in Latin.

"Hail and farewell, Caesar," he said. "The whole world owes you a debt of gratitude it can never repay. I am glad that you have at least seen evidence that your glory blazes ever brightly these two thousand years since your own time."

"Hail and farewell, great teacher," Caesar said. Dr. Martinelli flushed with pleasure.

Accompanied by the guards who had been waiting in the kitchen, he departed. A moment later, Alex vanished into his bedroom. Caesar and Cassandra were suddenly alone, and it wasn't even eleven o'clock.

"He is a generous man, your Alexander," said Caesar, breaking the silence Alex had left behind him. He picked up the gold medallion and turned it over in his fingers. "To Cassandra, he gives gold. To Caesar, he gives Cassandra."

"I am not his to give," Cassandra might have protested, but this was no time for indignation. She moved closer to Caesar. He kissed her forehead.

XCV

Cassandra awoke with a start, unaware that she had fallen asleep. Looking toward the window, she realized with despair that the sky was tinged with pink. Caesar's head was nestled next to her heart, and he was breathing deeply, peacefully.

What kind of monster are you, Cassandra? she asked herself silently. Today, you will escort Caesar to his death. You might as well be holding a bloody knife. You're as guilty as Brutus, as hideous a traitor.

God, I really am, she thought. Her motives were identical. If Caesar died, their lives went on unchanged. If history had it right, all Brutus ever wanted was to preserve the Republic, to keep Caesar from becoming a tyrant. Maintaining the status quo, that was his lofty goal. Damn. That was Cassandra's own lofty goal.

But didn't Caesar's assassins get it wrong? By killing him, they achieved exactly what they hoped to prevent. They murdered whatever chance remained of restoring the Republic. They paved the way for tyranny.

Cassandra's thoughts raged on.

Idiots! How could they be so stupid as to think they could put things back? Time moves in one direction, and it's never backward.

But wasn't Danicek trying to put things back? That's what he'd said. "We'll put Caesar back exactly where we got him. Nobody will ever be the wiser."

But *I'm* wiser, you bastard! You can't put *me* back! I'll live the rest of my life with a Judas kiss on my conscience!

Caesar stirred and smiled in his sleep. Cassandra's tears fell on his forehead, and she softly kissed them away. "Forgive me," she whispered. "Forgive me." She lay there, watching the sun do battle with the neon, and wept silently until no more tears would come.

Caesar was still asleep when Cassandra slipped out of his embrace. She crept across the hall to the facing bedroom, where she showered and dressed. It was six o'clock when she emerged. Rachel Tan was standing near the door, barking orders into her headset. Their long day had begun.

If everything went according to Rachel's well-oiled plan, they would be arriving back at the IDES Lab four hours before Caesar had to meet his date with destiny. Alex had guaranteed Andrew Danicek that they'd get there in time for dinner.

Cassandra dreaded the last supper. Could she really keep up the pretense when she knew what awaited Caesar back in Rome? It was too hideous to think about. She almost wished she could stay in Las Vegas.

She sighed as she watched Rachel snap commands over her radio. She knew there was no avoiding their return to Pasadena. The only thing to do was to keep on moving forward, and be grateful that the day ahead of her would be logistically challenging. She'd have to concentrate, and that meant she couldn't be wallowing in sorrow. Careful to avoid disturbing Rachel's one-sided dialogue, Cassandra sidestepped her and headed into the kitchen. After an evening of champagne and a night with little sleep, she was desperate for a cup of coffee.

There were four burly, dark-suited guys in the kitchen, none of whom Cassandra recognized. They stopped talking and stared at her when she walked in the door. She felt as though she had invaded their private lair.

"Coffee," Cassandra said. "I'm looking for coffee."

"Uh, yes, Miss Fleury," said one of the bulgy boys as he sprang into action. "How do you take it?"

"Black," she said. "No sugar."

A mug appeared in her hands, and Cassandra retreated to the living room. Rachel was still talking to her radio, and Cassandra sat down on the sofa facing the window. The gold coin Alex had given her the night before still lay on the coffee table. She picked it up, hefting its weight in her fingers. How much is it worth? she wondered as she slipped it into the pocket of her new leather pants.

She was wearing a new leather jacket, too. Skins seemed to make the appropriate statement for a day of walkie-talkies and rapid transportation.

When Alex came in, Cassandra saw that he'd opted for leather, also, in the form of a black bomber jacket. It suited him, and as he walked across the room toward her, she could see the young helicopter hero in his smile.

"Good morning, Cassandra," he said. "I hope you're doing okay."

Cassandra shrugged and tried to smile.

"I guess Caesar's still sleeping?" Alex asked. "It's okay if he is. We don't have to wake him up for another half hour or so. By the way, you look wonderful."

"Your doing," she said. "Thanks again for the shopping spree."

Just then, Caesar appeared in the archway. He was draped in a sheet.

"Oh, there you are, Cassandra," he said. "I was wondering where you had gone."

"I'll be back," Cassandra said to Alex. She and Caesar retreated into their bedroom.

"Cassandra," Caesar said when she had closed the door, "you have told me I may take nothing from your world with me when I return."

"Yes," she said. "It is dangerous enough that you will take knowledge."

"So you keep telling me," he replied, "but here is another question. May I leave something of mine in your world? May I leave Cassandra a gift?"

What was this? Her heart skipped a beat.

"Caesar," she said quietly when she found her voice. "There is nothing that would please me more. But again, I must say no. If you leave something of yours here that belongs in the past, it could alter history in ways we cannot predict. You must return with all the possessions you had when you arrived. We must part with only our memories."

Caesar did not reply. Instead, he rose from the edge of the bed and let the sheet he'd been wearing fall to the floor. He stood there in naked silence, and it was clear that their conversation was over. Cassandra took off her jacket and pushed up her sleeves. It was time to draw Caesar's last bath in the twentieth century. She tried not to think about the fact that it was also the last bath of his life.

XCVI

When, half an hour later, Caesar and Cassandra emerged into the living room, they joined the day's proceedings already underway. Breakfast had appeared on the bar, and the four black-suited guards Cassandra had met in the kitchen were tucking into big plates of eggs and bacon. Rachel, now clad in black cargo pants and a combat-equipped utility belt, looked like a Special Forces commando. She and Alex were engaged in heavy conversation, but Alex broke away when he saw Caesar.

"Good morning!" he said, moving toward him with a smile. Cassandra was about to translate when Caesar replied.

"Good morning!" Caesar said in English. God. Another week or two and he'd be bilingual. He didn't even have much of an accent.

After they ate, it was time to get ready to depart. Two brand-new leather suitcases had magically appeared in the atrium, and Cassandra knew from the logistics powwow that they were for her use. They'd be trucked, along with Simone's Corvette, back to Beverly Hills. She folded all the new clothes into them, along with the outfits she and Caesar had arrived in.

At eleven-thirty, they were ready to roll. Rachel ushered Caesar, Alex, and Cassandra into the hall. Instead of the elevator facing them, she directed them to the service elevator twenty feet away.

"Please move to the back," she said as they stepped inside. They complied, lining up against the stainless steel wall with Caesar in the middle. Three of the guards moved in next, turning their substantial backs toward them. Rachel squeezed in next. The doors slid shut.

As the personal bouquet of their bodyguards filled the compartment with the aroma of old cigarettes, nervous sweat, and Juicy Fruit gum, the reality of their departure suddenly hit Cassandra. Her reprieve was over, and a pang of fear seized her stomach. They were leaving their ivory tower, and Hank Morgan knew where they were. Would his goons ambush them as soon as they left the building? A sour taste of coffee and scrambled eggs rose in Cassandra's throat, and she fought off a wave of nausea.

Get a grip! she commanded herself. You can't throw up in here! The thought of annoying Rachel scared her stomach into submission, and by the time the elevator doors parted on the lowest level, Cassandra was fairly sure its contents would stay put.

"Don't move until I tell you to!" Rachel commanded as the car slowed to a stop. The doors slid apart to reveal a wide corridor lit by harsh orange lights and two more steroid-enhanced members of the dark suit gang.

Rachel held the elevator open. The guards stepped out. At Rachel's signal, everyone else followed them into the corridor. Cassandra took Caesar's right arm, Alex took his left, and Rachel fell in behind them. Five black suits surrounded them like a cell wall, and they proceeded in formation through the catacombs of Caesars Palace.

Three right turns, one ramp, and two sets of double doors later, they found themselves in the security office, a square, gray room full of armed men at metal desks. The man at the desk nearest the door leapt to his feet when he saw them. Guiding them to another door on the far side of the room, he ushered them into the employee parking garage in single file.

Three huge black SUVs were lined up nose to tail right on the other side of the security office door. All three had been hired by Rachel, one for Caesar and two decoys. Rachel was taking no chances. If Hank and Steve's men were watching, they'd have no way of telling which car held their quarry. With luck, the bad guys would follow the wrong car, but there was still a large chance they'd be in direct pursuit. What Rachel expected was that they'd split up. "We'll divide and conquer," she'd said. Considering the legion of operatives she had hired for the maneuver, it seemed like a fool-proof plan, and Cassandra's nerves quieted a little as she slid next to Caesar on the leather seat in the back of the third SUV. Alex climbed in next to her. Rachel and two guards took the middle seat. Another guard shut the door and climbed into the front passenger seat. A minute later, the car began to move. Thanks to the action plan Rachel had required everyone to memorize, Cassandra could report what happened next even though she couldn't see, and even though Caesar was distracting her by rapping his knuckles on the ceiling.

At exactly eleven-fifty a.m., three black Chevrolet Suburbans exited the employees' garage at Caesars Palace. All three turned right on Industrial Road. Anyone observing would have thought they were a convoy, but the parade was soon over. The first one made a sudden, hard left under the freeway and headed south to join Interstate 15. It was on a beeline for Los Angeles. The second vehicle split off at Fashion Show Drive.

A block later, it turned left on Spring Mountain and right onto Paradise Road. As any taxi driver would confirm, it was the obvious route to McCarran International Airport, where Alex's private jet was parked at the executive terminal. The third SUV stayed on Industrial to Wyoming, where it turned left. It made a right onto Rancho and then slowed at the corner of Cheyenne. It was a path that looked like it had nothing to do with getting to Pasadena, but it actually did. The third black Excursion, the one that held Julius Caesar, was headed for the Cheyenne Air Center.

XCVII

Rachel talked nonstop into her radio as the SUV zoomed north. Cassandra listened to the one-sided dialogue, grateful that Rachel seemed so competent. Everything seemed to be going smoothly until she heard Rachel say, "Shit! Take cover and call Metro!" Cassandra listened in horror as Rachel told Alex that three armed thugs had opened fire on the SUV that had gone to the executive terminal.

"Step on it!" Rachel commanded the driver. She twisted her head around. "If we aren't being followed yet, we're probably about to be."

The SUV sped faster, but the waits at traffic lights seemed interminable.

"I'm worried about that white Honda," Rachel said. "It's been with us since Sahara."

Cassandra turned to look. A white sedan with tinted windows was following them a car or two back. But it didn't get any closer, even as they approached the airport.

When the SUV finally pulled into the airport driveway, the gate to the airstrip opened automatically. Rachel was barking instructions before the vehicle pulled to a stop.

"Get out and head directly to the ladder under the tail as quickly as you can," she said. "Do not stop. Keep moving." She pushed the door open while the driver was still braking. Everyone tumbled out into bright sun, strong wind, and the roar of propellers. Cassandra squinted through her whipping hair, and sure enough, there in front of her was a shiny silver airplane, all revved up and ready to go.

Fortunately, it looked pretty good to her aeronautically untrained eyes. She knew they were going to be flying in a plane that belonged to Alex's old commander in Vietnam, a museum piece of which he was very proud. When she heard the word "museum," Cassandra braced herself for an open-cockpit biplane with canvas wings. This plane, although not exactly a 747, was at least a product of the second half of the twentieth century. It was cigar-shaped, about the length of a school bus, and its name, as evidenced by carefully painted cheesecake near the nose, was "Miss Mitzi."

Cassandra didn't have the chance to inspect the exterior further. The entourage covered the short distance between the SUV and the tail end of the plane. They clattered up a short ladder into carpeted darkness.

It took a minute for her eyes to adjust to the low light inside the cabin, but when they did, all thoughts of the Wright brothers were permanently erased. Cassandra found herself in a compartment of paneled luxury. The floor was covered with Persian carpets. The walls were finished in polished hardwood, and the chairs and sofas they sank into were velvet and mahogany masterpieces. The room glowed in the warm light of wall sconces, and a small, mirror-backed bar had a rack of crystal wine glasses suspended above it.

The noise from the engines was still overpowering, and no one attempted to speak. They had just caught their breaths when an unfamiliar silhouette darkened the doorway.

"Welcome, friends!" a deep voice shouted over the roar. "Please make yourselves at home. *Mi avión es su avión*, as they say. Ha, ha."

Alex greeted his old commander. He was wearing an olive drab flight suit and a maroon beret jauntily pulled down low over his left ear. He was probably past seventy, but he was still slim and fit, another old soldier whose military bearing Caesar would recognize immediately. "Meet Marty Aiken!" Alex shouted.

A younger man in a flight suit followed Marty into the cabin. He pulled the door—or was it a hatch?—up behind him, which cut the engine noise substantially.

"This is your pilot, Mike Darling," he said, slapping the Tom Cruise look-alike on the shoulder and stepping behind him. "And it's time for me to say, '*Bon voyage!*'" Opening the hatch again, Marty Aiken disappeared in a blast of dusty turbulence.

"Buckle up," Mike said after he'd secured the hatch once more. "We'll be taking off momentarily." He really did look like a movie star, with his finely chiseled features and wavy dark hair. Mike and Rachel, who would be the co-pilot, moved forward to the cockpit. Cassandra could see the instrument panel from where she was sitting. It was ablaze with lighted dials and little lights. *It looks modern enough,* she thought with relief. She was not a happy flyer at the best of times, and she'd certainly never had the slightest desire to go barnstorming.

Cassandra tried not to think about the fact that this plane would be not taking them all the way to Pasadena. They'd be landing at Brackett Field in La Verne, where a helicopter would be waiting to fly them the rest of the way. *Oh, God.* The future that only yesterday had seemed a long way off had arrived. A stiff drink suddenly sounded very tempting, or a double dose of Valium. At least, Cassandra told herself, nobody seemed to have followed them between Caesars Palace and the airport. With any luck, the excitement was over, and the rest of the trip would go exactly as planned.

She looked at Caesar, who was sitting next to her on a burgundy velvet love seat. His face was flushed, but Cassandra could tell he was enjoying himself. Damn! She envied him his ignorance of exploding fuselages and jets falling out of the sky. She took his hand and squeezed it, for her own comfort. As if he understood, he squeezed back and said, "My dove."

So then Cassandra was ready for an even stiffer drink. Not only was she dreading the possibility of plummeting to her death in the middle of the Mojave Desert, she was reminded of her terrible errand. Caesar and I have only a few more hours left together, she thought as she helped him fasten his safety belt, and he had little more than that to remain alive.

Cassandra was afraid she might cry again, but fortunately no tears came. She rested her head on Caesar's shoulder, past caring what anyone might think about so familiar an act. She closed her eyes, and the engines roared even louder as the plane taxied down the runway. The bumping stopped as the wheels left the tarmac. They were airborne.

Cassandra could tell by the sudden light in the cabin that everyone else had slid up the shades on the windows. She had the fleeting thought that it might be interesting to see Las Vegas shrink below the plane. But she kept her eyes closed as she wished once more there were some way to freeze time, some way to keep the future at bay.

Then Mike Darling's voice forced her eyelids apart. "What the hell?" she heard him scream. "We're taking fire!"

What was going on? They all stared at each other in disbelief, and two of the guards even pulled their weapons.

"Calm down!" ordered Alex, and Mike's voice cut through the roar again.

"I don't think we were hit, but a goddamn sniper was taking potshots at us from the parking lot at the end of the runway!"

XCVIII

"It's okay! Everything's fine!" It was Rachel's voice this time, and she was moving toward Cassandra and Caesar. "We weren't hit," she said. "No need to worry." She headed back to the cockpit.

A few minutes had passed when Mike Darling yelled again. "I'm going to have to put her down! The hydraulic system's down! We must have taken a hit after all!"

Alex unbuckled his seat belt and rushed forward.

"We might be able to make it to the strip at Sky Ranch!" Cassandra heard Mike say.

"What about the one at the Chicken Ranch?" asked Alex, which, even amid all the excitement, made Cassandra wonder. How did Alex know about a landing strip at one of Nye County's best-known brothels? Was the chicken king a regular? Or maybe—what poetic irony—the owner?

But she couldn't keep her mind on trivialities. They were about to crash! They were about to fall out of the goddamn sky!

"We're too far south of Pahrump," Mike shouted, "And at the rate we're losing altitude, we won't make Sky Ranch, either. I'm going to put her down when I get my chance. Seat belts, everybody! Brace yourselves!"

Alex lurched back into the cabin, and Cassandra's confidence was not raised by the grim look on his ashen face. Fastening his seat belt, he barked a simple command.

"Lean forward, and clasp your hands around your knees. Keep your heads down."

She linked arms with Caesar and tried to make him follow Alex's directive. She buried her face in her lap. Hadn't Alex left something out? Weren't they supposed to be kissing their asses good-bye?

Cassandra couldn't tell how long she sat that way. She kept waiting for the engines to sputter and die, for the plane to make a spiraling nosedive. But the only thing that seemed out of the ordinary was that the plane bucked a couple of times, and once it leaned a little too far to the left. She could hear Mike yelling at Rachel over the engine noise, but everyone else was silent.

And then the plane touched down, almost as neatly as if it had been at an airport. Its contact with the ground was a little rough, but Cassandra had endured bumpier landings in commercial jets. As the plane slowed to a stop, she raised her head and peeked out the window. A whirling cloud of white dust engulfed the plane. She turned to look at her fellow passengers, and as they slowly grasped the happy truth that they had not become a buzzard's lunch, a palpable wave of relief filled the cabin, as though they had all expelled one big "Whew!" in unison.

Cassandra's feeling of relief soon dissolved into "Oh, hell!" as the dust subsided outside, and she realized they were stranded in the middle of a vast and arid wasteland. Had they landed safely only to become the Donner Party of the eastern Mojave?

Don't be an idiot, she told herself sternly. That's what radios are supposed to prevent, and sat phones. They had plenty of both, and Alex was a man with connections. And they couldn't be very far away from

Las Vegas. They hadn't been airborne for more than fifteen minutes.

While Cassandra was still trying to quell her fears, Rachel appeared, followed closely by Mike. Before either one could speak, the cabin erupted in a burst of cheering and applause.

"Well done," cried Alex above the noise. "Good work!"

"Everybody out! Now!" Mike commanded, and they all fell silent. Rachel opened the hatch, and Mike lowered the ladder.

"You first," said Mike, looking at Cassandra. "And watch out at the bottom. It's a big step."

So much for my nice new clothes, she thought as she turned her back to the opening and lowered her foot tentatively to the top rung. The wind buffeted her as she descended, and she landed on both feet in a cloud of dust. She had just stepped away from the ladder when Caesar hit the ground.

"Get away from the plane!" Rachel yelled from the doorway above, when everyone had made the descent. "We have to make sure it isn't going to explode!"

She had a point, Cassandra thought, remembering that *Miss Mitzi's* fuel tanks must be pretty close to full, but she couldn't say she was happy about running across the desert while Alex, Rachel, and Mike stayed on board. If they vanished in a fireball, she'd be left with Caesar and three armed brutes who did not consider Cassandra their superior. If *Miss Mitzi* exploded, Caesar's chances of getting to Pasadena in time to preserve history would be reduced to zero.

They'd covered five hundred yards of swirling dust when Cassandra paused to survey their surroundings. Mike had landed in what looked like a dry lake bed, which was why the surface was so surprisingly smooth. The flat, bare depression was several miles wide, and they had walked in the direction of the nearest edge, where a rocky red hill rose up sharply. Cassandra looked back when they reached the base of the outcropping. The plane had shrunk to the size of a toy. The three guards sat down on rocks and pulled out their cigarettes, but when Cassandra turned to look at Caesar, he was scrambling up the boulders.

"No!" she yelled, her voice losing against the wind. "Come back!" But he ignored her, and she had to follow.

"Why are you doing this?" Cassandra panted when she reached him. "You can't just run off into the desert."

Caesar didn't say anything, and Cassandra followed his gaze as he looked down on the other side of the rocky ridge. There, not far in the distance was a little ranch house flanked by two big cottonwood trees. A curl of smoke drifted up from the chimney, and a two-lane road stretched off in both directions.

"That house isn't far off," Caesar said. "We could walk there easily." Was he actually suggesting they go there?

"We must stay near the fixed wing," Cassandra said. "It's our only hope to get you back to Rome."

"To my death, you mean," Caesar said.

Shocked, Cassandra stared at him.

"You think you've been careful not to reveal your secret," he continued, "but I'd be a fool not to have guessed the truth. You have been mourning me ever since we stood together in the sand and gazed at the Great Bear."

He turned and took her hand. They looked again at the little enclave on the desert plain. As they watched, a white pickup truck grew out of a dot on the horizon. It pulled to a stop beside the ranch house, and the door opened. A man in a cowboy hat was still climbing out of the driver's seat when a little boy and a woman holding a baby emerged from the house. The boy threw himself into his father's arms and sent his hat flying.

"Papa's home," Caesar said.

Cassandra looked at him. He was still gazing at the timeless vignette below them. The man was kissing his wife and baby when

Caesar spoke again.

"Cassandra, what history reduces you to tears? What tale have you been forbidden to relate?"

"Are you certain you want to know?" she asked.

"I want to know what causes you such pain, my dove," Caesar said. "We have shared too much to keep secrets."

But what had they shared? Cassandra wondered. Four days, and they'd spent half of that as sparring strangers. Two days as lovers—that was it. She was only doing the job she'd been hired for: show Caesar a good time, give him a nice reprieve before he was slashed to death by his so-called friends.

No! Cassandra shouted silently to herself. It hadn't been like that at all! Of course there was a cultural abyss between Caesar and her, but they had shared more than emotionless physical intimacy. Somehow, in spite of two thousand years, six thousand miles, and what should have been insurmountable differences in language, world view, manners, and social custom, they had connected on a level so deep she knew it would change her life forever.

"If you truly wish to know, I will tell you."

Caesar didn't reply, but he squeezed her hand. The wind died down, leaving them in silence. Cassandra took a deep breath and turned to face him.

XCIX

"It's a story that has been told for twenty centuries," she said. "Julius Caesar went to the meeting of the Senate on the Ides of March, even though he was warned that he should stay home that day." She paused, then drew another breath.

"While he was there, a group of forty senators gathered around him, and at a signal from their leader, they drew knives. Caesar died from twenty-three stab wounds. The last blow was dealt by Marcus Brutus."

Time seemed to freeze as they stood there. Caesar stared straight ahead, and Cassandra stared at him. Part of her wanted to hug him, kiss him, comfort him. Part of her wanted to punch him as hard as she could and scream, "Why did you make me tell you? Men were never meant to know their own futures!"

She looked again at the house below them. As Caesar had said, it wasn't far off. They could go there, use their phone, get a ride, disappear ...

"Let's go there," she said, pointing down at the house. "We shall make a new future together."

Yes, it was crazy, and yes, she was suggesting that she and Caesar risk the future of the whole world on the chance that the two of them might steal a few years together. Because if Caesar had to die, Cassandra felt like dying, too, and she really didn't care if she took the whole world with her. The world was going to end someday, anyway, right? All she'd be stealing was time.

"Cassandra," Caesar cut into her raging thoughts. "Cassandra." He was speaking more to himself than her, and she had the distinct impression he was thinking of someone else—that other Cassandra, maybe, the gloomy Trojan one. He stared straight ahead, and at last he spoke.

"Your story is not true. My son is not a murderer."

His son? What is he talking about? Caesar turned to face her, and he read the startled question in Cassandra's eyes.

"Cassandra, I know I have told you that I have no living children, and I can never make Servilia my wife. But Brutus is indeed my son. He could never be guilty of patricide."

She stood there dumbly as Caesar continued.

"It is difficult, Cassandra, to hear your words without being tempted to believe them. Even though they are untrue, they still wield peculiar power. When I return to Rome, your story will return with me. Until events prove otherwise, I am forced to doubt."

"Don't go," she said. "Stay with me."

"You know not what you ask, my dove."

"I'm asking you to live."

"No, Cassandra. You are asking Caesar to give up his life."

She stared at him. Then, looking again at the ranch house below them, she suddenly understood. If the two of them walked down there and knocked on the door, that couple wouldn't be greeting Julius Caesar. To them, he'd be nothing more than a homeless illegal alien who couldn't speak English.

Tears sprang to her eyes, and she hung her head. Caesar put his arm around her shoulders, and if she had thought he could say nothing more surprising to her, she was wrong.

"Those who surrender to fear perish a thousand times before their deaths. The brave die only once."

Why did his words sound so familiar? Cassandra looked at him, trying to remember.

"Sweet Cassandra," he said, smiling and gently raising her chin. He kissed her, and as she rested her head on his chest, it came to her. It was Shakespeare.

Cowards die many times before their deaths; the valiant never taste of death but once.

It seemed too fantastic to be true, but somehow Shakespeare had peered into the haze of ancient history and teased out the essence of Caesar's character so perfectly he could quote him. Caesar was right about poets. They cut through facts to tell far more important truths.

The wind whipped up, and a minute later Cassandra heard a voice rise faintly above it. One of the guards was calling them.

"Come on!" he yelled. "We've got to go back!"

Scrambling back down the rocks, Caesar and Cassandra headed back to *Miss Mitzi*.

They ascended the ladder, but the guards decided to stay outside and sit in the shadow of the plane.

"Okay," Alex shouted down at them, "but you can't smoke. Don't even think about it."

After dusting themselves off as well as they could, Caesar and Cassandra reassumed their places on the velvet love seat.

"Rachel's arranging for a helicopter," Alex said. "A big Sikorsky, and there won't be any other stops. It'll get us all the way to Pasadena." He patted Cassandra's hand. "I know you're worried, but we've still got plenty of time."

Plenty of time. Where had she heard that before? But she didn't say anything, and in a way, Alex was right. It couldn't be much more than two o'clock, and they had until six before things got tense. Four hours was still more than ample.

"There are drinks back here," continued Alex as he gestured toward the bar, "and probably some snacks. Help yourselves to whatever you can find. I'm going back up front to see what the prognosis on the Sikorsky is. Let me know if you need anything, and really, we shouldn't be here too long."

Once again, Caesar and Cassandra were left alone.

C

As soon as Alex was gone, Cassandra turned to Caesar. She was about to tell him about the helicopter when he put his arm around her shoulders and laid a finger on her lips. "Cassandra," he said, "you carry a dark cloud with you, worrying as you are about death and time. Let me share with you another truth this warrior has learned. Life is but a short and turbulent pleasure, grasped only in its moments. Let us seize this moment and the joy it offers us."

Turning her face gently to his, Caesar kissed her on the forehead. "Cassandra," he said, "May I ask a favor?"

"Anything."

"Will you tell the world the truth about my son? Will you reveal the secret that has been so well kept these many centuries?"

Cassandra sighed. "I can try, but it won't matter what I say. I am the only person who heard your words. My colleagues might believe me, but the world never will."

Caesar smiled at the frustration in her voice. He seemed slightly sad as he spoke.

"Your society has conquered many physical challenges, Cassandra," he said. "You can fly, both in the air and over the ground. You can talk across great distances, freeze water inside a house. Had I seen all this without your company, I might have thought you were a country of wizards, or even gods.

"But looks are deceiving, are they not? In spite of all your technology, you have not conquered your humanity. You, my dear, still chafe at the knowledge that others will ignore your words. You struggle to increase your power, only to find that you still stand in the shadow of those who work with equal diligence to keep you weak.

"It is my story, too, Cassandra. You cannot know how I have longed to tell the world that Caesar has a son. If only I could claim Brutus as my heir! But forces stronger yet than Caesar keep me silent."

When he turned to look at her, she saw the pain in his eyes. She looked down, gathering her thoughts.

"It matters little that the world remains ignorant," Caesar said. "The real tragedy is that Brutus does not know. A child should know who his father is."

Cassandra looked at Caesar as he struggled with his thoughts. Did he really disbelieve the story of his son's treachery and his own death, or was he just pretending? She couldn't help thinking back to the words Suetonius claimed were Caesar's last, the ones he uttered when Brutus stepped forward, knife drawn. Not Shakespeare's famous "*Et tu, Brute*," but a phrase in Greek, "*Kai sou, teknon.*"

You, too, my child. Could he have meant …? But she knew it was futile to ask. She had already proved herself a Cassandra, and to reprise the role would only cause both of them pain.

"Perhaps you can still find a way to tell him," she said.

"Perhaps."

They sat there silently, lost in their separate worlds.

"Caesar," Cassandra said at last. "Julius Caesar. No name has ever risen to rival it in power and authority. The greatest emperors in all the centuries since your birth—all have claimed your kinship, assumed your name. In a sense, you have a thousand heirs. Your legacy lives on, vast in glory and influence. You are immortal in the hearts and minds of people everywhere."

Caesar didn't reply at first, but just as she was wondering whether she had been a fool to try to comfort him, he took her hand.

"Fragments, Cassandra, fragments," he said quietly. "We see only broken pieces of the great whole. Only the wisest men are able to draw completed pictures from this mortal glimpse." He was silent for a moment. "Thank you, my dove. You will not let Caesar leave bearing thorns alone. You have insisted on giving him the rose as well."

There didn't seem to be anything left to say. Cassandra could have spent her final hours alone with Caesar asking questions, but what difference would it have made? She could tell the world that Brutus was his son, but who would listen? Historians decided long ago that Caesar and Brutus couldn't have been related. They would never sacrifice all their conclusions just because she claimed to know better.

And it wasn't just historians who wouldn't believe. People don't want their fondest histories rewritten. They don't like having their foundations rattled, their assumptions shaken. They like their cherry-chopping Washingtons and apple-catching Newtons just the way they are. The same goes for Cleopatra. They want her to look like a movie star. They want her rolled up in a rug.

Cassandra thought about the lists of questions she and her colleagues had taken such pains to compile. She knew them by heart, and perhaps Caesar might have given her some of the answers they had hoped to get. But what good would it have done? Without the kind of corroboration scholarship demands, no one would believe anything Cassandra reported. As she sat there in *Miss Mitzi*, the only thing that made any sense was to seize the moment for what it offered best. It offered respite. It offered peace. She and Caesar just sat there holding hands. She could hear him breathing. She could feel his heart beat.

◉◉◉

The Sikorsky was late. It finally showed up at about four-thirty, its advent announced by a vibrating roar, steadily increasing over the wind. "It's the spiral-wing," Cassandra said to Caesar as Mike, Rachel, and Alex emerged from the cockpit and climbed down the ladder to meet Marty. "Come, let us watch its descent."

Caesar and Cassandra stood at the open hatch and watched the chopper drop, beating up a great circle of dust as it neared the surface of the lake bed a hundred yards away. Here is our last hope, Cassandra thought. If this machine can't get us to Pasadena, we'll have to take our chances with the great unknown.

But she wasn't frightened any more, she realized with surprise. Cassandra looked out over that unforgiving landscape with Julius Caesar at her side, and for the first time in her life, she felt absolutely calm in the face of whatever the universe was about to dish out.

CI

M arty was mad, and he wasn't doing anything to conceal it.
"Jesus H. Christ!" he said as soon as Alex was standing
next to him. "Who the hell are you running from, Alex? What the
fuck is going on? I loan you my goddamn pride and joy, and you sons
of bitches get her shot full of holes and stranded out here in no man's
land. Do you have any idea how much it's going to cost to truck her
back to Vegas?"

"Get a mechanic out here first," Alex said. If you and Mike can't fly
her back, get as many haulers as you need. I'll take care of everything."

Still fuming, Marty turned to Caesar and Cassandra.

"Don't you have an appointment to keep?" he barked. "The chopper's waiting."

Cassandra didn't try to translate. She just grabbed Caesar's hand
and pulled him toward the hatch. Marty lobbed another salvo of invec-
tive at Alex, who stood silently on the receiving end. They must be
very good friends, Cassandra thought as Caesar lowered himself onto
the first rung. Either that, or Alex has a streak of masochism in him.

"I'll be right behind you," Alex said as Cassandra turned to follow

Caesar down the ladder. Marty was yelling something about "nuts in a vise" when the wind drowned out his angry tirade.

The gusts seemed even stronger than when they'd run across the lake bed an hour earlier, but Cassandra couldn't tell whether it was the weather or the helicopter making the difference. The roar from the rotors was deafening, even a hundred yards away.

Rachel and the three guards were waiting for them in the shade of *Miss Mitzi*.

"We'll go together," shouted Rachel. "Follow me, and don't look up. Keep your heads down."

Cassandra translated for Caesar, and off they went, approaching the helicopter from the front. Cassandra had never ridden in a chopper before, and she'd never had the desire. As their ears and bodies reverberated with the pounding vibration of the propeller, she was reminded that she'd been wise to avoid a trip in a whirligig. The noise and dust were awful, and she had suddenly remembered reading that spinning blades create a strobe effect that can trigger epileptic seizures. Keep your head down, Caesar, she prayed. Don't look up.

Things were better inside. The cabin was actually pretty luxurious. She'd been bracing herself for sitting on the floor of a stark metal pod, and she was pleasantly surprised to find six big cushy airplane seats, four against the back wall, and two against the wall facing them. There was thick carpet on the floor and walls, and it seemed to cut the roar slightly.

Rachel directed Caesar and Cassandra to the two backward-facing chairs, and the three guards lined themselves up in the seats against the rear wall. They had just slid onto the cool gray leather when Marty's silhouette filled the hatch. Alex was right behind him, and they were laughing. Old army pals, Cassandra thought. One minute they're busting each other's chops, and the next, they're the best of buddies. Must be what a couple of years of dodging punji sticks can do for a friendship, she guessed.

"Welcome to my velocicopter," Marty said jovially. "Sorry it wasn't available earlier, but the president of MGM had an appointment in L.A. Anyway, you're in the best of hands with Alex here—he's only crashed one plane today!" Marty slapped Alex on the back when he climbed aboard. "Fly between the bullets this time, you old bastard!" he said. "This chopper is my bread and butter!"

Marty disappeared back into the dust and roar outside. Alex shut the hatch behind him, and Cassandra was surprised to find that the noise level was cut by at least half. They'd actually be able to talk without shouting.

"Fasten your belts," Alex said. "We'll be taking off in just a minute. I figure we'll be in Pasadena in just under an hour." He glanced at his watch. "Still plenty of time, Cassandra," he added.

Plenty of time. Right.

"We'll be landing on the roof of an office building next to the freeway," Alex continued, "And I better say good-bye to you and Caesar now. I have to get this chopper back to Vegas tonight. Marty's got customers first thing in the morning. But you're in good hands. Rachel's staying, and a security team will be meeting you. And of course these guards are staying, too," he added when he saw Cassandra's look of surprise.

Stupidly, she hadn't thought about what might happen to the helicopter when they arrived in Pasadena. Alex had told them that Marty's business was flying VIPs back and forth between Las Vegas and L.A., and that the chopper they were sitting in was his air taxi. Damn. It just hadn't occurred to her that she would be getting back to the IDES Lab without Alex as a buffer.

"Farewell, Caesar," Alex was saying as he stretched out his right hand. Caesar knew immediately what his words and gesture meant.

"*Vale, Alexander,*" he said, rising. Ignoring the proffered hand, Caesar opened his arms, and the two men embraced. When Alex turned to give Cassandra her own farewell, she saw tears glistening in his eyes.

"I'm forever grateful, Cassandra," he whispered as he hugged her.

Rachel had already disappeared through the hatch, and Alex followed her. Once outside, they climbed into smaller doors on either side of the cockpit, which was separated from the passenger compartment by a wall with a sliding glass window in it. By turning in her chair, Cassandra could see the instrument panel from where she was sitting, and the view through the windshield. The sun was blinding, now that it had begun its western descent, and they'd be heading straight into it.

Although Cassandra had claimed that she no longer felt afraid, she realized her fear of flying was still alive and well when Alex took his place in the left-hand pilot's seat and started flipping switches. She had hoped to live her whole life without riding in a helicopter, and she avoided airplanes whenever possible. Damn! Why does life always drag you into the path of the things you hate the most?

She looked at Caesar. She didn't hate him, she told herself, and life had thrown her into his arms. His face was calm as he looked through the window toward the horizon, and he smiled when she caught his eye. Hell. Knowing him was worth a ride in a helicopter. A little prayer of thanks rose in her heart.

A minute later, the engine roar increased in volume and pitch, and Marty's "velocicopter" began beating its ascent over the desert floor. As she looked out the side window and watched *Miss Mitzi* shrink below, Cassandra had to admit it wasn't as bad as she'd imagined. It was more exciting than scary, and she was suddenly enveloped in a feeling of privilege.

And then she remembered. In sixty minutes, she'd be face to face with Andrew Danicek, and who could tell what their eleventh-hour reunion might hold? Cassandra waited for a fresh attack of fear to seize her, but nothing happened. She let out a breath, and she smiled as she realized that even though she'd admitted Danicek into her brain, it was still remarkably free of dire thoughts.

The helicopter gained altitude, rising easily over a low range of treeless hills. As the definition of the earth softened below, Cassandra gradually drew her attention back inside the cabin. The first thing she noticed was that her seat belt was too tight. She'd cinched herself in firmly when she first sat down, and now her right leg was falling asleep. She shifted to relieve the pressure and realized that part of the problem was something hard in her pocket. She reached inside to move whatever it was that was digging into her thigh.

It was the coin, the large gold medallion Alex had given her the night—last night! —after they played craps in the private room at Caesars. She pulled it out and gazed at it once again. It would probably be her only souvenir of her time with Julius Caesar, she mused. Too bad it bore a likeness of Augustus.

"May I?" Caesar's voice broke into Cassandra's thoughts. She handed him the coin, and he turned it over in his fingers. "It is beautiful," he said.

She waited for him to make another attempt to keep the coin, but Caesar handed it back to Cassandra without a word. She slipped it into her right jacket pocket and turned her attention back to the view outside. They were flying over inhabited areas now, and taller, snow-capped mountains rose on their right. To the left, the land flattened out to the ocean, which, caught in the blaze of the descending sun, gleamed white. What a view, she thought. Far better than an airplane. And Caesar seemed to be enjoying it, too.

Cassandra knew they were nearing their destination when she looked through the cockpit window and spied the Rose Bowl. She would have liked to explain to Caesar that they were near the scene of their first great escape, but the helicopter was descending now, and he seemed mesmerized by the Foothill Freeway. Alex was following its path, and the vehicles below looked like toys as they sped along the ribbon of pavement.

Cassandra thought their landing would be bumpy and terrifying, but it was nothing of the sort. The engine noise increased as the helicopter hovered above the painted target on the roof of an office building, but she barely detected the moment it touched down.

Almost as soon as the helicopter landed, Rachel opened her hatch and leapt out. The wind lashed her hair, and she crouched down as she hurried around the front end of the craft and made her way to the cabin door. The guards were already on their feet when the hatch opened, and Caesar and Cassandra were out of their belts. Following the guards, they stepped down to the roof. Keeping their heads tucked into their chests, they scuttled quickly to the door Rachel was holding open. There was no time to wave to Alex before they disappeared into a stairwell.

CII

Caesar and Cassandra clattered down a flight of concrete stairs and emerged into a carpeted hallway lined with closed doors. A security guard wearing a black uniform and a gold badge was punching the down button when they caught up with Rachel at the elevator. He joined them in the car, and soon they were descending rapidly, the floors counting down above them in red electronic digits. They reached the ground floor without stopping on any levels in between. The doors slid apart, and the guard led the way into a polished granite lobby. Cassandra could see from the directory on the wall next to the reception desk that the building housed lending agencies, stock brokerages, and law firms, but no one was hanging around for introductions. They marched lockstep across the slick stone floor and exited onto stairs leading down to a loading zone. Parked in the middle of it was a black van with tinted windows. Just as Caesar and Cassandra reached the sidewalk, a man emerged from the front passenger seat. He slid the side door open, and two more men stepped out.

Rachel, in full logistician mode, orchestrated the loading process. Caesar went in first, and Cassandra took the captain's chair next to him.

Two of the guards took places on the bench seat behind them. Rachel folded down a little jump seat and sat facing everyone else.

After the third guard slid the side door shut and locked it, he climbed into the front passenger seat. "Ready?" he asked, turning to Rachel.

"Ready," she said, and the van began to move. The driver made a U-turn, and soon they were heading south on a one-way street.

The van made a right turn, and by the time they turned again onto Raymond Avenue, Cassandra had gotten her bearings. They were only a few blocks from the IDES Lab.

She looked out the window and watched as the van slowed down and turned right into the IDES Lab's driveway. God, they were almost there. Within a minute or two, they'd be inside, where she'd have to face Danicek and the others. Suddenly, she wished with all her heart that she and Caesar had disappeared together in Boxcar's Corvette or run down to the house on the edge of the dry lake. Why were they back? Why had they headed so eagerly into the jaws of death?

The van pulled into the same parking space from which they'd departed on the fateful trip to the Illingsworth estate. Rachel slid the side door open almost before the van stopped rolling and started barking orders.

The guard sitting in the front passenger seat stepped out first and moved to the back of the van. Following Rachel's instructions, Cassandra got out next. Caesar followed, and Rachel stood facing them while the two other guards in the back seat disembarked and took places behind them.

"Okay," she said when everyone was in proper formation. "Let's go." Then everything happened at once.

On her left, Cassandra saw a large gloved hand slap itself around Caesar's face. In front of her, a big black handgun appeared at Rachel's throat, held by a massive dark-haired man behind her. Cassandra heard scuffling behind her, and a "Shut up or I'll waste you!" followed by several loud grunts and dull thuds. Cassandra wanted to scream, but she knew better.

Where were their guards? Cassandra turned her head slightly. She could see one of them spread-eagled on the ground in back of the van. Judging from the lack of activity, she decided that the other two were probably down, too.

Cassandra was beginning to wonder what the bad guys were going to do next when she caught sight of a blond head emerging from around the side of the building. She was not surprised when she recognized Hank Morgan. He was wearing a tan coat that blew open to reveal a gray suit and a red tie. He ascended the steps to the IDES Lab as though he were an after-dinner speaker, and leaned casually on the pipe railing before he spoke.

"So glad you could meet me here," he began, "and this shouldn't take long—"

Just then, the door of the lab opened behind Hank, and Elizabeth stepped out.

"Hank!" she screamed. "Don't!"

Judging from Hank's reaction to his wife's sudden appearance, this wasn't part of his script.

"Just give it up!" Elizabeth cried. "It's not worth it!"

When Elizabeth reached her arms toward her husband, Cassandra felt whoever was holding her relax his grasp a tiny bit, as though he was readying himself to protect Hank.

"Please, honey! Please!" Elizabeth was bleating now, and tears were rolling down her cheeks. Hank looked horrified as she threw herself upon him and wrapped her arms around his neck.

Just then, the door opened again. Eric stepped out, and John Reynolds was right behind him, brandishing his cane.

Before Hank could turn around, John brought the eagle head down on his head with an audible thwack. As Hank staggered, Elizabeth jerked her knee up into her husband's groin.

Cassandra watched Hank pitch forward. Beside her, Caesar seized the moment of confusion to wrench himself free. As he ran close to the ground, Cassandra caught sight of something in his right hand.

Simone's kitchen knife! He still had it! He lunged at an assailant who was trying to run away and caught the man by the ankles. Smashing him face first to the ground, he leapt onto the man's back and pinned him down. Cassandra saw the knife blade glint against the man's neck.

Rachel was right in front of her, still a prisoner. The man holding her dug his gun even farther into the base of her skull as he stared straight at Cassandra. She froze, wondering what in hell she could do. All she could think of was what Caesar had told her. "There's always something you can do, Cassandra," he'd said.

Always something. But what? Her mind raced.

Cassandra's hands were in her jacket pockets, and the fingers of her right hand closed around the gold coin from Caesars Palace. It was all she had. She pulled it out and flung it as hard as she could at Rachel's captor. It caught the light as it flew toward his head.

It was enough! The man holding Rachel dropped his gun-toting arm slightly when he saw the coin—just enough for someone like her to gain advantage. As quick as a cougar, she was on top of him, and almost as fast, he was spread-eagled on the asphalt, his own gun shoved into his back.

"Don't move!" Rachel commanded. She sprang to her feet, brandishing the gun in her right hand and pulling a zip-tie from her belt with her left. In a flash, the man's hands were cinched tightly behind his back.

When Cassandra looked around, she saw that the entire scene had done a flip. All five assailants lay immobile on the ground, their hands bound tightly behind them. Eric was kneeling next to Hank. John held his cane flat across the back of his neck until Rachel arrived with another zip-tie.

But where was Caesar? Cassandra scanned the parking lot. Damn. He was nowhere to be seen.

She was about to alert Rachel when Caesar rolled out from under the van only a few feet away. She rushed to help him to his feet. Elizabeth hurried to join her. Eric and John weren't far behind. As they brushed Caesar off, they all spoke at once in a cacophony of English and Latin. "*Esne sanus?* Are you all right?"

CIII

Caesar didn't answer the unanimous question. Instead, he reached for Cassandra's hand, and as he grasped it, he pressed the gold coin into it. Caesar was smiling at her when she looked back up.

"Well done, Cassandra!" he said. Drawing her toward him, he planted a kiss on each cheek.

Just then Rachel strode up. "The lab is now secure," she said, emphasizing the "now" ever so slightly. "I recommend you proceed inside immediately. I must attend to our uninvited guests before the local police arrive. Our engagement was far from silent, and you can be sure that someone in the neighborhood has summoned them." Pausing, Rachel looked at Cassandra and reached for her right hand. Shaking it firmly, she added, "Good job. Thank you."

They all headed toward the lab steps as Rachel began overseeing the task of stuffing Hank and his henchmen into the black van. Cassandra had no idea where she planned to offload them, but she was glad they weren't her responsibility.

As soon as the door closed behind them, Eric took Cassandra's arm. "Go to Caesar's suite immediately," he said. "We don't have much time."

She glanced at the clock behind the security desk. 6:34. Damn. They were down to the wire, after all. They had twenty-seven minutes to get Caesar back to Rome. The procedure itself took less than a heartbeat, of course, but cutting it this close had never been part of Danicek's plan.

They rushed through the airlock and down the hall. Eric opened the door to Caesar's suite, where Faith stood near the sofa. Cassandra heard Caesar draw in a breath, but he didn't say anything.

"Faith will stay with you while Caesar changes," Eric said. "I'll be making final preparations with Danicek in the transport chamber. Join us there as soon as you possibly can." He vanished down the hall, and the door swung shut behind him.

"Here's his toga," Faith said, pointing to the garment draped over the back of the sofa, "and here's his hardware." She sounds almost robotic, Cassandra thought, almost envying Faith's lack of emotion. Her own feelings were almost too much to bear.

Opening a wooden box on the coffee table, Faith removed Caesar's four gold *fibulae*, the pins Cassandra would be using to fasten his toga. She set them on the table.

"I'll go get his undergarment," she said as she strode toward the bedroom.

Without a word or any prompting from Cassandra, Caesar pulled the paring knife from his pocket, laid it on the table, and began to undress.

"Take it with you," Cassandra said. "I shall not try to stop you."

"No, my dove," Caesar said. "As I told you already, I am neither ruffian nor coward. I refuse to carry weapons to conduct state business. Return the knife to your friend with my thanks. It has served me well."

There was no point in protesting. Cassandra fell silent and watched Caesar's every small action as he disrobed. Caesar was silent, too. He seemed distant, as though he were already gone, already back in Rome.

By the time Faith stepped back into the room carrying his tunic,

Caesar was naked.

"I can do it," Cassandra said, taking the garments from her.

"I'll let them know we're almost ready," Faith said as she moved to the door.

One more time—one last time—Caesar and Cassandra found themselves alone. As she held up his tunic, her hands were shaking. Caesar covered them with his own, and when she saw two tears standing in his eyes, her own eyes filled, too.

But there was nothing to say, nothing to do but the task at hand. Wordlessly, she gathered up Caesar's toga. The smell of it—the exotic fragrance that still lingered in its folds—brought fresh tears to her eyes. Like a lamb to slaughter, he was going back.

How had she not saved him? Why had he insisted on returning, even when she had divulged what fate awaited him? Why would a man so willingly return to his own murder? Why was he not even tempted to take the knife?

As if he had read her thoughts, Caesar threw the toga over his shoulder, took Cassandra in his arms, and held her head against his chest.

"Peace, my dove," he said, stroking her hair. "Blame is everywhere, but you need not cloak yourself in it. Caesar returns to Rome of his own free will. He leaves Cassandra nothing but thanks."

Just then, the door burst open, and Faith entered with Elizabeth and Reynolds right behind her.

"We're almost ready," Cassandra said, wiping her eyes. She grabbed the edge of the toga and busied herself trying to drape it properly. Caesar laughed at her ineptitude.

"You are a far better soldier than you are valet," he said. "Here, place it like this, and pull it up here, like this."

In spite of Cassandra's clumsiness, Caesar was ready in a matter of minutes.

"Let's go," Faith said as soon as the last *fibula* was in place.

"No, wait," Cassandra replied. "He's got to put on his sandals."

Caesar sat down on the sofa and began tying on his footwear. Cassandra knelt to help him, and at last he rose, dressed exactly as he had been when he arrived. Had it really been only four days?

"I am ready," Caesar said as he turned toward the door. "Lead the way."

But Caesar himself took the lead with a confident stride. Cassandra rushed to keep up with him, tucking her hand through the folds of the toga covering his right arm as they reached the door to the control room. TESA was roaring, but that wasn't what made her pause. Danicek was in the hall.

This was it. The confrontation she had been dreading. She opened her mouth to speak, but Caesar beat her to it.

"Good morning," Caesar said, and he extended his right hand. Danicek, astonished, grasped it. "Good morning," he replied, even though it was after sundown. "Are you well? Are you prepared for your journey back to Rome?"

Cassandra translated, and Caesar, facing Danicek, spoke once again in English.

"Yes," he said.

Danicek looked slightly stunned, but there was no time for chitchat. "We will all join Caesar in the transport chamber," he said. "Cassandra, tell him what to expect."

Cassandra did her best to explain, and Danicek opened the door. The roar was loud, but the door to the transport chamber was already open. She gripped Caesar's arm as they stepped inside.

As if they had been choreographed, Danicek, Eric, Elizabeth, Reynolds, and Cassandra all formed a circle around Caesar, who stood in the center of the chamber, inside the transport zone. Cassandra was standing next to Danicek, and as she looked from face to face, she couldn't shake the thought that they were no different from the assassins waiting for him in Rome. They, too, would gather round as though in friendship. Were they less guilty because their means were bloodless?

Caesar turned to face Cassandra. Placing one hand on each shoulder, he gazed at her with eyes of steel.

"Victory in surrender," he said. "The greatest generals know when to find it there." His eyes softened then as he spoke gently. "You are the sweetness I bear with me on a bitter path."

"It is time," said Danicek, and Caesar turned his eyes on him. Slowly, his lips curved up at the sides in a sly grin.

"*Moriturus te saluto*," he said.

I who am about to die salute you. Oh my God! It was what gladiators said when they entered the arena. Elizabeth and Reynolds reacted with shocked gasps, but there was no time for anything else. Danicek was giving the order to begin the countdown when Caesar shifted his gaze to Cassandra.

"Five, four, three, two, one—"

Cassandra could swear that Caesar's eyes lingered an instant longer than his body. They were staring straight into hers. They were utterly unafraid.

Gradually she felt Reynolds' eyes boring into her from across the chamber, along with everyone else's. But no one said a word until Danicek broke the silence.

"We will meet in ten minutes in the common area," he commanded. "As soon as Eric and I have finished here."

CIV

C assandra was the first one out of the transport chamber's door, and she left the rest of the IDES team standing in the hall. She had no plan, but she found herself walking through the airlock and foyer to the main door, and outside into the gathering darkness. She stood on the concrete step and looked out over the parking lot. It revealed no clue to the confrontation that had occurred there less than an hour before.

I could leave, she thought. I could walk up to Starbucks and call a cab. It was chicken-hearted, but hell. Caesar was gone. Maybe it was the perfect time for Cassandra to disappear as well.

A chilly breeze blew across her face, and she stuffed her hands into the pockets of her leather jacket. She was still debating about whether to stick around for Danicek's post-mortem when she felt an unfamiliar object next to her right hand. Closing her fingers around its irregular shape, she drew it out.

Cassandra gasped. Even in the failing light, she could easily see what lay in her palm. It was Julius Caesar's signet ring.

She felt in her pocket again, and the rest of the truth dawned. Her gold coin was gone. Caesar had pulled a switch. He'd taken a souvenir and left her a gift, in spite of everything she'd said.

As she stood there with his ring in her hand, she could almost hear him laughing.

Unbidden, a smile took hold of her face. She was still here. The present appeared to be intact, even though Caesar had returned to the past with a modern object and left a fabulous memento in its place.

Cassandra's relief vanished in a wave of overwhelming sorrow. Caesar was bleeding now, dying now, murdered by traitors, slaughtered by his son. Had he known, when he slipped the gold medallion from her pocket, that he was taking a coin for the ferryman?

She bowed her head, expecting tears. But no tears fell. Her eyes stayed as dry as she felt empty.

She didn't hear the door behind her open, didn't realize she had company until she felt a hand on her shoulder.

"Cassandra." It was Danicek's voice, and she jerked her head up.

"Cassandra," he repeated. "It is time."

Her fingers closed around Caesar's ring inside her pocket. Then she squared her shoulders and moved through the door Danicek was holding open for her.

CV

P ollio's foul breath was the first indicator that Caesar had returned not only to Rome but to the exact moment from which he had been abducted. In the moment that his eyes once again connected with the yammering old man's, Caesar wondered if he had imagined the chain of peculiar events that had now ended so abruptly. Perhaps a seizure was the explanation, or a fever dream. But he had obviously not lost consciousness. Here he was, still standing in the *curia* with Pollio's shrill grievances falling on his ears. Was it possible that Cassandra and all the rest were just a strange phantasmagoria?

Caesar tightened his fingers around the object in his right hand, hidden under the folds of his toga. Without pulling it into view, he could tell beyond a doubt that it was a coin. The absence of a signet ring on his forefinger offered further proof that whatever was the truth about his recent experiences, he had not been dreaming.

Caesar was about to pull his hand into view for visual affirmation when Pollio's whiny monologue abruptly ended in a yelp. Shoved from behind, the old man lurched forward. He would have collapsed onto Caesar if his attacker had not immediately yanked him back and thrown him aside. Caesar turned his head to watch Pollio stagger a few steps, then sink to his knees, whimpering. Turning back, Caesar found himself staring into a familiar face.

"Decimus," he said. "Tell me what transpires here."

Caesar's friend did not respond. Instead, he turned his head. Caesar followed his gaze to Casca, who had just moved into view.

Caesar did not repeat his request. He watched, transfixed, as Casca drew a dagger from under the folds of his toga.

A dagger.

Had Calpurnia been privy to some intelligence after all? Caesar had no time to ponder this possibility. Casca raised the weapon. Caesar watched in shocked silence as Casca glanced at Decimus, and Decimus inclined his head.

Caesar closed his eyes as he felt Casca's dagger pierce his right shoulder. The searing pain was still shooting through his body when a second blow struck him in the chest.

Caesar opened his eyes to ratify what he already knew. Decimus was his second attacker. Decimus, whom he had always considered his most loyal friend.

In that moment, Caesar also saw that the conspiracy was far larger than two men. The others pressed forward. His friends, his colleagues. Daggers drawn, they struck Caesar again and again, in the abdomen, on the arms, wherever their daggers could make contact.

Caesar was still standing when the one face he had hoped against hope he would not have to count among this terrible fraternity moved in front of his own.

Marcus Brutus.

"My child." The words jumped out in Greek, with the intimacy Caesar would have used when Brutus was young.

The face in front of Caesar froze for an instant. In that moment, Caesar recognized the features that confirmed his belief. Without question, this man was his son. The nose, the brow, the chin. And most convincingly, the gaze. And in that same moment, Caesar saw that Brutus shared his recognition.

Maybe you will have the opportunity to tell him. You spoke the truth, Cassandra.

"My son." The words jumped out, again in Greek, just as Brutus's blade plunged into Caesar's breast.

In the frenzied moments after Caesar fell, no one noticed the gold coin that rolled from under the blood-soaked fabric of his toga. No one saw it disappear into the space between two slabs of travertine.

A NOTE FROM JULIAN

December 27th, 2020

O n my eighteenth birthday, my mother told me I was a little like Theseus. She didn't mean I would have to fight monsters on my way to Athens. What she meant was that I would find out the truth about my father, now that I was old enough. Then she slipped off the chain she always wore around her neck and placed it around mine. There's a heavy gold ring hanging from it.

"You'll understand when you read these pages," she said, handing me a brown cardboard box. I stayed up all night reading.

You have just read the same pages, so you already know what I learned. Eric Barza is not my biological father. Julius Caesar is. I was born in Los Angeles nine months after his four-day visit to the year 1999.

Cassandra Fleury—my mother—and Eric Barza got married a few months before I was born. My legal name is Julian Barza. We lived in

Pasadena, California, until Mom got her bachelor's degree from USC. We moved to Las Vegas just before I turned two.

Alexander Hunt, or as I call him, Uncle Alex, bought us a house in Summerlin. My grandmother, Margot Lewis, moved in with us. My dad had to stay in Pasadena to sort out the aftermath of the IDES Project. Later, he got a job at the Naval Air Weapons Station in China Lake, California. He spent weekends in Las Vegas with us. My parents divorced when I was eight. My dad still lives in Ridgecrest and still works at China Lake developing weapons.

While I was growing up, Mom worked as the communications director for Chasen Chicken, Uncle Alex's company. She mostly worked at home, but we went to Arkansas pretty often. I always looked forward to the trips, because we flew in a private jet and I had my own room at Uncle Alex's estate. I learned how to fly fish there.

I went to the Meadows School, a private school in Summerlin, from kindergarten all the way through high school. Dennis Martinelli, who was my mom's Latin teacher at Rancho High, got a job there, so I took Latin from him, too. I can't speak Latin as well as she can, but I can read it pretty well. I've started rereading Caesar's books. It's a whole different experience now. When I read them in school, I was worried about passing grammar tests. Now I am much more interested in the author.

Faith Hopper, the IDES Project's doctor, is now a good friend of my mom's. They didn't get along at first, but after Andrew Danicek was diagnosed with brain cancer, my dad and Sonia Illingsworth worked with Faith to dismantle TESA. They saw that Dr. Danicek was losing his mind and might do something dangerous. My mom helped, too. She was good at calming Dr. Danicek down. Dr. Danicek died in 2002. Faith lives in Cleveland now.

We used to visit Sonia Illingsworth in her big house in Pasadena until she died last year. We still visit my mom's former landlady.

Simone Babcock moved into a retirement home when I was about ten. She asked if we would like to have Cléopâtre, her blue macaw. Cléopâtre has ruled over our family room ever since.

John Reynolds is still chairman of the classics department at USC and my mom's close friend. I met him a few years ago when he came to Las Vegas to get married to Warren Scott, an architect from Santa Barbara. The wedding was in our backyard, and Dr. Martinelli was the best man. It was a great party. After dark, I got to set off fireworks out by the pool.

Elizabeth Palmer is still a professor at USC and still in touch with Mom. She divorced Hank Morgan right after the IDES Project was over. He later went to prison for a few years for securities fraud. Now he lives in Europe.

I'm taking some time off from school since I graduated from The Meadows. I was working as a parking valet at the Cosmopolitan until the pandemic came along, and the Strip shut down. I'm planning to go to college, and thanks to the Hunt Foundation, I can go anywhere I'm accepted. I'm thinking about majoring in political science at USC.

A couple of weeks after I read Mom's manuscript, I went to Arkansas with her. I took the box of pages along, and Uncle Alex read them. The morning before we left for Las Vegas, he told me the book could be published. He wanted to know whether I would like that. I didn't have to think long. I said yes. I think it's great that anyone who's interested can read the story of the IDES Project. It seems right for the world to know that a successful time-travel experiment really did happen back in 1999.

Even though it's based on real events, my mom says this book has to be called fiction. She had to imagine some things and fill in gaps. Like for example, Mom obviously doesn't know for sure whether Caesar was able to tell Brutus that he was his father. We don't even know if Brutus really was Caesar's son. Historians don't think so, and nothing my mother tells them is likely to change their minds. I don't think it matters whether Brutus was really—biologically—Caesar's son. What matters is that Caesar believed it.

Believe whatever you want. I'm just glad I know who my father was.

A NOTE FROM FAITH HOPPER

MAY 3, 2021

I knew that Cassandra Fleury had decided to write some sort of
memoir about the IDES Project, but it wasn't real to me until the
publisher wrote to ask me if I would be willing to read and respond to
it before its release. Of course I said I would, but by the time the manuscript arrived in my mailbox, I was having serious second thoughts.
I left Pasadena in 2002, not long after Andrew Danicek died. I had
stayed to help Sonia Illingsworth and Eric Barza dismantle TESA and
everything related to the IDES Project. It was tragic and exhausting,
and by the time I escaped to my mother's house in Wyoming, all I
wanted to do was to put the last few years behind me.

When I left California, it was with the understanding that the
nondisclosure agreements that everyone on the IDES Project team

had signed with the Illingsworth Corporation would always keep us quiet about Julius Caesar's visit. This was particularly difficult for Eric, who had been looking forward to collaborating with Andrew on the publication of IDES Project results. Once Andrew was incapacitated, however, suppressing his research was the only responsible path. It is only now, with the passing of Sonia Illingsworth, that Cassandra has decided to share this fictionalized account. She has the support and cooperation of all the remaining members of the team, including John Reynolds and Elizabeth Palmer.

Cassandra and I were good friends by the time I left. I was on good terms with Sonia and Eric, too. Shared trauma forges strong relationships, I guess. We all suffered through Andrew's illness.

I can't say that reading Cassandra's book was a pleasant experience. In fact, it was excruciating at times. When I first met Cassandra, I was suffering horribly from my breakup with Andrew. I loved the man. When he discarded me, I was angry and hurt, but I couldn't leave the project. I regret my behavior toward the team now, and especially toward Cassandra. Even though it was painful to read her characterization of me, I must admit she got it right. I am grateful that we spent enough time together after Andrew's diagnosis to become friends. She deserves more credit than I do for hanging in there.

I live in Cleveland now, where I work at the Cleveland Clinic doing research in epidemiology. Before the SARS-CoV-2 pandemic refocused my research, I traveled to Las Vegas fairly frequently to consult with a colleague at the Lou Ruvo Center for Brain Health, another Cleveland Clinic research center. I loved those trips, because I got to visit Cassandra. I am sorry that things ultimately didn't work out between her and Eric. Fortunately, they are still friends, and they both love Julian. So do I. One of my favorite things in the world is that he calls me auntie.

And now, we have this book. I'm grateful to Cassandra for writing it. How many amazing things have happened, only to vanish unremembered into the past? Without this account, the IDES Project would have been one of those things. For many readers, of course, it will be just an interesting story. Because she chose to write it as a novel, and the publisher is releasing it as fiction, readers are left to decide for themselves whether to believe it. My only comment on that subject is that it rings truer than many history books I've read.

I am especially glad that I told Cassandra about Andrew's early childhood and that she included the details in this book. I know it's a long shot, but I can't help wondering if an old man somewhere will recognize himself as the Andrej Novotny who unwittingly turned a little German boy into Andrew Danicek. It was Andrew's greatest disappointment that, even after the rise of the Internet, he never found his friend.

As for Julius Caesar, it's tempting to use his own words to encapsulate the IDES Project.

Veni. Vidi. Vici.
I came. I saw. I conquered.

But if I recall enough of my high-school Latin, and you don't mind a little flexibility in my translation, I think a slightly different version sums it up far more accurately.

Venit. Vidit. Vicit.
He came. He saw. She conquered.

ACKNOWLEDGMENTS

When a book takes twenty years to get itself written, the list of those who contributed to its contents and helped the author grows long. The names below are just a few of the wonderful people without whom this story would never have been brought to completion. My thanks to everyone who interacted with this story, from its inception in 1999 to its current form. Your comments, suggestions, ideas, knowledge, and encouragement were vital to this book's long and circuitous path to publication.

If I got anything right or convincing about ancient Romans, time travel, and the locales in which this tale takes place, I owe thanks to all those who took the time to share knowledge with a writer who wanted to bring Julius Caesar alive, send him to Las Vegas, and not have the story be a joke. Any errors are mine alone.

Paeans to my editors, Maureen Baron, Nancy Zerbey, Kristen Weber, and David Johnstone, who so brilliantly helped me shape and polish this tale.

Tributes to Michael H. Dickman, Steve Glass, Sandy Glass, Bruce Jones, Ellen Finkelpearl, Brian Rouff, Jimmy Upton, Eric Chiappinelli,

John Tsitoras, Mark Helmlinger, Bob Abrahams, Donald Maass, Monterey Brookman, Jeff Brookman, and David Mickey Evans, who offered invaluable insight and suggestions.

Panegyrics to Mark Sedenquist, Margaret Sedenquist, H.G. McKinnis, Ruth Mormon, Tom Martin, Ivy Sun, and Jamie Erlich for inspiration, support, and encouragement.

Lastly, laurel wreaths and encomia to all teachers of the classics who, day in and day out, keep the glory alive.

ABOUT THE AUTHOR

The idea for Caesar's visit to our world occurred to Megan Edwards when she first visited the Getty Villa in the hills above Malibu back when she was a classics major at Scripps College and had just returned from a semester at the Intercollegiate Center for Classical Studies in Rome and a summer at the American School of Classical Studies at Athens. What would a real ancient Roman think? she wondered. This question became her go-to mental challenge whenever she had time to ruminate. She kept on thinking over the fifteen years she spent teaching Latin, and she continued after a wildfire destroyed her house and all her worldly possessions. Seizing the opportunity her sudden "stufflessness" offered, Megan spent six years as a nomad on the highways and byways of North America. In 1999, shortly after the publication of her first book, she started writing this one.

Megan soon realized that while her former life had given her some insight into Caesar's world, she knew almost nothing about Cassandra's hometown beyond the ubiquitous stereotypes. Because her peripatetic lifestyle made it easy, she traveled to southern Nevada, where she believed she would stay, oh, a month at the most. She's still there, two decades later. And while she will agree that Las Vegas can't yet be called an eternal city, she now also knows it wasn't built in a day. She hopes she captured her adopted hometown accurately in these pages as much as she hopes her portrayal of Julius Caesar rings true.

Connect with the author online:

🌐 MeganEdwards.com

🔲 @megan.edwards.author

🔲 @ MeganEdwards

🔲 @meganfedwards